Long Night Moon

Long Night Moon

a novel

Sue Boggio · Mare Pearl

UNIVERSITY OF NEW MEXICO PRESS | ALBUQUERQUE

Library of Congress Cataloging-in-Publication Data
Names: Boggio, Sue, author. | Pearl, Mare, author.
Title: Long night moon : a novel / Sue Boggio and Mare Pearl.
Description: Albuquerque : University of New Mexico Press, 2017.
Identifiers: LCCN 2016018374 (print) | LCCN 2016023246 (ebook) |
ISBN 9780826357946 (pbk. : alk. paper) | ISBN 9780826357953 (electronic)
Classification: LCC PS3602.A395 L66 2017 (print) | LCC PS3602.A395 (ebook) |
DDC 813/.6--dc23
LC record available at https://lccn.loc.gov/2016018374

Cover illustration: *Salute the Moon*, pastel on panel, 16 x 20 inches, by Barbara Clark
Photograph of authors by Kyle Zimmerman
Designed by Catherine Leonardo
Composed in Palatino LT Std 10.25/14
Display font is Voluta Script Pro

For our loved ones here, there, and everywhere.

In loving memory of

my brother,

Samuel Mark Pearl

October

HUNTER'S MOON

Chapter One

SANTIAGO SILVA COLLAPSED onto the sofa he and his two room-mates had negotiated up three flights of stairs to their penthouse apartment in San Francisco. The steep, ornate stairs had seemed quaint when they first found the place, but with the reality of schlep-ping, Santi groused they needed Sherpas for the ascent.

"Shove over, Silva," Kat said, smacking his legs and flopping down next to him. Her hair, currently cut with little girl bangs and dyed black, made her seem even more white, if that was possible. She was one of those girls who were naturally a bit on the plump side, which Santi thought was cute, but Kat did not. She had a love-hate relation-ship with food that Santi and her brother, Reggie, found tedious. When she ate, she scolded herself between mouthfuls.

Reggie stood huffing and sweating over them. "Gravity might be the law, but it is not our friend. Not today."

"It's all the fucking books," Kat said. She moved closer to Santi so her brother could sit on her other side. Her soft hip and shoulder pressed against him in a comfortable way. Santi knew Kat didn't mind squeezing in closer to him. He wasn't sure how he felt about his former arm-punching buddy transforming into a girlfriend wannabe. When he'd agreed to this roommate situation, he was still dating Tori, but she broke up with him the day before graduation from UCLA, announcing she was returning home to Maine. The breakup sur-prised him less than her decision to move back to her family. He loved his family in New Mexico, but he could see them on visits. Tori told him he didn't understand how strong her pull to go home was because he was adopted, which was bullshit. It had zilch to do with bloodlines. At least not his.

Gordon Hopkins, Kat and Reggie's father, had published a quarterly literary journal, *Polydactyl*, for decades, but when his offspring graduated from college he had decided to branch into book publishing and started Polydactyl Press. Back in high school, Santiago's passion for literature and writing had ignited his dream to work in publishing; he figured he could support himself as an editor while writing on the side. This became his single-minded purpose, and as with all things, Santiago drove himself to succeed. It was scary perfect how everything had fallen into place, just as his adoption had after his nightmarish first decade on the planet.

"The problem is, you two are old-school. Instead of lugging twenty boxes of books, you could have carried your books in your pocket, like I did," Reggie said. He waved his phone to demonstrate.

"As if I'm going to let these original built-in bookcases go to waste," Kat responded. "Or part with my books. Sometimes I think mommy dearest must have dropped you on your head when you were a baby. What with juggling a cigarette, a martini, and a newborn, something's gotta give. I'm afraid it was your soft little cranium."

"Why are we not drinking a cold beer?" Santi asked.

"Because we have half a truck left to unload, unless someone has stolen it by now." Reggie swam his chubby self from the depths of the sofa as if coming up for air.

"We could hope." Santi stood and offered his hand to Kat. She smiled that new version of her smile that seemed created just for him, still sardonic but now sultry as well. She put her hand in his, and he pulled her up to face him. Her eyes locked on his and conveyed even more than her smile had. Maybe this shift from buddy to something else was not entirely a bad idea.

Rosalinda Ortiz stretched her long brown legs, peeling back the top sheet with her heels. Jesse's naked white-boy legs reminded her of chicken flesh. He was the first non-Hispanic guy she'd been with, and even after the year they had lived together, she still wasn't used to how skim-milk pale and circumcised he was. Her most handsome ex-boyfriend was Santiago Silva, whom she had met when he was freshly graduated from high school and still a virgin—miraculously, since he was so drop-dead gorgeous. At twenty-three, she had been well equipped to relieve him of his innocence. She shifted in bed with the memories of their one summer together: his sweet eagerness and smooth brown skin, the way he looked at her with puppy love oozing from his beagle-brown eyes. One summer with Santiago Silva was the closest she had come to loving any guy. So how could she not think of him, even after four years? Especially since she saw his beautiful face every day on Diego, her son.

Jesse put down his paperback book and switched on the television that sat atop the dresser in their cramped two-bedroom apartment. He never missed the news. Rosalinda thought he was checking to see if one of his sketchy friends had gone down for anything or to make sure his own likeness wasn't the subject of some police artist's rendering. He'd either given up his petty-crime ways, as promised, or he was just getting away with it. He brought home money from his series of shit jobs and was generous with it, helping to support her and her son. She didn't know how she would make it without him. Her minimum wage job at Diego's day care couldn't pay the rent on this nice of a place, even with the employee discount she got on his care. Jesse was tolerable, so despite his chicken flesh and her lack of love for him, she stayed.

Jesse fired up the bong and passed it to her. "Hang on," she said. "I need to check Diego first." She got up from the bed, feeling Jesse's eyes on her. She knew she looked good; men had been telling her that since she was eleven. And no one, except maybe a doctor, would guess her body had ever been pregnant or given birth. Few people did know. She had moved away from the prying eyes in the village of Esperanza to the anonymity of sprawling Albuquerque as soon as she found out she was pregnant. No one from her previous life knew about Diego. Especially Santiago Silva.

She padded barefoot the short distance to Diego's room. Rosalinda knelt at the side of his bed to be at eye level with her son, though his were closed, his long lashes casting shadows on his cheeks in the soft glow from the Spider-Man night-light. Her love for him rose as an ache in her chest. Before Diego, she'd never known true love was equal parts joy and terror. Now her life depended on this fragile, unexpected miracle of a son. She tried not to think about her own mother, a nasty old repeat offender who didn't even bother getting Rosalinda's father's first name, let alone his last, but could say for certain he was "some kind of Indian."

Rosalinda did not learn mothering from her mother. She learned it from deep within her rending soul. She worked every waking moment to make his life on earth as good as she could. With no family to count on, it had been a struggle until Jesse came along. If she waitressed she could make three times the money she was now earning, but that would mean long hours away from her son. And who could she trust to watch him? She ended up deciding to work at the first day care that wanted her and Diego as a package deal. The lesson she had learned growing up was: when you don't have love or money, money is not what you need the most.

Rosalinda leaned over to smell his sweet puffs of breath and kiss his cheek. Anyone who knew Santiago Silva would see this was his son, even asleep. Diego must look precisely like Santiago had at three and a half. But there might be no one left alive who knew Santiago when he was that age, since both of his birth parents were dead.

Rosalinda could tell he had inherited more than his father's handsome face. Diego was smart, too. He was already starting to read his storybooks along with her and could write his name clearly with all the letters facing the right way. But what pleased her most was that Diego had inherited his father's goodness. He sure as hell didn't get any of that from her sorry side of the family. Even though Santiago's father had been mean and violent, Santiago was nothing but kind. Maybe he got it from his long dead mother, or maybe his adoptive mother, Abby Silva, had instilled it in him, but Santiago was the kindest person she had ever known. And now Diego was the one who helped the other kids at the day care, kissing their boo-boos, soothing their temper tantrums, and making little presents for them out of pipe cleaners, Popsicle sticks, and tinfoil. Everyone loved little Diego. Rosalinda scrutinized his development as if he were a rare and exotic flower blooming before her eyes. She took no credit for his perfection but only counted herself lucky that fate had given her son the perfect sperm donor to spark his existence. It nearly made her believe in God.

She smoothed his straight, dark hair from his forehead to plant one more kiss. Her own long, straight hair tumbled forward, creating a veil that enveloped her son. Her lips lingered against his warm skin, and that brief connection filled her. "Mama loves you," she whispered in his ear. He stirred; one small fist rubbed his face. She pulled up the sheet to cover him, since the nights were getting cooler and he was sleeping in only his Spider-Man underwear.

Rosalinda tiptoed out and left the door ajar in case he called for her in the night.

"He asleep?" Jesse asked when she returned. He wore his stoned expression, his blond hair standing up in gravity-defying tufts from his habit of running his hands through it.

"Yes," Rosalinda said and accepted the bong. She never drank anymore, since her mom was such a worthless drunk, but a tiny toke at bedtime eased her overactive mind into sleep. She took a taste and handed it back to Jesse. The news was still on, so she leaned back onto her pillow to watch. Just as the slight buzz took hold, she gasped at what she saw. It was a human interest story about Abby, Santiago's adoptive mother, donating money to set up a children's literacy program back in Esperanza. "Shit!" she blurted. "That's Diego's grandma!"

"What? That rich white woman?" Jesse asked.

"She's Diego's father's adoptive mom. She married the Silva name. Santiago's father killed her husband, and she ended up adopting Santiago," Rosalinda said. As soon as she said it she realized the pot was making her spill the carefully concealed secret of Diego's paternity.

"Are you shitting me? I'm busting my hump to pay for Diego's shoes when he comes from money? What the fuck?" Jesse was way stoned but not unable to put two and two together.

"I don't want her money. I never told Santiago I was pregnant," Rosalinda said. "I'm doing this on my own."

"No, we're doing this on our own, and now I find out not only do you know who Diego's daddy is, he's rich. It's not fair, Rosalinda. You deserve money from the father—it's the law."

"Like you care about the law. Santiago isn't rich; he's a college student, far away from here. I didn't want to ruin his life then, and I'm not going to ruin it now. So forget about getting your grubby hands on any of their money."

"Grandma has so much she's giving it away to other people's kids—don't you think she'd want to know she has a grandson? Aren't you cheating them out of knowing Diego? This is all wrong."

Rosalinda sighed and did the only thing she knew for sure would shut Jesse up and get his mind off of Abby's money. She stripped off her tank top and straddled him. As he reached for her, she caught his hand in hers. "Forget I said anything, Jesse. I mean it."

"Whatever," he said, and she released his hand.

After several days of nothing further from Jesse about Abby Silva, Rosalinda figured he'd let go of the notion. On Saturday, she did the laundry and the grocery shopping with Diego as her little helper. Jesse had left without saying when he'd be back, which was fine with her. She read to Diego and settled him in for his afternoon nap. Just as she was putting away the laundry, Jesse came home, but not alone. He had that nasty Caden Owens with him. She didn't know he was out of prison. Jesse had once confessed to her that he had been the getaway driver on the job that landed Caden in prison. Caden didn't rat him out. Rosalinda was grateful for that, but Jesse told her it meant Jesse owed Caden a favor he could never refuse. She eyed the pair with a rising sense of unease.

"Hi, babe," Jesse said. "Look who I ran into—Caden."

"Where'd you run into him? An ex-con convention?" Rosalinda said. "And there's no smoking in my house."

Caden glared at her and swaggered into the kitchen, stubbing out his cigarette in the sink. "I thought this was your place, bro."

Jesse shrugged. "She's got the kid to think about."

"Don't we all," he said, throwing Rosalinda a wink. Caden's red hair was sheared short. Angry zits dotted his pale complexion. A former Texas football linebacker, it looked as though he'd made good use of the gym during his latest stint at the state pen for armed robbery.

"What's that supposed to mean?" Rosalinda said.

"Let's sit down over here and talk," Jesse said.

The three sat in the tiny, toy-strewn living room. Rosalinda kept her gaze boring into Caden. She would not be intimidated. Shit, she'd grown up with the Hispanic version of these lowlife criminals—her cousins and her mother's various associates—and held her own just fine, putting them in their place, not taking any bullshit, and managing to stay out of trouble even as they circled through the revolving door of the state penitentiary. Her toughness had earned their respect, and that had kept her safe, at least after she was old enough to defend herself against drunken rages and sexual advances.

"I did my homework on Abby Silva," Caden said. "She's all over the Internet, man."

"Shouldn't have wasted your time," Rosalinda said.

Caden ignored her, pulled out small notebook from his jeans pocket, and began to read: "Abigail Gibbs, only child of billionaires Paul and Virginia Gibbs of San Diego, California. Abby was disowned when she married Roberto Silva from Esperanza, New Mexico. He was in the navy, stationed in San Diego. They met when Abby was in college. She made her own money as a chef, started her own successful restaurant, Abigail's. She's still part owner, and the place is going strong. She was a local celebrity, did a lot of TV and shit. But when Roberto's dad died back in Esperanza like twelve years ago, he talked her into moving there for a year while she was pregnant. After burying his old man, Roberto picked a fight with Joseph Baca, who was squatting with his kid, Santiago, who's like nine, in a rental Roberto and his dad had built on their land. Joseph wasn't going to let Roberto evict his ass, so he shoots him dead and buries him in his rooster house. When Roberto doesn't come home, Abby goes to the neighbors, who had been tight with Roberto's old man and his late mother, so it's all like family. After his dad kills Roberto, little Santiago hangs out there, too. He gets to know Abby, and she mothers him since, let's face it, he has no mother and his father is a cockfighting criminal and not around a lot. So, long story short, Santiago spills the beans about his dad killing Roberto Silva, and the sheriff corners Joseph Baca but Joseph blows his own brains out—in front of the kid and Abby. She decides to stay in Esperanza, has her baby, and adopts Santiago. Abby Silva remarried a couple of years back to a UNM professor, bought up some foreclosed farms in the area to save them from developers, and now she leases them out. Her net worth is over ten million. Abby, Ben, and her daughter still live in Roberto's dad's little adobe house and drive older cars. She doesn't live like she's rich, but she is. Meanwhile, her adopted son, Santiago, who spawned Diego with our Rosalinda here, is now in San Francisco and is starting up a book publishing business with some friends and their father."

"He's not Diego's father. I was just stoned and making shit up," Rosalinda said.

"Oh, but he is," Caden said. "And it's time to pay up."

"I'm not doing this," Rosalinda said and rose to leave.

Jesse grabbed her hand. "Just hear his plan." The pleading look in his eyes convinced her to sit back down. She tried to appear bored, though her heart was exploding in her chest.

"I'm thinking Rosalinda shows up with Diego down at Abby's place and tells her she has nowhere else to turn," Caden continued. "Her live-in boyfriend has a gambling problem, and he borrowed money from the wrong people. So boyfriend tells her to get somewhere safe until this blows over, and he goes on the lam. And by the way, Diego here is Santiago's kid."

Rosalinda shook her head. "Abby never liked me or wanted me anywhere near her precious Santiago."

"One look at Diego, and all that goes away," Caden said.

"She just hands me money?"

"She takes you and Diego in. You stay there a week or so, long enough for Grandma to get all attached to her grandson. Then, one day, you and Diego are somewhere alone, and Diego gets kidnapped by the bad guys, who hold him for ransom since boyfriend can't pay them what he owes. Only it's just Jesse bringing him back here for a few days until Grandma pays up. I'm thinking a million ought to do it. That's like the minimum to be a serious ransom. And we split it."

"She won't even miss that million, so it's not like we're being all greedy," Jesse said.

Rosalinda looked straight at Jesse. "Read my lips. No fucking way!"

Caden put away his notebook. His hair was like a thin, red sheen hovering over his pink scalp. A swastika tattoo adorned the top of one hand. He had run with the white supremacist gang for protection in prison.

Rosalinda jumped up to lean over Jesse. "You bring home this Nazi to kidnap my son? Are you insane?"

"I'm the one taking Diego. It's not a real kidnapping. We'll just come back here and chill for a few days. Caden will set up the exchange," Jesse said. "All you have to do is act all freaked out when he's taken. Abby will pay up fast."

"What about my job? Diego's day care? We can't just not show up," Rosalinda said. "And they have this address on file."

"Good thinking, Rosalinda. You'll have to destroy his records and quit before this goes down," Caden said. "You won't need a job after this anyway."

"Just to be safe, I could take him to a motel or something," Jesse said.

"The kidnapping would be all over the papers. His picture would be everywhere. The police would be looking for you." Rosalinda paced. "This is ridiculous."

Caden stood to block her path, filling the small space. Rosalinda was five foot eight, and he towered over her. "Our conditions for Diego's safe return are: no police involvement, no publicity. Abby will want his safe return. And you will be there to make sure they don't try anything stupid. You give a fake name for the boyfriend. He's on the run, remember? Hiding out from the bad guys who want him to pay up. They take matters into their own hands. If I can find out all this shit about Abby Silva and Santiago, don't you think our fake crime syndicate could, too? Or maybe they find the gambler boyfriend and torture him to get him to talk. Doesn't matter, the story works. She'll pay up fast, and it's over. Then you and Jesse and your half a million dollars go start a new life somewhere, never to see those people again."

"And nobody gets hurt," Jesse added. "Diego is all happy with me; we'll have a great time. You come back after the ransom is paid."

"They'll figure out I was part of it and come after me," Rosalinda said.

"You disappear," Caden said. "For a price, I can hook you up with new identities, passports, drivers' licenses. Untraceable. They won't be able to find you."

"Maybe we should go to two million on the ransom, clear a million each," Jesse told him.

"I see your point. I was trying to keep it down so Abby could get the cash together fast, since a lot of it is tied up in real estate and shit. Let me go back over the numbers."

Rosalinda's thoughts were like an electrical storm, arcing and crashing. How could she stop this? Shit! Her big mouth! "I won't do it. I won't use my son like this. I just want my normal life—Jesse, we don't need this. Come on!"

Jesse put his hands on her shoulders, smoothed her hair. "Look at me, babe. We won't have to struggle anymore. Think of the great schools you could afford to put Diego in—he'd have the best of everything. We're just talking about what's owed to Diego from his father's family. They'll still be rich. And there's nothing keeping us here. You always wanted to live on the ocean—we could do that. Think of the life Diego could have. Do it for him."

Rosalinda backed away from him. "Your plan won't work without me. What if I say no?"

Caden's eyes narrowed into slits. "If you won't cooperate, there's plan B. I always have a plan B. But I don't think you'd like it."

"What is it?" She almost couldn't get the words to leave her constricted throat.

"If you and Diego want to stay healthy, you'll go with plan A. Jesse, get your woman on board. You don't have a choice in this—you feel me?"

Rosalinda couldn't eat or sleep. Jesse kept pressing her about how he owed Caden, how he would have done some serious time in prison instead of being free to help her and Diego these last few years.

She was so preoccupied at work that despite doing a head count, she accidentally left a toddler outside in the enclosed play yard when it was time to go inside. Mason had fallen asleep in the playhouse, and no one missed him until snack time, half an hour later. Even as her director was chewing her out, all Rosalinda could think about was how to get out of Caden's insane kidnapping plot.

She couldn't go the cops. She had no proof of Caden's scheme. It was nothing but talk at this point. And if she did that, no more Jesse. The pragmatic side of her was terrified about how she would survive financially without Jesse's help—that's if Caden didn't kill her as a part of plan B. She didn't want to have to run away and start over somewhere and be looking over her shoulder for Caden. She didn't think Jesse would ever hurt her or Diego, but she doubted he was capable of stopping Caden from harming them.

Rosalinda knew Caden would kidnap Diego and hold him for ransom with or without her cooperation. He could call Abby and tell her she had a grandson and that he had been kidnapped. When she demanded proof, he would send her a picture of Diego, along with an ear or a finger Abby could use for genetic testing.

She saw no way out. She would have to go along with the plan, stay with her son, and make sure it went off without a hitch. It was too dangerous to go against them. But sure as hell, once this was over she would be done with Jesse.

The brisk October morning helped wake CeCe Vigil as she carried her steaming coffee cup to her spot at the table on her flagstone patio. A meringue of white clouds dotted the Manzano Mountains to the east. Pretty Boy, their peacock, cried out and flew from the barn roof, landing near her.

"You looking for Papa?" CeCe asked, tears stinging her eyes in the cold air. She hadn't stopped crying since her father, Mort, died two weeks ago. Everything here on Sol y Sombra, their chile farm, reminded her of him. In his last years with dementia, he had found a new life with her and her husband, Miguel; and she had discovered a new father. His suffering in the Treblinka extermination camp never stopped torturing him, but thanks to his short-term memory loss he forgot his PTSD episodes soon after having them. Near the end, at almost ninety-five, he would sit outside, wrapped in blankets in winter or donning a big straw hat and holding a paper fan in summer, to watch and feed Pretty Boy. She looked over at the skeletal remains of her vegetable garden. Her papa, too feeble to help her his last summer, had observed from his chair, still kibitzing her every move. The blue sky overhead promised that it would warm into an ideal New Mexico autumn day—a day Papa would have loved.

Her tears dripped like hot wax along her cheeks. In her youth, she had prayed for her angry and abusive father to die. For years he made everyone's life miserable. The family would have been glad to see him go, back then. But after spending these last four years with him, she missed him. Grief was complicated.

"Cecelia! *Gevalt!* You want to catch your death! I just buried your father, I don't want to bury you next," CeCe's mother, Rose, yelled from the porch. Her voice was hoarse as she leaned on her walker. CeCe could see the neon-green tennis balls on the feet of the walker as her mother pushed forward on swollen ankles.

After Mort's funeral, Rose had suffered a heart attack. CeCe had just gotten rid of her three sisters, their husbands, and their grown children from Brooklyn, who had stood disdainfully at her father's grave. Papa died with nothing except the love of his Esperanza family, so there was no will to read. Her sisters clung to their outdated memories of Mort, still blaming him for losing their investments when his dementia destroyed the family business, not fathoming the man he had become since moving to New Mexico.

Rose coughed and held her chest. When she left the hospital after her heart attack, the doctors handed CeCe a pamphlet about her mother's weakened heart along with a bag of medicines for her to take around the clock.

"You're the one who should get inside, you crazy old woman! Ninety years old and you act like you're five." CeCe stood. How fleeting her moments of peace had become. Pretty Boy began a defensive *honk-honk-honk.* "You tell her," CeCe said, mimicking Mort. By the time she reached the back door, her urge to strangle Rose had subsided, and she ushered her mother inside.

"I'm not dead yet," Rose said as she deflated into a kitchen chair. "And I'm not five years old, so don't talk to me like I am." She brushed imaginary crumbs from the table. A Jewish mother's tic.

"I'm making you some of Rachel's hawthorn and hibiscus tea, Ma. She says it's good for your heart. It's a diuretic. Do you want it with honey?"

"She dotes on me, my Racheleh. I am blessed to have such a granddaughter to care for me," Rose said with a soft clap of her hands toward heaven. "Honey would be nice."

"We all love you, Ma," CeCe said, feeling as if her mother was blind to her efforts. After all, CeCe was the one who had asked her partner, Abby, to keep their café closed so she could take care of her mother—not that Rose gave her any credit for that sacrifice. The whistle of the teapot shook her out of her momentary emotional fragility, a sure sign of her exhaustion. According to the doctor, Rose likely had a few short months left of her life. This was no time to nurse her resentments.

CeCe brought Rose her mug of tea and joined her at the table with a fresh cup of coffee. Rose's hands trembled as she brought the mug, which read, "If you can't say anything nice, say it in Yiddish," to her pale lips. Her fluffy hair, dyed bright red for years, was now stark white, like a dandelion in seed. Small and frail, she looked like a doll sitting in the chair, albeit one possessing a will still larger than life.

Rachel watched her ten-year-old daughter, Hattie, poke at her breakfast as if it were a voodoo doll, her egg bleeding out its fresh canary yellow into her bacon. Purple circles, pale as columbine blossoms, bloomed under Hattie's eyes. "Honey, what's wrong?"

"Nothing," Hattie said, her pokes at her plate turning to stabs. Her sun-bleached hair hung in her face. Other than the blue eyes inherited from her mother, she looked like her Anglo father's side of the family.

Rachel figured this was about Hattie losing her great-grandfather. Hattie had grown close to both her Great-grandpa Mort and Bubbe Rose over the past four years, so on top of losing Mort, Hattie now had to deal with Rose's decline.

"I need to go," Hattie said, picking up her backpack as though it were a cross to bear. Her kiss on Rachel's cheek felt like a passing breeze as she hurried out the door.

Rachel lingered at her kitchen table. The past weeks had been hard on everyone, and Rachel, the self-appointed emotional rock of the family, needed her healing herbs and quiet time to indulge in her own grief.

After the bosque fire destroyed her and husband's home four years ago, they had rebuilt the house she now sat in from the original plans. On the outside it looked the same, except it was positioned closer than before to the home of her parents, CeCe and Miguel, and not tucked deep into the trees of the bosque, where it would be vulnerable to fire. They had to purchase everything new, so it didn't feel the same. Her Navajo rugs, Charlie's family antiques, her late Tía Maria's notebooks and belongings—all gone. Up until Zeyde Mort's death, she had helped as much as she could with him while continuing her goat dairy and cheese business, a labor of love that wore her down. And now Bubbe Rose was failing.

Rachel sipped her calming maypop tea, made from the leaves of the passionflower. From the time Rachel was younger than Hattie, Tía Maria had taught her the ways of the traditional Hispanic healers known as *curanderas*. What she couldn't find growing wild in the secret spots Maria had shown her, Rachel grew herself. She made sure Hattie had her daily tonic to cure anything and everything . . . except the pain of losing a loved one. She hadn't found the remedy for that yet.

None of her herbs were used for spells or curses. That had been Maria's sideline. As Maria aged, she turned toward her dark *bruja* side, making good money providing the locals with love spells and revenge curses. Gone twelve years now, Maria still inhabited Rachel's thoughts and healing rituals, her presence defying death.

Rachel heard her husband's whistling before his boots clomped up the porch steps.

"Hey, babe. Surprised to see you're still here," Charlie said with a wide smile. At forty-five, even with gray at his temples and then some, he still looked like an over-six-foot-tall kid.

"I'm wallowing." She downed her tea. "After I did the milking, I told Jenny and Leticia I wouldn't be around today. They can cover for me with the cheese deliveries." She smelled the sweat in his old Stetson as it hit the table with a huff.

"You deserve it, Rachel," Charlie said, opening the fridge door. "Loaded up all that alfalfa in the barn. Mighty thirsty." He poured himself a big glass of lemon balm iced tea.

"I'm worried about Hattie. She still looks so sad."

"Babe, it's only been a couple of weeks since Mort died. It'll take her some time."

"Then what? Rose dies, and she goes through it all over again."

"We can't keep her from life. Or death." His warm brown eyes met hers. "She's a strong girl, just like her mother."

"You mean to say stubborn." Her husband's usual bone of contention and often the trigger for an argument.

"I got to slop me some hogs." Charlie headed for the door, plopping on his hat as if taking cover.

"We don't have any hogs."

It was past noon by the time Rachel walked across the pasture to her parents' house. CeCe had already fed Rose her lunch of salmon salad, and the smell hung in the kitchen. "Ma," Rachel called out.

"In here, *mi'ja*," her father called from his study. She found her parents sitting at his desk, their heads together, looking over some papers.

"*Mi'ja*. Come see the nice card and letter Santi sent. A little late for my birthday, but he remembered." Her father chuckled. "After four years of college, he doesn't need an old man like me anymore. But I'm glad he doesn't know that." He folded the letter and placed it back in the envelope, handing the card to Rachel. "It sounds like he's got his hands full trying to start up a new business along with a new girlfriend."

"Another girlfriend?" Rachel said. "He goes through them kind of fast, doesn't he? I notice he never brings them home." She smiled at the funny card and handed it back to him.

Rachel thought at sixty-six her father was as dashing as ever, though the New Mexico sun had done its damage, leaving small scars where skin cancer had been burned or cut out. A decade of drought, his chile farm barely surviving, created a weighted slouch in his shoulders and back. "I told him to shop around until he finds a woman he would be proud to bring home. Santi's a man now, but he's still young. He'll find his way."

"Knock, knock," said Rachel before opening the door to Rose's room. "Hi, Bubbe, how are you feeling today?"

Rose sat at the sunny window, crocheting. She looked half-asleep as her fingers worked. She came to with a start. "Ah, Racheleh, I'm fine, just a little tired."

Mort's clothes still hung in the closet; his things were still laid out on his dresser. "Ma and I are getting ready to string the last of the chile *ristras*," Rachel said, wanting to get Rose out of her room for a while. "Do you want to help?"

Rose put down her crocheting. What was it? An afghan? It seemed to go on forever. The bright sun made Rose's translucent skin resemble a road map of blue byways. She planted her feet firmly to stand.

"Let me help you," Rachel said.

"I don't need help." Rose waved her off. She walked gingerly, holding onto the bedpost, the footboard, then to her walker. "What do those doctors know? I'm getting stronger every day. Racheleh, I want you to get me a pair of those Nikes."

"I'll put it on my list, Bubbe."

CeCe had brought a couple of bushels of late-crop red chiles to the porch by the time Rachel and Rose had made the trek across the sprawling adobe house to the back door. Rachel guided her grandmother to a chair.

"I'll go ahead and cut the twine and hang it. You guys start with the cotton cord and tie on some chiles," said CeCe. She secured the twine to a hook embedded in the beam of the porch overhang.

Rachel pushed a bushel basket of red chiles in front of Rose and cut her long pieces of cotton string. Rose would select the best chiles, feeling them for firmness and sturdy stems. She had worked at a produce stand as a kid in Brooklyn and could pick out the best of anything. "Pull from the back," she would tell strangers at the grocery store in Los Lunas.

The rooster crowed, the peacock screamed, but Rose did not tell them to shut up as she usually did. Rachel and CeCe looked at each other and then at Rose. Rose continued to tie chiles. Maybe her hearing had gotten worse. Rose looked up to see them staring. "*Vas?*"

"Did you hear them?" Rachel asked.

"Of course I heard them. I'm not deaf. Beautiful, isn't it? The sweet music of life." Rose continued her stringing. She had been stringing chiles faster than Rachel, and CeCe barely kept up with tying them onto the hanging twine.

"Bubbe, what's your rush?" Rachel said.

"I don't want to miss Jerry Springer. He's dreamy. If only I was thirty years younger."

"That's a horrible show. People fighting, sleeping around," said CeCe.

"Did you see him dance with the stars? He glided across the floor." Rose looked like a swooning teenager. "And, boy, he makes me laugh."

"Ma, Pa's only been gone two weeks, and you're getting all cougar over Jerry Springer?"

"A nice Jewish boy who lost most of his family to concentration camps and immigrated here like your family did," Rose said.

"Sounds like a pattern, Bubbe," Rachel said with a grin toward CeCe. "You have to watch those rebound romances. Ever thought of nice non-Jewish men?"

"Go ahead, make fun. Yes, Mort has been gone two weeks, I had a heart attack, and now you look at me as if I'm going to kick off any minute. But I feel more alive than ever. You get to be as old as me, you start thinking about everything in your life. Things you did, didn't do, couldn't do. So much time was spent married, taking care of children, catering to Mort. Now that's over, and it's just me and my life. Mine. What's left of it."

Rachel said, "You go, girl."

"I'm kicking up my heels before they're planted in the earth," Rose said. "Ask Bonnie to come over to color and set my hair." She patted the white cloud on her head. "I want to be a redhead again."

Rose's medicine timer beeped frantically in her robe pocket. CeCe looked at her quizzically. Rachel knew her mother was vigilant about Rose's medication. Never had she forgotten, not one pill, so why was Rose's timer going off in between doses?

"Jerry Springer's starting! Help me up!"

Chapter Two

SANTIAGO CAREFULLY EXTRICATED himself from Kat's limbs so as not to wake her. He found his boxers, put them on, and grabbed his shirt, pants, and shoes from the floor. He crept from her moonlight-drenched room, managing to close the old door without it creaking.

As he was tiptoeing across the living room to get to his room, a voice startled him. "What the fuck, Silva?"

Santi froze.

"I can see you," Reggie said from the sofa.

Santi took the chair opposite the sofa. Some light shone through the windows, casting Reggie in silhouette. It unnerved Santi that he couldn't read Reggie's facial expression. He felt blindfolded. He braced himself for the firing squad and kept his mouth shut.

"Dude. Come on. She's my sister."

"Uh, yeah."

"Which, interestingly, is not the part I'm pissed about. We're in business together. That alone should have made you keep it in your pants, dude. Now all of our livelihoods are at stake and hanging in the balance of whether you guys will end up hating each other. This cannot end badly. You know this."

"Look, Kat and I have been friends for like four years now. We know each other very well. She wanted this, by the way—it was totally her idea. I did not make the first move."

"Of course she wanted this. She's wanted this for like four years now. This is not something she's going to take casually, like friends with benefits or something."

"This just happened tonight. We're just going to see how it goes. Worst case, we go back to being friends."

"Have you ever even met a woman? Women do not go back to being friends. You're on the interstate, friendo. There's no U-turns, there's only off-ramps. There's only keep the fuck going or get the fuck off."

Santi began to panic. Shit. Reggie was right. Unless Kat was the one who decided not to be lovers and to go back to being friends and business partners, he would end up married to her. And then she'd want kids, and he wasn't sure he ever wanted kids, and his life was now completely out of his control. Permanently. Before it had even started.

"So I hope you just had the best sex of your life, that's all I can say." Reggie got up and walked to his room, his flip-flops slapping against his heels.

The best sex of his life . . . no, it wasn't that. It was nice. It was comfortable. It was Kat. So, weirdly, it felt familiar, not like a first time. But then, he did remember the best sex of his life. The summer just out of high school. He had been eighteen. She was twenty-three. Nothing since then had surpassed or even come close to that one summer with Rosalinda Ortiz. His first, totally insane love.

He forced the images from his mind. He was an inexperienced kid then. Now, at twenty-two, he understood life a lot better. He and Rosalinda never would have worked out, even if he hadn't gone away to college. When they were children their criminal relatives had formed some sort of dysfunctional extended family. Rosalinda's mother and Santiago's Uncle Manny had been together. He'd been too young to remember any of that, including Rosalinda. Five years' age difference was insurmountable back then, even for friendship.

After he was adopted by Abby, his life had detoured onto the law-abiding, success-oriented track. When he and Rosalinda met again after he turned eighteen, he was working out some shit from his traumatic past, and that meant sticking his toes back into some dangerous waters. Hooking up with Rosalinda had been part of it.

He calmed down then, looking at it from that perspective. Being with Kat meant he had evolved enough to have his priorities straight.

They were compatible; they shared a vision for their work and their lives. Kat was smart and funny and creative. Last night happened because it was meant to happen. Reggie had gotten his panties in a wad over nothing.

Santiago looked down at the clothing and shoes in his hands and smiled, remembering how he and Kat had laughed at their awkward disrobing, turning it into a joke. The therapist Abby had hired for him when he was ten—after all the abuse, neglect, and violence—had worked with him on learning how to trust. He was still working on it, on believing he was a good person who deserved a good life. Just as loving Rosalinda had meant venturing into darkness, learning to love Kat meant he was embracing the light. He would love Kat—the seeds were there. He only needed to nurture them, and while that might take some time, he wasn't going anywhere.

"Abigail Gibbs Silva *Frasier*." Her husband, Ben, put the emphasis on "Frasier" as he patted the spot next to him on the sofa. His Aussie accent was as thick as the day they'd met over four years ago, when he had crashed a farmers' emergency meeting at her café and nearly started a riot with his defense of the endangered silvery minnow, his life's work. The Esperanza farmers were struggling against a perpetual severe drought, and the notion that the feds had declared the right to divert some of their rationed water to save a four-inch fish did not sit well. It had taken all that summer for her farming friends, the Vigils, to accept him and realize they were really all on the same side, that keeping the Rio Grande healthy and vibrant supported both the silvery minnow and the farmers' traditional irrigation methods.

Abby sat next to him. She let her tired muscles relax, her head resting against his shoulder. He shifted to put his arm around her, and they sat a moment in the quiet.

"I wish you'd let me remodel the kitchen, get a dishwasher installed. Or at least let me help with the washing up." With her ear pressed against him, Ben's voice reverberated through his chest.

She lifted her head to look at him. "You've been teaching all day. With the café closed, I'm just a lazy old housewife."

His eyes crinkled with his grin. He played with her hair. "Old? My dear, we are barely entering the threshold of middle age—in fact, if we live to be as old as Mort and Rose, we're not even at the halfway mark. Early forties is the new thirties."

"I saw Rose today. She looks pretty good. It's hard to believe the doctors said her heart is going to give out. CeCe looks awful, though. She just buried her father, and now her mother gets a death sentence."

"Good thing CeCe has her husband and daughter and son-in-law and granddaughter and you and me and Maggie and her friends gathered around to help."

"Even with all of that support, it's her mom. You know, you lost your mom. Even though I never had that bond with my mother—"

"Mom!" Maggie's voice preceded her entrance. Her nearly twelve-year-old daughter strode into the living room carrying her math book, her pretty face squeezed into a contorted knot. Maggie looked nothing like Abby's fair, Anglo-Saxon side of the family. She was all Silva. Abby knew him only as Bobby in San Diego, but when they moved here to his home, everyone called him Roberto. Maggie looked so much like her late father it made Abby gasp sometimes, right down to Bobby's facial expressions, which Maggie had never seen since he was murdered months before she was born. Her two Hispanic kids, Magdalena and her adopted son, Santiago, looked more like dark-haired, perpetually tanned Ben, and he wasn't related to either of them.

Maggie held up her math book as evidence. "That stupid teacher gave us five pages of homework and didn't explain anything and it's taking me all night to do one page and it's already eight fifteen and I have required reading to do still!" Tears spit from her dark eyes. Her tangle of dark curls waggled in emphasis. She was Bobby's kid, right down to the frequent dramatics. Abby often made the mistake of smiling when Maggie got like this, which was of course the wrong response.

Ben kissed Abby's hand and stood up, knowing his cue. "Let's have a look at that and see if I can make heads or tails out of it."

"You better, because I'm hopeless!"

Ben put an arm on her shoulder and took the offending math book from her outstretched hand. Abby watched as they made their way to Maggie's room. Ben's voice low and calm, Maggie's strident with pubescent angst. Thank God for Ben. She had that thought at least fifty times a day. He arrived on the scene when Maggie was seven and a half and ripe for a dad's love and attention. Once Ben won her over, they were inseparable.

Abby decided she would take a hot bath. October had arrived with a cold wind that was starting to strip the golden leaves from the cottonwoods in the bosque. She dreaded their bareness every year, a sign of coming winter, but she did relish hot bath season. The thought of a bath in candlelight and another glass of wine from the bottle they had opened at dinner inspired her to stand up. But as she stood, the front doorbell rang. No one used the front door. Her friends and neighbors, Rachel and CeCe, always entered through the back kitchen door, knocking as they let themselves in.

She walked over to the front door and hesitated. The bell rang again. She turned on the porch light and opened the door a crack. It was a woman holding a young child. "Abby?" the woman said.

"Who is it?"

"Rosalinda Ortiz. I'm sorry to bother you—"

Abby processed the name. Santiago's old girlfriend, for lack of a better word. The older woman who had seduced her innocent son and involved him with her criminal cousin, that awful James Ortiz. "What do you want?"

"I didn't know where else to turn. Can I come inside? I have my little son with me."

Abby opened the door and stood back as Rosalinda carried the sleeping child, bundled in a hooded jacket. Abby led them to the living room, motioning to the sofa and taking a chair for herself. She watched as Rosalinda carefully settled her sleeping son onto the sofa and sat beside him, her hand resting on his back. "I know I'm the last person you want to see."

Santi had been sneaking around with Rosalinda before Abby had busted him and finally met her, so Abby had seen Rosalinda only a few times that summer. She was beautiful then and looked the same now, four years later. Her long, straight black hair reached her waist. She was tall and thin, but shapely. She looked clean and not obviously like a druggie or a drunk. "What's going on?"

"Like I said, I had nowhere else to go. My boyfriend, Jack, he started to gamble, and he lost a lot of money, and he borrowed from the wrong people. Now they're making threats. He told me to go somewhere safe until this blows over. We live up in Albuquerque, but I don't know anyone there that well. I don't speak to my mother and don't even know where she is. So I came here."

"You want money, is that it? To pay your boyfriend's gambling debt?" Abby wasn't surprised Rosalinda had hooked up with some lowlife. It was obvious that was where she was headed back then, which was exactly why Abby hadn't wanted her anywhere near Santiago.

"I don't want your money." Rosalinda said it with such vehemence that Abby almost believed her. "I need a safe place to stay for a couple of days. I'd never ask, except for my son."

"Maybe you should go to the police," Abby said. "How do I know you weren't followed here? Did you bring your danger to my home?"

"I'm not stupid. I wasn't followed. No one knows I came to you, not even Jack. That's why I thought we'd be safe here, since no one would make the connection."

"What connection?" Abby was ready to throw her out. Child or no child, this smelled like a scam.

"I never was going to say anything," Rosalinda said, her voice quavering. "I'm raising my son on my own. But then this happened, and I don't have family. So I came to you, my son's father's family."

Abby burst out laughing. "Seriously? That's how you're going to play this? One paternity test, and the jig is up."

Rosalinda stared at her. "I'm not looking for money or anything from you. If you want a paternity test, that's fine."

"Santiago did not get you pregnant. He knew to use protection and be responsible."

"We were very careful. Except for the time I guess we weren't. Do the math. Diego is three and a half. He was conceived in mid-June, four years ago, when I was with Santiago and only Santiago. He was born March 22."

The child stirred and sat up. The hood of his jacket slipped off. The face of Abby's son peered at her and yawned. "I need to pee pee," he said.

Abby felt as if she were falling backwards, down some dark tunnel that opened up beneath her. Her hands gripped the chair.

Rosalinda stood up with her son. "Can we use your bathroom?"

"It's . . . right there in the hall." Abby blinked and tried to focus, but none of this was making any sense. She watched Rosalinda slip off her son's jacket, take his hand, and walk him toward the hallway, speaking to him in a soft, reassuring tone.

When she heard the bathroom door close, she sprung to life and got up to find Ben. She stood in front of Maggie's closed door, hearing their voices and then laughter. Ben's transformational magic. She knocked and opened the door.

Maggie sat at her desk, the math book opened in front her, her hand holding a pencil poised over her spiral notebook. Ben stood next to her. Both were grinning. "How's it going?" Abby tried to sound casual.

"We're fine," Ben said. "Maggie's conquering the evil math empire. We thought we heard the doorbell. Is someone here?"

"Could I borrow Ben for a moment?" Abby said and managed to smile at Maggie.

"I guess, but come back and check my work," Maggie said.

Ben followed her from the room and closed the door. "What—"

Abby put her finger to her lips to silence him. The light still shone under the bathroom door, and she heard water running. She led Ben back to the living room.

"Who's in there?" Ben asked.

"Rosalinda Ortiz. With a three-and-a-half-year-old son she claims is Santi's. She says they're in danger, and she had nowhere else to go." With Ben by her side, she wanted to cry.

Before Ben could respond, Rosalinda and Diego returned.

"I'll just go to a motel or something. I'm sorry I bothered you." Rosalinda began to help Diego with his jacket.

"Wait," Abby said. "You don't get to show up here and make these claims and then leave. We need to get to the bottom of this."

Ben walked over to Rosalinda, putting out his hand. "Rosalinda, I'm Ben, Abby's husband. We met once, but it's been a long time."

"I remember you from that summer," Rosalinda said, shaking his hand.

Ben knelt in front of Diego. "Who's this, then?" He smiled at the boy.

"Diego." The little boy smiled back, revealing his perfect seed-pearl teeth and Santiago's dimple.

Ben ruffled Diego's hair, eliciting a giggle. "We have a perfectly good spare room, so I don't see any need for a motel. Why don't you get this lad settled in, and we'll all talk in the morning? Rosalinda, do you and Diego need a snack?"

"I'll put out some fresh towels. The sheets on Santi's bed are clean," Abby said, taking Ben's lead.

Rosalinda looked at Abby. "Are you sure—about us staying the night?"

Abby nodded, not sure she could speak around the big lump forming in her throat.

"I brought some snacks. I'll just go get our bag from the car. Diego, Mama will be right back. Stay here with these nice people."

"Pull your car around to the back," Abby said. "You can come in the kitchen door—it's right next to Santiago's room."

Rosalinda nodded and left them. Diego watched her and then smiled up at them again.

"How old are you, big guy?" Ben asked him.

Diego looked down at his hand as he extended three fingers and held them up. "Three."

"Wow. You are a big guy. Want to see the room you and your mum will be in tonight?" Ben took his hand and walked with him to the hallway. Abby followed. She stood in the doorway while Ben showed him some of Santi's old toys, which still sat on his shelves.

Diego was drawn to the same model ship and airplane that Santiago had been enthralled with as a child . . . the model ship and airplane that Bobby had built in that room as a little boy.

Abby fled to the bathroom, shaking and unable to hold back her tears. She felt all the hopes and dreams she'd had for Santiago's carefully planned future threaten to evaporate like Scotch mist, as Ben would say, gone by morning.

Rosalinda leaned against the extra pillows Abby had brought after she'd turned into the hostess with the mostes'. The house was quiet, so different from her apartment with its thin walls. Diego slept next to her. The room was dark except for the light seeping in through the curtains. She pulled her phone from her purse and called Jesse.

"Finally! How'd it go?" he asked.

"Abby was real pissed and like, challenging, but once she saw Diego's face, I could tell she was freaking out, but trying to be all cool. Her husband, Ben, is really good with Diego, and he's even nice to me. I'm in Santiago's old room, Diego's sleeping. I'm too wired."

"You can sleep on satin sheets when this is over. Remember to suck up to them. Get Abby to do stuff with Diego—give him his bath, read to him, all that grandma shit. We need her to get good and attached. Did she bring up getting a paternity test?"

"I told her to go for it."

"Sweet. See, this is going to be way easy," Jesse said. "I miss you guys. Be careful about calling, though. We don't want to fuck this up."

"I'll call in a few days. Good night," Rosalinda said.

She stashed her phone and pulled the covers up around them. The wind had kicked up again, and she felt a draft from the old casement windows. She listened to the rustling of the leaves on the giant cottonwood that cradled the house. She had been in this room once before, in early June, four years ago. Her cousin James had been staying with her at her mom's piece-of-shit house while her mom was doing time for identity theft. James had brought Santiago home, and they drank beer. Poor Santiago didn't know what he was doing, so he had way too many, and it wasn't even nine thirty. James was too drunk to drive, so she had driven Santi home and had to half-carry him inside. Luckily, as it turned out, Abby was out on a first date with Ben. She'd left a note on the kitchen table saying Maggie was sleeping at a friend's house. Santiago was sloppy drunk, telling her how much he loved her. She'd thought he was cute in a little brother kind of way, even as she was helping him out of his clothes and tucking him into bed. Within days, they were lovers. And later that summer, without either of them knowing, he had given her Diego.

She curled up on her side to face her son as he slept. She lightly touched his head, stroking his hair. "I'm doing this for you," she whispered.

"Come to bed," Ben said for the second or third time. "You're all wound up."

Abby was perched in front of her computer at the desk that served as her office in the corner of their bedroom. "They do the paternity test with a cheek swab from the mother, the child, and the possible father. There's even a home test kit if you don't care about using the results in the courts; otherwise there has to be something called 'a chain of custody' with the samples. So you go to the testing site—they have them all over the country—and they overnight the sample to their lab in San Diego. Santiago could go to their testing site in San Francisco. You get the results in about a week; you pay more if you want them in three days."

"I think Santi will want to come here and sort this out for himself."

Abby shut down her computer and crawled into bed. "I'm going to try to get him to stay there for now, until this is confirmed, at least. I wish there was a way to handle this without him even knowing about it." She sighed. "He's getting settled into his new place in a new city and starting a high-pressure job. He said he already has a huge stack of manuscripts to evaluate. The timing of this is terrible. He doesn't need this distraction right now."

"At least he got through college before she showed up with his son," Ben said.

"Alleged son."

"I think we both know that boy is Santiago's. Maybe you're afraid he'll get distracted by Rosalinda. A first love is a powerful connection, and adding a son to that equation, well, could be life altering."

"I don't want his life altered! Santi was born into terrible circumstances—you know how bad his life was. When I adopted him, I swore I would give him the life he deserved. He's done so well, despite everything, and now, when he's finally starting the career he's dreamed of—she shows up. Maybe we don't have to tell him. Maybe there's an old toothbrush with DNA, or hair from a comb—"

"That would only delay the inevitable. Santi is nearly twenty-three. He's not your fragile little boy, Abby—he's a man. He can cope. You never know, this could all end up being a blessing in disguise. Come now, let me rub your back. You need to calm down, get some sleep."

She turned away from him so he wouldn't see the new wave of tears forming in her eyes. She couldn't wait until morning, when she could talk to CeCe and Rachel. They would get this; they would validate her. Ben's optimism was only frustrating at this point. His hands began to knead her back, finding every knotted muscle and trigger point. She took some deep breaths and blew them back out. His words might not be helpful, but God, those hands sure were.

At first light Abby gave up trying to sleep. She dressed and went to the kitchen. The house was quiet. She scribbled a quick note and left it on the kitchen table.

She grabbed her jacket and let herself out the kitchen door. Rosalinda's small silver sedan sat next to her and Ben's cars. She peered inside to see it was neat and clean, with a booster seat in the back. The light steadily grew as the sun began to rise over the Manzano Mountains. The sky was clear and colorless; the wind had died down during the night. She stopped to look up into the branches of the giant cottonwood that sheltered her home. A scattered layer of its gold-coin leaves was beginning to settle on the green grass beneath its canopy.

As Abby walked briskly across her property to the access road that separated her land from the Vigils' sprawling farm, she thought of that terrifying morning twelve years ago when she woke to find her husband, Bobby, had not come home. They had only arrived in Esperanza a few days before, to bury his father. Bobby had been distraught, blaming himself for not being there when his dad needed him. Months later she learned he had gone drinking and ended up at the house on their property he and his dad had built together the summer before he joined the navy. He had been furious to find out that Joseph Baca, Santiago's father, was paying no rent, had intimidated Bobby's father into doing nothing about it, and was claiming the house as his own. Instead of involving the authorities, Bobby had confronted Santiago's dad and tried to evict them.

Abby looked over at the spot where that house and the rooster house had once stood behind a cloak of overgrown trees and weeds and a tall barbwire fence. After Bobby's body was unearthed, along with Santi's mother's body, from beneath the rooster house, she had had everything bulldozed and hauled away. A natural meadow grew there now, dotted with wildflowers and waving native grasses.

The morning after, when Bobby still hadn't come home, she had run to the Vigils' for help, four months pregnant with Maggie and nearly hysterical with the knowledge her Bobby was not the kind of man who would abandon his wife. And she ran to them now, her closest friends, who had seen her through so much over the intervening years.

Miguel sat in the back on a lawn chair, drinking his coffee and watching the sunrise spread streaks of yellow and pink above the mountains. Roosters began to crow, and Abby could see the lights on in the goat barn where Rachel and her hired help, Jenny and Leticia, would be milking. Miguel smiled at her as if there was nothing strange about her showing up at that hour.

"It got down to forty-three degrees overnight," he said. "I'm still playing chicken with the first freeze. I have a nice fat crop of red chile for one last picking and a stack of orders for it."

"Ben will help; just let him know," Abby said. "Is CeCe up?"

"She doesn't sleep much. Ever since Rose came home after her heart attack she gets up about every hour to make sure her mother is still breathing. I tell her she'll be no good to Rose if she wears herself out and gets sick. CeCe's no spring chicken, either. Don't tell her I said that."

Abby smiled at Miguel despite the burdens on her own mind. CeCe and Miguel were her surrogate parents, which contributed to her sibling-like relationship with Rachel. She and Rachel were the same age, forty-two now, only thirty when they met, when Abby and Bobby had come to Esperanza. Rachel was completely hostile in the beginning. She was divorced from Charlie at the time and wanted to believe her "Roberto" had come back to rekindle their teenage affair. As the months after his disappearance wore on, Abby and Rachel searched and waited together. Their rivalry dissipated the moment they learned of Roberto "Bobby" Silva's brutal murder. In their shared grief, and especially after Rachel reconciled with Charlie, their friendship had grown and deepened as the years went by.

Abby let herself into the Vigil house. CeCe and Rose were seated at the large kitchen table, drinking coffee. Rose's hair was back to red, shocking since in the months prior to her husband's death she had let it go white. She appeared better than Abby was expecting and wore a perky little smile on her face.

CeCe looked at Abby in horror. "Lord, no, what's the matter now?"

Abby poured herself some coffee. "Why do you think anything is wrong?"

"Because it's not even six o'clock in the morning, and you are dressed and in my kitchen."

"Oh, I can feel it from here. It must be something real bad," Rose said, practically rubbing her hands together in anticipation.

Abby sat and glanced from one to the other. "Rosalinda showed up at our house with a three-year-old son she says is Santi's, and he looks just like Santiago, and her boyfriend is on the lam from some bad guys he borrowed money from for gambling debts, and now he can't pay them back, so she and the little boy are in danger, and they came to me."

"Holy cow," Rose said.

"We knew that girl was trouble. Never was I more relieved than when their relationship ended and he went off to college," CeCe said. She was Santi's designated grandma.

"We're going to get a paternity test, of course," Abby said. She pressed her hands to her temples. "But, God, Diego looks just like him. And the dates work."

"What does Santiago say?" CeCe said.

"I haven't told him yet. This just happened last night. I don't want to turn his world upside down." Abby gulped her coffee for fortitude.

"You have to tell him. This is his problem, not yours," Rose said. "He danced to the music, now he's got to pay the fiddler."

"Ma!" CeCe said. "Abby, why do you think Rosalinda didn't show up until now? If the boy is Santiago's, wouldn't she have told him back then—four years ago—when she got knocked up?"

"She says she wanted to raise him by herself. She denies wanting any money. She says she just needs a safe place and has nowhere else to go, and from what I know about that Ortiz family, I can believe it. But I still spent half the night trying to figure out what her game is."

Rose grabbed Abby's hand. Her skin was cool and smooth, as if time had worn away even her fingerprints. "She risked her own neck to squeal on those gangsters who started the fire by the river that burned down our Racheleh's house and told the sheriff Santiago was not there when it happened. She did that because she cared about him and wanted he should go to college, am I right? Then she finds out she's knocked up, and she keeps Santiago out of trouble again, and it couldn't have been easy to be a single mother. There must have been plenty of times she wished she had some more money or the help of her kid's father. If you ask me, she's only here because she has no choice, it's a last resort."

"Ma, why all this sudden love for Rosalinda?" CeCe said.

Rose snorted. "No love, *bubeleh*. If she was after Santiago or Abby's money, why would she wait four years? That's old news. Whatever this *tsimmes* is, it's happening now." She released Abby's hand after giving her a meaningful look.

"Poor Santi. Miguel just got a nice letter from him, so excited about his new job and dating some new girl. Just as he's getting his legs underneath him, this happens," CeCe said.

"So he has a son—who are you to say that's a bad thing?" Rose was always ready to debate the opposite side of an issue. "When you get to be my age, you learn that what you think is bad can end up good and what you think is good can turn out bad. No use in getting all *farklempt*."

Abby finished her coffee and took her cup to the sink to rinse it. CeCe reflected her stance in this, Rose reflected Ben's. But she did feel stronger now, more ready for whatever came next, which for the moment meant going home and fixing breakfast for her guests. After that, she would figure out how and when to tell Santiago.

Santiago looked out of his North Beach office bay windows. Columbus Avenue stretched out below him—the Italian quarter—and on a clear day like this, he could see Telegraph Hill and Coit Tower; the wharf was only eight blocks away. Gordon had spared no expense on their top-floor suite of offices for Polydactyl Press.

"Dad wants a meeting," Reggie said, sticking his head in Santi's doorway.

Santiago followed Reggie to Gordon's corner office, a massive, light-filled space. Kat smiled at him from her seat on the sofa. Reggie plunked down beside her, leaving Santi the chair.

Gordon was on the phone at his desk, nodding at them and holding up one finger. His assistant, Bev, brought in a tray of coffee and placed it on the table in front of them. Santi noticed Reggie had his laptop and Kat had a notebook and pen. Just as he was leaving to find something to write on, Gordon got off the phone.

"Well, initial press releases have been issued. Polydactyl has listings in *Publishers Marketplace* and ads in *Publishers Weekly* and some writers' magazines, literary journals. I'll email you the marketing details. We're on board with Ingram for distribution. But we'll need product to deliver. Santiago?"

"I've looked at maybe fifty manuscripts, some agented, most direct submissions from authors. I have maybe two I'd like you guys to take a look at. The rest are just not worthy."

"With word getting out, you can expect a sharp increase in submissions. I want a list of five initial releases ASAP, and as you've already seen, you have to wade through a lot of crap to find the gems. Reggie, do you agree we can push our production schedule to twelve months?"

"For all five books at once, or staggered?" Reggie asked.

"They can be staggered, maybe a month apart," Gordon said.

"Since we're each one-person departments, I like staggered," Kat said. "Especially for our first year."

"Sure. But to be honest, this is going to be an intense schedule for at least the next six months to a year, and a lot is going to fall on your shoulders. That's how it goes in the start-up phase. Expect long hours, pretty much every day. Eventually we'll be expanding our personnel, but not before—"

Santiago's phone began to ring. He hit "Ignore" after seeing it was his mom. He'd call her back after the meeting. After a short pause, it rang a second time—his mom again. "Sorry," he said and switched off his phone. He flushed with embarrassment, as if his boss and colleagues could somehow know his mommy was interrupting their meeting right when Gordon was giving the speech about commitment and work ethic.

"Do you need to take that?" Gordon asked, his tone sounding concerned.

"It was just home. I'll call them back. My phone is off now. Sorry."

"Santiago." Gordon smiled. "The first priority in this family business is family. Step out and call home. I promise we'll be just fine without you for a few minutes."

Santiago stepped out. This had better be good. He turned on his phone and hit speed dial.

"Santi?" Abby said before it even rang on his end.

"Yeah, mom. Look, I'm at work and—"

"Santiago, I wouldn't be calling during business hours if this wasn't important. Do you have a few minutes?"

Gordon's words replayed in Santi's mind. "Sure."

"I wish I didn't have to tell you this, but I have to, because you have a right to know. It impacts your life, and I can't protect you from that."

"You're making me nervous here—what is it?" He could hear her rapid breathing for a long moment. His pulse ramped up in response.

"Rosalinda came here last night with a three-year-old boy she claims is yours. He was born March 22, nine months after you and Rosalinda were together that summer. We need to do a paternity test."

"That's impossible."

"That would be why we do a paternity test. Rosalinda says she wants it done, she's that sure. Santi, little Diego looks exactly like you. This might be happening."

Santiago leaned against the wall as his legs threatened to buckle. "Mom, I can't do this."

"I know, son, but you have to. We're using a national company—they do it with an inner cheek swab. They have a testing site you can go to over in the Financial District, and we can have the results in less than a week. I'll give you the address and phone number. Santi, however this turns out, this doesn't have to alter your career or your life. We will figure this out as a family. Please try not to worry."

Santi hung up after taking down the address. He could barely write, his hands were shaking so badly. It was such a cliché, but getting this call, hearing her words, seemed like a nightmare. He even felt slow-witted, unable to move. But there was no waking up from this. He might be royally screwed. All of his hard work, this opportunity in the publishing world, Kat—he could lose it all and just be another Hispanic guy with a baby mama in Valencia County, New Mexico.

"Santi?" Kat materialized in front of him. She grabbed his arm and led him into his office, shutting the door behind them. She sat him and then herself on the plush armchairs in front of his desk. He bent forward, his gaze locked on the oriental rug beneath his feet, the intricate pattern swirling. She leaned toward him and held his hand. "Santi, did someone die?"

"No, no one died . . . someone was born. I told you about Rosalinda. She showed up at my house last night with a boy she says is mine. I have to do a paternity test. How's this for timing?"

"He's probably not yours. This comes from having a wealthy family. My family deals with this kind of thing from time to time. Some crazy will show up and make some kind of allegation, and our lawyers pay them to go away. It's this game everyone plays." She rolled her big brown eyes. God, she was cute. Could she be right?

"My mom said the kid looks like me."

"What—Hispanic, with dark hair and eyes? Male? Three or four years old? You can probably order one off of Craigslist."

Santiago laughed. "How can you crack me up at a time like this?"

"I'm just cool that way. I'm so cool that even if this rug rat turns out to be yours, I'll be the coolest dad's girlfriend there ever was." She stopped laughing. "I'm serious . . . I'd be cool."

"Will you come with me and hold my hand when they swab inside my cheek?"

Her hand migrated up his thigh as she kissed him back. "Are you sure they don't need a sperm sample?"

This kid, this Diego, might be all the sperm sample they need, he thought.

Chapter Three

ROSE HAD BECOME adept at working the remote on her new flat-screen TV. She watched it from her bed or in her easy chair when she crocheted. Flipping through channels, she landed on *The Westerner* starring Gary Cooper. She remembered seeing it at the Oceana Theater in Brighton Beach in 1940. The repetition of her swift crochet hook and the drone of Gary Cooper's voice made her eyelids heavy . . .

Rose is eighteen, holding her father's bible, dark blue velvet with spots worn thin from the devotion of past family members. Papa didn't bring much when he fled Russia in 1914, but his bible was his priority. Mameh's was her Shabbat candlesticks. Rose rubs the not-so-soft velvet with her hand. The mother-of-pearl Star of David in the center is still smooth on her fingertips as she stares at it.

"Bring it here, Rose," she hears her father say. He sits at the head of the table, dark brimmed hat, long beard, and *payots* curling down his cheeks. Her rabbi uncles are around him as her mother serves them wine. The smells of *tsimmes* and chicken waft from the kitchen. Her mouth waters.

Rose brings her father the bible and sits at the table. Almost every man she has known in her life in Brighton Beach looks the same—except the kosher butcher, who is bald and wears a tiny yarmulke. Her father and her uncles speak in Yiddish. Everyone does. She sees her mother stab her fingers under her *sheitel* to scratch her head on her way back to the kitchen, a tired hitch in her step.

She had been one of the Jewish immigrant women who did hand sewing and made baked goods to help raise funds to open the first synagogue there. Now her mother assists the war effort by collecting toothpaste tubes and taking them to Radin's Pharmacy on Brighton Beach Avenue. When she's not cleaning and cooking and serving the men, she's walking the neighborhoods collecting. Rose tries to be a good Jewish daughter, but at eighteen she feels more like taking flight. She and her friends like to go to the Brighton Beach Baths and dance to the bands playing there. That's the closest she's come to flying.

"Baruch atah Adonai, Elohaynu melech ha'olam," her father begins the wine blessing. Rose recites along in her head. She speaks Hebrew, as she was sent to Hebrew school and was bat mitzvahed at thirteen. But she can't hold a conversation in it like she can in Yiddish. She moves her feet under the table and thinks of Frank Sinatra. He's dreamy.

In the city, Friday nights are big nights. Not everyone observes, like in Brighton Beach. Nor is everything centered on being Jewish. Thirty-five minutes away by the Brighton Beach Line that whips through the neighborhoods, the city is a different world. Not that *she* knows, but friends tell her. Friends who are brave enough to defy their parents. Friends who don't have rabbi uncles lurking around every corner of the apartment like watchdogs, making it hard for a gal to sneak anywhere.

Rose's family doesn't blame her for going to the beach for entertainment. That's the only place poor kids go in the summer. That or walk the fifteen blocks of Brighton Beach Avenue looking in storefront windows. She can't afford Coney Island. Most of the Jewish young men here have been shipped out to war, so anything that could be considered a date is slim pickings. Seems everywhere she turns, she sees someone sobbing over a lost loved one. The Brighton Beach Baths is her happy place, even though she hears it is not what it was in its heyday.

On Saturday night, she puts her bathing suit on under her cotton floral dress and yanks the puff sleeves around straight, slips on shoes she can easily kick off to dance barefoot. Her heart beats with the thought of Glenn Miller playing in the pavilion tonight. She loads her makeup into her purse to put on later, once she's out of the house. She likes to wear the bright red lipstick of the stars, and she has been told by friends she resembles Rita Hayworth, although she's much shorter. If only she could get away with tinting her hair red like Rita's. She sticks her purse in her beach bag, hoping one of her girlfriends will have money for a locker.

She makes a corned beef sandwich and wraps it in waxed paper to go in her bag. "Going to the beach now, Mameh," she says and walks down the four flights of stairs in their six-floor apartment building on Brighton 4th Street. To the north she hears the rumbling of the aboveground train and to the south, the crashing sounds of ocean waves.

On her way to the beachfront a block from her apartment building, she weaves in and out of the tables and chairs of the elder Jews on the sidewalks who schmooze and play board games. By the time she gets to the bathhouse, she feels wilted from sweat and humidity. Her once flouncy hair, held back in tortoise combs, is frizzy. She cranes her neck over clusters of women mah-jongg players, groups of people singing Yiddish songs, open umbrellas, caned push chairs, and men listening to the Brooklyn Dodgers game on tube radios, but she doesn't see her girlfriends. The beach itself is full of children splashing and adults swimming, picnicking, and taking pictures. Coney Island's beach is always busier. But tonight Glenn Miller plays in the band shell, so she notices an ocean of strange faces in the growing crowd. She squints at the tiny gold-plated watch she got for her bat mitzvah.

She decides to sidle up to Mrs. Rabinowitz, who sits under a comfortable canopy in her canvas lounge chair watching her grandchildren play. Rose doesn't have an actual membership to the baths, even though practically every Jew in Brighton Beach belongs. Mrs. Rabinowitz lives on the floor below them, and sometimes Rose takes care of her cat when she's away. Rose plays cards with her neighbor until her excitement over the approaching time for the big band grows too great. She decides to make her way closer to the band shell, even though she can never hope to actually get down front. But she will be able to hear the music and dance right outside. There are posters of the Glenn Miller Orchestra slapped everywhere. She sees her two girlfriends running off with the Perlowitz twins and sighs. Stood up again.

"He plays a mean trombone," a young man says to her. He looks like he's from the city in his white shoes and loose-fitting pleated pants. She figures he's in his early twenties and definitely not Jewish. Gary Cooper handsome, with his unassuming big blue eyes and slicked-back hair. "You going in?" Rose shakes her head no. She hasn't had much experience talking to guys like him. She never even went to school with non-Jews. "I've got an extra pass to the show," he says, producing two white pieces of paper out of his pants pocket. "By the way, I'm Nick."

"I'm Rose."

"Let's go in," he says, pulling her by the hand. He guides her through the crowd until they are right up near the big white band shell. He smiles broadly at her.

"How did you get passes?" Rose asks. She has never heard of such a thing.

"My buddies and I are union musicians. Some have sat in with the band, so they get passes."

"What do you play?" Rose asks. Her stomach growls, but she is too embarrassed to take her corned beef sandwich out of her bag.

"Clarinet, tenor sax, some drums if they can't find a real drummer," he says with a laugh.

"You live in the city?"

"That's where the work is. But I like coming out here to the beach. I'll like it even more now."

Rose feels herself blush. He's no doubt a wolf, but in a crowd of people, who can he hurt?

The band enters the stage, and Rose ignites like a match. She feels Nick watch her more than the band as she sways to the melodies of her favorite songs. She's so close she can see the trumpet players empty their spit valves and feel the heat from the musicians as they play. Nick takes her onto the dance floor. He's much taller than she is, but they fit somehow. He glides her around the floor to "Moonlight Serenade." She has never been in the arms of a real man. She doesn't count her awkward pubescent dancing with pimply boys at all the bar mitzvahs and Jewish weddings in her past. She waits for him to get fresh, for in the back of her mind she hears her father say that goy boys are only after one thing. But he's a perfect gentleman. "Pennsylvania 6-5000," the band's newest big hit and the last song of the night, gets the entire crowd up and dancing. Rose yells along with the rest of the audience, "Pennsylvania six five thousand!" She has no idea that it's the telephone number of the Café Rouge at the Hotel Pennsylvania in New York City until Nick yells in her ear. His breath gives her chills and feelings in places she's never felt before.

"I have a surprise," he says as he grabs her hand and leads her behind the band shell. The band is packing up, smoking cigarettes, cleaning off their instruments, and laying them in their cases as if putting babies to bed. Nick takes her over to Glenn Miller, who shakes Nick's hand.

"Good to see you again," Glenn Miller says to Nick while Rose stands dumbstruck.

"This is my friend, Rose. She's a huge fan."

"Nice to meet you, Rose," Glenn Miller says and reaches for her hand, which seems like it weighs a ton as she lifts it to meet his. "I've a train to catch, but you two have a good night."

She and Nick run out to the beachfront. Rose is laughing hysterically, and she realizes they are still holding hands. Suddenly he kisses her. Overhead the summer fireworks burst and light up the sky.

"I want to see you again, Rose," he says.

"Ma, Ma, wake up. It's time for your medication." CeCe gently patted Rose's arm. She must have fallen asleep in her chair. Rose shifted, the TV still showing the same cowboy movie. At first Rose tried to stand without her cane or walker. Hadn't she been dancing on air moments before? But the heavy pull of gravity and sharp hip pain jolted her back to reality. So did trying to catch her breath.

"Ma, what are you trying to do?" CeCe said, grabbing Rose by her elbow as she collapsed back in her seat. "Are you still asleep?"

"*Farmisht*," said Rose, shaking her head for clarity. Her heart still felt the tenderness of the dream, the searching Gary Cooper blue eyes of Nick, the suddenness and excitement of his kiss. It made Rose's body feel things that in this world she could not and had not for decades. Maybe this was the beginning of her dying process.

"The meds you're on can cause dizziness. You scared me. You practically shot out of your chair like a rocket," CeCe said. "Here, drink a glass of water."

"Funny how your mind can think one way and your body another. Sometimes I still feel eighteen inside my head and heart, *fershtay*? I forget I can't leap out of a chair like I used to."

"The spirit's willing, the flesh is weak. I know how it is."

"You think your flesh is weak?" Rose said, flapping the loose skin of her arms under her robe sleeves. "Not to mention what's giving out on the inside of me." Even weakened, her heart seemed determined to wring out what lay buried.

39

"Well, your mouth isn't giving out, that's for sure." CeCe handed Rose her pills. "So put these in it."

Rosalinda turned her face to the sun as she stood at the rail fence of Rachel's goat pasture with Diego. They had been at Abby's for a few days now and had driven with her into Albuquerque yesterday for their cheek swabs. Santiago was going in for his today, according to Abby. Rosalinda hadn't spoken to him yet but knew how pissed he must be. Abby told her all about his great new life in San Francisco, which included a girlfriend. Rosalinda responded that she never wanted to disrupt Santi's life. Abby had looked at her long and hard, but then thanked her. It had almost seemed as if Abby believed her.

"Mama! Look at those goats—they are bonking their heads!" Diego laughed and pointed to the goats that were rearing up and diving into each other headfirst, producing an audible *conk*.

"That's how they play." Rosalinda kissed the top of his head as he hung from the top rail, his little tennis-shoed feet perched on the lower rail. Goats rushed over to inspect them, using their mouths to explore their clothing and whatever else they could reach.

Rachel came over carrying a bucket. "I have some old apples. Would you like to feed them to the goats, Diego? You hold your hand flat, like this, with the apple sitting on top."

Diego nodded and put out his hand the way Rachel demonstrated, but as soon as the goat's searching lips tried to take the apple, he shrieked with laughter and dropped it. Rachel picked it up and helped him try again, but not before smiling and making eye contact with Rosalinda, startling her with such intensely blue eyes. Then Rosalinda remembered Rachel was half-Hispanic, from her father, and half-Jewish, from her mother. Was it her Jewish side that gave her those blue eyes? She appeared Hispanic otherwise. Maggie looked completely Hispanic and nothing like Abby. Hattie, Rachel's daughter with Charlie Hood, her Anglo husband, was a total blondie, what Rosalinda had grown up calling a *güera*. Since becoming a mother, Rosalinda had become fascinated by genetics, and right there on Sol y Sombra—Sunlight and Shadow, what they called this farm—all sorts of combinations made up their extended family. Just like the name said, light and dark. In the world she had grown up in, lines between races were firmly drawn.

Everyone here was treating both her and Diego with such kindness it was making her stomach ache. She was surprised by how quickly Abby, Ben, Maggie, and now the Vigils were welcoming them into their families. Of course they were nice to an innocent little boy who might be their precious Santi's son, but they were equally nice to her. It made her wonder how things would have gone if she had come to them when she first knew she was pregnant. At the time, she had only imagined anger, resentment, and blame. Maybe she had been wrong.

Rosalinda clapped and cheered with Rachel as Diego held still long enough for a goat to take an apple. The warmth of the sun beat through her jacket. Dappling through the yellow leaves of the cotton-woods, the sun bathed everything in golden light. She loved October in New Mexico, although she had never been anywhere else. She had grown up not far from where she stood but had not been out of Albu-querque in four years. Living in the city blunted the experience of autumn—or any other season, for that matter. Here, she remembered how much she loved the crisp air, the stark blue skies, the hulking Manzano Mountains. She could smell the lingering, spicy scent of chile roasting and the earthy, musty smell of harvested hay and alfalfa.

Being suspended here in time was like living in a dream. When the harsh reality of Caden's terrible plan intruded, she felt the pain and panic of her regret and fear.

Diego's giggling snapped her out of her thoughts. Rachel, her long, curly, dark hair flying, twirled Diego through the air and loudly smooched his exposed, round toddler tummy. These people exuded the kind of love she had never experienced. Not as a child and cer-tainly not now. The closest she had come to knowing what love felt like was in Santiago's arms that long-ago summer, which would now seem like nothing more than a fantasy if it weren't for the solid evi-dence grinning at her from Rachel's arms.

Santiago took Kat to Trattoria Pinocchio on Columbus for dinner to thank her for going with him to the paternity testing lab. He could still feel the swab swiping his inner cheek, collecting epithelial cells for the test. He swished his wine on that side, trying to rinse the entire experience away. His mom said she had taken Rosalinda and Diego into Albuquerque yesterday for their tests and Diego had sat very still and cooperated with the tech when his sample was col-lected. He could hear her becoming attached to this child, which only freaked him out further. He was counting on the test proving he was not the father and refused to consider any other outcome.

Kat snapped her fingers. "What's going on? You completely checked out on me."

"Sorry." He took another gulp of his Chianti.

She reached for his hand across the table. "Look, worst case scenario, you're on the hook for child support."

"Let's talk about something else. I'm halfway through a manuscript that I'm really excited about. The author has won some regional awards and has published some short fiction in journals, but this is her first novel. It's called *Black Cat Alley*, and I'm totally hooked."

"Santi. Please don't shut me out. I know you are dealing with a lot, but I'm here for you." She stroked his hand with her fingertips.

Her soothing tone grated on his nerves. His anger over all of this was barely containable, and he could feel himself wanting to lose it and yell at her, but this wasn't about Kat. She was just the person in front of him. "Kat, I really can't do this right now. I just want to eat dinner and put it out of my mind for a while. Can't you get that? Please."

Her eyes filled with tears, and her pale skin flushed. "This isn't easy for me either, you know. Shit! My boyfriend might be some kid's father. I've risked everything to take this step with you—have you thought about that? I love you, Santi. I've loved you for a very long time, and I've had to watch you be with Tori and all the other chicks who were all wrong for you, and finally I have this chance—we have this chance—and it's getting blown to hell!" Now her tears were streaming down her face.

Santiago shook his head, feeling his control slip away. "I'm sorry. I can't do this." He pulled out his wallet and threw a handful of cash onto the table. He downed the last of his wine. "I need some air."

He heard her say, "Wait" as he rushed out of there. He couldn't face her pain, even though she was entitled to it. Their apartment was only a few blocks away, but when he reached the turn, he kept walking, heading south on Grant Avenue until he found himself in Chinatown. It was after dark but only seven thirty. Tourists, whole families, collected in front of shops and milled around under the streetlights, holding out maps or consulting their phones. Laughter, kid's voices, music swirled around him. He had to dodge people taking selfies or posing for group shots in front of paper dragons and lanterns.

He finally stopped when he reached the Chinatown Gateway. It was going to be uphill all the way home, but he wasn't ready to go there yet, not physically and not mentally. He only existed in the present moment, breathing the incense-laden air, looking up at the moon, keeping his focus tight until he could calm down. He turned and walked the block and a half back to St. Mary's Square, where he gazed up at the huge metal and granite statue of Dr. Sun Yat-sen, the founder of the Republic of China, and the nearby statue honoring the Chinese Americans who died in both world wars defending their country, the United States.

He looked across California Street to see Old St. Mary's Cathedral lit up, its spire cross jutting into the darkness. He crossed over and stood on its steps. The plaque said it was the first Catholic cathedral in San Francisco, built by Chinese laborers and dedicated in 1854. He looked up to the clock face: 8:50 p.m. Beneath it an inscription read: "Son, Observe the Time and Fly from Evil." As much as he had struggled against evil in his life, the message seemed meant for him. It made him think of Miguel Vigil, the most virtuous and wise man Santi had ever known. Miguel never gave him the answers, but somehow he opened the doors inside of him to reveal the answers he was seeking. He sat on a bench and pulled out his phone, calling the Vigil's landline before he had time to think about it.

"Good God who's calling at this hour!" CeCe's voice exploded in his ear.

"Oh, it's later there, I forgot—I'm sorry, CeCe," Santi said.

"Santiago? It's almost ten o'clock. But don't worry, kid, you didn't wake us up."

"How's Rose doing?" He hadn't talked to CeCe since he'd heard about Rose's prognosis.

"Better than I am, I think. Physically, she doesn't seem that different yet. Gets tired quickly, sleeps more. But she seems happy, and I think that's real odd. I mean, she just lost her husband and was told her heart is failing, but Miguel says to be happy she's happy and try not to analyze it. I bet that's who you called to talk to, am I right?"

"Yeah."

After some fumbling, he heard Miguel's voice. "Hola, *mi'jo*. How are you?"

"Scared shitless," he said.

"I bet you are. Abby tells me you won't know anything for sure for three more days, though," Miguel said.

"What do you think, Miguel? You've seen Rosalinda and the kid. Do you think he's mine?" Santiago closed his eyes as he waited for Miguel's response.

"Santi, he's a cute little boy, but he's only three, so how can I tell who he looks like? Little ones all look alike, no? Only when they grow older and develop jug ears or a pointy nose do they display the physical traits that run in a family. Thank God we have scientific tests these days. *Hasta que lo veas, no lo creas.* Until you see it, don't believe it."

"I don't know what to do," Santi said, regressing into a young boy at Miguel's knee.

"For now, wait until you know the results of the test. If you are the father, you will have responsibilities to face, but now is not the time, *mi'jo.* You can give yourself an ulcer and make yourself crazy with your worry, but what will that accomplish?"

"I want my life here. I've worked for this for so long. I feel like I could lose everything for a mistake I made four years ago."

"You aren't alone in this. It's not all on your shoulders. *La familia,* Santiago. We will help you. But consider this, you may have made what you call a mistake, but the child, he is no one's mistake. He is an innocent little boy, just as you once were not that long ago, *¿comprende?*"

"What's Rosalinda like for a mom?"

"Rachel's seen more of them, but she tells me Rosalinda is a loving mother and he seems like a happy, healthy boy who is very close to his mama. Abby could tell you more."

"I better let you go, Miguel. But thanks. Sorry to call so late."

Miguel laughed. "CeCe's jumpy these days. You call me anytime, *mi'jo.*"

"Good-bye, Miguel." Santiago stared at the phone as a major wave of guilt washed through him. He had abandoned Kat. When she was crying. Shit. At least talking to Miguel had the grounding effect he had hoped for. Just saying his fears out loud gave them less power. Now he could focus on Kat and her feelings that he had so soundly trampled. But if his behavior cooled things off on her end, maybe it was for the best. He shouldn't be anyone's boyfriend right now.

Chapter Four

IT WAS FRIDAY. Ben was teaching at UNM. Maggie was at school. Abby heated up some homemade chicken noodle soup for her, Rosalinda, and Diego's lunch. The paternity test results would not be available until Monday. Rosalinda had taken it upon herself to clean the bathroom. Abby could hear the fervent scrubbing and caught a whiff of bleach wafting down the hallway. Rosalinda was not one to sit around; Abby gave her credit for that. Diego was scooching the new red tractor Miguel had given him along the faded linoleum floor. He looked up at her and grinned. "This tractor goes fast, see?" He gave the toy a shove, and it traveled about two feet before toppling over on its side, which delighted Diego even more. "Crash!" he said.

Abby dropped down to sit cross-legged on the floor. Diego propelled the tractor to her, and she sent it back to him. In the four days he had been there, Abby had grown increasingly fond of the little guy, even as she still hoped with all her heart he was not Santiago's son. Hearing the stress in her son's voice over the phone had rattled her. He might be approaching twenty-three, but she was still hardwired to react as his mom.

Diego crawled over to her lap, rolling and wiggling like a puppy. She laughed and tickled him while he giggled and shrieked in delight. When she stopped, he lay panting in her lap and looked up at her with his big, brown Santiago eyes. "You are my friend, right?"

She nodded, her hand still on his tummy. "Yes, and I'm so glad you came to visit."

The smile faded from his face. "But mama and me don't go to my school anymore so I don't see Oliver and Emma and Reynaldo and those other kids."

"You miss your friends at school?"

"And Miss Nicole. She sings songs and helps me paint." Diego scrambled to get up. "Mama!" he yelled into the hallway. Abby got up to follow him.

Rosalinda appeared, taking off her yellow gloves. "Yes, *mi amor?*"

"I want to go back to school now."

"Oh, baby, we talked about that. We're going to stay here with Abby a little bit longer, and then we'll see." Rosalinda picked him up, and Diego buried his head into her neck and began to cry. "I think you are very tired. After lunch we'll rest on the bed and read some books. Let's wash hands." She held him up to the kitchen sink and helped him soap and rinse his hands.

Abby quickly ladled some of her soup into three bowls, buttered a slice of her homemade wheat bread for Diego, and set everything on the table. She poured milk for Diego. "I didn't let the soup come to a full boil, so hopefully it isn't too hot for him."

Rosalinda stuck her finger into the bowl and then licked it off. "It's fine."

They sat down together and began to eat.

"Abby, why do you still live in this little old house? I mean it's cozy and all, but, well . . ."

"That's what my husband wants to know. Eventually we'll renovate—I just dread all the chaos," Abby said. "But that's not the whole truth."

Rosalinda raised an eyebrow.

"I grew up in a mansion. I don't even know how many rooms, but there were three wings and three stories. That house had everything, indoor and outdoor swimming pools, game rooms, a theater, a humungous indoor kitchen that opened to an outdoor kitchen—this was in San Diego. But the one thing it never had was love or even attention from my parents. I was close to Lupe, our Mexican cook. She was my family."

"Is that why you became a chef?" Rosalinda asked.

"Yes, and that's why I am so comfortable in this house. It's little and old, and I do my laundry in the kitchen, but it feels real and honest. I'm afraid to change it, I guess."

"It's full of love—with Ben and Maggie—that won't go away,"

Rosalinda said, her expression open and reassuring. "It's your family that makes it feel the way it does."

"Mama, I'm all done," Diego said with a yawn.

Rosalinda began to clear the table. "Go ahead, I'll do this," Abby said.

She cleaned up and put things away, hearing the drone of Rosalinda reading to Diego in the nearby bedroom. She didn't know why she had opened up to Rosalinda. Four years ago, she practically hated the girl and certainly didn't trust her. But there was this strange thing happening between them that Abby wasn't sure she could name, let alone understand. It felt important.

One thing she didn't reveal to Rosalinda was her reluctance to obliterate her first husband's boyhood home. Bobby grew up in this house, scooched his toys on these floors, slept in one of these rooms. When she moved here with him, he disappeared so quickly they barely had a chance to live in the house together. She spent long, tortured months alone under this roof, waiting for him to come home before learning that would never happen.

But then Maggie was born, named for Magdalena, Bobby's long-deceased mother and CeCe's best girlfriend, who had died in a car crash when Bobby was young. Abby converted Magdalena's old sewing room into Maggie's nursery, and Santiago moved into Bobby's boyhood bedroom. For seven years she was a single mom, grieving and healing in these rooms.

Then Ben came along, and even though she could bring herself to move on from Bobby, she kept her attachment to the house just as it was. It filled her with fresh grief to think about knocking it down to build something new, even if that included a more functional kitchen, a separate laundry room, walk-in closets, and enough bathrooms for everyone. It was silly, she knew. But when she couldn't sleep, she walked these floors at night and felt the reassuring presence of the spirits who still shared the house with her. They would wrap their arms around her and ease her worries. She could hear Magdalena whisper words of encouragement, and though Abby had never met her, she recognized her immediately from CeCe's stories. Bobby's father, Ricardo, whose death had brought them to this place, often wandered through the house at night alongside her—she knew it was him from his gentle strength. And even Bobby himself came by to check on her and Maggie, to reassure her it was okay to love another man. What would they think if she destroyed their home? How could she do that?

Rosalinda joined her, looking out the kitchen door window, and said, "The leaves are starting to fall. Naked trees make me sad."

With the recent death of Mort—even though it was his time—and with Rose going bit by bit, death seemed linked to the coming winter. When trees were blown bare and flowers shriveled in their beds, it was hard to remember spring's renewal. Winter gave Miguel and the other Esperanza farmers a well-deserved break from their labors, but it tested Abby's faith. "Rosalinda, would you like some tea? I was going to put the kettle on, and then maybe we could talk."

"Sure."

They waited in companionable silence for the kettle to boil. Abby laid out a tray with Magdalena's china teapot and two cups. She spooned the loose tea into the pot and then poured in the water that had come to a boil and carried the tray into the living room.

"Do you take sugar or milk?" Abby asked.

"No, this is fine," Rosalinda said. She took a sip from the delicate flowered cup. "This is my first tea party in real life. I used to have them at the day care with the little kids—even the boys liked them—but that's just at work."

Abby smiled. "Maggie and I used to have tea parties all the time with her dolls and stuffed animals. We'd even bake scones or little cakes to serve. Now she's nearly twelve and too old for such nonsense."

"She's a great girl. I remember when she was seven and Santiago called her his annoying little sister, but I could tell how much he loved her."

"He was so much help when she was born. He was only ten, but he took care of both of us. Changed her diapers, made me scrambled eggs after I was up all night with her," Abby said. She paused and took a breath. "I wanted to ask you, if the paternity test shows Santi is Diego's father, what do you want from him?"

Rosalinda set down her teacup. She looked at her hands for a moment and then looked up to meet Abby's gaze. "He's welcome to be in Diego's life as much as he wants. But I wouldn't be here at all if we weren't threatened. And as soon as this mess with Jack is over, I'm breaking up with him. Putting Diego at risk with his gambling, that's the last straw."

"Would this Jack hurt you—I mean if you break up with him?"

"No. He'll be hurt, but he'd never harm us. I haven't even heard from him, and I have no idea where he is or if he's even coming back. Whoever these guys are, they said they'd kill him. That's why he took off, and that's why he sent me away. He didn't tell me anything about them—to keep us safe. I might never see him again, and that would be just fine."

"But what will you do? You left your job at the day care. Where will you live?"

"I want to move back down here, find a little place. The rent is cheaper here than in Albuquerque. James is still in prison for the bosque fire, and the rest of the family has scattered, so the coast is clear—I don't have to worry about running into any of their sorry asses. I've missed Esperanza. It's so different here than in the city. I want to find another job at a day care, maybe over in Los Lunas, where I can be with Diego like before. I like working with kids, and even though the pay is bad, it saves me on childcare for Diego until he starts school in a few years."

"What are you now, about twenty-seven?"

"Yeah. How old are you?" Rosalinda asked.

Abby smiled at her boldness. "I was only three years older than you when I first came to Esperanza, pregnant with Maggie. I'm forty-two. I warn you, it goes faster than you can imagine."

"I was going to go back to school and become a dental hygienist or something. But then I found out I was pregnant. I had morning sickness all day long, and I had to work full-time, so there was no way I could go to school. After Diego came, I knew I couldn't hand him off to strangers to watch, so that's how I started working in a day care, just so I could be with him. I want to go back to school, maybe when Diego is in kindergarten."

Abby poured herself another cup of tea. "If you believed Santiago was Diego's father, why didn't you come to us when you found out you were pregnant? We would have helped you."

"What I loved about Santiago were all his big dreams, his drive to become something. You gave him that, and I didn't want to take it away from him. So I did it on my own, and I'd still be doing it on my own if it weren't for stupid Jack. It kills me that Diego misses his friends at the day care—I miss working there. I'll just have to start over. I've done it a million times, I can do it again."

49

"You won't be alone this time. If the paternity test comes back positive, we'll set up child support. I'll be Diego's grandma, and I expect to be in his life and yours. I'll be advising Santiago to stay in San Francisco for his career, but I know he'll want to be a part of Diego's life. We'll figure out the details once we know for sure, but I wanted you to know where I stand on this. I care about you, and I care about Diego—even if he isn't Santi's son. I'll help you get away from your boyfriend and start a new life. In case you haven't noticed, we're all one big family around here. Once you're in, good luck getting out."

The paternity testing organization had given Santiago a code to use on their secure website to find out the results after they were posted on Monday morning. He woke at five, but the results were not up yet. After compulsively hitting "Refresh" about a hundred times, he got ready for work.

He and Kat had sort of made up, though, through some unspoken agreement, they were not sleeping together at the moment. He figured they were on hold. When he emerged from his room, he found her making coffee. She looked at him, her eyes wide and fearful.

He shook his head no, but then saw her relief and realized she misunderstood. "No, I mean the results aren't up yet."

Her face resumed its worried expression. "Coffee?"

"Thanks." He stood behind her, wrapped his arms around her waist, and hugged her. She leaned against him. They stood that way for a long moment.

Abby and Rosalinda sat next to each other at Abby's desk while Diego rolled around on Abby and Ben's bed, singing something about goats and chickens. Abby logged onto her computer and went to the secure website the paternity testing company had given her. She tried to type in the code but messed it up in her nervousness, then tried again. She could feel Rosalinda lean in closer, though she seemed completely calm.

The results page appeared. Abby's eyes scanned down past the tables and graphs until she read: "Probability of Paternity: 99.9999%." She stared at the screen until her tears blurred all those nines into meaningless loops. She thought she had been prepared, but now that she saw the truth in black and white, she was stunned.

"I don't want anything from Santiago, I promise," Rosalinda whispered.

Abby nodded, unable to look at her. Yet even as her heart ached for Santiago, she felt something else begin to rise within her—a lightness, a giddiness—and she began to laugh. When she looked at Rosalinda, who appeared seriously concerned, she laughed harder. Abby stood up and pulled a startled Rosalinda into her arms for a hug. "I'm a grandma. I'm Diego's grandma," she said into Rosalinda's ear. She looked over Rosalinda's shoulder to see Diego jumping on the bed and flapping his arms like a bird. Abby let go of Rosalinda and tackled Diego on the bed. "Who's this little monkey jumping on my bed?"

Diego wrestled with her and giggled maniacally. "I'm a flying monkey, that's what."

Abby pulled him onto her lap, and he did not resist. The feel of his warm skin, the faint scent of him, seemed deeply familiar, and Abby knew she would love him for the rest of her life.

Santiago stared at his office computer screen. "Shit." The parade of nines on the paternity probability score mocked him until he closed the damn thing. He kicked his wastebasket. He paced, running his hand through his hair. Of course he'd knocked up Rosalinda. Why should he be surprised? His life was fucked. He was cursed. The Baca curse that his father passed on to him after he murdered Santiago's mother and then Roberto Silva had laid low long enough for him to think he had escaped it. He'd gotten lucky after Abby had adopted him, enjoyed some great years, and even made it through college and landed this job. All the better for karma to pull the rug out from under him now, when he had so much to lose.

He looked around his office at the piles of manuscripts stacked here and there, the art on the wall he and Kat had picked out together when life was still good, when his future was still his. He couldn't believe it when, in his freshman year, his new college friends, Reggie and Kat Hopkins, told him their father published the quarterly literary magazine *Polydactyl*, a reference to Ernest Hemingway's six-toed cats. Santi not only subscribed to the magazine, it had published one of his short stories when he was still in high school, leading to his getting a scholarship to UCLA. Then Gordon Hopkins decided to branch into book publishing. Gordon recruited him to be the editor after reading his collection of short stories and the first draft of his novel in progress. When he hired Santi, he emphasized it had nothing to do with his friendship with Kat and Reggie. He made it clear that it was Santi's literary aesthetic he was after, not a playmate for his children. Gordon said he chose him rather than one of the seasoned editors who applied because he wanted Polydactyl Press to be innovative, and when he read Santiago's work he felt the excitement he was seeking. Santiago didn't think twice about deferring his MFA pursuit for the opportunity. It seemed like divine providence. But it was only a mirage.

He strode out of his office and over to Gordon's doorway. Gordon was sitting at his immense antique desk, his reading glasses perched on his tan nose. The sun streaming through the windows glinted off the silver mane of hair that somehow made him seem younger than his fifty years, though his constant marathon training didn't hurt. Santiago, a high school cross-country athlete, had run with Gordon a few times and was challenged to keep pace.

Gordon looked up from the paper he was reading. "Santiago, come in."

Santiago sat down and leaned toward Gordon. "I need to tell you something. I found out a girl I dated right after high school had gotten pregnant and never told me. So there is this three-and-a-half-year-old kid back in New Mexico that's mine—I just now saw the paternity results."

"Must be a shock," Gordon said. "What are you going to do?"

"I don't know. I'm totally blown away at the moment."

Gordon nodded, and Santi found it impossible to maintain eye contact with him. His mentor, his boss, his hero, would see what a loser he was after all. "How many manuscripts have you completed?" Gordon asked.

"One hundred and seven. I have twenty or thirty more I want to go through. I have five I like a lot, but I wanted to have at least eight or ten for you guys to read, and then we can hone them down to our final five choices."

"This is Monday. Do you think you could have that ready for us by the weekend?"

"Sure."

"Forgive me if I'm overstepping, but this is what I'd tell my own son. Get your picks done this week and fly home on the weekend and stay a couple of weeks—say, until the end of the month. We'll spend that time reading your choices, and we can talk about them with you as we go. As long as we have our list set by early November, we'll be fine. Kat can contact the agents and authors. Next step would be to do your editorial notes for revisions, and like we said, we'll stagger those deadlines so they don't all hit at once. You need to go home and meet this child and figure out some things. To my mind, that's going to take at least a couple of weeks."

"I'm sorry," Santi said. "The timing is terrible—but I don't need to be away that long. I'll set up child support and deal with the legal stuff and come right back."

"Priorities, Santi. This is only work. You just became a father, and that involves more than paperwork, let me tell you. I'm serious. I don't want you back here before the end of the month. You have to trust me on this." Gordon's mouth was set in a hard line. His chin tilted slightly as he looked Santi in the eye. One did not defy Gordon Hopkins.

"I will," Santiago said and watched Gordon's face soften.

"Good luck, then. And I look forward to reading your choices."

Santiago stood in the doorway of Kat's office, watching her. Her dark hair was twisted into a loose topknot, held in place with two pencils. She wore her black-framed glasses and red lipstick. She smiled as she listened to someone on the phone. "That sounds great. I'll get back to you once we have our release calendar set. Okay, bye, Pete." She hung up, her smile fading as she took in Santi's expression.

"What, no cigar?" she said.

"I talked to Gordon. I'm going to finish up the manuscripts and fly home this weekend. He told me to stay a couple of weeks. I don't think I need that long, but he insisted. Kat, I'm sorry about this." Santi stood awkwardly, unsure if he should say any more, hug her, or what.

Kat stayed in her chair, the desk between them. "I might get over this. I might not. You might go home and realize you're still in love with Rosalinda, get married, have ten more kids, and live happily ever."

"I'm going to set up child support and meet the kid. I suppose that's going to lead to figuring out visitation, because I'm his dad, and I owe it to the kid for him to have his dad in his life. Because that's the decent thing to do, and I want to at least be decent." His words came out more intensely than he intended; he felt his hands squeeze into tight fists. God, he wanted to punch a wall, and he'd never been a wall puncher. But now he understood the appeal of slamming flesh and blood into plaster and wood. "I do not love Rosalinda."

"You don't love me, either," Kat said under her breath.

"Seriously? When has there been time? It's been like a week. I'm sorry you carried around some thing for me all through college while I thought we were just friends. This is new for me, so give me a minute, will you? I'm sorry one of my gazillion sperm got past a condom and fertilized an egg over four years ago—I just got the memo. Can you give me a couple of weeks to take care of this? Isn't that what you'd want? Or would you rather be with some asshole who'd call his lawyer to make it all go away, sign away his paternal rights, pay child support but never meet his son, just go on like nothing happened?"

"That might be for the best. He's done all right without you so far," Kat said.

"I don't know that. I don't know how he's doing. That's what I have to find out. And if you can't get that—"

"I get it. I hate it, but I get it." Kat stood up and walked around her desk to him. "And you're right. The guy I want to be with would never be such an asshole."

"You said you could be cool with this. That you would be the coolest dad's girlfriend ever," Santi said, his anger a receding tide.

She put her arms around him and nestled her face under his chin. He could feel her eyelashes strumming his neck. "That's when I thought it couldn't be true. But being cool is the objective, it is the shining beacon on the hill, I have it in sight. While you're gone I'll be making great strides in that direction."

Rosalinda watched as Abby read to Diego. He was cuddled up on her lap, his face becoming slack and dreamy, like it did before his nap. She marveled at how comfortable Diego was with Abby, especially since the paternity results had become known and Abby seemed to let down her guard and take Diego fully into her heart. Diego didn't know yet that he was in his grandma's arms or that his father would arrive in a few days. Rosalinda and Abby had decided to wait until Santiago arrived to explain things to Diego.

But Diego did know how much he loved it there. Rosalinda saw him flourish with the attention from Abby, Ben, and Maggie. He loved visiting Rachel to play with the goats or Charlie to pet the horses. Miguel took him on a tractor ride, and CeCe sang him songs and baked cookies with his "help." Rose's face lit up when Diego played peekaboo with her or showed her the plastic horse family with real manes and tails that Charlie had brought home from the feed store. Diego hadn't asked about Jesse, even once.

From their first day there, Rosalinda knew she would not cooperate with Jesse and Caden's ridiculous plan. She played along with Jesse to buy time. She had to figure out how to stop them. The more time she spent with these people, the more she knew she could never betray or terrify them with a fake kidnapping to extort money.

Abby finished her story in a whisper as Diego slumped in her lap. She carried him to the bed, and Rosalinda patted his back as he turned onto his tummy and sighed in his sleep.

Rosalinda and Abby came out of their room into the kitchen. Abby put the kettle on. It had become their tradition to share a cup of tea and talk while Diego napped. "I think I'll take a quick walk first," Rosalinda said, reaching for her jacket on its hook by the back door, in among Ben, Abby, and Maggie's jackets.

Abby smiled, her lightly freckled face glowing in its natural beauty. Her hair, a light auburn brown, brushed her shoulders in no particular style. She was thin and toned from her daily runs. She wore very little makeup, causing her to look younger than she was, certainly too young to be anyone's grandma. She wore simple clothes, but they were probably ordered from one of the upscale natural fabrics clothing catalogs Rosalinda had seen around the house, maybe Abby's only indulgence. "I'll keep the kettle warm."

Rosalinda walked through the cottonwoods on the running path she knew Santiago and Abby had formed over the years. The sky was a vibrant blue with chalky white clouds, like something one of her day care kids would create with their tempera paints. Once she was safely out of sight, she called Jesse.

"Rosalinda—about time you checked in. What's going on?" Jesse said. "When are we going to do this thing? You've been there a week and a half already."

"Patience, Jesse. Everything is going perfectly. But listen, Santiago is flying in this weekend, and he going to stay about two weeks. This is good, because he can be with Diego and get all attached, too. It will make the plan work even better." The words tasted foul in her mouth.

"How do you figure?"

"I think we can up the ransom to more like three million. The time we invest now will make for a bigger payday later. After a few more weeks, they'll fork over any amount, I swear."

"Caden's getting antsy," Jesse said.

"I'm sure you can cool his jets. Trust me, Jesse. This is a long con, and you have to play it with patience. It takes time to do it right. You want quick, go rob a bank."

"I guess. I'll deal with Caden. It's not like anyone's going anywhere. We'll just sit tight while you work your magic."

It would take magic to make this all go away. Right now, she needed time to figure out how to stop them, and she had just bought some.

On the flight to Albuquerque, Santiago stared out of the window and wondered what he would be walking into in Esperanza. It was hard to wrap his head around the fact that there was a little kid he had fathered staying in his old bedroom, with a woman he had fallen hard for when he was eighteen but thought he'd never see again. He had been obsessed with her, driven to flaunt Abby's rules and sneak around, anything to be with Rosalinda. He was such a kid then. No wonder his mom had been so freaked out, and yet she had stopped fighting him about it, probably on Miguel's advice. Santi had realized on his own how different they were the night she brought him to the banks of the Rio Grande to party with her gangster cousin, James Ortiz, and his nasty friends. The bosque was officially closed to people and vehicles because of the terrible drought. Open burning and fireworks were banned, so naturally, James and his homies lit a bonfire and set off fireworks. Santi remembered how repulsed he was that these lowlifes could be so arrogant as to threaten the land he loved.

The memory was surreal after four years. The sounds of the drunken gangsters lurching around the bonfire like crazed demons, the pops and fizzes of the fireworks hitting the river, Rosalinda's furious face telling him if he left, she would never forgive him, and neither would James. And him telling her if he didn't leave, he would never forgive himself. Those were the last words they had exchanged, and that was the last time he saw her.

Yet Rosalinda had sworn to Sheriff Ramone Lovato that Santi did not attend the river party where the fire started. Ramone, one of Abby's closest friends, had known better, but he told Santi not to contradict his star witness and then proceeded to arrest James Ortiz and the rest of his crew. At the time Santi thought sparing him was the least Rosalinda could do. But now, he fully grasped that if she had chosen to be vindictive, or even just told the truth, he could have faced felony arson charges alongside James and the others. The ensuing trial would have delayed college and perhaps derailed him altogether.

Rosalinda must have learned she was pregnant soon after that. Again, she spared him, and off he went to Los Angeles to start college. As much of a pain in the ass finding out about this now was, the news would have been more devastating then.

He drank his complementary soda and listened to a little boy seated behind him chatter to his mother. He tried to tune out the innocent voice that interrupted his thoughts. This disruption into his life was not the kid's fault—he even had trouble calling him by name—or even Rosalinda's, since he knew she wasn't trying to get pregnant. He could blame himself, he supposed, or the condom manufacturer, but ultimately blame was a useless exercise. Shit happens. Especially to him.

The garbled voice on the speaker reminded passengers to secure their seatbelts for their descent into Albuquerque. Descent as in decline, deterioration, degeneration . . .

Charlie met him at the airport curb, gave him a hug, and threw Santi's bag in the back of his truck. "Good to see you back so soon," Charlie said as they climbed in the cab.

Santi pulled his sunglasses out of his pocket. Even at the beginning of the third week in October, the sun was painfully intense, especially in comparison to foggy San Francisco. "*Good* is not the word I'd use."

Charlie merged onto the interstate heading south to Esperanza. "I'll try not to take that personal."

"Sorry," Santi said. "The whole thing is just, well, not what I planned."

"Yeah, but while you've been off bettering yourself at college, dating a slew of those California girls, having the time of your life, Rosalinda's been raising your son by herself." Charlie cast him a smile to soften his words. His hair, curling beneath his cowboy hat, was getting grayer, and his craggy face appeared older than his midforties, but he still looked like a movie star hired to play a cowboy. Charlie, along with Miguel, was a father figure to him, so he expected the jab.

"So if I want any sympathy, I've come to the wrong place?"

"I can conjure up a certain amount of sympathy. But not if you're bent on a pity party."

"It's not about pity. It's about how much pressure I'm under, launching this publishing house. My boss has invested a ton of money—and it's all riding on me, the editor, to pick the right books and edit them into shape for publication. The clock is ticking. Gordon, my boss, is big on family, or I'd probably be fired. He basically ordered me to come home and stay two weeks to sort everything out. I've got my laptop so at least I can get some work done while I'm here."

"I guess this job means a lot to you. I hear there's a girl involved, too."

Santi looked out to watch the dry, earth-toned landscape fly by. Below and off to the west, he could see the strip of cottonwood forest along the river, the bosque, its bright golden leaves infiltrated with patches of brown. The peak fall colors must have been a week or two ago, a few weeks after he'd returned to San Francisco following Mort's funeral. Too early then, too late now. "Her name is Kat, short for Katrina. We've been friends since freshman year, but we've just started dating, so it's new. She's Gordon's daughter."

"The boss's daughter? Aren't you living with her and her brother— and you all work for their dad? Man, you got a lot riding on this relationship. What does she say about all this?"

"She's cool. I mean, none of us wants this, but she's supportive," Santi said.

"I don't know about 'none of us wants this.' Abby seems on board with becoming a grandma. Hell, all of us like the little guy. Maggie's excited to be an aunt. She's going to be bunking with Hattie at our place while you're here. Rosalinda and Diego are settled into your old room, so you'll be in Maggie's purple palace room. She shoveled it out for you, special."

It unnerved him there'd been all this bonding with Diego before he'd even had the chance to meet the kid. Shouldn't it be up to him what this kid's place was in the scheme of things? Rosalinda should have told him first, so he could have decided when and how the kid got introduced to his family. But no, she had to run down there behind his back and get in good with everyone. Talk about being put on the spot. Her excuse about being in danger was probably just some drama she made up to orchestrate this whole thing and get to Abby's money.

"You haven't asked about Rosalinda," Charlie said as they exited I-25 at Isleta Pueblo. "Aren't you curious about your great first love and all?"

"I was young and stupid."

"That's the definition of first love, isn't it?" Charlie said. "She may have led you into trouble with her cousin James, but she got you out of it, too, as I recall. Not even knowing the trouble you'd gotten her into yet."

"Why is it always the guy's fault? I used protection. She's equally to blame for getting pregnant." Santi could hear the resentment in his voice.

"I hope before we get there you can adjust your attitude. It won't help you any to show up loaded for bear. Rosalinda has turned into a responsible young woman and a darn good mother to your own flesh and blood. I think that deserves your gratitude, if nothing else."

"If she's so responsible, why did she hook up with some lowlife with a gambling problem who put her and her kid in danger? Has anyone even checked out her story? One paternity test, and common sense goes out the window."

They passed the massive Isleta Resort and Casino, with its full parking lot and a stream of cars still turning in to get their Saturday fix with Friday's paycheck.

"Rosalinda doesn't know who the bad guys are; her boyfriend kept her in the dark. He's on the run from them. She hasn't told him or anybody else where she and Diego are staying. She told Abby she's breaking up with the guy and wants to start a new life back down here."

"How convenient."

"We're almost there. Whatever grudge you want to keep about his mama is separate from Diego. Your son is waiting to meet you. Try to be nice."

Chapter Five

CHARLIE PULLED THE truck around to the back of the house where Santiago could see Abby, Rosalinda, and the little boy hanging out around the picnic table under the immense cottonwood tree. Golden leaves spiraled down like dying birds, covering the still-green grass. Santi's chest tightened as he watched the child kick the leaves, running with his open jacket flapping like wings.

"Thanks for the ride," he said as Charlie set the emergency brake with a loud squeak. Charlie nodded and got out to greet Abby, who was walking toward them. Rosalinda stayed where she was with Diego. Santiago made himself busy, grabbing his suitcase from the back of the truck and slinging his laptop bag over his shoulder. Watching Abby hug Charlie, her smile wide, caused Santi to remember how, when he was a kid, Abby and Charlie had been so close he had hoped they might get together as a couple. Charlie and Rachel were still divorced at the time. He realized now that his ten-year-old self was holding that hope out of his secret guilt, knowing Abby's husband was never coming back. He'd watched his father bury Bobby under the earthen floor of his rooster house. He had wished Abby would love Charlie so that the baby, huge in her belly, would have a father. Even though his own father was a mean son of a bitch, he knew how things were supposed to work.

Abby was upon him with a hug. He looked past her to see Rosalinda rise from the picnic table and pick up her son, who seemed smaller and younger than he'd been imagining, but what did he know about three-year-olds?

Standing twenty feet away from them, Santiago froze. He wondered how he was supposed to react to meeting his son and managed to render himself incapable of feeling anything but self-conscious. And then Rosalinda began to approach, so slowly it was nearly imperceptible.

She stopped an arm's length in front of him. Diego regarded him solemnly, blinking his large, dark-lashed eyes. "Diego, this is Santiago. Sometimes we call him Santi. He's Abby's son and mama's friend from before you were born, when I lived down here," she said.

Santiago smiled, hoping Diego would smile in response. Instead he buried his head against Rosalinda. Her long hair lifted on the breeze and swirled around her son like a dark cape.

"You don't want to say hi?" Her voice was soft, her words meant for Diego. And then to Santi, she said, "He's missing his nap right now. I better put him down, or he'll have a hard time." She began to walk toward the house but then turned back and met his eyes for a moment. "I'm sorry."

Rosalinda carried Diego through the kitchen door that Abby held open for her and settled him on the bed with his beloved tractor and a stuffed purple unicorn his Aunt Maggie had given to him from her large stuffed-animal collection. His eyes were fluttering closed as she kissed his forehead.

"Poor, tired little guy," Abby said from the doorway.

Rosalinda wanted to hide away with Diego but instead got up and joined Abby in the kitchen. "I hope Santiago isn't upset that Diego wouldn't meet him."

Abby was making tea. She turned to smile at Rosalinda. "There's plenty of time for that. He's putting his things in Maggie's room."

Rosalinda looked down the hall, where Maggie's door was ajar. "Should I go talk to him?"

"Let's have our tea, and he can join us if he wants to," Abby said.

Rosalinda nodded, grateful Abby seemed disinclined to force things. Rosalinda felt the pressure of the situation like a vise around her head and neck, yet Abby seemed cool as she carried the tea tray to their spot in the living room. Rosalinda curled her legs up, sinking into the comfy chair, holding her cup of tea, watching the wisp of steam wind its way into nothingness. Santiago was all grown up, a man, now. His face had filled out. His ponytail was gone; his hair was trimmed short on the sides but longer on top, loosely pushed back from his face. She had loved to play with his long hair, freed from its tie, when they were in bed together.

"How are you doing?" Abby asked.

Rosalinda shrugged, too overwhelmed to pick one feeling. If her hands weren't gripping her cup, they would be shaking.

"Me, too," Abby said.

Rosalinda appreciated Abby's ability to not fill silence with meaningless chatter. They sat and sipped their tea.

Santiago emerged from Maggie's room in the hall and did a double take when he saw them together in the quiet of the living room. He'd changed into some faded blue jeans and boots, and his shirt was untucked. "Where's Maggie?"

"Off running around with Hattie. She had her bag packed and was out of here before nine this morning," Abby said. "Tea?"

Santiago's gaze shifted to Rosalinda. She glanced away.

"I thought I'd go over and say hi to Miguel and CeCe and see Rose if she's up to it. I didn't really get a chance to talk to her much at Mort's funeral. Where's Ben?"

"At his office, catching up on some work. We're just going to have a quiet dinner here tonight, around six. Rosalinda and I made a tray of green chile chicken enchiladas to heat up. CeCe and Rachel are hosting a dinner at the Vigils' tomorrow night for all of us," Abby said.

"Sounds good." His expression contradicted his words. He nodded awkwardly and left.

At the sound of the kitchen door closing, Abby said, "He's pretty freaked out at this point. He just needs a little time."

Rosalinda thought all the time in the world would not put a dent in Santiago's freaked-out-ness, which was fine by her. Better that Diego's father wanted to keep his distance than intrude and try to take over his life. Sharing him with Abby and the rest of her extended family was fine, but it scared her to think what the law could decide if Santiago wanted to exercise his paternal rights. Damn her for spilling the truth that night with Jesse, and damn Jesse and Caden for forcing her to come to Abby. She longed for her old life, as imperfect as it was. At least she'd never had to worry about losing her son.

Santiago closed the kitchen door carefully behind him so as not to wake up the napping boy in his old room. He stood outside for a moment, just breathing in the autumn air, full of the scent of ripening pumpkins and the last of the red chiles, which hung like Christmas ornaments on drying stems. The sky was that shade of blue he'd never seen anywhere else.

Despite the captivating view, he kept returning to the image of Rosalinda, her beauty untouched by the last four years, her body as slim and graceful as he remembered. Her eyes meeting his still incited the same irrational desire they had when he was eighteen. But now there was a little boy in her arms. His little boy. And that was why he was there—the only reason he was there—torn away from his real life and Kat.

He hiked to the Vigils' house, hitting Kat's number on his phone as he walked. He would let her know he'd arrived and listen to her voice to remember who he was now, instead of who he used to be.

Rachel poured the bottle of Coke into the bowl of ketchup and stirred the foaming concoction until it became a sweet red sauce. She smothered the brisket with it, sprinkled onion soup mix over the top, covered it, and popped it in the oven to cook for hours, until it pulled apart. Brisket was one of Santi's favorites. "Remember when Charlie and I got remarried he hid under the table skirts and ate a stack of little brisket sliders he made with dinner rolls? He must have eaten about five or six of them," Rachel said to her mother with a hint of melancholy.

Since Zeyde Mort's decline in the prior months, big dinners at the Vigils' had become a thing of the past. Even Shabbat dinners on Friday nights had dwindled, as Mort and Rose could not always wait for the late summer sunsets to have their meal. But with Santi's return, the Vigil women reentered the kitchen to prepare his welcome-home feast.

"How do you think he's handled meeting Diego?" CeCe asked. "I wish I could be a fly on the wall over at Abby's."

"Abby said Santi is hanging back, just watching Diego for now. She's hoping this dinner with everyone will help loosen him up."

Rose was stationed at the kitchen table peeling potatoes. "At least Rosalinda knew who the father was. On Jerry Springer there was a woman who had been on five times testing men, looking for the father of her baby. Still no luck. In my day when you *shtupped* someone, you were *chosen kalleh*, engaged."

"Who in their right mind would go on national TV and do that?" CeCe said. "That show is *drek*. I keep telling you."

"What's it to you? Afraid it's going to turn me into a crazy ho? It's entertaining to watch a bunch of *meshugoyim* while I do my crocheting. Oy, one gives a *zetz*, then the other gives a *zetz*, and they end up pulling each other's wigs off." She balled up her fist and jabbed it overhead. "Jerr-ee, Jerr-ee, Jerr-ee!" Rachel could still see the bruises on Rose's wrinkly forearm from the hospital stay, now a sickly purplish yellow.

"Rachel, your *bubbe* is *gornisht helfn*," said CeCe, throwing in her dishtowel.

Rose gave her a satisfied grin. "At least you have the good sense to say it in Yiddish."

This love-hate relationship between her mother and her *bubbe* had been going on forever, and it exhausted Rachel. Tired of playing referee, she let the barbs fly back and forth between them, wondering if CeCe could ever get over Rose vehemently opposing her marriage to Miguel and the hell it had caused. Rachel knew that what her mother had to swallow to allow Rose and Mort under her roof had not completely gone down, although CeCe denied it.

"What else can we prep?" asked Rachel.

"You can make the flan and get the ramekins in the fridge, so that will be out of the way. I have the empanada dough already made, so I have to bake one of the small pumpkins from my garden to make the filling. I always made them for Santi around this time of the year when he was a boy. I wonder if Diego will love them as much." Rachel heard the excitement in her mother's voice every time she mentioned Diego.

"Charlie's going to fry a turkey and bring it over. You want him to make the red chile sauce? He said he didn't mind." Her Charlie made the best.

"That would be great. Tell him to use one of those *ristras* hanging on the porch."

Diego sat between Santi and Rosalinda at the big dining table on Hattie's former booster seat. Hattie and Maggie, more inseparable than ever, sat at their own small table nearby. Miguel carved the deep-golden fried turkey at the head of the table, while Diego watched, big eyed and grasping his hands.

Rachel tried not to stare at Santi sitting stiffly next to his son. She remembered when Santi was a little boy and she had asked him to help her pick cherries. He had been a skinny child whom she wanted to rescue from his cockfighting drunk of a father, so she found ways of drawing him into their lives. He flinched when she came near him to ask him to help her pick, and it broke her heart. He climbed the cherry trees like a little monkey, and she caught a glimpse of the playful boy he would become. After Abby adopted Santi, they became the village that raised him. Miguel and Charlie were the strong father figures. They taught him about women, fixing tractors, and how hard work in the chile fields would not kill him. But most of all they showed him how to be a good man and how family ranked above everything else.

Rachel watched as Charlie got up to check on the girls at their table. Hattie and Maggie were goofing around, so he wanted to make sure they remembered to eat. She might not have ever reconciled with Charlie if Santi had not come into their lives. In her growing love for Santi, her hardened heart had opened, and he taught her how to mother a child and not just her goats. She fell in love again with Charlie while watching him with Santi, demonstrating what a patient and loving man he was, and there was nothing more attractive than that. Her entire view of him shifted. Soon after, she became pregnant with Hattie.

Abby and Ben talked to her papa about his plans for spring planting. Rosalinda focused on Diego at the table. Santi gave them a sideward glance every so often. Rachel tried to read his mind; he seemed so quiet and guarded. Jesus, he looked better grieving at Mort's funeral than he did now. He caught Rachel looking and gave her a brief, pained smile. He resumed pushing his food around with his fork before she could react. Even the brisket lay cold and forgotten on a sliced dinner roll on the side of his plate. Diego happily ate mashed potatoes and turkey, oblivious to his tense father next to him. Rosalinda kept wiping Diego's mouth and occasionally scooped some acorn squash or green beans on his little fork for him to eat. "Drink your milk," Rosalinda said, handing him his SpongeBob sippy cup.

"Who wants dessert?" said CeCe, bringing out a tray of flan and empanadas. "Santi, honey, I made your favorites." She gave him a loud cartoon kiss on the top of his head as she put the tray in front of him. Diego squealed with laughter. "Oh, you want one, too, mister?"

CeCe planted big smooches on top of his little head. "What a *shayna keppel kroit!*"

By this time, the turkey had knocked Rose out in her chair. Ben and Abby were eating flan. Papa boned the rest of the turkey right there on the platter. Charlie was on his second empanada. Hattie and Maggie took their desserts and ran off.

"Who wants the wishbone?" Miguel asked.

"Me! What is it?" Diego held out an eager hand. Miguel brought it over to him.

"You pick someone to make a wish with, and you each take hold, like this. Then you make a wish and snap the bone. Whoever gets the bigger end gets his wish. *¿Comprende?*"

"I want to wish with Santi." Diego thrust the bone in front of Santi's startled face.

Rose could hear the din of the family at the table, but it lulled her, even more than her belly full of turkey . . .

She dares not tell a soul about meeting Nick. Not even her very best friend, Ida Goldblatt. If it gets back to her family, Rose knows it's considered a *shandeh un a charpeh.* She hears the words spit sharply from her father's mouth: a shame and a disgrace. She hopes no one sees the way she's completely over the moon, how she sits at the radio listening to big bands, imagining Nick at the helm of each one. She relives his kiss over and over again, remembering his soft, parted lips, a teasing lick of his tongue. Just by thinking of him, she tingles. She holds the telephone number he wrote on his backstage pass from the other night. She is to call him to set up their next date. If she never calls him, he will be out of her life forever. He doesn't know where she lives. She told him she doesn't have a phone, even though they do, with a gossiping party line. She shouldn't follow through, but he begged her with those ocean blue eyes.

She walks with her mother up M Avenue toward Emmons Avenue on Sheepshead Bay to buy fish, as the markets sell their excess there at cheaper prices. Rose counts blocks and pay phones as kids play chalk games in front of their apartment buildings, bored shoeshine boys yawn in the shade under barbershop awnings, and shop owners sit outside their storefronts reading Yiddish newspapers. Her mother walks the two miles to save a nickel. Occasionally Mameh stops to examine fruits piled high on sidewalk carts. In the heat, Rose wears the same light cotton dress she wore when she met Nick; she is forbidden by Jewish law to wear shorts or even pants. She wants to. She longs to dress like Katharine Hepburn in her flouncy trousers or Ginger Rogers in her tap pants. She passes shop windows with all sorts of things she cannot wear. Rose puts her hair up in her silk scarf that covers her head, but there is no breeze to cool her neck. She reaches into her dress pocket and feels the paper with Nick's phone number on it. It's worn as soft as tissue paper, and she wonders if the numbers are still legible. No matter; she knows it by heart.

When they get to Emmons Avenue and the docks, Rose tells her mother she has to use the bathroom and heads for a restaurant. Her thumb rubs a hole in the paper in her pocket as she finds a phone booth without a line of people and enough pennies for the call.

"Hello?" a male voice answers.

"Is Nick there?" Rose says, summoning her courage. She looks around as if there are Nazi spies lurking.

"Just a minute," the voice says. "Hey, Nick, some broad's on the phone for you." Nick told her he shared a cheap hotel in mid-Manhattan with other union musicians who came and went.

It seems like hours before Nick comes to the phone. "Hi-dee-ho!" he says. "What's buzzin', cousin?"

"It's not your cousin," Rose says, "It's Rose."

"Rose! You finally called. Can I see you?" His anxiousness sends waves through her. She can hardly hold herself up, her knees shake so. She doesn't know what to say. She hears wolf whistles in the background from his peanut gallery. "I'm playing at a club Friday night. You could come hear me play, and afterward we could get a bite?"

"No! I mean, I'd like to, but Friday night I have plans." Her heart feels like it's trying to break through her chest wall. "Sunday. I can meet you somewhere Sunday. Coney Island?" She needs to put more pennies in the phone. They wait as the *clink-clink-clink* of the phone eats the coins up.

He speaks as soon as he can. "I'll meet you anywhere, Rose. Just say where and when."

Rose hands her father the tobacco they picked up for him on the way back from Sheepshead Bay. Whenever there are two nickels to rub together, Papa gets his small tin of pipe tobacco. Forbidden to even strike a match on the Sabbath, he abstains from smoking at that time but is allowed to use snuff. Other days he puffs on his pipe until his beard turns yellow, which many rabbis still disapprove of. Yet her two rabbi uncles guzzle vodka behind closed doors and gossip at the dinner table. Clearly, rules were meant to be broken or at least bent.

She tells herself as long as she doesn't marry Nick there's nothing wrong with what she's doing. After all, she's eighteen, of legal age, has just graduated high school, and wants to experience life beyond the shtetl of Brighton Beach before she gets a job and settles into adulthood. With the war on, she knows what is expected of her. Still, she longs to light her life on fire. Just not on the Sabbath.

If he asks, Rose will tell Nick she's twenty. That sounds far better than eighteen, she thinks, as she readies herself to meet him at Coney Island. She steps into the dress she borrowed from her best friend, Ida, who has much nicer clothes. She puts her hair up to look older and carefully maneuvers her red tube lipstick over her full lips, finishing with a smack and a blot on a tissue.

"Rose, you look like a *nafke*," her papa says upon seeing her. He disapproves of makeup. Mameh, Papa, and her uncles sit in the main room listening to Brooklyn Yiddish Radio, a small fan whirring at them from the table.

"Oh, Papa. Don't be an old fuddy-duddy," Rose says, kissing him on his scruffy cheek. "It's so hot. Ida invited me to go to the movies at the Tilyou. At least it's air-conditioned." Her lies slip out more easily than she expected. "After, as long as we're in Coney Island, we'll probably walk around the amusement park awhile." She thinks of Nick, the touch of his hand in hers, and her armpits begin to sting. She hurries out before she ruins Ida's dress.

She told Nick to meet her under the Nathan's neon hot dog Take Home Food sign. Sunday at Coney Island is so crowded, she wonders how they'll find each other. Hundreds of people line up around the block at Nathan's, like cattle at troughs, while she anxiously waits under the neon weenie sign. The greasy, sweet, pungent odor makes her stomach roil. Kids and adults alike leave the stand heavy fisted with ice cream, seafood, hot dogs slathered with thick mustard, ice cream malteds, corn on the cob, or burgers and thick-cut fries and any juice-ade you can imagine to drink. Some of the crowd is clothed, and some are in swimwear, smelling of the salty ocean and sand. None of them are Nick.

"Hi, Sugar, are you rationed?" she hears Nick say from behind her, his smile broad as he hones in for a kiss. It is like a drink of water in the desert. "You look beautiful."

She wants to say he makes her feel beautiful. Not like that Miss Frum she's been the last eighteen years (but twenty if he asks). His white shirt is as light as tissue paper, tucked into his pleated linen pants. "You look beautiful, too." He laughs and takes her by her elbow. She doesn't even know this man's last name. She's given up all hope he could by some miracle be Jewish. Not with a name like Nick. "What's your last name, Nick?"

"Do you want my musician union name or my real name?"

"I suppose your real name."

"Mancinelli, but I go by Nick Mann."

"Why a different name? Don't you want people to know you're Italian?" Rose could understand that. They could be scary.

Again he laughs at her, and she feels too stupid for him. Unworldly. "No, if you can believe it, there's already a union musician by the name of Nick Mancinelli, so I had to use another. Everyone knows I'm Italian." Catholic, too, but he didn't need to add that. "And yours, Rose?"

She hates to lie to him, but this entire fantasy is a lie. He just doesn't know it yet. "Burke," she says, anglicizing Burkowitz. It didn't taste like a lie that way. "Rose Burke."

They hold hands as they walk on the boardwalk. Servicemen on leave stroll with their sweeties, lifting them on the merry-go-round horses or holding them tight on the ninety-foot drop of the Cyclone. She is proud for people to think Nick is her sweetie, even though he is not in a uniform.

"In case you're wondering why I'm not serving, I have a blown eardrum," he says. "One crazy night on the tenor sax with an ear infection."

"I knew you couldn't be perfect," she says. But he is.

They stop for candied apples and gnaw at them on a wrought-iron bench on the boardwalk, watching the swimmers and sunbathers, and then they walk to Lillie Santangelo's World in Wax, where they also advertise a headless woman from London, and in the window are animated wax monkeys playing cards and labeled "Cheating Cheaters." Nick offers to take her in, but the thought of a woman without a head and a man who electrocutes himself frightens her. "I have a hard time looking at my father and uncles without their teeth," she admits. Nick laughs and leads her away because she's covering her eyes. When she drops her hand, a dwarf in a clown suit, Elizabethan collar and all, takes it and leads her to a small gated entrance, where the skirt of her dress blows up around her hips. Startled and mortified, she falls against Nick, laughing so hard he holds her to keep her from collapsing. Her laugh, an unfettered beast bursting from its confines, flies with new abandon. It's wonderful to feel this way. She tucks the images of her disapproving family away like an underground war note. She couldn't believe a man her parents would approve of could ever make her feel like Nick makes her feel.

They walk hand in hand, his fingertips callused from long nights of sax playing in low-lit, smoky clubs, and yet his grasp feels gently possessive as they walk, he on the curbside like a gentleman. She loves his clean-shaven profile, short sideburns showing a chiseled jaw she attributes again to his sax playing. "This time I'm going to walk you home," he says, breaking her google-eyed trance. "I know you must live within a mile or two from here. Some tough neighborhoods north of here." She knows he's referring to the Italian gangs, which she would swim to Brighton Beach to avoid.

"Don't worry, silly. I go that way. See how crowded the avenue is? I'll be fine."

"What kind of man am I if I don't make sure you get home safe?"

"I'll call you tomorrow and let you know. Here, let me walk you to your train," she insists and hooks her arm in his.

"Rose Burke, I will dream of you tonight," he says under the aboveground tracks. He kisses her. His body is warm against her, the smell of Vitalis on his neck, his ear. She feels him grow through his linen pants. "Sorry," he says. "You're just so damn beautiful."

"There's your train," she says, blushing, as its headlight appears in the distance. "I'll call you!" she yells as he darts up the stairs to catch it. The doors of the train swallow Nick.

Rose waves, but the train whisks him away, along with a piece of her heart.

Chapter Six

SO FAR, IN the few days since his arrival, Santiago had enjoyed the insulation of a group whenever he interacted with Diego. Abby had taken him aside and told him he was hanging back too much, being too passive. It pissed him off because he knew she was right. He preferred to observe his son from a safe distance, but tonight, with Abby and Ben visiting Maggie at Rachel and Charlie's house for the evening, there was nowhere to hide.

Santi sat in the living room, holding the *Esperanza News* in front of him like a shield. He could feel Rosalinda and Diego enter the room.

"Abby and I made turkey meat loaf earlier, so I'm heating it up, and I'm going to make mashed potatoes and cook some peas Abby froze from CeCe's garden. Maybe you could play with Diego while I'm doing that," Rosalinda said, her tone light.

He lowered the paper. Diego hung onto her legs and smiled at him. They still hadn't had the talk with Diego about Santiago being his father. Abby said they should wait until the two got to know each other better. Santiago thought they should wait until after the meeting with the mediator scheduled for Friday, the day after tomorrow, when they would figure out what his role would be in Diego's life. "Sure. What would you like to do, Diego?"

Diego ran over to him. "I have new puzzles. Do you know how to do puzzles?" He blinked his brown eyes, waiting for Santi's response. Everyone said Diego looked like him, but he saw Rosalinda in the boy's expressions.

"I'll try. You could help me if I have any trouble," Santi said.

Diego cocked his head to the side and stared into Santiago's eyes for a moment, as if sizing him up. "I can help you. Miss Nicole at my school says I'm the best helper. I got three gold stars, like this." He held up three fingers, holding his thumb and pinkie down with his other hand. "That's how many I am." He turned and began to run toward his room, and then he stopped to look back at Santi. "Wait and I will bring the puzzles."

Santiago sat down on the oriental rug Abby had brought from San Diego when she moved here with Bobby. He remembered playing on this rug growing up. Even though he was almost ten when he met Abby, his time with her in this house comprised the full repertoire of his boyhood, at least the memories he wanted to keep. His life predating that was buried pretty deep. He knew the contents those years held—no gift of amnesia—but he had no reason to revisit or examine any of it. As far as he was concerned, his childhood began in this house.

Diego came skidding in on his socks against the polished wood floors, and Santiago felt the sensation of his own socked feet gliding for long stretches as if on roller skates. He smiled at the memory, and Diego smiled back. "I'm fast."

"Yeah, you are. I used to slide on these floors, too, when I was a kid."

"Because Abby is your mama. But who is your daddy? Ben?" Diego set the wooden puzzles on the floor and sat near Santiago.

"Well, I don't have a daddy anymore. But Miguel and Charlie are like dads to me, and now Ben is, too." Santiago felt his heart rate surge, discussing daddies with Diego.

"You have lots of daddies. I don't have one. Jesse was kind of one, but I don't know where he is. I think he went away." He pointed at the two puzzles on the rug in front of them. "Do you like this one with zoo animals or this one with planets?"

Santi's thoughts were stuck on his son telling him he didn't have a daddy. His eyes tried to focus on the puzzles. They were the kind cut from thin wood, twenty-four large pieces for ages three and up, the label said. Diego waited patiently for him to decide. "Uh, I like both." But he saw his avoiding a choice did not please Diego. "But I like the planets one the best."

Diego dumped the puzzle and began turning the pieces over and mixing them up. Santiago helped, noticing how large his hands were next to Diego's and how their skin was the same shade of milky brown. Diego worked quickly and quietly. "Find the edge pieces. They are flat on the side, see?"

Santiago saw this was serious business, so he began to try. He managed to find a few edge pieces that fit together, and he located their place on the wooden tray. His experience with jigsaw puzzles had been with Miguel, who always set up a card table and began a fifteen-hundred-piece puzzle immediately after the last chile harvest. Miguel would play some traditional New Mexico Hispanic music, usually Cipriano Vigil, and they would work at the puzzle for hours. It was as if they entered a puzzle-working trance, transporting them to whatever exotic place the puzzle depicted. Sometimes, they wouldn't even notice CeCe bringing them milk and hot-from-the-oven cookies.

He looked up to watch Diego, the little boy's tongue curled slightly between his lips as he concentrated. Santi could see his mind working behind those big eyes as he tried and discarded pieces until he found the right combination to pat into place. He didn't stop to celebrate, but kept going as if he were being timed and was determined to beat the clock.

When they got to the last few pieces, Santiago hung back so that Diego could be the one to finish it. "We did it!" Diego said, putting up his hand to smack Santi's in a high five. Santiago laughed as Diego kept on high fiving.

Rosalinda stood in the dining room. "Time to wash those hands, boys."

"I will beat you!" Diego jumped up and ran to the bathroom.

When Santiago got there, Diego was standing on Maggie's old step stool to reach the sink. He'd pulled his sleeves up in preparation.

Santiago turned on the tap and adjusted the temperature. "Okay." He grabbed the bar of soap and began to suds his own hands. He enveloped Diego's hands inside of his own, and they began to laugh as they soaped each other's hands, the bar of soap squirting from their grasp and landing back in the sink to spin circles around the drain.

They rinsed and dried them on the hand towel. Diego looked up at Santi with his wide smile, his perfect, tiny teeth so white against his skin. Baby teeth. He would start losing them in a few years. Santi used to hide his loose teeth from his dad, who chased him around with a pair of pliers. He never had a visit from the tooth fairy—or saw a dentist, for that matter—until he moved in with Abby. Luckily he still had had some back molars left to lose for a few more years after that, earning him a dollar each, and after all his rotten baby teeth fell out, he never had another cavity.

"Do you go to the dentist?" he asked Diego.

Diego nodded. "I went one time with Mama. He gave me a toy that's a top you spin and a toothbrush and toothpaste. Some of my teeth didn't come to me yet, but mama says they will if I drink my milk."

Santiago looked up to see Rosalinda in the doorway, watching them. He wondered how long she'd been standing there. Diego ran to her, and she scooped him up, planting loud kisses on his neck. He giggled and waved to Santiago over her shoulder as she carried him away.

After dinner, Rosalinda insisted on cleaning up while Diego and Santiago completed the other puzzle. She joined them just as Diego put in the last piece. "It's time for your bath, Diego."

"Can Santi come?" Diego asked.

"Of course," Rosalinda said, walking Diego toward the bathroom.

Santiago noticed Rosalinda rarely made eye contact with him now, but when she did, it was powerful, almost startling, as if their connection had not diminished at all over the last four years. When their eyes met, he felt weirdly vulnerable.

He joined them in the small bathroom. Rosalinda was rinsing out the tub and starting to fill it, carefully feeling the water, adjusting the temperature as if this was some sensitive scientific experiment. "Bubbles?"

"Yes," Diego said, trying to pull the knit shirt off over his head. It became stuck over his eyes, and he began to giggle and blindly stumble around.

Santiago held him by his shoulders. "Careful, buddy, you might hit your head on the sink or fall down." He pulled the shirt the rest of the way off. Static electricity caused Diego's dark hair to stand up. Santi laughed and grabbed the hand mirror Abby kept on the small wooden shelf. He held it up to Diego, who laughed, his scrawny, naked chest heaving, his ribs showing like rows of pretzels beneath his skin.

Rosalinda shut off the water as bubbles billowed nearly to the tub's edge. "Come on, little man. Get those pants off and get in."

Diego pulled down his elastic-waist jeans and underwear, but instead of climbing into the tub, he darted past Santiago and began to streak naked through the house, giggling frenetically.

Rosalinda followed. "You come back here, naked boy!" She laughed and chased him through the living room and dining room and kitchen, circling back into the hall.

Santiago secretly rooted for Diego to evade her grasp. His perfect toddler body was agile and quick as he jumped and spun past Rosalinda, his face lit with pure joy. Santi put out his arms to pretend to catch him, leaving plenty of room for Diego to run past him. Instead, Diego dove into his open arms. "Save me from the monster!" He hugged Santi's neck, his breath rapid, his heart thumping as his chest pressed tight against Santi, his cherub body so light and smooth in Santi's arms. Reflexively, Santi inhaled Diego's sweet scent. He wanted to tell Diego that he would keep him safe from the monster, but his voice caught in his throat as Rosalinda led them back to the bathroom.

"I should have warned you about toddlers and streaking. The books say it's a normal part of their development," she said, taking the boy from Santi and lowering him into the bath. She knelt in front of the tub, washcloth in hand.

Diego was calm now, playing happily with a little boat in the bubbles as Rosalinda washed him. Santi's gaze drifted to Rosalinda. She read books about child development to be a good mom, he supposed, and for her work at the day care. Her long, dark hair was in a loose braid down her back, reaching to the gap between the bottom of her shirt and the top of her low jeans, exposed now because she was kneeling and bending forward. He remembered kissing that place. He remembered how his hands had felt holding her there, just below her thin waist. He wondered if she still wore a twinkling gem in her pierced navel or if that was just a symbol of her wild youth, gone now that she was a mother.

Rosalinda had changed. She used to have a chip on her shoulder, an edge to her attitude. Raised by gangsters, Rosalinda had worked hard to not become like them, yet a few mannerisms had rubbed off. But now, the chola rhythm was gone from her speech, and her makeup was nearly nonexistent. She seemed softer, almost younger, less prickly. She resonated hard-earned wisdom and strength of purpose.

She was a mother, and it blew his mind.

After the bath, Rosalinda and Santiago lay on Santi's old double bed with Diego between them, taking turns reading to him from the bag of well-worn picture books Rosalinda had brought with her. Soon, Diego began to yawn. Santi carefully got up and stood by the door while Rosalinda kissed Diego good night.

Rosalinda followed him from the room after switching on the night-light and turning off the lamp. She looked at her watch. "Eight-fifteen. Not bad. Eight is his usual bedtime, unless he doesn't nap; in that case, he goes down by seven or seven-thirty. But that's how our evenings usually go: dinner, playtime, bath, story time, bedtime. He'll sleep until maybe six-thirty or seven. But don't worry, I'll write everything down for you."

"Why—as if I need you to prove it? You're obviously doing a great job with him."

Rosalinda looked at him as if he were one of her slower students. "So that you'll know how to take care of him. I figured you'd want to. Am I wrong?" She walked through the house, picking up random toys, the puzzles, while he followed. "It's fine if you don't want to. We've been getting along just fine without you."

"I hadn't thought about it yet, I guess. Sure, I want to visit him when I can get away from San Francisco. I'd be staying here, so Abby and everyone would be here to help. But you're right, I need to know his schedule." He could tell Rosalinda was angry but wasn't sure what he'd done wrong. "Look, just sit down. We haven't even talked about any of this yet. Let's talk."

She dumped the toys onto the ottoman and sat. Her arms were folded across her chest.

"We—I would have been there for you if I'd known," he said, sitting down.

"That's why I didn't tell you." She seemed to be blinking back tears.

"I appreciate you letting me go to college, but it didn't have to be that way. I'm sure it was hard to be on your own."

"I don't regret one second."

"But now that I know I have a son, I want to help support him financially, and I want to be a part of his life, so I'll figure out how to do that."

"He's too little to go to San Francisco without me."

"Right, no, I'd only visit him here until he's older. I wouldn't take him away from you like that. Abby said you wanted to move back down here."

"I'm breaking up with my boyfriend. I want to be out of the city and live back here where I grew up. I want Diego to have your family around him, since I don't have one to give him."

"The boyfriend, is that Jesse?" Santiago said.

Her eyes widened.

"Diego mentioned him."

"What did he say?"

"He told me he didn't have a daddy. He said Jesse was sort of a dad, but he didn't know where he was anymore, that he went away. You need to tell me about this guy and how he put you and Diego in danger." Santiago realized how intensely he felt about the issue, when before it had only been a minor footnote to the headline news that he'd fathered a child.

"Jesse isn't a bad guy. But I never loved him. He had a decent apartment in a better neighborhood than I could afford, so he invited me to move in. He helped a lot financially, and he was good to us." She stopped, her eyes darting about as she seemed to be trying to find the right words. "Then he started gambling, and I didn't know it. He borrowed money from some bad people—I don't know who, he kept me out of it. They made some threats to him when he was having trouble paying them back. He told me to take Diego somewhere safe, and he took off. That's all I know about it. I told Abby everything." Rosalinda looked down at her lap. "The people who are after him, I don't know if they even know about me and Diego, but we left just to be safe. And I couldn't stay in that expensive place by myself anyway. I didn't have anywhere else to go, so for Diego, I came here."

"I'm glad you did."

"Yeah, right."

Santiago got up to pace. "I'm all over the place on this, all right? I'm shocked. I'm pissed that, just as I'm getting my life the way I've worked so long and hard to make it, it gets all shaken up"—his hands grabbed something imaginary and shook it—"like a freakin' snow globe. I wasn't planning on snow. I'm not prepared for snow— but now I have to be. Don't take it wrong, Diego is amazing and perfect—but that doesn't change the fact that there's one hell of an impact here, and I'm still reeling. But I am glad you came to Abby for help."

Rosalinda hung her head and stared at the floor. "I would have been fine if Abby had just let us stay here for a few days and never told you."

"I would never expect—or ever want—her to keep that kind of secret. And she never would." Santiago sat back down, wishing she would look up. "We'll work this out. The mediator will help us work out all the details and get it right, so everyone's happy."

When Rosalinda finally lifted her face, her eyes were red and puffy from crying, her expression a million miles from happy. "Good night, Santiago."

He watched her walk away, pulling the clasp from the end of her braid, raking her fingers through the long ripples of crimped hair, shaking her head back, setting it free. When he could no longer see her, he realized he hadn't said good night back to her.

Abby looked at her watch: 9 p.m. She'd give Santiago and Rosalinda another hour. They'd been playing rousing back-to-back games of UNO with Maggie, Hattie, Charlie, and Rachel, after a dinner of Rachel's spaghetti with marinara made from CeCe's garden tomatoes.

"Hattie won three games, I won two, Ben won two, Rachel and Charlie each won once, and Mom—you won zero games!" Maggie said. "Oh, poor Mommy!" She put her arms around Abby for a hug.

"I'm just a loser," Abby said, hugging her back. "Your looser mommy misses you, Maggie Moo."

"I haven't let you call me that since I was like ten."

"Doesn't change the facts," Abby said, running her hands over her daughter's dark, wavy hair. She knew Maggie would stop her in a second, but she craved these tactile moments with her. And now that Maggie was turning twelve, Abby knew there would be fewer and fewer of them.

Hattie, such a fair-skinned blond that Maggie reported Hattie was sometimes on the receiving end of a little bullying from the tougher Hispanic girls, pulled Maggie away from Abby. "She's all mine, now. You can't have her back," Hattie said as they bolted from the room.

Rachel was putting the cards away in her dining room hutch. "I think it's wine o'clock."

"Beer for the gents?" Charlie asked Ben. They headed to the kitchen.

Rachel opened a bottle of Pinot Noir and put out a jar of her smoked salmon goat cheese, which was selling so well, and some crackers. "This stuff is like crack, so be careful."

Abby took a swig of her wine. "This feels good. God, to just relax for a little while."

Rachel clinked her wine glass with Abby's. "Tell me about it. CeCe's been so tense, she makes me tense. And the two of them with their constant bickering and pushing each other's buttons. I know they have a lot of baggage, but Jesus, get over it already."

Abby swallowed a delectable bite of smoked salmon cheese and cracker. "CeCe will get there. We'll help her. But it's her *mom*, you know? A complicated relationship even under the best circumstances."

"I guess I know a little something about that."

"Not me," Abby said. "I got that shit sorted out, what, like decades ago? I was still in college. Our mutual agreement to never see or hear from each other again is working quite well."

"Don't you miss having a mom, even one who makes you crazy sometimes?"

"I have yours for that." Abby smirked and drank more wine.

"It's made my life easier for her to have you to mother. All that beyond-necessary mothering has somewhere else to go. And now you are a grandmother! An *abuela*! A *bubbe*! You're making me feel prematurely old."

"Well, I'd be a biological grandma if I'd given birth to Santi when I was a teenager. But he came to me already ten years old. This way, I get to be a very young grandma to my Diego."

"You are completely smitten, aren't you? Too bad, so sad for Santiago, as long as you get a cute grandson out of the deal," Rachel teased, in her wicked tone.

Abby poured herself another half glass of wine. "Santi's going to be all right. I worried at first, but he's a big boy. With technology, air travel, he can still be a good dad and have his new life. Meanwhile, I'm going to help Rosalinda get back on her feet and be there for her. We meet with the mediator on Friday to get it all worked out."

"He's lucky he has you."

"He has all of us," Abby said.

"Are you talking about our wayward son?" Charlie drawled as he and Ben joined them, swigging their local Tractor Brewing Company beer from the bottles. "You know, I hounded him all that summer about using condoms. So did Miguel. I thought we got through to him."

"Condoms aren't perfect," Abby said. "Especially in the hands of an eighteen-year-old."

"I was hoping her experience would make up for his ignorance," Charlie said. "Where I grew up, she would have been every Texas teenage cowboy's dream, an older woman to show him the ropes."

"From dream to cold, cruel reality. He's having to do some quick growing up, college lad to dad," Ben said, his Aussie accent always thicker after a beer.

"As we were saying before you men interrupted, Santiago has all of us to help. I adopted him, but we all raised him together. We can do the same with Diego," Abby said.

"If Rosalinda sticks around and lets us," Charlie said. "I still get the feeling there's something she ain't saying."

"Like what?" Abby put down her glass. She knew enough to trust Charlie's instincts.

"Here's a girl who got pregnant and didn't tell the father, just disappeared, and then reappears four years later saying she needs to lay low, and—ta-da!—here's Santi's son. Seems to me there are some missing pieces here, and I'm not sure we should take her at her word."

"I've been meaning to talk to Ramone, as my friend, not as the sheriff, to see what he says," Abby said, deciding more wine was in order since they wouldn't be driving. "Maybe he could check out Rosalinda's story about the boyfriend and see what she's been up to since we saw her last. I feel like she's telling me the truth, but maybe I just want to believe her."

"Ramone screened my background before our first date, as I recall. Your own personal Homeland Security," Ben said.

"Well, you were a dang foreigner," Charlie said, pointing his beer bottle at his friend. "Spouting your radical notions about saving the river and the silvery minnow and all."

"I should call Ramone first thing in the morning, right?" Abby asked, her head swimmy from the wine.

"Yes," Rachel said. "Ramone should know about this. Like papa says, *En la confianza esta el peligro.* In trust is the danger."

Chapter Seven

WHEN ABBY CALLED Ramone, she suggested they meet for coffee at Yvonne's diner in Los Lunas. Ramone was already seated in one of the old, cracked-red-leather booths when she arrived. He stood to hug her. Her arms easily wrapped around his lithe frame. He had possessed an impressive Buddha belly when she first grew to love him, the summer of Bobby's disappearance. He was not sheriff at the time, having quit to care for his infirm father, but after he died, Ramone decided to run for sheriff again, get into shape, and start dating. Now in his early sixties, Ramone had kept off the weight and was still considered the most eligible bachelor around by any woman over forty and by some under.

Abby held onto him, her surrogate father and Miguel's buddy. "Thanks for meeting me."

"I was hoping to go to your place and see Santiago, meet the little boy, and check out Rosalinda. I already ordered the coffee. Have a seat."

"I wanted privacy, so I could speak freely. Miguel told you the whole story—Rosalinda showing up saying she and her son might be in danger?"

"He didn't mention the danger part. What's Rosalinda got herself mixed up in now?" Ramone smiled at the woman who brought their coffee. "Thanks, Yvonne." Yvonne blushed like a schoolgirl, despite her age, and grinned at Ramone before scuttling off to her kitchen.

"She says it's the boyfriend, a gambler in trouble with loan sharks. He's on the run and told her to take Diego and go someplace safe. I was her only option, apparently." Abby took a sip of the coffee from the vintage mug. This place looked like a historically correct recreation of a 1950s diner, but its nostalgia wasn't intentional—Yvonne just hadn't changed a thing since her parents opened it back then, naming it after their newborn baby girl.

"Do you believe her?" Ramone's eyes drifted over to the bakery case, where every delectable and sinful pastry, cookie, cake, and pie appeared to be calling his name. Abby saw his resolve threaten to weaken just before he turned his eyes back to her and sighed.

"I want to believe her, but now everyone thinks I should ask you to see what you can dig up. She was telling the truth about Diego being Santiago's. But I'm not sure about the rest."

"Could she have invented that as an excuse to look you up? Maybe she was just tired of going it alone and wanted some help from her kid's father."

Abby looked at her friend while she considered this possibility. His wavy silver hair was thick on his head; his face was aging but still handsome, with his neatly trimmed goatee. She didn't see him ever settling down, at least not as long as he was still in high demand. "Well, on the one hand, Rosalinda tends to be pretty direct, so it's hard to imagine her being coy about the real reason for coming to me. On the other hand, she has a lot of pride, so I could see her hiding the fact that she just needs some help raising her son. She has no viable family."

"When I heard she was back, I checked up on the Ortiz family. James Ortiz is still locked up from the arson conviction. Her mom is out but living in Texas now, so she's not our problem. The other cousins seem to have scattered on the wind. Probably up in Albuquerque doing their gangster thing." He pulled his little notebook from his pocket and opened it up, pen poised. "What else have you got?"

"She says she's been working at a day care in Albuquerque since Diego was born, so for around three years. She referred to the boyfriend as Jack but didn't mention a last name."

Ramone finished his coffee and nodded to Yvonne for a refill. "How about I come home with you and I can interview her myself? That way I can read her face and body language."

"I think Rosalinda would freak out, and I'm trying to forge some trust with her, which is probably why I waited two weeks to call you. I'm the grandma. I don't think it would help to bring home the sheriff to interrogate her."

"Then you'll have to get some more out of her. Like her boyfriend's last name. The name of the day care for her employment records. I can look her up through MVD and get an address, but it might not be current. If I knew what apartment complex they were in, I could get the rental contract and the boyfriend's last name. I already ran Rosalinda. No busts, no warrants, pristine as a nun."

Abby declined a refill from Yvonne. "I'll try to find out more. We're meeting with the mediator tomorrow—maybe that will bring up something useful."

Ramone leveled his gaze into her eyes. "The paternity results are important, but the fact that Santiago fathered this child might be only part of the story. Before he goes before a judge to finalize everything, the more we can find out about Rosalinda and the boyfriend, the better."

Rachel arrived at Abby's by 9 a.m. after seeing Hattie and Maggie off to school. "Those two were a trip the morning. They had me laughing so hard. I think Maggie is having too much fun to ever come home. Sorry, but I think you've lost your daughter to me."

Abby felt too nervous about meeting with the mediator to play along with Rachel's teasing. "Diego wants to visit the goats and horses if you want to. His jacket is there on the hook if you take him outside. He usually has a snack around ten, some fruit, and then lunch at noon. There's sandwich stuff in the fridge and carrot sticks. We should be back before nap time. His toys are in a laundry basket in their room, and his books are in the bag next to it."

Rachel stepped closer, put a hand on her shoulder, and spoke in a low voice, as if Abby was one of her spooked animals. "It's going to be okay."

Abby nodded, suddenly close to tears. She blinked them back and took a shaky breath. Since meeting with Ramone the day before, Abby couldn't stop worrying about what they didn't know about Rosalinda's life and how what they didn't know could harm Santi.

Santiago and Rosalinda followed a running Diego into the kitchen. Diego stopped when he saw Rachel. "Can we play with your goats with Mama and Santi?"

Rosalinda picked him up. "Babe, we told you we had to go with Abby into Albuquerque today for a few hours. Rachel is going to take good care of you, and we'll be back soon."

"We better get going," Santiago said. "Mom, I can drive us in your car, if you want."

Abby dug out her keys while Rosalinda kissed Diego and handed him over to Rachel.

The mediator's office was adjacent to downtown Albuquerque in a converted Victorian house, walking distance to the courthouse. The receptionist escorted them into a room with a round table. Less adversarial, Santiago figured.

He felt his tensions rise as they sat down at the table. He'd worn his professional clothes, a suit and dress shirt, though Abby and Rosalinda were dressed casually. The silence, with each of them processing their own thoughts, was anything but tranquil. Rosalinda licked her lips and stared at the painting of one of the Indian Pueblos, her leg jiggling beneath the tabletop. Abby produced a small notebook from her purse and a pen she absently clicked.

After about ten minutes, a man carrying a file and a woman with a yellow legal pad entered the room. Introductions were made. The man, Dave Garret, fortysomething with a country club tan, smiled at them. "Our goal here is to support Rosalinda and Santiago in defining a mutually acceptable custody, visitation, and child support agreement within the parameters of New Mexico state law, to be submitted to the Thirteenth Judicial District Court, which covers Cibola, Sandoval, and Valencia County. Rosalinda, you are a resident of Valencia County?"

"Right now I'm staying with Abby in Esperanza. I'll be finding my own place there."

"Which is in Valencia County, so the Thirteenth District Court applies. The courthouse is in Los Lunas, and depending on what you decide, you may or may not have a hearing to finalize the agreements. Or the judge may sign off on the Parenting Plan and Child Support Obligation without a hearing. If the judge has questions, there will be a hearing," Dave said.

The woman, Roberta Cruz, who looked like a prim schoolteacher from decades ago, spoke. "We made copies of the relevant and required forms for each of you. I'll pass those out now. First we have the Parentage Flowchart, which explains what is required for a notarized signature; a packet on developing a parenting plan, which goes into things to consider and recommendations based on the age of the child; and, finally, the fourteen-page Parenting Plan and Child Support Obligation paper work, which we will complete together and submit to the judge for final approval. That one has all the nitty-gritty details spelled out after Santiago and Rosalinda have agreed about custody, child support, and visitation. It includes the required Worksheet A, which calculates the child support and must be reviewed by the judge." Roberta paused to smile her encouragement. "Since this is not part of a dissolution of marriage, and since paternity has already been legally determined, this can be a straightforward process. But I want to stress that now is the time to get any disagreements out on the table so we can find solutions together. Don't agree to anything just to get it over with. What you agree to will determine your future lives with your son. I urge you to consider not only what is in each of your own best interests, but what is in the best interests of your child, Diego. He is who we are here to serve."

Santiago began to flip through the forms and then set them aside. "Like I said on the phone, I live out of state. And I only just found out about Diego, so we've just met. I agree to Rosalinda having custody, and I'll pay whatever child support I'm supposed to. I can't really be specific about a visitation schedule, because that will depend on my workload and when I can get away to visit him here, since he won't be traveling to California to stay with me until he's older."

"New Mexico favors joint custody," Dave said. "Sole custody requests always require a court hearing. Santiago, it would help me if you tell us your understanding of the terms *sole* and *joint custody*."

Santi could feel his dress shirt become damp under his arms. "*Sole* means Rosalinda would have custody, Diego would live with her. *Joint* means he'd go back and forth between us."

"Actually, with sole custody, Rosalinda is responsible for all the major decisions, such as residence—where he lives—religion, school, health care, and activities. She can confer with you if she likes, but it isn't required. You would be allowed visitation. With joint custody, parents must consult and agree about major decisions. Each parent has defined times with the child—doesn't have to be equal time—and is responsible for the child's needs during that time. Do you see the difference?"

Santiago nodded.

"I am open to joint custody if that's what Santiago wants," Rosalinda said. "I would rather share the responsibility of major decisions.

I've been doing it alone; I want to know what Diego's father thinks, and if we disagree we can talk about it."

Dave turned to Santiago. "What do you think about what Rosalinda said?"

"Joint custody would be better, I guess. That way we don't have to have a court hearing?"

"Not automatically, like with sole custody. The judge might still have other questions for you, but that doesn't always happen," Dave said.

Roberta took off her dark-framed glasses. "Rosalinda, I need to ask you, why did you withhold knowledge from Santiago that he fathered your son? It's important to tell me if you had any safety concerns about allowing your son near Santiago or any fear of retribution or abuse of any kind if he had possessed that knowledge."

"God, no! He was only eighteen and going off to college when I found out I was pregnant. I was twenty-three, old enough to take care of myself and a baby. I didn't want to mess up his life like that."

"And now that he has graduated, you decided to tell him?" Roberta asked.

"Yes," Rosalinda said quickly.

"If you are more comfortable elaborating on any of that in private, we can arrange that," Roberta said.

Santiago wanted to shoot Roberta a nasty look but contained the impulse. Implying he was some kind of sociopath who would hurt Rosalinda or Diego. He felt his neck flush hot beneath his collar.

"Then do I understand you two are in agreement regarding joint custody?" Dave asked.

Santiago and Rosalinda said, "Yes" simultaneously.

"When you look at the packet, you'll see you will be deciding things like what health and dental insurance Diego will have and which of you is providing it. Also the names and numbers of your chosen doctor and dentist. And who will be providing child care and how much it costs. Then it gets into time sharing, choosing holidays, and vacations. Even though it says the usual plan is splitting time fifty-fifty, that's not mandatory. There is a section on how weekends are divided. Given your out-of-state residency, we can put something in there estimating how often and for how long you would travel here to spend time with your son on a monthly basis," Dave said. "Remember, today is just to get oriented with all of this and talk about the big decisions. We'll be meeting back here next week to try to finalize the paper work, since, Santiago, you said you're flying back to California the following Saturday. Use this time to read it carefully, answer what you agree on, leave the rest blank. Write down any questions or concerns you have."

"I've read ahead to the Child Support Worksheet A," Abby said. "I see what Santi would pay is a percentage of his income. He just got hired in a new position and, frankly, his starting salary is not that much, given he lives in one of the most expensive cities in the world. I want to pay the child support for him. I have the money, in fact I could pay more than what the state requires. Diego is my grandson, and I want to help Rosalinda as much as I can, since I live here and Santiago doesn't—"

"Mom! No way!" Santiago spoke too loudly for the small room. "We wouldn't even be here right now if I'd listened to you. Quit trying to bail me out. This is my screw-up, and I have to pay the consequences. I don't care how rich you are—I'm an adult, and I can pay for my own goddamn mistakes."

"Diego is not some 'goddamn mistake'! He's the best thing to ever happen to me. Don't you say that! You don't deserve to be in his life if that's how you feel. See why I never wanted to tell you people?" Rosalinda grabbed her purse and headed for the door. Roberta intercepted her.

Santiago stood. "I didn't mean Diego was a mistake—I'd never say that. I'm sorry, Rosalinda, don't leave. I was mad at Abby, and it came out wrong." He was horrified at how fast everything had tanked. How fast he had managed to fuck it all up. So fast he felt dizzy and sat back down. He stared at Rosalinda, who had stopped with her back to him. Roberta whispered something into her ear, her hand on Rosalinda's shoulder. Something calming, no doubt, something she learned in mediation training.

"It's my fault," Abby said, still trying to save him. "I was only trying to help. I don't want my grandson's mother to have to struggle or for Santi to be strapped. There's no reason for it. I'm sorry, I never intended to make things worse. You were doing fine. I'll go wait in the car."

"Don't leave," Santiago said. "You should be here. You're going to be spending more time with Diego than I will, and I'm glad you want to. I just can't take any more of your money. I can do this. I can support my son. I want to."

Abby sat back down, her pale complexion blooming patches of scarlet red.

Rosalinda turned around and allowed Roberta to guide her back to her chair.

"I'm actually glad to see some honest emotion from you all," Dave said. "I get nervous when everyone is too polite in here. These are tough issues we have to tackle, and it's bound to push some buttons. I want you each to feel safe enough to express it: the good, the bad, the ugly. Well, not too ugly, I hope." His tan face crinkled with his smile. "So, Santiago, you will bring in your financials for when we do the child support worksheet. Rosalinda, I understand you are currently not employed outside of the home?"

"I'll be looking for another day care job. I don't want Santiago to have to pay more when I can work, too. If I work at a day care, I can be with Diego like before and get a discount."

Abby started to say something, but Santiago gave her the Don't Do It look.

"Abby, did you wish to add something?" Roberta asked.

"Just that Rosalinda and Diego are welcome to stay with me while she's looking for her new job and apartment." She looked at Santiago and raised her eyebrows, as if to ask him if that was allowed. He nodded, still feeling like shit for his outburst. Roberta was probably even more convinced he was an asshole.

"Thank you, Abby," Rosalinda said. "It shouldn't take me long to get a job."

Dave said, "So, to review—and stop me if anything is not accurate or you want to discuss it further— Rosalinda and Santiago have agreed to joint custody. Before our next meeting, you will discuss time-sharing ideas. You will carefully read the parenting plan and fill out what you already agree with and leave any sticking points for us to discuss together. Next time, we will complete the Child Support Worksheet A, so do your homework regarding health and dental coverage, child care costs, anything else that affects the financials. And that should do it. So let's meet on Thursday morning—would that work? Gives you five days to go over everything. And if we can wrap it up and get your notarized signatures, we can submit it to the court on Friday."

That night, after he and a subdued Rosalinda put Diego to bed,

Santiago retired to Maggie's purple palace to try to get some work done. After the stress of the mediation meeting, he needed to get away from everyone, away from Abby's concerned gaze and Ben's eager cheer.

He responded to emails that had been piling up and talked to Gordon on the phone, who assured him Polydactyl Press was surviving without him. They were reading his chosen manuscripts and getting excited about them.

When it got late and he could tell everyone had gone to bed, he finally called Kat.

"Santiago. How did it go?" Kat said as soon as she picked up.

"I guess we'll be doing joint custody and I'll be paying child support for the next fifteen years or so—and then college. How weird is that? I just graduated from college and we're planning my son's college education? I'll be putting him on my health insurance and flying back here every month for a visit. It's just a matter of writing it up and submitting it to the court. Hopefully, the judge will sign off on it and I won't have to come back for a hearing."

"You sound tired," she said.

"I can't wait to get back to you and work and San Francisco, you know, my world. It feels weird and wrong to be here, like I'm going backward instead of forward."

"Soon, babe. But I hate that you'll have to fly back so often. I hate sharing you."

"When Diego's older, he'll be able to travel to visit me. I can picture how it can be when he's older and he's more of an actual person. He's so little right now. Rosalinda is going to find her own place and a job down here near Abby, so when I visit, Diego can come stay at Grandma's with me. You know, I just have to keep up the contact so we have a relationship that grows as he grows. It won't be that bad."

"A week from tomorrow," Kat said. "You know what I going to do to you?"

Santi turned out his light. "What?"

She proceeded to engage him in some pretty hot phone sex, vividly reminding Santi that Kat's creativity extended well beyond her writing. The problem was, instead of imagining Kat, his mind kept replacing her with images of Rosalinda. Finally he couldn't fight it anymore, and it was Rosalinda's lips he kissed, Rosalinda's body in bed with him.

After saying good night to Kat, Santiago couldn't sleep. He checked his phone: 1:35 a.m. He got up and decided to get a glass of milk and one of the cookies Diego had made with CeCe and Rose. The house was quiet. He opened Maggie's bedroom door, willing it to not squeak, and trod carefully, avoiding the boards he knew creaked, until he was lightly hopping back and forth, as if in a game of hopscotch.

When he looked up, he could see Rosalinda in the hall, silhouetted by moonlight, watching him. He heard her soft laugh. He stopped and stood in his boxer shorts. "This isn't the least bit awkward," he said.

She turned, and he followed her into the kitchen, where he switched on the dim light above the sink. She got out the milk, and he grabbed two glasses. They sat at the table, the plate of cookies in front of them.

"Sometimes, I just can't sleep," Rosalinda said, dunking her chocolate chip cookie into her milk. "I remember you having terrible nightmares. You'd thrash around and cry out. Do you still get them?"

"Not like those. Those were beyond nightmares. I didn't get to tell you about that, did I? We never talked again after the night of the fire. That night, James came and found me on the spot where my old house used to stand. He beat me up bad, bruised my ribs, and threatened Maggie. After he left, I had like this vision—my mind was finally letting me remember what really happened the night Bobby died. And once I remembered it and dealt with it, I never had those bad dreams again. I still get the kind where I'm hopping around in my underwear in the middle of the night in front of the mother of my child. No, wait, that really happened. Shit."

Rosalinda laughed but then became serious. "What did you remember that had been messing you up for so long?"

"It was like watching a movie, so detailed and vivid. I saw Bobby come to our house. I was nine. And I watched him yell at my dad, about how we never bought the house from his dad—how my dad had bullied his old dad into letting us live there without paying rent. They fought, and my dad pulled out a gun and taped Bobby's arms behind his back and took him to the rooster house—it was during a terrible thunderstorm, raining like crazy. I didn't want to go with them—I was scared and had to pee—but my dad made me. He had Bobby kneel on the ground, and he was about to shoot him and Bobby's pleading for his life . . . my dad noticed the duct tape he'd put around Bobby's wrists was coming off, from getting soaked in the rain. So he hands me the gun and has me point it at Bobby while he's cinching up the tape and tying it. I'm only nine, I'm scared, I'm peeing my pants, and this huge bolt of lightning strikes right over us. The gun goes off in my hands and hits Bobby in the stomach, but he's not dead. My dad cusses at me and finishes Bobby off with a few more rounds to the head." His heart pounded just as it had that night. He looked down to his shaking hands.

"My god. You never remembered?"

"The morning after it happened, I didn't even remember going to the rooster house. I thought I'd gone to bed. I never knew I was there and shot Bobby until the night of the fire, after your cousin almost killed me." He paused and looked up to meet her eyes. "And then I had to tell everyone I shot Bobby," Santiago said, the shame fresh and searing.

"You were just a little boy. It was an accident. And your dad was the murderer, not you." Rosalinda reached for his hand, which still held his cookie.

The cookie dropped to the table as he opened his hand to receive hers. "That's what everyone says, and I know it's true. But I was only a kid, and I felt what it's like to shoot someone, see their blood and their agony. Knowing it was an accident doesn't take that away."

Rosalinda squeezed his hand. "The only thing that helps me with my bad memories is focusing on making new good ones. Sounds corny, I know, but there's a lot of shit I could obsess about from my past. But that just takes away from my life now, no? So I fill my heart up with Diego, and the little kids I worked with, stuff like that."

"That's easier to do if you're someplace new, like going to college, meeting new people, making a whole new life."

"And then you get pulled back here. I'm sorry, Santiago."

"Not your fault. And this is home, the good and the bad," he said.

"Whether you're here or in California, the peace you need to find is in your own head, your own heart. When I left here after the fire, I wanted to put the past behind me. Living in Albuquerque was a distraction, but not the cure, you know? Coming back here with Diego is me saying those assholes from my past—and my mother is number one on that list—do not get to control me anymore. They don't get to keep me away from the place that I love." Her hand squeezed his once more, and then she let it go.

Santiago listened as the wind gusted and rattled various vents and trembled the giant cottonwood over the roof. He finished the cookie, imagining Diego's little hands caked in cookie dough, and drank his milk. He stole glances at Rosalinda, her hair loose and tousled from tossing and turning, her face determined, even as she nibbled her cookie.

She caught him looking. "What?"

"I admire how you've been taking care of Diego, how strong you are. I'm proud of you—I hope that doesn't sound patronizing. But after the life you've had, to be so resilient and come out of it with such a big heart, capable of so much love . . . you're a good person, Rosalinda."

Her eyes filled with tears, and her mouth quivered at the edges. "Don't admire me." She got up and put her glass in the sink and started to leave.

"Rosalinda, wait." He stood and tried to reach for her, stop her from leaving. But she was quicker. She disappeared into the hall, and he heard her open the bedroom door and close it behind her. Then he remembered. After he knew he had shot Bobby and confessed it first to Miguel and then to Abby, his shame was so complete that the worst thing they said to him—and they said it over and over—was they were proud of him and he was a good person.

Chapter Eight

CECE TOSSED AND turned. Whatever *mish mosh* of herbs Rachel had given her for sleep and anxiety wasn't working. She got up and noticed the streak of light under Rose's door that meant Rose's TV was still on. CeCe entered Rose's room, checked her oxygen tank, and listened to her breathing. The television glared the twenty-four-hour Home Shopping Network. Rose's cup of chamomile tea sat cold on its saucer next to her bed. She had the most peaceful smile as she slept. CeCe wondered what made her smile so. She looked younger, as if her dreams pulled the years away. CeCe gazed upon her mother's angelic face before shaking her head and turning off the TV.

She padded her way to the kitchen cupboard for a mug to make some hot cocoa. She dare not turn on the kitchen lights because Charlie had been up nights tending a sick horse, and if he saw her kitchen light on, he'd be sure to come over to check on them. But the fridge had a light to help her find the milk and chocolate syrup, and the microwave had a light, too, so she was in business.

After crawling back into bed, she sipped her cocoa as she watched her husband sleep. Just as she had predicted over forty years ago, this amazing man made her happy every day of her life despite the rebuke of her family in Brooklyn. She would not have traded her hot Hispanic man for any of their measly milk-toast husbands. What could they know about being held in the dark, muscled arms of a gorgeous chile farmer?

And he was still gorgeous to her. His hair was mostly silver, like the patina of old sterling. With every breath she loved him still. Thank

God she had had the strength to defy her parents, or she would have missed out on marrying the love of her life. Missed out on Rachel and Hattie. Love was worth fighting for. Worth losing everything for. CeCe hoped her mother saw that now.

Over the week, Rosalinda had received a series of increasingly angry messages from Jesse. Hearing his voice had felt like such a jolting intrusion, she'd deleted them. She wished she could delete the entire situation. Her anxiety had been building to the point where sleeping and eating were almost impossible. She was jumpy and prickly all the time and often caught Santiago and Abby looking at her with concern. She couldn't think of how to stop Jesse and Caden, yet it was becoming obvious she could no longer stall. Her time was up.

She asked Abby to keep an eye on Diego while he napped, grabbed her jacket, and took off on a walk. The strong afternoon sun warmed her, even as the breeze brought the unmistakable chill of autumn. Her boots kicked through the cottonwood leaves, their gold coins fading and drying, succumbing to their fate, ready to serve the earth in their decay. She looked to the mountains for strength.

She phoned Jesse.

"About time," he said.

"Santiago has only been here a week. Our strategy is working," Rosalinda said, putting false cheer into her voice. "He's getting real bonded to Diego. Everyone here is."

"Caden wants to move on this. He said for you to pick a time and place where you can be alone for the handoff. All you have to do afterward is convince everyone it's for real. He'll call Abby's landline—she's listed—with the ransom demand and instructions for payment."

"I don't want to scare Diego, so only you should come," Rosalinda said. "Like you're taking him for a visit—that's what we'll tell him. This better not drag out—he needs his mom." Rosalinda felt her voice crack and took a deep breath to try to get through this.

"How long it takes depends on how fast Abby gets the cash together and makes the exchange. We're going to hide out in Caden's family's cabin in the Sandia Mountains. The whole thing only needs to take a couple of days—that is, if they don't try to pull anything, so make sure they don't. After you get Diego back, you'll stay like one more day and then skip out on them. By the time they figure out you're gone for good, we'll be long gone."

At the thought of doing something so heinous to Santi and his family, Rosalinda had to lean against a tree trunk to steady herself. She recited the lines she had planned. "Friday is Halloween. They're all going to the Esperanza Halloween Carnival that's held at the grade school. Diego and I are invited, but I'll make up some excuse at the last minute, and we'll stay back at Abby's by ourselves. I'm sure you've looked up the address online."

"I know exactly where it is," Jesse said. He sounded as if he was buying her act. "I'll run it by Caden, but I like it. We can make it look like there was a struggle, knock over some shit. We decided to demand three million, one for each of us."

"Sure, whatever." Rosalinda reminded herself it was never going to happen anyway.

"So I'll confirm the plan after I talk to Caden. I can't wait to be with you again. I miss you, even the little rug rat."

"Oh—I need to go." Rosalinda abruptly ended the call. She couldn't make herself say she missed him. She wasn't that good of a liar.

The breeze gusted. She wrapped her jacket tightly around herself and stepped out of the cottonwood's shade into the warmth of the sunlight, even though her shivering had nothing to do with being cold. Somehow, in the next five days, she had to figure out how to stop Jesse and Caden for good and how to keep her son and herself safe without anyone ever finding out.

Abby holed up in her room to wrap Maggie's birthday presents. She always thought of Bobby when picking out the presents, wrapping them, celebrating the birth of their child. It was her duty and privilege to carry out these rituals as the parent left behind. She mothered Maggie, cognizant of channeling Bobby's love for her, along with that of his parents, Magdalena and Ricardo, as their spirits reminded her to do in the night.

She stacked the boxed gifts and rolled out the purple with silver stars wrapping paper on her bed and got to work. How could Maggie be twelve? In six fast years she would be leaving home for college, too.

After wrapping the clothes that Maggie had basically picked out for herself on their last shopping trip, Abby wrapped the gift she thought of as coming from Bobby. She had been walking past a jewelry store in Albuquerque's Nob Hill when she felt Bobby pull her in. She walked straight to a case holding a delicate ring, opal and aquamarine set in silver. Opal for Maggie's birthstone, aquamarine for Bobby's. The fiery opal in the center captured both Maggie and her father's temperaments, and the surrounding circle of aquamarine lent serenity and balance.

The birthday party would be at Rachel's again. Rachel and Charlie's house had all the room and amenities her home lacked. The big kitchen with its humungous island would fit the circle of Maggie, Hattie, and their friends making their own pizzas. The generous den with its deep pile carpet would hold all of the girls' sleeping bags and provide enough privacy for the tweens' secret conversations and enough distance from the master bedroom to stifle the noise of late-night giggle fits. The big, wall-mounted flat-screen television with Charlie's-top-of-the-line sound system would play Maggie's favorite movies or stream music to keep them entertained.

She opened the large gift bags and carefully arranged the wrapped gifts into them for the walk to Rachel's house. As she looked around the small room, she thought about the plans to expand the house that she and Ben had hired an architect to make. They had never followed through on the expansion; the time never seemed right. Ben said she hung on too tightly to the past that this house contained within its faded walls. It held the thwarted dreams and collective memories of Bobby, Magdalena, and Ricardo, and she had always respected that. But how could she continue to honor their wishes at the expense of Ben and Maggie and of her expanding family, Diego and Rosalinda? The living had to come before the dead.

Santiago sought out Maggie an hour before her party. He wanted to have a few private moments with his sister before the onslaught of pubescent-girl party chaos. Rachel directed him to the horse barn, where he found Maggie visiting a few of Charlie's boarding horses, petting their noses and sneaking them some extra feed. He watched her for a moment, dust motes swirling in the one shaft of light angling down from the hayloft's open window. Her wavy hair was woven into a complicated braid, probably Rachel's handiwork. She wore faded jeans and boots with a ratty sweatshirt that did not conceal her blossoming figure. How could this be the baby he'd held in his arms after helping Abby through her twenty-hour labor? Even though Charlie and Rachel and CeCe had been with her, too, Abby had cried for her dead husband. When she finally gave birth to the baby with big brown eyes and a mop of curly, dark hair, she had thanked Bobby, over and over, for her daughter. But it was Santi who had walked the floors with Maggie at night to let Abby get a few more hours of precious rest. It was Santi who had made eggs and squeezed oranges for juice so that Abby could produce healthy milk and keep her strength up. He felt something beyond an adoptive brother bond with his little sister. She was his baby, too.

"All dressed up for your party, I see," he said.

She set down the feed bucket she was carrying and walked over to him, wiping her dusty hands on her sweatshirt. Straw and god knew what else clung to her. She smiled a fiendish smile, tipping her hand as she always did, giving him time to evade her lunge. "Where's my birthday hug, big brother?"

"You just want to get barn gunk all over me." Santi laughed and darted past her reach.

"You've turned into such a city boy," Maggie said. "Breathe deep, Santi, this is the best smell in the universe."

He inhaled: musky horses, straw, green hay drying in the hayloft, old wood, Charlie's stale coffee in the coffeemaker, hand-rubbed leather saddles and tack, farm equipment, and engine grease. The smell hadn't changed a whiff since he was a kid. "It's a pretty good smell. Where's Hattie—spying on us from the hayloft?"

"She and Rachel are wrapping my presents. I got bored, so I came out here."

"Big twelve. Almost a teenager. But don't rush it. Stay a kid as long as possible." Santi sat down in one of the folding chairs.

"I can't believe you have a kid," Maggie said, taking a seat opposite him.

"Me neither," Santi responded. "So let that be a lesson to you. Even when you think you are being careful, stuff happens."

"I'm not getting anywhere near a boy until I'm old, like twenty or something. And forget about sex. Sex is the grossest thing ever invented."

"It's how we all got here. But that's many, many years away for you. Decades."

Maggie rolled her eyes. "Diego is cute, though. I like being an aunt."

"I'm glad he has you for his aunt."

"I think Rosalinda is beautiful, and she's really nice to me. Are you going to marry her?" Maggie looked at him intently, her face so innocent, asking the obvious question.

"It was four years ago when we broke up. I loved her, but I was only eighteen, which might sound old to you, but I was an inexperienced kid. She's a good mom to Diego, but I have a girlfriend back in San Francisco."

"But if you loved Rosalinda again, you could move back here, and Diego and I could see you every day. You've been away from home too long already."

Santi reached over and worked a piece of straw from her hair, carefully removing it so as not to disturb her elaborate braid. "I'm making a new home for myself in San Francisco, new job at a brand-new publishing house."

"With a new girlfriend," Maggie said, in her semi-snotty tone.

"Yeah, with Kat. You'd like her, she's cute and funny."

"Santi, there is more to life than cute and funny. There's Abby and Ben. There's CeCe and Miguel and Rose and Rachel and Charlie and Hattie. There's your son. And there's me." She counted it off on her fingers as if she could win the argument with him through sheer numbers. "And most of us are cute and funny, too."

"You're the cutest and funniest." How could he explain what it was like to want a life far away from home? When he was twelve, he never would have imagined such a thing, only two years into his new life with Abby and the rest of them, just across the field from where his old house had been bulldozed and hauled away like trash. Maybe she would know the feeling of needing to escape a great thing when she got older. Or she might stay here forever, the next generation on the Silva homestead, where the grandparents she'd never met raised the father she never got to meet, thanks to Santiago's dad.

"It's my birthday, so you have to do what I say. I command you to move back to Esperanza." She waved an imaginary wand.

"I can promise you this: I'm going to be back here so often, you'll get sick of me."

"I want to be sick of you. I'm your sister—I'm supposed to be sick of you. But I can't be sick of you if you aren't here to be sick of. Then, all I can do is miss you, and that sucks."

Santi smiled, and she pouted and kicked his shoe with her dirty boot. "You better get ready for the ball, Cinderella," he said. "Forty minutes until the pumpkin coach arrives."

"Crap!" She ran out of the barn, yelling over her shoulder, "You better bring me a whole big gob of presents!"

Rosalinda watched as Diego made the rounds at Maggie's birthday party. He ran to the clump of men who stood in the open dining area, holding their beer bottles, talking and laughing. Santiago, Miguel, Ben, and Charlie immediately stopped their conversation to give Diego their attention. Santiago picked him up so that the guys could give him high fives.

How much bigger Diego's world was here in Esperanza, with so many people constantly giving him attention. Diego squirmed out of Santiago's arms and ran over to where Maggie, Hattie, and their friends were up to their elbows in pizza fixings at the kitchen island. His Aunt Maggie stopped to dab stripes of flour dust onto his nose and cheeks, war-paint style. He giggled and ran over to where Grandma Abby, Rachel, and CeCe were gathered around Rose, who sat regally on a living room chair. The women turned their attention to Diego, who resisted Abby's efforts to clean off his face with her napkin.

Rosalinda hung back, watching everyone, trying to believe this was her and Diego's new life. This was her son's birthright, and it was high time she allowed him to claim it. She and Santiago had sat Diego down the day before to tell him Santi was his daddy and would be visiting often. Santi showed him on a map where he lived in California and told him that when Diego was older, he could visit him there. "I'm older now," Diego had said. He took the news in stride, probably not even sure what it all meant.

Despite the abrupt change, her son was thriving in his new world, basking in the affection that came at him from every direction. She just had to get them through this week, sever all ties with Jesse, and then she could feel more worthy to receive all the blessings that seemed almost within her reach. With Abby's help, she would find a decent place for her and Diego to live. She would explore going back to school. She would become the mother her son deserved.

Just as her chest swelled with hope, it deflated when she saw Sheriff Ramone Lovato arrive, loudly calling out to everyone, hugging each who greeted him. Even in his civilian clothes, he reeked of law enforcement. She remembered giving him her sworn statement, which had landed her cousin in prison and cleared Santiago of any wrongdoing in the terrible bosque fire. That was the last time she had seen Sheriff Lovato, who now approached her with a big smile. "Rosalinda, it's so nice to see you again and finally meet your son." He reached for her hand with his, so she gave it. He clasped it strongly, keeping his eyes fixed on hers, trying to read her, no doubt. She felt stupid for not realizing Abby's close friend would come to Maggie's party.

"Hi, Sheriff." She managed to smile.

"Please, call me Ramone. I'm here as a family friend, not in any official capacity."

Rosalinda smiled again. "Maggie's really growing up fast."

"She's a good kid, but that's not surprising, since Abby is her mother. The apple never falls far from the tree, no?"

Rosalinda felt his remark like a sock to the gut, an obvious dig about her notorious mother. "This apple fell and rolled as far away from the tree as possible."

Ramone nodded. "The same could be said for Santiago, though he had the benefit of Abby's influence at a young age."

Rosalinda felt her temper rising. "Are you trying to get at something, Sheriff?"

He smiled that smile Rosalinda knew worked on the ladies. "When I heard you arrived on Abby's doorstep saying you and your son were in danger, of course I had to wonder what you might be bringing to my loved ones."

"I brought them my son—Santiago's son—and nothing else."

"Let's hope that is true."

Rosalinda realized she had to relieve him of his doubts. "Look, my ex-boyfriend—I broke up with his sorry ass—was the one in trouble. He's long gone and took his trouble with him. So, see? No worries. I'm starting a new life here near Diego's family, and I'm the last one who wants any trouble." She drilled her gaze into his.

"I could check into it, make sure everything has resolved favorably. I'm sure that would bring you even more peace of mind. What is your ex-boyfriend's name?" As Ramone waited for her response, Ben showed up.

"The men folk are wondering when you'll be joining them," Ben said, handing him a beer and slinging an arm over his shoulder.

"It's hard to tear myself away from the lovely Rosalinda. We were just catching up."

Rosalinda smiled again and playfully tapped Ramone's arm. "We're all caught up. You can run along and play with the boys now."

Rachel swept the flour that seemed to have exploded in her kitchen. The smell of dying embers from the *horno*, a traditional Pueblo wood-burning oven made from adobe, wafted in the open door while Charlie retrieved his pizza paddle and tongs. Rachel had offered to be the cleanup crew, since Abby was head pizza chef, prepping all the veggies, meats, and cheeses for the girls to create their own pizzas. Ben served as her *sous* chef, which to Rachel was French for "fetch monkey."

When she and Charlie had rebuilt their house after the bosque fire, she'd redesigned the kitchen, adding double farm sinks and a commercial fridge and stove. A brick-floored sun-room opened up from the kitchen, where Rachel babied her herb and plant gardens. Hattie's turtle, Slo-poke, had an impressive habitat Charlie and Hattie made out of river rock, dirt, and plants that had become lush over time. Sometimes he'd come out to sun and smile at Rachel as she groomed her plants and communed with the spirit of her Tía Maria.

Maria, an aunt of Miguel's, was the only relative who didn't desert him after he married Rachel's Jewish mother. Papa had sacrificed too, something Rachel believed her mother didn't fully acknowledge. CeCe had never liked Maria, believing correctly that Maria undermined her. That was only one of the many things that had polarized Rachel and CeCe for years. More than a mother-daughter conflict, it was a cultural one. Growing up in a largely Hispanic community, along with Maria's influence, Rachel rejected her mother and her own Jewishness. She would identify only with her Hispanic side, making her one hell of a papa's girl and a real brat to her mother. After the arrival of her *bubbe* and *zeyde* and some serious growing up, however, Rachel had finally explored and embraced her Jewish half.

She pictured Tía Maria in her broom skirt and big Nikes on her feet. Arms like tanned hide and splinters of chewed osha root visible in her mouth when she talked. Rachel couldn't imagine not having the expertise of natural healing the old *curandera* had carefully taught her. It was central to who she was, a Hispanic-Jewish earth mother, her two halves in balance and whole.

In the family room, helium-filled happy birthday balloons with dangling colorful ribbons snuggled against the high ceiling like spirits watching from above. Abby was gathering Maggie's gifts from the sofa table to start handing them to her. Rachel joined Charlie, scooching him over to share his seat, his arm automatically draping around her.

Oakley, the black cat that Charlie had saved from their burning house, jumped out of nowhere onto strewn wrapping paper. The girls squealed while Oakley thrashed through the paper as if a mouse was running underneath. "Damn cat," mumbled Charlie, but he laughed along with everyone else. Rachel knew he couldn't look at Oakley without reliving his painful injuries and the year of rehabilitation that had resulted from the cat's rescue. The cat might not exhibit appropriate gratitude, but Hattie did.

Abby observed Maggie closely as she opened her presents, her relief evident when Maggie and her friends raved about the opal and aquamarine ring. Ben sat on the arm of the couch next to Abby, still in his apron. Abby's falling in love with Ben had been like crossing an angry picket line at the time. Rachel admired that about Abby. She had crossed the line for the right guy. Twice in her life.

Even Santi seemed relaxed as Diego bounced on his knee. Diego held the small truck Abby had wrapped for him so he would have something to open, too. Rosalinda gazed at Santi with their son as if she couldn't take her eyes off of them.

Rachel caught her own father watching Santi with Diego, a subtle smile on his lips. Santi vroom-vroomed the truck in the air for Diego, who giggled and reached for it. CeCe and Rose wore matching expressions of amusement as they beheld the boundless energy of Diego and of Maggie and her friends. She heard Rose remark that it wore her out just watching them.

If she could only freeze-frame this perfect moment. Where all the pieces fit and her family was happy under her roof. Rachel imagined Zeyde Mort in spirit, wearing a silly birthday hat, cake frosting smearing his mouth and shirt, leading them all in a chorus of "Happy Birthday."

CeCe gathered up plates and glasses as the girls picked out movies to watch for the slumber portion of their party. Six sleeping bags sat off to the side of the room like rolled hay.

"We need to get this one bathed and into bed," said Rosalinda, standing up and holding a fussy Diego.

Without thinking, Rachel kissed Rosalinda on the cheek, like one would any family member. She tried to kiss Diego, too, but he buried his head in the nape of Rosalinda's neck, so Rachel shook his little tennis shoe. "Bye-bye, you."

Santi kissed Rachel on her cheek. "Have fun," he said, nodding toward the chaos of the girls. "Love you." Rachel watched him follow Rosalinda and Diego out. Now that they had gone through mediation, he would be leaving soon. Back to a life and a girl who was waiting for him. Would he bring that one home someday? Selfishly, Rachel wanted things to stay the way they were at that moment. She called upon all the magical powers of her Tía Maria. Freeze-frame.

Chapter Nine

HALLOWEEN TURNED INTO one of those quintessential New Mexico autumn days. The sky was a vibrant cornflower blue, and the sunlight came at a slightly softer angle, lengthening the shadows. Santiago had to stop to look at the mountains as he walked over to say good-bye to Rose, CeCe, and Miguel. When he had first gone to college in Los Angeles, he was surprised at how much he missed the Manzano Mountains, almost as much as the people. It occurred to him now why that was. When he was little, during his years before Abby, he would stare trancelike at the mountains. When he was alone and scared, when his father had been drinking and his behavior had escalated to yelling and punching things, Santiago would look out of his bedroom window facing the mountains. He would pray to them to make his father pass out before he could get around to beating Santi. He prayed to them that he would have enough to eat until his father and uncle came home after days of cockfighting. The mountains didn't always listen, but sometimes they did. Even if the beating came or he had to make one stale tortilla last four days, he still turned his eyes to the mountains.

The drying grasses crunched beneath his boots as he began to walk again. Would he even still be alive if Abby and Bobby hadn't moved into the house across the field? He doubted it. And if he had somehow physically survived, his mind and soul would both be wrecked. He never would have been able to succeed in school, would never have had love and a supportive family, and would never have attended college, landed a great job right after graduation, and been able to live in San Francisco. When he pulled the thread, everything good in his life originated with Abby. Sometimes, his appreciation was almost too much to bear.

Now, she guided him through this new turn of unexpected fatherhood in his life, opening her home to Diego and Rosalinda, embracing them as family, and hiring the best mediators she could find, who made the process go smoothly. When he got on the plane in the morning, he would go back to his life knowing his son and Rosalinda were in good hands, Abby's hands. There were none better.

Rosalinda settled Diego in for his afternoon nap. Santiago was visiting with the Vigils and Rose. It was Friday, so Ben was at work and Maggie was at school, no doubt counting the hours until the big Halloween bash that night. Abby was helping Rachel with a large goat cheese order after one of her employees came down sick. CeCe and her friends—the cabal, as everyone called them—were finishing the Halloween costumes.

The house was so quiet she thought she could hear her heart pounding, instead of just feeling it in her throat. Her fingers trembled hitting Jesse's number on her phone. "Yeah," he answered on the first ring.

"It's me. We need to talk," Rosalinda said.

"We're on for tonight."

"It's not going to happen, Jesse. I'm not going to do this, and you can't talk me into it. This is Diego's family, and we're going to stay here with them. I'm sorry, but we're over. It's all over." Her voice was strong, but her legs were shaking so much she had to sit down on a kitchen chair. "I can't do it, and I won't do it."

"You just have cold feet. It's going to be fine—think of the life we can give Diego—"

"The life I'm going to give him is right here. You know I don't love you."

"Yeah, but we're good together. And if you want to go separate ways, then we do that after this is over. You can't back out now. Caden would be so pissed," Jesse said.

"If I have to tell everyone here what's up, I will. Abby's real cozy with the sheriff—he'll keep us safe somewhere. I've made up my mind, Jesse. Don't come down here—I mean it. Tell Caden to find someone else to steal from. He's not getting money from Abby."

"You think he's going to just forget about a million dollars? Take no for an answer?"

"If he wants to get arrested, I'll talk to the sheriff. Caden better forget the whole thing, or he'll be charged with conspiracy to commit kidnapping of a child, a federal offense. He'd be looking at some hard time. I looked it up."

She knew Jesse believed her. They didn't love each other, but he had enough integrity to accept defeat. She listened to him breathing into the phone while he thought.

"You still have stuff here, winter clothes and shit."

"I'll come up and clear out my stuff sometime tomorrow. I'm sorry, Jesse. You've been good to us. It's just time to move on, you know?"

"Caden is going to freak. I don't know how to tell him without him going all ballistic, and you know I owe him."

"That all happened before I even met you. It has nothing to do with me or Diego. So I don't owe that piece of shit anything. Tell him the sheriff was on to us. He could pay Caden a visit. He'd convince him to back off real fast."

"That's gasoline on the fire, man, getting the sheriff after him. I brought Caden into this, I'll handle him. It's not like he's part of a crew anymore, he's just some lone badass. Fuck it. I'm sick of New Mexico. There's nothing for me here. I think I'll take off for Nashville. My brother's been telling me to join him there. He's getting regular gigs in the music scene. You could come with me. We could leave tonight."

Rosalinda blinked back tears. "I have a couple hundred left in the bank, if you want it. I don't need it here. For your gas and food."

"You keep it." Jesse sounded more sorrowful than angry. "Are you hooking up with Diego's father again? Is that what this is about?"

"Jesse, it's hard to explain if you've never been in a real family. I never had that; you never had that. But now Diego can—with grandmas and grandpas and aunties—all these people who just want to look out for him and love him. That's what I'm giving him, and that's worth way more than money."

"I've been missing my brother. Him and me, we're all that's left. To tell you the truth, I'm kind of relieved we aren't going through with this. I was getting pretty tense about it, you know, taking care of Diego without you, the whole exchange deal. Having to lay low for like the rest of our lives, changing our identities—that's some hard-core shit. It's one thing to think about it and talk about it, but to actually do it . . ."

"I'm so relieved you get it, Jesse. The whole plan was just nuts. It just wasn't worth it. You have this address. Send me a postcard once in a while, let me know how you are in Nashville. Does that mean you're going to start talking with a twang and play the banjo?"

Jesse laughed. "Might have to. I'll send an address after I get settled. Maybe you could send me Diego's school pictures so I could see him grow up."

"Yeah, sure. You're a good guy, Jesse."

"We had us a pretty good run. Won't forget you, that's for sure. Don't worry about Caden. I'll tell him the sheriff is watching you like a hawk and knows the gambling story was a lie. He might be nuts, but he ain't stupid enough to walk into a trap, especially since he just got out of the joint."

"Be careful, Jesse. Let me know how it goes with Caden—don't underestimate that asshole."

"Like I said, I can handle him," Jesse said. "But I'll check in with you before I hit the road in the morning. You take care of yourself, Rosalinda. And take care of Diego. Tell him I said he's a good kid. Bye, Rosalinda."

"Bye, Jesse." Rosalinda ended the call. She heard a catch in Jesse's voice, and she felt sorry for that. He would tell Caden and then leave for Nashville in the morning. She wouldn't see him again, and while she wished him well, she felt nothing but relief. Tomorrow, they would see off Santiago, knowing he would be back to visit in a few weeks' time. By then, she should have her own place nearby and, she hoped, a new job at a good day care for Diego. With the child support, she would finally have a little breathing room.

After a month of hell, it was over. She could finally relax.

"I can't thank you guys enough," said CeCe to her best friends, the cabal, in her living room. Hazel, Carmen, and Bonnie came loaded with fabric, sewing boxes, and a potluck dish for lunch. Usually they met once a month to make crafts for charity, but today they were gathered to make Halloween costumes for Hattie, Maggie, and Diego. "I still have cakes to frost for the cakewalk for the school party tonight."

"This is our first time back together since Mort was here sewing with us," sighed Carmen. "I miss him." She made the sign of the cross.

Hazel set up the portable sewing machine on the coffee table and sat on the floor in front of it. She worked the pedal with her knee as the machine whirred through perfect seams. Though seventy-seven, she kept limber from practicing yoga and had recently, to the surprise of no one, started marching in gay pride parades.

Bonnie went to Rose, who sat in her usual easy chair, her walker next to her like a faithful sidekick. Bonnie raked her long, painted acrylic nails through Rose's mop of half-red, half-white hair. "*Hijola,* girl. You're all scary for Halloween! Time for more color." Rose's tired hair couldn't hold onto color very long anymore.

"Oy, I should cut it all off and wear a *shmata.*"

"You're still one hot mama, chica." Bonnie gave Rose her flamboyant, bosomy hug. Rose rolled her eyes at the torture of such affection.

"So Maggie's the bad witch, and Hattie's the good?" Carmen said, wrestling through yards of black fabric. "That makes sense with their hair color."

"I'm afraid they've given us drawings." CeCe handed Carmen two sheets of paper. "They'll be over after school to try them on."

"Two designer dresses in one afternoon? What is this, *Project Runway?*" said Carmen, taking the drawings. "Luckily, I have a dress pattern I can alter for the basic shape of these."

"What do you think about this for Diego's flying monkey suit?" Hazel was rummaging through a box of old costumes she had made in the past. She pulled out a Curious George costume and held it up.

"Look at the close-set eyes. It's George W. Bush," Rose said.

"I could cut the mask part out, and we'd do scary flying monkey makeup on his face," said Hazel. "I'll put wire into the wings and tail so they'll stick out."

"He's going to look so adorable!" CeCe said. "He's obsessed with *The Wizard of Oz.* The girls have seen it with him three or four times this week. He loves to be scared and watches through his fingers most of the time. Hattie and Maggie were the same way. I was, too."

"I was obsessed with Dorothy," Hazel said. "My first crush."

"I liked the way Dorothy could get all bad and up in peoples' faces," Bonnie said. "It's those swarming dwarves that freaked me out."

"I never saw it as a child. My parents said it was the work of the devil," Carmen said, scratching through her football-helmet hair with a fabric ruler.

"My parents didn't want me to see it, either," Rose said. "Not because it was the devil's work, but because they thought it a waste of a dime. I was fifteen when it came out. Ida Goldblatt and I snuck out to see it. On top of that, we flirted with the nonkosher ushers." Rose gave a guttural laugh. "They gave us free candy."

"Whoa," CeCe said. "I wonder what else I don't know about you."

"I could have never gone against my parents' wishes. I wouldn't have been able to live with myself. Jesus would know, even if my parents didn't," Carmen said, twisting her crucifix.

CeCe waited for the usual jab from Rose, about how CeCe had been the poster child for going against her parents' wishes. But Rose stared into her lap.

The cabal had been coached to not grill Santi about Diego or Rosalinda, so when he came in from carving pumpkins with Miguel, they all smiled at him dumbly.

"What?" he said. "It's scary when you are all so quiet."

"It's so good to see you," Hazel said. "I can't get over it."

"So grown up," blubbered Carmen. "A father." She blew her nose in her hankie, probably thinking of little Diego born out of sin.

Bonnie sidled up to him. "Hey, *mi'jo*. I wish you would have knocked up one of my nieces instead, but I'm happy for you all the same."

"Um, thanks, I think. It's great seeing all of you. I better get back. Just came in for a glass of water. I want to get one more pumpkin done before Diego wakes from his nap." CeCe imagined a cloud of dust at his boot heels when he took off.

"Are he and Rosalinda getting married, since they share a child?" asked Carmen, working pins into the black fabric. Her pursed lips conveyed her concern.

"Actually, he's leaving tomorrow, back to San Francisco. But he'll come to visit Diego regularly. They have it all worked out," said CeCe.

"I know what you're thinking, Carmen. But not every Catholic is as narrow-minded as you," Bonnie said. "In my barrio, virginity is celebrated with Our Lady, while babies are born out of wedlock soon after *quinceañeras*. Time to come out of the dark ages, Saint Carmen."

"I believe in abstinence until marriage," Carmen said. "There's nothing wrong with that."

"Carmen, weren't you ever a teenager in the backseat of a car with a hot boyfriend?" Bonnie's lips purred in Carmen's ear. "Hormones pounding through your veins, the heat of your bodies fogging up the windows. He reaches up your shirt . . . maybe down your pants." Carmen swiped at her as if she were an annoying insect. "You love him, and you want it so bad," Bonnie goaded. Carmen looked at her blankly. "Well, I'm only fifty-one, and I still want it," Bonnie declared. "I keep it interesting for him." Bonnie turned to pull out the black lace of her thong underwear and flash the black and red flower tattoo at the base of her spine. It distracted the eye away from her protruding love handles.

CeCe laughed. She didn't want to toot Miguel's horn, but he had never lacked in the lovemaking department. She wasn't about to brag about it with him right outside on the porch.

"When did you and Mort stop having sex?" Bonnie asked Rose. "I hear some old couples never stop. He seemed pretty frisky to me."

Rose squinted in thought. "Nineteen-fifty. Right after CeCe was born."

"Over sixty-four years ago? Ma, that can't be right." CeCe could never go too long before she wanted to feel intimate and safe in Miguel's arms.

"I was done having kids, so I was done having sex with your father. We didn't exactly start off in love, you know. More Jews than you'd think married like that. Ida Goldblatt married for money. Before I married Mort, my mother's words of wisdom to me about sex were to just lie there. So I did. Now you know my dirty little secrets," Rose said, sewing an arm onto the white witch dress. She worked her lips as she sewed, and for a second, CeCe saw her chin quiver.

"Ooh, Rosa. Let's get you all dolled up and me and you go to the Caravan and find you a hot guy to dance with?" Bonnie slithered like a snake temptress around Rose. "What do you say, ¡mamacita!" She shimmied and gave un grito, one of those mariachi yells.

"Don't let this old face fool you," said Rose, obviously amused by Bonnie. "I was a real looker in my day. Some people thought so, anyway."

"Did Papa?" CeCe had seen old pictures in which young Rose resembled Rita Hayworth. "I thought you were gorgeous."

"You know, I don't remember him ever saying it, but I'd catch him staring at me, so who knows. He wasn't one to kvell." She gave a big sigh, the kind that comes after a long, grueling job. "My eyes are tired. I'll go rest in my room."

CeCe helped her mother out of the chair and steadied her on her walker. "Loved our little *butchke*, girls," said Rose, thanking them for their chat. She got herself going, scuffing and pushing slowly toward her room. "*Drai zich. Drai zich,*" CeCe heard Rose say to herself as she turned the corner out of sight. Keep moving. Keep moving.

Rose leaned against the sink basin, splashing cold water against her eyes to soothe them. The years made her face feel foreign to her. She peeked in the mirror around her terry cloth towel. Who was she really? A grieving widow? An empty old woman at the end of her life?

She could hear Bonnie's cackles from the front room, so she turned on the television. It was easier getting around in her room because she could steady herself on the furniture, going from here to there like a monkey on a vine. It gave her a sense of independence, which she realized she never had in her long marriage to Mort. The look of pity on the women's faces after she told them about her marriage got Rose thinking. Had it not been for her children, she would have been the loneliest woman on the planet. Never feeling a man's loving touch. Even when she and Mort still had sex, it was never amorous. He wasn't about such things.

Rachel had given her a thermos of yarrow tea for her circulation. It tasted a little bitter, but it helped her relax, so she gulped it down. She settled into her chair, her weary eyes closed . . .

She's in her mother's kitchen peeling beets for borscht over the sink to have with tonight's Shabbat dinner. The prettier beets Mameh will can for the winter months. Rose's hands are stained magenta, and she prays to a god who's not mad at her for dating a gentile, asking for the stain to wear off before her date with Nick tomorrow night.

She has done nothing else but think of him, reliving every moment they've had together. Something connects her to him in a way she never thought possible. She looks over at her mother, who rhythmically chops her beets, just happy she's not stuck in a Jewish ghetto or dead in the ground. How dare Rose want so much more? She had been raised to be humble and serve God and her community. To honor thy father and mother. She goes to the radio and turns on a swing station. Now she peels beets eight to the bar. To Rose, Brighton

Beach is her ghetto. Everywhere she looks, things are the same. People look alike. Believe the same things. Can't they see it suffocates her? Her best friend, Ida, plans on marrying rich, and she has her claws in the furniture store owner's son, Jacob Epstein. Jewish parents still participated in choosing their children's mates—if not directly arranging their marriages, at least pointing them in what they believed was the right direction. Girls marry up if they can. To other Jews. That goes without saying.

Whenever Rose can get out of the house, she phones Nick. Sometimes he's sleeping from playing out late the night before, and she hangs up right away to save pennies, even though one of his roommates calls her "doll face" and wants to talk. She feels like she'll explode if she doesn't hear his voice.

Rose keeps up on the Roseland Ballroom venue in the *New York Times*. Just last year, Harry James and Frank Sinatra did a CBS Radio broadcast from there. What she would have given to sit at Frank Sinatra's feet and watch him croon into his microphone.

She hates the subway ride to the city—the way the train travels under the river as the lights flash on and off. She has to wait until sunset, when the Jewish Sabbath is officially over, to lie her way out of the apartment. Nick is to meet her at her stop on 50th and Broadway. Roseland is two blocks from there. She can see the bright neon marquee down the street as soon as she ascends the subway stairs.

Nick comes out from under a newsstand canopy and scoops her in his arms. He kisses the top of her head. "I've missed you," he says. He tips the newsman, grabs his sax case from behind a stack of newspapers, and reaches for her hand. They head toward the bright lights of Roseland's air-cooled comfort and the Dolly Dawn and Her Dawn Patrol band. Rose loves seeing her name in lights: ROSELAND. It is her land and she, its princess.

She realizes she is squeezing the life out of Nick's hand as they stride onto the large wooden dance floor. The lights remind Rose of the flying saucers in *Science Wonder* magazine. Nick slips his sax case behind the bandstand as the drummer gives a nod.

"Do all you musicians know each other?" asks Rose.

"Not so many of us around since the draft." He grabs her around her waist. "Let's show these dead hoofers how it's done." He dances her around, using more of the floor than anyone else. She tries to follow, but bar mitzvah dancing is nothing like this. She sees a man signal to Nick, who swings her out to the gentleman cutting in. He dances more like he's got ants in his pants, and she laughs the whole time, until he swings her out to another partner, and then another. She dances so much her legs become weak. Finally, Nick takes her back in his arms, where she knows with all her heart she belongs.

They sit at the Ham and Egg restaurant on the corner. She orders a chicken salad sandwich, while Nick eats his Adam and Eve on a raft. She watches as he chews his bacon and imagines kissing him afterward. She has never touched nor eaten pork. Does secondhand count? Does it matter at this point? Italian tongues are not kosher, but she has acquired a taste for his.

"Rose, I know we haven't known each other long, but do you believe in kismet? I believe we're destined to be together, that a force beyond ourselves has set us up." He stops for a moment, picks up her hand, and looks into her eyes. "I wanted to tell you . . . I think I love you."

She sits stunned, in the middle of a chicken salad chew, long enough for him to look uncomfortable and embarrassed. "I don't mean to put you on the spot," he says. "You don't have to say anything. I just wanted to tell you how I feel."

She swallows. It goes down hard, like her lies. She lies to her parents. She lies to Nick. Most of all, she's been lying to herself. But now she tells him the truth. "I think I love you back."

He throws cash on the table and pulls her up and out of the diner.

Stars are hard to see through the dazzling lights of the city, but the full moon follows them wherever they walk. She should have headed home long before now, but she can't bring herself to leave Nick.

"I have to do a gig in Boston for a couple of weeks," he says.

"What? No!"

"My train leaves in the morning. It kills me to have to go. I wish I could put you in my sax case and take you with me."

"I'm pretty small. I might be able to fit." She realizes she is crying in the middle of Columbus Circle. Nick leads her to a bench by the park, lit by a small lamppost. He opens up his sax case, and for a second she thinks he really is going to stuff her inside; but he takes out his sax, the brass gleaming in the soft light like fireflies. He plays in a whisper, some notes not strong enough to take flight. She recognizes it immediately as "I'll Be Seeing You," a song popular with lovers separated by the war. His fingers make their way along the mother-of-pearl full moon keys. As he gets to the last verse, Rose sings softly to the song she knows well, conveying all of her wistful yearning for him.

Nick sits down on the bench next to her and kisses the tears that run down her cheeks. "Here's the number where I'll be staying. We'll be back together in no time." He kisses her, and his mouth tastes a little musty from his reed and mouthpiece. "Look up there, Rose," he says, indicating the full moon above Central Park. "That's our moon. We'll look at our moon every night when we're apart and send out our love to each other." He produces a silver pendant holding a round moonstone surrounded by diamond chips, like glittering stars. "Promise me."

He sounds like a kid who believes in magic. That a huge, glowing orb in the sky could keep them close. But then again, that is what love songs are made of. He puts the pendant around her neck. It feels heavenly, yet heavy as an albatross. "I promise," she says.

Rose lies in her bed, but because the buildings are so close together, she cannot see the full moon. She wonders why she keeps making promises to Nick she may not be able to keep. What started out as a secret summer fling has spiraled into full-blown love. She finally admits it to herself. She's in love with Nick. She grabs her pillow, stifling her giddy giggles. How romantic this night was! Who in his right mind would play a saxophone to a girl in Columbus Circle? She squeezes her pillow tight and rolls from side to side, as if hugging the Jesus out of Nick. If she could do that, she would not be in this *tsimmes*.

She climbs out onto the fire escape outside her bedroom window. She has done this since she was a kid. It's a cramped little iron platform, but she's still small enough to sit hugging her knees. She hears the ocean waves, like familiar voices, and looks up to see the moon, as full and as promising as Nick. She touches her pendant. Two whole weeks. She doubts she will have enough change to make a long-distance call. She has no income. She could get a job in the city and move there. Then she could do anything she wants without anyone judging her. Perhaps she would still be able to sneak back to see her Mameh, as Papa would never ever let her inside his door again.

She will have to find a way to make this work. Her parents will have to understand, once she states her case: we can't pick and choose who we fall in love with. God is love. What is wrong with honoring God with true love? She will tell her parents Nick will eventually convert. And maybe he will, if that's what it takes.

She thinks of his blue eyes wherever she goes and compares all other blueness to his. Singing "I'll Be Seeing You" has become her suste- nance when she languishes at the Brighton Beach Baths or splurges at Coney Island. She fantasizes about having his children, the ones who would never know her parents. It seems as if every daydream about Nick comes with a knife twisting in her gut.

What is worse to confess? Nick's not Jewish, or he's a musician? Papa will not think that is steady, reputable work, even though Nick has gotten recognition from some big band leaders and fellow Ital- ians, Guy Lombardo and Louis Prima. "Tough guys," Papa calls the Italians. She realizes what Papa and other immigrants didn't expect after coming to America: their children want to become Americans. There are a million different reasons people pair up now besides reli- gion. Shouldn't love be enough?

She needs to talk to somebody. Someone who can relate to what she's going through or at the very least be sympathetic. The women she knows were brought up in the sheltered Jewish world, where if you can't speak Yiddish, you are distrusted. Maybe she could speak to Mildred, Brighton Beach's yenta. But Mildred has a big mouth. It would get back to someone who would spill the beans to her parents.

Ida Goldblatt, her best friend, has broken a few Jewish rules with her. They've eaten nonkosher food and done things on the Sabbath they are not allowed to do. Ida might understand, though when it comes to marriage, come hell or high water, for her it would be Jacob Epstein. "Why put yourself through it?" Ida would say about marry- ing outside the religion. "It's just a lonely place to be. Having our families around is more important than you think." Ida wouldn't tell Rose what she wants to hear. Maybe she should go to one of the fortune-tellers on MacDougal Street in the Village. For money, they'll tell you what you want to hear.

One morning she is eating cheese blintzes with her parents when her mother gets a call from her half sister, Ruth. Ruth is much younger than Mameh, and the poor thing is a tad cross-eyed. Rose used to think Ruth's eyes were crossed from trying to look around her large hook nose. Short and pigeon-toed, Ruth is nevertheless the family cutup. She says what she thinks and has shocked Papa down to his socks and slippers at times with her jokes. Papa always says Aunt Ruth looks down her nose at everyone, but she can't help it. Ruth never married, lives alone, and is an operator for the telephone company. She used to listen to big band music on the radio with Rose, and they would dance and laugh. One time, when Mameh and Papa were out, she and Ruth, who was babysitting, made the famous nonkosher cheeseburgers in Mameh's *Fleischer* pan. They laughed until their stomachs hurt as they tried to keep the melting cheese from hitting the meat-only pan. Ruth said there wasn't a Jew alive who wouldn't love to taste a cheeseburger.

As usual, Mameh's Yiddish becomes faster and louder into the receiver. Ruth and Mameh's conversations inevitably end in arguments. Mameh is more like a mother to Ruth than a sister.

Papa wipes his mouth and beard. "I've never seen two people love each other as much as those two yet disagree on everything."

Rose smiles behind her napkin, realizing Ruth is the one she can trust.

Aunt Ruth lives in Brighton Beach in a little apartment that Rose has never visited until now. Aunt Ruth is very private, and Rose wonders if she holds some deep, dark secret. "Come on in," her aunt says, swinging the door wide. It's an efficiency apartment, and Rose can see washed hose hanging from the shower rod, the seams snaking down each one.

"You want coffee or tea with *mandelbrodt*? I didn't make them. Mrs. Mandelbaum did." They laugh at the irony.

"Coffee, please." Rose feels better after her laugh. A sudden reconnection to her aunt.

"I was surprised to get your call," Ruth says. "This must be serious if you couldn't talk to me at your apartment or on the phone."

"Party lines and family with ears like owls." Rose sips her coffee. Her heart is pounding. She can feel her hidden moonstone pendant against her breast, egging her on. "Aunt Ruth, why haven't you ever married?"

Her aunt looks shocked. "Is that what you needed to talk to me about?"

"No, but I'm leading up to something." Rose takes a bite of her almond cookie, chewing like a nervous squirrel.

"I never found the right person. I'd rather be alone than marry someone I don't love."

Rose takes a breath. "I'm wondering if it's possible to . . . to let the cheese hit the pan."

Her aunt scrutinizes her. "You're in love with a gentile? You poor thing."

Rose produces the pendant, warm in her hand, and breaks down sobbing. At the same time it feels freeing to let her secret become real to someone else. "I didn't mean for it to happen."

"That's the best kind of love," her aunt says with a sigh and a look of longing.

"I think I can change Papa's mind. What God frowns on true love? It shouldn't have to be based on their stupid old rules! I'm sure Mameh would be on my side. She'd convince him."

"You know as well as I do that she wouldn't have a choice. Your Papa makes the rules. He would disown you."

"No, no, he wouldn't. He loves me. I'm the apple of his eye. Everyone says so. He'd be mad, but he'd come around. Especially if Nick would convert."

"No rabbi converts just because two people want to get married. And to your papa, it wouldn't change Nick biologically—he still wouldn't be pure. I can hear your papa spit the Torah verse at you: 'You shall not intermarry with them, you shall not give your daughter to his son, and you shall not take his daughter for your son!'"

"There should be a clap of thunder after that." Rose rolls her wet eyes.

"You wanted the truth. To your father, dating is for marriage. So there's a *halachah* against even dating a non-Jew. He will not deviate from Jewish law. You will have a *shidduch*, like everyone before you, because enchantment wears off and only an outsider can be the best judge of who you should marry." Aunt Ruth takes Rose's hands in hers. "Believe me. Your papa will disown you, and he and your mother, the entire family, will sit shiva for you. Except for me. I wouldn't be there."

"Why can't they be like you? Aunt Ruth, what would you do if you were me? I know what Nick and I have is real. We believe we are meant to be together. I don't need anybody's outside opinion to know it for sure. I can't live without him."

"Then you need to ask yourself if you can live without your mother and father and live with being shunned by your community. You will be a ghost to all of them. What does your Nick think about all this?"

Rose's head falls forward. "He doesn't know I'm Jewish. I can't tell him where I live or my phone number. I sneak out to meet him. He has a lot of Jewish musician friends, though, so I'm sure he'd accept it."

"He needs to know what you two are up against. What you'd have to sacrifice to be with him. If you're looking for a happily ever after, I'm afraid you aren't going to find it. Ah, honey, my heart breaks for you, but I can't tell you what to do. It's a terrible choice to have to make, and there will be terrible pain either way. I'm so sorry." Ruth pulls her into tight hug, and together they weep.

As Nick puts it, their time apart feels like blowing one long, whole note without ever taking a breath. Rose secures a post office box just to be able to receive the love letters he writes every day; sometimes they arrive two at a time. They will still be arriving even after he returns. She can faintly smell his hair tonic when she opens them. She imagines embracing him and the feel of his hardness in his trousers every time they dance close. And how can she forget the look in his eyes that goes beyond race or religion, reaching straight into her soul? She can't stop wanting him, even after her talk with Ruth. Nick makes her so happy that it would be worth taking a chance on marrying him. Mameh could sneak to see her and the future kids. As long as Papa never found out. But then Mameh's life would be misery. Like Ruth says, there are no happy endings. But what is the happiest of endings? Nick is being bold in his letters, hinting at sexual things now that they are "practically engaged." He promises they will travel the country together as he tours with the bands. He wants her to name their children and promises he'll never let her regret for one minute she married him. Maybe they will live in the Village, in the bohemian crowd of artists, writers, and musicians. She could openly eat pork and shellfish at restaurants. Wear pleated pants as she pleases and finally dye her hair red, like Rita Hayworth. She could step into that wide, wonderful world and say good-bye to her parents and her old world forever.

Chapter Ten

THOUGH THE CARNIVAL would last another hour, Diego was cratering by 8 p.m. He had played the games, won a handful of plastic Made in China toys, walked the cakewalk, ridden an elderly pony, participated in the costume contest in his age division (beaten out by a boy dressed as the Hulk) and trick-or-treated through the classrooms, filling his sack with enough candy to last until Christmas. He refused Maggie and Hattie's invitation to go through the haunted house with them and laid his head on Santiago's shoulder, his eyelids fluttering.

"I should take him home," Rosalinda said. "My poor, tired monkey."

"I could go with you, help you settle him in," Santi said.

"No, you said you'd go through the haunted house with us," Maggie said. "And you're leaving in the morning."

"He's just going to conk out in the car, Santi. Besides, I wouldn't cross the Wicked Witch," Rosalinda said. Maggie cackled her Wicked Witch laugh on cue.

"You guys wait for me, then. I'm going to carry Diego to Rosalinda's car for her. I'll be right back. Do you have enough tickets, or do I need to buy more?"

"The haunted house takes three for each of us," Hattie said as she and Maggie counted their mangled strip of tickets. "Better get some more. I want to try the cakewalk again."

Rosalinda followed Santiago as he carried Diego, carefully making his way through the crowds of sugar-hyped, costumed kids and their smiling, talkative families. She noticed a few women looking at Santiago with Diego and smiling their approval to Rosalinda. She smiled back. They might not be exactly the family these women thought they were, but they were family, and Rosalinda felt an unfamiliar sense of pride.

As they emerged from the building, the full moon hung above the Manzano Mountains. "What a beautiful night," Rosalinda said. Kids chased each other along the walkways, parents' voices cautioning them to slow down and watch where they were going.

"You seem a lot happier. Is it because I'm finally leaving tomorrow?" He gave her a teasing smile as they reached her car. Rosalinda unlocked it. Santiago managed to get Diego buckled into his car seat without waking him. Then he faced Rosalinda.

"I am happy," she said. "I just can't believe how we got everything all worked out already. And that we can be friends." She wanted to pour out her relief about Jesse and the glorious freedom she felt, and tell him that in fact this might be the happiest night of her entire life, and that she felt like she was finally on the right path for her and her son, and how deeply she loved his family for loving Diego. Instead she stood in the moonlight and grinned like a fool.

They stood smiling at each other, and Rosalinda felt him almost reach out to hug her. Instead he looked up at the moon. "Hunter's Moon. Some Native tribes called it that because it was time to stock up on meat for the winter. Miguel taught me all the moons, their names and meanings. Someday I'll teach Diego."

"Before you came, Miguel took Diego to his chile fields and told him all about how to grow and harvest chile. Diego listened, all serious. Miguel explained how the irrigation ditches carry water from the river, how the rains and temperatures affect the chile crop. We walked the fields for over an hour. This was before his last picking in one field, so there were still red chile pods left on the dried-out plants. Diego picked one and handed it to Miguel, all proud, and said, 'This chile is red, like our hearts.' Miguel held it up to his heart and said, '*Chile por vida.*'"

"Chile for life," Santiago said. "I hope Diego gets to spend a lot of time with Miguel. He'll learn so much about everything. And Charlie can teach him about horses and Rachel can teach him about goats and making cheese. CeCe and Rose will teach him Yiddish words and how to make latkes and matzo ball soup. Abby, well, Abby will teach him to love himself and believe in himself and to do the best he can. Ben will teach him about nature and conservation and how to love the earth. Maggie and Hattie might paint his fingernails purple, but they'll teach him how to be a little brother. Promise me you'll make sure he gets to spend time with all of them." Rosalinda put her hands on his shoulders and looked into his eyes, which were glassy in the moonlight and perhaps from a few sentimental tears. "Santi, I promise you. Diego will know your family as well as you do. That's why I'm so happy tonight."

He put his arms around her waist and hugged her. She held onto him tightly and then leaned away to look at his face. For a moment she thought they might kiss. Instead, she put her hand on the side of his face and said, "You better get back, or you'll have two angry witches."

He leaned down and chastely kissed her forehead. "I'll see you in another hour or so."

After getting a conked-out Diego stripped of his costume and into his pajamas, Rosalinda tucked him into bed. She was even able to remove most of the monkey makeup from his face without waking him. It was a good thing she'd be getting his winter pajamas and clothes in the morning, if they still fit. November would bring colder weather. She realized his sack of candy and toys was still in the car. She went out to get it, since otherwise she'd probably forget and the chocolate would melt in the sun the next day and ruin her upholstery. She looked up at the moon, visible through the nearly naked branches of the giant cottonwood, and thought about how it felt to be in Santi's arms. She closed her eyes, feeling his arms around her, his breath in her ear, their hearts pressed close. It was a kind of love, she guessed, to love each other as Diego's parents. An undeniable and unique bond. Whatever else, they had that.

Her eyes opened when she heard someone walking through the leaves. She could see a figure emerging from the cluster of trees across the yard where the path through the bosque began. She stood about ten feet from the back door. The figure began to run toward her. Was it Jesse, here to say good-bye? But where was his car? The figure drew closer, and she saw he was too big to be Jesse. Caden.

She ran to the door and slammed it behind her, locking it and drawing the curtains over the window. His black-gloved fist came through the glass, grabbed the doorknob, and opened the door in one swift motion.

"I told Jesse it was off!" she yelled.

"This is plan B. Where's the kid?"

"He's at the carnival. The whole family will be here any minute."

Caden smiled. "I saw you bring him back here. Get him, or I will."

"Get out of here!" She ran from the kitchen to the dining room, the opposite direction from where Diego lay sleeping. She grabbed her phone from her pocket and tried to hit 911.

Caden smacked it from her hand and grabbed her by the hair, yanking her head up to his lips. "This can go one of two ways. You bring me the kid, and you don't get hurt. Or fight me, and you *will* get hurt, and I'll get him anyway. What's it going to be?"

She kicked him hard enough that he let go, and she ran, knocking over furniture to try to slow him down. If she could just get to Diego and reach her car. But he was right behind her, twisting her arm behind her back, slugging her in the face. She fell backwards but got up again as he checked Maggie's room. She reached him, jumped onto his back, and scratched his face and eyes with her fingernails. He growled and knocked her into the wall, scraping her off of him.

She jumped him again as he reached Abby and Ben's room and flicked on the light. He elbowed her in the face and pulled out his gun as she hit the floor. He held it on her as he backed toward the last room in the small house. "Look, bitch, play your part, and you'll have him back in a few days. Ain't worth dying over."

She scrambled after him, the gun trained on her face. He switched on the light and grabbed Diego from his blankets with one arm around the boy's waist. Diego hung limply, his small, bare feet dangling from his thin summer-weight pajamas, his stuffed unicorn tucked under one arm.

"No!" Rosalinda screamed and lunged forward. She heard the gun discharge, felt searing pain rip through her abdomen. When she still came at him, he shot her again. She heard Diego cry out as everything dissolved into darkness.

Santiago rode in the back of Ben's SUV while Ben drove. He smiled when he noticed Ben and Abby were holding hands. It was so quiet in the car after the din of the carnival. He thought about Rosalinda and found himself eager to see her when he got home. Maybe she would stay up and talk with him after Ben and Abby turned in for the night. He didn't care if he slept tonight; he could always sleep on the plane, even though he should be catching up on emails and work. When Kat came to mind, it was jarring. He figured it was due to their several weeks' separation. Tomorrow everything would get back to normal.

Ben drove slowly up the drive, the moon so bright the headlights seemed superfluous. When the house came into view, it was lit up as if a party was being held. "What in the world?" Abby said.

Ben sped up as they all became uneasy. Why would Rosalinda have turned on every light in the house? The car skidded to a stop next to Rosalinda's sedan, and Santiago leaped out before Ben could cut the ignition. "Be careful!" Abby called after him.

"Call 911, the window's broken!" He opened the door and saw kitchen chairs knocked over and candy and toys scattered over the floor, the ripped Halloween bag in the doorway. He could see through to the dining and living room, where furniture was upended. Ben and Abby came through the door after him, skidding on the candy in their rush.

Santi ducked into the hall off the kitchen to his old room. In the open doorway, he saw Rosalinda sprawled on the floor in a large pool of blood. He knelt next to her, feeling for a pulse in her neck. His hand was shaking so badly, he couldn't find it. He couldn't breathe or think straight. Finally he felt a rapid, faint pulse in the groove of her neck. He put his head down to her lips and listened as a small whisper of breath caressed his ear.

"Oh, God! Is she alive?" Abby stood behind him. He could hear Ben tramping through the house.

"Barely—call 911 again for an ambulance—tell them to hurry!"

"Where's Diego?" Abby said, frantically looking around.

"He's probably hiding—find him," Santi said, covering Rosalinda with the blankets from the bed, first aid for shock he remembered from a college health class. He tried to apply pressure to her abdominal wounds but knew internal bleeding was the issue. "Come on, Rosalinda, wake up. You can do it, just wake up."

"I can't find the lad anywhere. I checked the closets, the bathtub, even under the kitchen sink. He's nowhere," Ben said, raking his hand though his hair.

"Oh God—he's been taken!" Abby cried.

"I'll take the torch and check outside. Maybe he was able to get out of the house while this was happening." Ben rushed out.

"I'll go with you and call for him. He might come to me," Abby said, running after him.

Santiago hovered over Rosalinda, trying to shake off his panic. He had to think. He checked her pulse again and made sure she was still breathing, ready to start CPR if he had to. "Don't die on me. Where is the fucking ambulance? She's going to bleed out and die." He looked around for Abby and then remembered she had gone outside with Ben. He couldn't allow thoughts of Diego to fully penetrate his consciousness, or he would lose it entirely.

Finally he heard sirens coming up the drive.

After shoving Santiago out of the way, the EMTs started an IV in Rosalinda's arm. They ripped open her shirt and plastered her chest with EKG leads. Then they quickly loaded her onto a gurney. Ramone stopped them to say, "I saw blood under her fingernails. That's evidence. Bag her hands and tape them closed until they can get the DNA samples collected. And bag her clothes, too."

The lead EMT drilled Santi with questions. All he could tell them was, as far as he knew, she was in good health, with no chronic illnesses or medications, and that he'd last seen her at about 8:30 pm.

After the ambulance sped off, Ramone sat Santiago down on a kitchen chair while his deputies combed the place for evidence. Santi looked down at his hands and realized he was covered in Rosalinda's blood.

"What can you tell me, Santiago?" Ramone, picked up an upended chair and sat opposite him. "Has she been acting suspiciously in any way?"

"She's the victim." Santiago gave him a hard look.

"I'm referring to her claim that she was in danger. Come on, Santi, I want to find this guy fast. We're searching outside, but he most likely took Diego."

"You have to find him!"

"You can help by answering my questions."

Santi tried to comply. "She's been kind of quiet and stressed lately, but we've been meeting with mediators and figuring out all the legal shit. But tonight, she was happy. Really happy. I don't know what else to tell you."

"Did she tell you anything about the boyfriend, Jack? Like a last name?"

"His name is Jesse. And they broke up."

Ramone flipped through his little notebook. "Abby said Rosalinda told her the guy's name was Jack."

"Diego called him Jesse, and Rosalinda called him that, too."

A young deputy interrupted them. "I found this in the dining room behind the potted plant." He held up a plastic bag with a cell phone inside.

Ramone reached for it and turned it on through the plastic. "Not password protected. Good girl, Rosalinda. Not much activity—just one number comes up a few times. The most recent call was this afternoon. To a Jesse, no last name in her contact list." He pressed the number and held it to his ear. "Ringing and ringing. Then goes to voicemail." He handed the phone back to his deputy. "Get this to the lab. Tell them it's a stat—a kid's life could depend on it."

"Jesus! This is a fucking nightmare! I can't believe this is happening!" Santiago jumped up from his chair.

"Sit down and try to keep it together, Santi, and I'll tell you what I'm thinking."

Santi sat and tried to breathe, looking to Ramone for answers, anything to hold on to.

"If we can believe her—and it's all we got, so for now I'll go with it—she said the boyfriend borrowed money from some loan sharks for gambling debts. Let's say they gave up finding Jesse and traced Rosalinda here. It's no secret Abby's loaded, so it would make sense they would take Diego for ransom, to recoup their losses. We'll set up a tap on Abby's phone and wait. Meanwhile, we issued an AMBER Alert, and I've contacted the FBI."

"Good." He clung to the hope that the FBI and AMBER Alert would rescue Diego. "At least Maggie wasn't here to see this."

"From the looks of the place, Rosalinda fought like hell to keep her son. Diego was probably in bed asleep. Rosalinda took the guy on a chase through the house—kitchen to dining room to living room, then back up the hallway, checking bedrooms, until he found Diego. He was through fighting with Rosalinda; he had his prize. So he shot her while she was trying to stop him from leaving," Ramone surmised.

"Diego is her whole life. Come on, Ramone, there must be something I can do—this is killing me to just sit here."

Ramone scrutinized him for a long moment. Santiago tried to look calm and coherent.

"Earlier today I got an address from MVD for Rosalinda, and I'm assuming it's for the boyfriend, too, since she said they were living together until he supposedly took off. My guys will need a few more hours to go over this place. Want to take a little drive with me up to Albuquerque? We can check out the address, see what we can find out before involving APD and obtaining a search warrant, and then stop by the hospital after that."

Santi stood up. "Well, let's go."

Ramone pointed to Santiago's blood-soaked clothing and hands. "I'll talk to my men while you clean up and change clothes."

"I wonder why Rosalinda gave two different names for her boyfriend," Ramone said as he drove them north on I-25 to Albuquerque. Ramone sped with his lights flashing but no siren, weaving effortlessly through minimal traffic.

"Maybe he goes by both," Santiago said. "Like Billy Bob. Jesse Jack."

"I believe Diego. A three-year-old child is not a good liar. I think Rosalinda deliberately gave a false name to Abby. The question is, why? What was she trying to hide?"

"To protect the guy in case someone came looking for him?"

"Hopefully we'll be able to locate a rental manager and find his name on the lease," Ramone said as they crested a hill and the lights of Albuquerque came into view.

The address took them to a small complex in the Northeast Heights. It looked like a box: flat roof, two units up some wrought-iron stairs and two units down, facing a parking lot that held three vehicles. Ramone parked his marked sheriff's vehicle on the street. "They're in the C unit, so upstairs on the left."

Even though it was Halloween, all four of the units were dark. It was nearly midnight, Santi realized. The street was quiet. Some kids' bikes and toys were huddled up on the lower units' porches. Ramone led the way up the stairs, which rattled and shifted more than Santi thought they should. On the balcony, Ramone first looked at the apartment marked D. The curtains were open, and the place was entirely empty. He turned back to the C unit. The drapes were closed, but as they drew closer Santi could see the front door was standing open several inches. Ramone took the flashlight from his belt and aimed it through the gap. "Somebody's down. Stay here."

Ramone pulled his weapon. "Hey! Anybody in there? Police! I'm coming in." He entered, aiming both the flashlight and gun into the darkness. Santiago stood in the doorway, following the beam of Ramone's flashlight as it illuminated a figure sprawled on the floor. Ramone called out again, but there was no response.

Santiago watched as Ramone knelt by the figure and after a moment got up and resumed checking the place. Ramone reappeared. "Come in, but don't touch anything."

Ramone had secured his weapon and had his phone out. "This is Esperanza Sheriff Ramone Lovato. I am at 10045 Hilltop Drive, apartment C. I found the apartment door open with an adult white male in full view on the floor. I entered the apartment to render aid and found the individual is deceased from what looks like multiple stab wounds. A bloody kitchen knife is next to the body. No one else is in the apartment. I believe this crime scene is related to the one I'm investigating in Esperanza, the one with the Diego Ortiz AMBER Alert issued at 21:55. I have a civilian associate with me. Yes, we'll be here. Thanks."

Santiago stared at the dead body lying on its side. Ramone pulled a glove out of his pocket and put it on his right hand. He knelt and drew a wallet from the back pants pocket of the corpse, flipping it open and reading with his flashlight. "Jesse Schroeder. Well, Jesse. You didn't run far or stay away long enough."

Santiago walked past, drawn to the hallway. "Don't touch anything!" he heard Ramone caution him again. Santi stopped in front of the first bedroom. With the curtains open, the window let in a generous portion of moonlight. He saw an unmade twin bed with Spider-Man sheets. Some toys littered the floor. Kid art plastered the walls, all with the same name in kid scrawl: Diego.

Ramone stood in the doorway.

"Diego's room," Santiago said, feeling his gut clench and tears stab at his eyes. He couldn't cry. If he started, he might not be able to stop. He cleared his throat. "What are you thinking, Ramone?"

"I found Jesse's phone all busted apart, but APD can probably still get something useful from it. This is their turf, but since the crimes are related, probably the same perp, we'll be collaborating. I'd say the perp came here first while the sun was still up, so no lights were on yet. With how congealed the blood is and the look of the body, I'd guess it's been a good six hours or more. Jesse either let the guy in, or he pushed his way past—no sign of forced entry. No other exterior doors on the place. No sign of a struggle, so the guy might have used a gun to keep Jesse in line, or Jesse wasn't expecting this to go down and was taken by surprise. Looks like the perp did some creative knife work on him before finishing him off, maybe getting some information out of him or just torturing him for whatever reason, payback, sending a message. Stabbing is quieter than using a gun, with people living downstairs."

"And then he went to Abby's for Diego," Santiago said.

"If it's the same guy. My hunch says it is. If he didn't already know where Rosalinda had taken Diego, maybe he persuaded Jesse to give it up."

Santi noticed one of Diego's shoes sitting by his dresser. He thought of Diego's little bare feet and toes and how Abby loved to tickle them with loud kisses. Diego would shriek and pull away, only to extend his foot toward Abby's lips for more. Suddenly he had to get out of there. Ramone stood back from the doorway to let him by, but Santi impulsively walked to the second bedroom. A double bed took up most of the floor space. In the moonlight, he could see the sheets and pillowcases were a flowered print. The open closet revealed some of Rosalinda's clothing had been left behind. A pair of high-heeled boots lay on the closet floor.

This was where they lived. When he was in California, this was his son's home. And Rosalinda had slept in this bed with that dead guy in the living room. The loser boyfriend who nearly got Rosalinda killed and Santi's son kidnapped. The one to blame.

"Santiago, I hear APD coming," Ramone called.

He came out to the living room just as two squad cars pulled up. Ramone met them at the door, identified himself, and let them by. "Aside from my retrieving his wallet with a gloved hand, nothing has been touched or altered since our arrival thirteen minutes ago. I kept the lights off, like we found them. This is Santiago Silva, a close family friend and father of the boy on the AMBER Alert that we issued at 21:55 in Esperanza." An Albuquerque officer began switching on lights, which seemed too bright.

Ramone briefed them on the Esperanza crime scene and explained they had driven there after running Rosalinda's car license plate. He gave them all the background information he knew while Santiago stared at Jesse's body in the stark light. Jesse looked like one of those white guy wannabe gangsters. Baggy pants with chain belt, graffiti art T-shirt, dark knit stocking cap askew over scruffy blond hair. His open, lifeless eyes stared back at Santiago, his complexion chalky from blood loss and death. The cops swarmed around the apartment, doing their cop thing.

The forensic team arrived and ushered Ramone and Santi out onto the balcony. While Ramone called to check in with his deputies, Santi stood gazing at the full moon and remembered how beautiful Rosalinda had looked under its glow and how Diego had slept safely in his arms, sweaty in his furry flying monkey costume. More than anything in the world, he wanted that moment back.

"Let's head over to the hospital," Ramone said, starting down the jiggling staircase. Santi followed. The downstairs neighbors were outside in a cluster now, in bathrobes and jackets, standing in the strobe lights from the APD vehicles. A female APD officer was talking to them. "I saw on the news about the missing boy, little Diego," a man was saying. "My boy played with him sometimes. A real shame."

Santi rushed over to him. "That's my son! Did you see or hear anything?"

The man shook his head. "We were out trick-or-treating with the kids all evening, and it's been quiet since we got back. We didn't go up there to trick-or-treat—since the lights were off, we figured they weren't home. I hope you get Diego back and he's okay."

His wife held a sleeping infant in her arms. She reached out her hand to touch Santiago's arm, looking into his eyes. "I'll pray for him."

Ramone grabbed Santi by the other arm. "The news vultures are arriving. Let's get out of here."

November

FROST MOON

Chapter Eleven

RAMONE PARKED IN an official vehicle space, and Santi followed him into the main entrance of University Hospital. As he passed a wailing family huddled outside the ER entrance, it hit him that Rosalinda could have already died, or could still die, from her injuries.

University Hospital was as lit up and frenetic after midnight as during the day, perhaps more so since it was Halloween. The waiting area was crowded with people, some in costumes that were the worse for wear. A drunken argument broke out over the last remaining empty chair. A woman dressed in a skimpy black cat costume vomited profusely in the corner while her male companion yelled at her in Spanish.

Ramone strode over to the safety-glass-enclosed reception station and picked up the phone to speak to one of the scrubs-attired staff inside. "Sheriff Ramone Lovato. I need information on patient Rosalinda Ortiz." He nodded as the man behind the glass spoke into the phone. "All right. Thanks."

He turned to Santiago. "She was taken straight to surgery. We can find out more at the OR waiting area—that's probably where Ben and Abby are."

Ramone knew his way around the labyrinthine series of hallways and elevators, and he led Santi directly to the surgical waiting area, which Santi was thankful to see was nearly empty. Aside from Abby and Ben, one Native American family, its members ranging in age from toddler to elder, sat quietly in the corner. Abby had her eyes closed, but Ben saw them walk in and nudged her. They both stood as Santi and Ramone approached. Abby grabbed Santi into a tight, wordless hug, the effect of which was to dissolve him into tears. He heard himself sob in his mother's arms for a brief moment, but then pulled it together. Ramone asked Ben if they had heard anything.

Ben shook his head. "All we know is she was rushed to surgery to find out where the damage is and stop the bleeding. On that board over there, she's patient 3507. It says she's still in the operating room."

"We went to her old apartment and found Jesse—that's his real name, not Jack—stabbed to death," Santi said.

Abby's hand went to her lips. "My God. We should have taken what Rosalinda said more seriously—I feel so stupid!"

Ramone put his arm around her shoulders. "Rosalinda was not exactly forthcoming or cooperative. But, with hindsight, I should have pressed the issue more with her. I'm sorry."

"We don't know if Rosalinda knew any more than what she told us," Ben said. "It seems safe to say she was as caught off guard as any of us."

Santiago felt his anger surge, a rising sense of power to combat the impotence of fear and grief. "Meanwhile, what's being done to find Diego? An insane killer has him."

"The FBI is sending a CARD team—that's Child Abduction Rapid Deployment—from one of their West Regional Offices. They'll head up the investigation for us. They're the best, Santi. They have all the latest technology to get Diego back. When I checked in, my deputy told me the Albuquerque FBI office updated him that the CARD team will be arriving any time now and will start their operation at Abby's house, where the abduction took place. I need to brief them when they arrive. Do you want to come with me or stay here?"

"We'll stay here for Rosalinda," Abby said. "We'll call you as soon as we know anything. Go with Ramone. Find Diego." Abby broke down and leaned into Ben.

Ramone took a gulp of his vending machine coffee as he drove. Santiago drank from the bottled water that Ramone insisted he down to avoid dehydration.

About halfway back to Esperanza, Ramone broke their silence. "What you said about the insane killer? I don't think he's insane. He's on a mission to get money, either for himself or people he works for, if we go with the gambling debt scenario. The FBI will run

Jesse's financials, and we'll see if there's any evidence of gambling—usually gamblers hit the ATMs at the casinos. If he was into private gambling, backroom stuff, we should still see something in the form of transfers, cash deposits and withdrawals, that kind of thing. If he did borrow money from some crime outfit and our perp is their guy, then he's under orders to get their money and give back the kid without any complications. See, that's good, because it means Diego is not in the hands of some crazy, unpredictable, rogue killer—he's in the hands of someone who views him as an important commodity in a business transaction. It's all about making the exchange now."

Santiago nodded, surprised Ramone could say anything that could help him feel even a little better about any of this. But it did help to think of it like that. It was something to try to believe in and hang onto: that this nightmare could be over soon and Diego would be back in his arms.

And Rosalinda would wake up to learn her son was safe with his father.

When Ramone and Santiago arrived back at Abby's, the place was lit up like a movie set and crawling with various law enforcement personnel. Ramone parked next to several vans. "The feds are here," Ramone said.

Santiago saw floodlights positioned away from the house in a cluster of cottonwood trees. Ramone walked in that direction.

The wind had kicked up, and the thin desert air permitted the temperature to plummet. Clouds roiled overhead, obscuring the traitorous moon. When he and Rosalinda had gazed at it together earlier, he had spouted the poetry of Hunter's Moon. The moment had seemed benevolent even as something evil was lying in wait, intent on destroying his family. Hunter's Moon was advantageous only to the hunter, not the prey.

Ramone introduced himself to a trio of agents collecting evidence in the clearing.

"Special Agent in Charge Williams." A tall, thin, fortysomething male agent shook Ramone's hand. "CARD team out of Texas. This clearing is where our perpetrator hid his vehicle. We found this." He showed them a sealed evidence bag containing the purple stuffed unicorn that Maggie had given Diego.

"That's Diego's. He sleeps with it." Santi recoiled from how macabre the toy seemed, contorted beneath a layer of plastic.

"We'll get whatever DNA off of it we can, but it will most likely just be the child's, since the perp probably wore gloves. But the tissue samples from Ms. Ortiz's fingernails are already at the FBI lab in Albuquerque. We'll be running the results through NDIS into CODIS, the national computer data banks of DNA-tested arrestees. If our perpetrator is in the system and we get a match, we'll have his name in a few hours."

When Ramone and SAC Williams began to debrief each other, Santiago turned away from them. His teeth chattered in the cold. He walked toward the house as the wind whipped his hair and clothing. He had to pee. Everything else receded as his mind could only attend to his basic physical needs.

One of Ramone's men was positioned at the door. He opened it for Santi and announced to some agents in the kitchen, "The father is here—Santiago Silva."

He stared at the row of coat hooks by the back door as voices greeted him. Diego's little jacket hung there. Santi grabbed it and waved it around, his voice bellowing from his throat. "This is Diego's only jacket! He's out there without his jacket! He's only three! He could freeze to death! You have to find him!" He flung the jacket at the nearest agent and ignored their response, and ducked into the hallway on his way to the bathroom.

He stopped in front of his old bedroom. The bed was stripped and the bedding, bagged. A female agent was photographing bloody footprints that emanated from the oval of blood that had collected under Rosalinda. For a second, he saw Rosalinda lying there, pale and still.

Before the agent could say anything, Santi backed away and stumbled to the bathroom. After he finished peeing, he began to gag and vomited violently into the toilet. He sank to the floor, shaking, wiping his mouth, and gasping for air. He leaned against the bathtub and saw Diego playing in bubbles, completely unable to fathom how vulnerable he was. The monster was coming, and his daddy couldn't keep him safe.

Santiago cried angry tears and then stood up to wash his hands and face, cupping mouthfuls of water to swish in his mouth. When he opened the door, Ramone stood in the hallway, eyeing him. "You okay?"

"What time is it?"

"Coming up on three thirty. Why don't you try to rest? I'll get you if anything happens. Right now, there's just coordination going on and agents going over the scene for any last evidence. They put a tap on the landline. And APD assigned an officer to keep guard on Rosalinda. Have you talked to Abby?"

"She said she'd call me when Rosalinda was out of surgery."

Ramone put his hand on Santiago's shoulder. "Grab some rest while you can."

When Santi entered Maggie's purple palace and switched on the light, he saw his packed bag with his airline ticket and boarding pass sticking out of a side pocket. He switched off the light and sat on the bed in the dark and then collapsed onto it, kicking off his shoes. He pulled the sparkly purple comforter over his fully dressed, shivering body. The old furnace in this house didn't cut it, especially with the door to the outside hanging open as the officers went about their business. To them, it was a job; and even if they were passionate about their work, it was still just a puzzle to solve before going back to their real lives.

Less than eight hours ago, he had thought he was returning to his real life. The image of his suitcase hung like an apparition in his mind's eye. In all that had happened, he had forgotten not just that he was going back to San Francisco but the entirety of his life there: Kat, Reggie, Gordon, his apartment, his job. Now, he reeled it in as if it were a fighting fish, this life he had cherished now seemed unreal. He put himself back into his office, back into Kat's arms, back walking the streets of the city he loved, and felt nothing.

After a night of feeling too much, it was a relief to feel nothing. In the morning, he would cancel his flight, call Kat, and tell her what had happened. They would just have to understand. Or fire him. As his exhaustion enveloped his mind like a dense San Francisco fog, he didn't care one way or the other what their reaction would be.

He woke with a start to find daylight seeping into the room. Shit! How could he sleep? He grabbed his phone to see if Abby had called and found it dead. He got up and lurched from the room, expecting to see the mob of law enforcement and their buzz of activity, but the house was quiet. In the kitchen, he found Ramone making coffee.

"My phone's dead—I never got the call from Abby," Santi said. The wall clock said seven twenty.

"Rosalinda is in critical condition in the Trauma Surgical Intensive Care Unit, TSICU they call it. She's hanging on for now, but the doctor's wouldn't promise anything. She lost a lot of blood, and they had to work on her liver and stomach and remove her spleen. Her kidneys could still fail. They have her in a medically induced coma and on a ventilator, so they're not sure about any brain damage yet from blood loss. Abby and Ben spent the night there. She doesn't want Rosalinda to be alone. I tried to tell her Rosalinda doesn't know if anyone's there or not, but you know Abby."

"What about Diego?"

"See this?" Ramone pointed to a rectangular black box mounted on the wall next to Abby's ancient landline. "It will record all incoming phone calls and store them on one of those SD cards they pop into a computer. No ransom demands yet. Agent McCoy has been assigned to stay here. He's taking a break while I'm still here, due to return in half an hour. SAC Williams is going to debrief us at nine at the Albuquerque Field Office, followed by a press conference at ten. I brought some breakfast burritos from Benny's there in that sack. I'm glad you got some sleep—now you need to eat."

Santiago noticed a bulging trash bag by the back door and realized Ramone must have swept the floors and picked up all the disposable coffee cups, fast food containers, and debris the agents had left behind. He saw a piece of Halloween candy by the refrigerator that Ramone missed. The furniture was all restored to its approximate configuration. "You didn't sleep."

The coffeemaker began to hiss and spit coffee into the carafe. "I can skip a night, no problem. I'll catch a nap later." Ramone unwrapped a burrito and took a bite. "Oh, yeah. This is the stuff," he said through a mouthful.

The scent of chile, eggs, and potatoes convinced Santi to unwrap one and take a big bite. He felt guilty that he could enjoy eating. Ramone poured them both some coffee. "The television networks are running the story, along with the connection to Jesse Schroeder's murder. Albuquerque police are checking his known contacts. SAC Williams said they've been getting calls on the tip line from the AMBER Alert, but nothing solid. I called the professional biohazard cleaning company I deal with; they'll be coming later to tackle the wood floor in your room. Once they sand it down and refinish it, you won't be able to tell."

The last bite of burrito wanted to lodge in Santi's throat. He forced it down with a gulp of coffee. He looked at Ramone, the man who had supported Abby through her ordeal when Bobby was missing. When Santi was a teenager, especially that summer he was associating with the gangster James Ortiz and sneaking around with Rosalinda, he'd considered Ramone a threat to his freedom, someone to evade. Some of that attitude he'd absorbed from living in the Baca household as a young boy, where cops were the enemy. But now, seeing the deeply furrowed lines on Ramone's face, the silver moustache slightly tinged with red chile, the sleep-deprivation evident in his eyes, Santiago couldn't feel more grateful to him. "Thanks."

"*De nada.*" Ramone waved him off.

"I better get to the hospital so Abby and Ben can come home." Santiago drank the hot coffee fast, flinching from the burn in his throat.

"I went over to CeCe and Miguel's this morning to fill them in. They didn't see or hear anything last night; neither did Rachel or Charlie. CeCe called her girlfriend Hazel—the former nurse. Hazel is already on her way up there to relieve Ben and Abby. We can go to the hospital after our briefing to check on Rosalinda. I'd like to know when they think they can ease her out of the coma, to see what Rosalinda remembers, if anything."

"I need to cancel my flight and call Kat. And take a shower." Santiago put his burrito wrapper in the trash bag.

"We need to head up to Albuquerque by eight fifteen," Ramone said, giving Santiago a quick clap on the back as he passed by.

Santiago plugged in his dead phone so he could make his calls. Kat answered in her sleepy voice. he knew she would pick up, since she slept with her phone. "Jesus! It's still dark. Are you at the airport?"

"I'm not coming—"

"Santi, you have to get home. We have you scheduled for lunch with those agents—we've already postponed twice. And you have that writers' conference starting Friday—you're on a panel discussion, and you're taking pitches."

"My son was kidnapped last night. His mom was shot and almost killed—she could still die. There's no fucking way I'm going anywhere until I get my son back."

"What? Your kid was kidnapped? For real?"

"I have to shower and go to the FBI for a briefing, so I can't stay on. I have no idea how long this could take. Tell Gordon I'll call him when I can. I'm sorry—there's nothing else I can do. If he needs to fire me—"

"Nobody's firing you. I'll take your meetings, and maybe Dad can stand in for you at the conference. I just can't believe all the drama."

Santi breathed into the phone, wanting to go off on her about the drama remark, but there wasn't time. "I need to go."

"Good luck, Santi."

When Abby and Ben got home after their night at the hospital, Agent McCoy greeted them at the door. Being welcomed home by a stranger was a bit unnerving, but he was large, wore a weapon, and seemed competent, so Abby decided to feel reassured.

Ben immediately headed for bed. She promised to join him for a nap in a little while. She felt her exhaustion like some muscular wasting disease that sapped her strength but kept her mind active. Too active.

While Agent McCoy studied something on his laptop at the kitchen table, she paced around in the quiet. The wind pounded her old casement windows, leaking through the loose caulking. Cold drafts swirled like poltergeists as the old furnace rumbled.

Someone had cleaned the chaos from the house and tried to arrange the furniture back into place. She adjusted the chair placements, moved the coffee table where it belonged, and saw that her pole lamp's stained-glass Tiffany shade would need to be sent for repairs. Otherwise, it looked as if nothing had happened.

She circled back up the hallway to Santiago's closed door and opened it to see the bloody mess still there, triggering a flashback of Santi kneeling beside Rosalinda. Abby shut the door, but the image lingered. She walked back down the hallway to Maggie's room, where the door was ajar. Santiago's suitcase gaped open on the bed, his clothing rummaged through, his airline ticket ripped into two and cast aside. Her heart ached for him. It seemed the more she tried to extricate him from his traumatic past, the more it reached its bony fingers from the grave to hold him tight and not let go.

Her gaze roamed over Maggie's purple walls, her artwork and posters precisely hung, just as her father would have done. Her love for Maggie exploded like a geyser, blasting through the stupor of her exhaustion. She had to see her daughter. She had to hold her in her arms.

Abby ran so fast to grab her jacket that Agent McCoy looked up from his laptop screen. "I'm going over to see my daughter—call me if you get a call or anything. Ben's sleeping."

"You should try to get some sleep, too—"

Abby was out the door. She jogged across the field, the wind gusting like ocean waves. Ice pellets so small at first she thought she was imagining them began to sting her face and eyes. Only November first, and they might see their first snow. The dark, winter-like sky seemed to have swallowed the sun.

When Abby reached Rachel and Charlie's house, she tried to smooth her hair and not look like such a wild woman before ringing the bell. Yesterday's shower and makeup had probably worn off, but her daughter needed to see she was okay, even though she felt anything but okay. It would take all she had not to weep hysterically while clutching her child to her bosom. She must be the one to give comfort, not the one taking it.

She rang the bell and opened the door, their usual protocol. Rachel rushed to her with a wordless hug, taking Abby back to the embrace they had shared twelve years ago when the private detective brought them proof of Bobby's death. Adversaries united in grief. Now Abby allowed herself a moment of weakness, crying into Rachel's strong shoulder, her fingers entangled in the long, dark curls that tumbled down Rachel's back.

"Where's Maggie?" Abby said, pulling back and wiping her tears.

"They're up in Hattie's room, making pictures for Diego to welcome him home and cards for Rosalinda. What's the latest? How is Rosalinda?" Rachel's ice-blue eyes bored into her.

"She made it through surgery and is in intensive care, still touch and go. Hazel is up there now, running them through their paces, I expect. Santi and Ramone went up to Albuquerque to get briefed by the FBI, and then there is a televised news conference at ten that we have to watch. Ramone said the story went viral, so we'll have even more press to deal with. Ramone's deputies have our joint road blocked off near the highway, so hopefully they won't make it this far. I can't believe this fucking nightmare!"

Charlie came over to put his arm around her back and kiss the top of her head. "Whatever you need, we're here for you."

"I need to hold my daughter without it pissing her off."

"I think she needs it as much as you do at this point," Charlie said. "How's your boy?"

"I don't even know. Ben and I just came home to sleep, and Santi is with Ramone in Albuquerque. Ramone said Santi got over three hours of sleep and he bought him a breakfast burrito. I know he's in good hands. Ramone seems to be including Santi as much as he can in the investigation."

"Mom!" Maggie cried as she scrambled down the staircase, Hattie right behind her.

Abby ran to intercept her just as she hit the landing. Maggie about bowled Abby over with her hug and then burst into tears. Abby held her, smoothing her hair, saying the things mothers say to soothe their children, what she desperately wished she could say to Diego: "Don't worry, baby, everything's going to be all right."

After the briefing and press conference, Ramone and Santiago headed to the hospital. The strong canyon winds whipped the vehicle and tossed trash and tumbleweed skeletons onto their path. The Sandia Mountains were obscured behind thick clouds, indicating snowfall. The sky was as dark as he felt, and it was not even noon.

Finding out the DNA under Rosalinda's fingernails matched a known repeat violent offender and ex-con, Caden Todd Owens, and seeing his menacing face, enlarged on a poster for the press and television, was equal parts reassuring and terrifying. Reassuring that they knew who to find, terrifying because the guy was a murderous monster who had killed Jesse Schroeder and tried to kill Rosalinda. And he had Diego.

"So Rosalinda lied about her boyfriend having a gambling problem, since his financials ruled that out. Why do you think she said that?" Ramone asked him.

"Maybe Jesse was in some other kind of trouble and she couldn't go into it. Obviously Jesse pissed Caden off, since Caden killed him."

"Jesse had been living the straight life, on paper anyway, since hooking up with Rosalinda. His priors were all minor stuff. Jesse's phone records show repeated calls with Caden Owens, starting just before Rosalinda showed up at Abby's, until the last call made the day Jesse got himself killed. Did Jesse double-cross Caden? Some kind of deal gone bad? What were they up to? And how much did Rosalinda know about it?"

Ramone's questions seemed more to himself than to Santi, as if he was processing the information from the briefing, but Santi felt obligated to try to respond. "Maybe Jesse knew Caden was going to kidnap Diego, and he tried to stop him—he lived with Diego for more than a year."

"Doesn't mean he liked the kid, maybe he just liked Rosalinda in his bed. Williams said Rosalinda called Jesse in the afternoon and they talked for over fifteen minutes. After their call, Jesse calls Caden. Then Caden comes over and kills Jesse, and later, he goes to Abby's to take Diego. I never could swallow Rosalinda's story. What was she really doing here? Having regular phone calls with the boyfriend who was supposedly on the lam, only according to neighbors, Jesse was at home the whole time, associating with Caden Owens, who ends up killing Jesse and kidnapping Diego. What's Caden's motive for killing Jesse? Remember they think Caden tortured Jesse before finishing him off— was he trying to get Diego and Rosalinda's location out of him? Too many questions and I only know one thing for sure," Ramone said, pulling into a parking spot. "Rosalinda has some explaining to do."

Hazel looked up from her iPad when Santiago and Ramone found her in the TSICU waiting area. "I just watched the live news conference. Great they found out who did this so fast. Now they can get him." She stood up to hug Santi.

"I just want Diego back." Hazel stood eye level to his six-foot height. She looked more than a decade younger than her late seventies, especially in her hiking pants and fleece pullover.

An older Albuquerque police officer stood next to the Do Not Enter double doors outside of the TSICU. He nodded to Ramone.

Ramone returned the gesture and then barked at a guy in scrubs seated behind the desk. "Can someone get that officer a chair?" The guy raised his eyebrows but quickly complied.

"Ramone, you look like shit. Get some sleep," Hazel said. "Or you won't be of any use."

"Yes, ma'am. How's the patient?"

"Hanging on. They're watching her kidney output real close. Blood loss is hard on kidneys. Vital signs are stable, except a slight fever, but you'd expect that with a GSW—gun shot wound."

"Is she awake?" Ramone asked a little too eagerly.

"Oh, no. They'll keep her sedated as long as she's got that tube down her trachea and she's on the ventilator. She's only about fourteen hours out from major trauma, and she underwent surgery all night. Allowing her brain and her other vital organs to rest is her best bet for recovery."

"How soon can they bring her around? She knows things that could help us get her son back." Ramone's exhaustion and frustration were evident.

"We want Diego to have a mama to come back to, Sheriff. You know who the perp is—go out and get him." Hazel dismissed him with a flick of her hand.

"Do I get to see her?" Santi asked.

"She's allowed one visitor for ten minutes about every hour, though they're not being too strict about it. They tried to pull that blood relative crap on me, but I got them sorted out. The head nurse was one of my students twenty years ago when I was still teaching at the College of Nursing. I think she's still scared of me." Hazel's lips twitched at the corners and finally gave in to a smug smile. "I got her to help me wash the caked blood out of Rosalinda's hair and put it into braids. I'd rather have cut it all off, like mine—so much easier while she's out of it."

Santiago must have looked horrified, because Hazel laughed. "I'd never do that to poor Rosalinda. Besides, you can't cut a nonresponsive patient's hair without a signed consent from the family."

After asking the APD officer if he could get him anything, Ramone turned back to Hazel. "I think I'll take off. Can you get Santiago home?"

"Carmen will be up after a while to relieve me. You know how CeCe's cabal is—we do for each other. I'll get him home."

Hazel had a word with her former nursing student, who then escorted Santi to Rosalinda's bedside. A forest of medical machinery and monitors surrounded the head of the bed. The tube in her mouth was strapped in place; her chest rose and fell as a machine breathed for her. Intravenous tubes delivered blood transfusions, fluids, electrolytes, and antibiotics, the nurse explained. The urinary catheter dripped into a container at the side of her bed.

"I just emptied it," the nurse said, following his gaze. "Her kidneys put out twenty-five milliliters last hour, which is close to what we want to see. More would be better."

Santiago's gaze flitted around all the equipment keeping her alive and finally landed on Rosalinda herself. The nurse wheeled a small stool next to the bed for him to sit on just as his legs went weak. "I'll be back in ten minutes," she said. Santi nodded.

Rosalinda seemed small in the bed. Her thick, Indian-style braids lay against her rising and falling chest. One eye was swollen and purple, her cheek was bruised, her lip was cut.

He remembered watching her sleep that summer. In their stolen nights together, he'd been too enthralled to sleep much, preferring to dream awake, seeing her face soften in sleep. When she was awake, twenty-three years old, brash, and self-assured, Rosalinda could be a little intimidating to an inexperienced eighteen-year-old—not that he hadn't liked the challenge. But when she slept curled up next to him, her head resting on his shoulder, his arm around her slender shoulders, he could feel protective of the little girl she had been, abused and raised by criminals. Like he had been, before Abby rescued him. Only she had never been rescued.

He felt protective of her now. Ramone seemed intent on blaming her for what had happened, when in fact she had nearly died trying to stop it. He knew how to measure love, and Rosalinda loved Diego more than her own life. She had come to them in some kind of trouble; the details weren't important. Whatever shit Jesse and Caden were involved in, Rosalinda was trying to escape it. She left the apartment where Jesse ended up murdered. Otherwise, she might have been lying dead next to Jesse, Diego taken, without Santi or his family having any idea he even existed until a demand came for ransom. She must have never imagined she and Diego were not safe at Abby's house, that the threat she was fleeing could track her there and strike so mercilessly.

As the machine breathed for her, each exhalation ended in a sigh. He reached for her hand and found it cold. He cupped her hand inside his and blew warm breath onto her icy fingers. His lips drew closer until they rested on her hand in something like a kiss.

Chapter Twelve

"I DON'T NEED a *farshtunken* wheelchair," said Rose, huffing and puffing as she pushed her walker into the living room.

"But, Ma, it's smaller than a clumsy wheelchair, see? It has a motor and a little thingy here you push for which direction you want to go. They had it in blue or gray, but I knew you liked blue." CeCe had noticed in the past weeks Rose's health had further declined, although if you held Rose's hand over a lit match, she'd never admit it.

"Just like a *maidel mit a klaidel*," said Rose, comparing herself to a young girl with a pretty new dress. "Me and Hi-Yo Silver do just fine." Rose tapped the handles of her walker.

"Ma, we just want you to have more freedom." Outside, the whirr of the circular saw and the pounding of nails started up.

"What's that racket?" Rose pushed her way toward the window. Her walker caught on the edge of the rug. The sun streaming through the glass caused her hair to shine like the red willow trees along the riverbank. "What are they doing?"

"Miguel and Charlie are building a ramp for your new chair. Look at the tread on the wheels, Ma. No more getting caught on the rugs or uneven bricks."

"You shouldn't go to all this trouble. I need all this like a *loch in kop*. There are far more important things going on than for you to be coddling me. Go help Abby and Ben and Santiago!"

"Abby and Ben would want me to stay here and take care of you. The cabal is helping them keep vigil over Rosalinda. Ramone and the FBI are looking for Diego. As much as I wish I could do something, I can't. So for Pete's sake, the least you could do is let me help *you*. Why does everything have to be a *farshtunken* struggle with you?"

Rose's knuckles whitened with her grip on the walker; her eyes seemed to be brimming with tears as she watched the ramp take form through the window. "Cecelia, my whole life has been a struggle. Why should my death be any different?"

CeCe pulled her pocket knife out of its sheath on the belt she wore around her faded jeans and cut open another bag of scratch, scooping up a coffee can full. The chickens charged toward her, and Pretty Boy, the peacock, swooped down from the top of the barn, landing a few yards away from her in a dusty cloud. She reached in the nesting boxes, pulled out enough green and brown eggs to fill her basket, and gingerly stepped through the sea of pecking chickens, the protective rooster threatening to attack her ankles if she got too near. He reminded CeCe of her mother when anyone dared to mess with her kids. Little snippets of memory popped into CeCe's mind; she'd remember the color of the lipstick her mother wore to her fourth grade band recital, or the times they'd played Monopoly for hours locked in her mother's sewing room while Papa had a flashback and tore up the house. Rose had distracted them with her loud Coney Island barker impersonation. "Step right up and roll the dice! Who's next! Don't be shy!" And no matter what Papa was doing, she never missed giving them their good-night kisses. She tried to make up for Mort, who could not show love for his children.

CeCe sat on a log watching her chickens, the spring chicks now old enough that the mother hen had nothing to do with them anymore. She thought of Rosalinda nearly dying in her attempt to protect Diego. And little Diego—who knew what he was suffering, or if he was still even alive? Her tears ran hot down her cold cheeks. She wiped them with her quilted plaid flannel shirt sleeve. The ferocious love Rosalinda felt for Diego was how CeCe loved Rachel and Hattie and how Abby loved her children. How mothers were supposed to love.

When she married Miguel, her mother and father took their love away from her. Her mother and all her good-night kisses and smothering ways vanished. For almost forty years. For marrying a "Mexican," though CeCe had tried to explain the difference between New Mexico Hispanics and Mexican nationals. They didn't care. It was all the same to them.

She sat there and sobbed like an abandoned child. Those years rolled over her like a giant wave, sucking her into that familiar painful void. CeCe had thought once she became pregnant, her mother would come around. "So now I'm supposed to be happy you're having a half-Mexican baby," her mother had said and hung up the phone. Shocked, CeCe had held the receiver and listened to the apathetic dial tone.

Dashed was her hope that Rose would hold her baby and coo the same Yiddish lullabies that CeCe remembered from her own childhood. CeCe had no one during her early pregnancy except Miguel's Tía Maria, who read the bumps on umbilical cords and insisted CeCe would eat her own placenta when the time came. She couldn't even understand what Maria was saying during her rituals. CeCe longed for her mother's Eastern European *bubbe maisses* about pregnancy and her yummy, homemade *luchen* chicken soup for nourishment instead of the threat of having her own placenta forced-fed to her by a cuckoo *curandera*. Tía Maria had been the only family member of Miguel's who did not desert him for marrying CeCe. But she had disliked CeCe from the moment Miguel introduced them. CeCe was not Hispanic, and Maria treated her as if she were a money-grubbing mail-order bride, even though Miguel was a dirt-poor chile farmer. Nonetheless, she was the only woman in the family who did not hang up on CeCe when she called.

One day CeCe was at Joe's Pharmacy to pick up some prenatal vitamins, because she could no longer force down the putrid concoctions Maria had bubble-bubble-toiled-and-troubled over. She watched a tall woman in her aisle checking out homeopathic tinctures. Reminding CeCe of Joan Baez with her cropped dark hair, the woman could squat all the way to her heels to read the bottles on the bottom shelf and push herself straight up from her toes. She wore scrub pants and a T-shirt that had a primitive-woman fertility symbol on the front. "Are you pregnant, too?"

The woman smiled. "No, I'm a nurse working as a doula on the side." From CeCe's hippie Grateful Dead days, she knew what a doula was. A pregnancy companion.

"I'm pregnant," CeCe said. "I could use a good doula."

"Hazel Diego," the woman responded, shaking CeCe's hand with a confident grip. It felt exactly like the hand CeCe had been waiting for. "Give me your name and number," Hazel said, handing CeCe her card. "I have an opening."

After that, Hazel introduced her to Carmen, whom Hazel knew from Carmen's volunteer work at the hospital where Hazel worked part time. Carmen, a mousy little woman, was devoted to her Catholicism and according to Hazel was married more to God than to her own late husband, even when he was still alive. And so it began.

Without their loving, helping hands, she would have never have gotten through that first year of motherhood. CeCe bonded with her new girlfriends, but they could not replace her mother. Neither Hazel nor Carmen had children, so they funneled their mothering onto newborn Rachel. CeCe sent baby pictures to her parents and never knew if they had been saved or thrown away. She sent canned beets and pickles every holiday, never to hear a thank-you. They missed all of Rachel's childhood because of the choice CeCe had made. Try explaining to a child why her grandparents didn't want anything to do with her. CeCe would have chosen to marry Miguel all over again. But there had been a price to pay.

CeCe let herself into the goat pen, where Rachel kept the young goats. Charlie had constructed a playscape, using large wooden spools from an electrician buddy and his ingenuity with two-by-fours and plywood. Rachel still treated her goats as the children she couldn't have after an emergency hysterectomy when Hattie was born. The goats screamed bloody murder, their frantic high-pitched cries all coming at her. They snuffled her, tasted and spit out her shirt tails, nibbled her fingers, searched her pockets, and screamed some more when they came up empty. One sneezed a blob of green snot on CeCe's hand. Just like human grandchildren.

She doled out pets and scratches when Rachel came from behind the goats' small wooden barn. "I wondered what all the crying was about," Rachel said, carrying a few tools on a tool belt slung low on her waist.

"Hi. Thought I might find you here." CeCe wiped her hands on her jeans.

"Sure, let me get a couple of things, and we can go up to the house."

"We can talk here, so I can visit my grandkids. But while we're on the subject of grandkids . . ."

"Ma, Hattie knows you have your hands full right now with Bubbe. Anyway, she's focused on Maggie and what happened to Diego—"

"No, it's not about any of that. I got to wondering how it felt to you growing up without your grandparents. How much collateral damage was there?"

"I've had more collateral damage since I've *had* my grandparents." Rachel laughed.

"No, seriously." CeCe sat on an old, dead tree log. Rachel joined her.

"They shunned me too, Ma. That time you took me to see them in Brooklyn? I was treated like a leper. It was better I wasn't around them."

"I should have been better at being a Jewish mom. I should've put my foot down more with your Tía Maria and taught you things about our Jewish culture, to help you connect with that side of yourself. I shoved it aside when my parents shoved me aside."

"I remember you were trying to be a good wife to Papa. You learned to cook traditional New Mexican food, learned all about Papa's saints and the history of his bultos and retablos. You immersed yourself into another culture for the good of your family. Tía Maria criticized you every chance she got, and I was stupid to listen to her. I'm sorry."

CeCe shivered in the cool breeze. Her daughter took off her jacket, toasty warm from her body heat, and wrapped it around CeCe while she wept.

Rose's electric chair turned out to be like the bumper cars at Coney Island. She chased CeCe with it, driving her to the kitchen and cornering her against the crook in the cabinets. She had to admit, it did give her more freedom. She felt like a kid again as she rode "Nellie" down her ramp. "Whoa, Nellie," she'd say as if she were Gary Cooper thundering down a riverbank.

Rose couldn't figure out was happening to her with these detailed dreams that became her addiction. If this was part of her death process, she welcomed it. To feel young again at the end of life. She wondered if she could change the outcome of the story this time.

She felt stronger now that she didn't have to waste energy pushing her walker, and getting outside did raise her spirits. Was this the place Mort had come to? Content to linger on the periphery of life? Where had he traveled in his sleep near his peaceful end? Back to his idyllic life in Poland before the Holocaust? While she could still taste Nick's kiss, feel his arms around her again, and see deep into his blue eyes, she wasn't going anywhere.

She supposed she was lucky to still have her own teeth at her age, but plopping them into a glass at night sounded easier. Brushing her teeth tired her arm. Her swing out arm. Lucky she didn't dislocate it dancing in her day. She took baby jitterbug steps to her bed, singing "In the Mood," her furniture guardians around her, eager to take her hand.

She poured herself a mug of peppermint tea from her thermos and checked her oxygen tank before nestling into bed. The mattress hardly indented with the weight of her tiny, frail body, as if she was floating on air . . .

Rose sits in the gigantic, Romanesque Penn Station. She reads in the brochure that the architect had studied Roman architecture, and it certainly is as if she were inside a great coliseum, with its honeycombed ceiling one hundred and fifty feet above the buzzing swarms of people catching and departing trains. Massive industrial-steel cathedral arches and paned windows, right down to the perfectly placed rivets, are the bones of this colossal building. The huge clock reads 5:45 in Roman numerals. She's early—Nick's train from Boston isn't for another hour—but she got away from home when she could. Military men sit on their suitcases, waiting; some stand in long embraces with their wives or sweethearts saying good-bye, perhaps for the final time. One couple hugs, and over the shoulder of her soldier, the woman wears a look of terror on her face, clutching a wilted white hankie in surrender.

Rose hates herself for giving thanks Nick does not serve. Band tours are hard enough. She wonders at this point how much she is going to spill about herself or if she'll say nothing and buy herself more time to think. His letters have only deepened her love for him. Despite Aunt Ruth's warnings, she wants Nick. And she is not throwing in the towel.

She sees him coming up the stairs from the lower tracks, sax case in hand; her knees are too weak to let her run to him. He drops his case to grab her in a tight embrace, swinging her once around. He kisses her, and she can feel his smile against her mouth. He holds her at arm's length, and his fountain-blue gaze washes over her. He picks up his case and leads her by her elbow through the crowds to the baggage claim area, where he grabs his bag, and then outside, where he hails one of the cabs lined up outside on Seventh Avenue. He holds her hand while they cuddle in the backseat of the cab that takes them to his Midtown room. With his roommates still out of town, they look forward to having a quiet place to spend time together.

There is no maid service in this particular hotel. "Flophouse" is more like it. Stacks of newspapers, magazines, and full ashtrays sit on every flat surface. The sink in the tiny kitchenette is full of coffee cups, the garbage full of take-out containers. "What do you do with your garbage?" Rose asks, crinkling her nose and picking up the full paper bag.

"There's a chute in the hallway. Here, let me get that," he says and takes it from her and into the hall. He looks embarrassed as he appears back inside. He turns on the radio, and they sit on the sofa. This is the first time ever she has been alone with a man in his apartment. She closes her eyes, listens to the music, and imagines herself married to Nick right now. Never to get on that D train back to Brighton Beach. Mameh and Papa turning into memories in old, dusty photographs on the dresser and mere hearsay to their future children.

"I want to meet your family, and I want you to meet mine. It's time," he says with excitement in his voice. "You're going to love them. It's a big Italian family who loves to be together, eat, and tell stories. My mama is going to love you. You'll be just like a daughter to her, you'll see."

At this moment, Rose realizes if she tells Nick nothing about her, she could pass for a non-Jew, marry him, and have a ready-made family to join. Would it be the same if she confesses she is a Jew? Can she take the chance of finding out? "My parents are very reclusive and set in their ways," she says. "My father is ill, so it can't happen for a while," she adds. Not a lie, since she sees her papa's stubbornness as a brain disease.

"We'll start with mine. My *nonna* is still alive. That's on Papa's side. She doesn't-a speak-a da English-a so well-a." He laughs. "But Italian is pretty easy to learn. You'll catch on in no time. If you really want to get on her good side, attend Saturday Vigil Mass with her. She's running out of people who'll go with her." He laughs again, and Rose sees how much he loves his family. Nick has never talked about being Catholic, but he wears a gold crucifix around his neck, she guesses now from his *nonna*.

"They sound wonderful," she says. She forces a smile. She wants him so badly. She feels she's at the edge of a cliff looking down, contemplating. Nick promises her love forever. Even her papa cannot promise that. Can she jump? Papa gives her no choice. But will she do it as a confessed Jew? It would be so easy to keep her mouth shut to Nick, slither into her new life as an Italian wife, and live the rest of her life as a lie. Even now she has to make a conscious effort to not speak Yiddish in front of Nick when English won't do. She would be shutting the door not only on her parents but on her entire identity, forever. Her Jewishness would have to be murdered; she imagines only sneaking the food she loves at Jewish delis. She would enter the world of Jesus for the rest of her life, a world where he's hung over beds, thanked before every meal, worshiped in large cathedrals, and used to keep children in line. Every time she would utter his name, she would see her Papa's disapproving eyes, void of the love he lavished on her as a child, when he promised her everything and bragged about her to anyone who would listen. Papa may be able to forget her, but she could never forget him.

After spending Saturday evening at Rachel and Charlie's, Abby and Ben retired early to their room. "How do you think Maggie is doing, really?" Abby asked as they bundled under the quilts for another subfreezing night.

"About as well as a girl her age could do dealing with all of this," Ben said. "Good she has Hattie. Good she has a little distance and healthy distractions."

Abby snuggled against him. "I thought we'd hear something today. You'd think that asshole would want to get his money."

"McCoy said kidnappers usually wait more than twenty-four hours before calling, to raise the desperation level of their targets and increase the amount of money they're willing to pay."

"I just don't know how to contain all of this—I'm so overwhelmed. I'm terrified of what little Diego is going through. I'm terrified something will go wrong and we'll lose him. I'm worried about Maggie and Santiago. I'm scared we'll lose Rosalinda—"

"Me, too, but my biggest concern is you. You haven't slept since Thursday night. You'll get ill if we can't find a way to shut off that relentless brain of yours." He pulled her closer, stroking her hair.

"I thought you liked my brain," Abby said.

"I love your brain. It's right up there with the rest of your physical entity. Like your lips, for instance." He kissed her, as if testing her response.

Abby closed her eyes as Ben's lips moved to her neck. She entered some kind of dissociated state where her body could not only respond but abolish all intrusive thoughts. The only awareness that lingered was one of gratitude.

Santiago held his phone, readying himself to call Kat. He thought back to his exhilaration at landing the job with Polydactyl Press, the excitement of moving to San Francisco, his growing affection for Kat. Maybe it was the effect of drinking three of Ben's imported Australian beers, but he was able to feel all of that again. He hit Kat's number.

"Santi! I was going to call you, I swear. I'm so sorry I was a complete bitch to you."

"I'm sorry I couldn't come back. I know it's a burden on you and screwing up everything—"

"Fuck the job shit! I mean it. I'm sorry I even brought it up, with what you're dealing with. We're all so sorry about what's happened. We caught the news conference on CNN. God, it's just horrific. How are you doing?"

Santi took another swig of beer. "I'm all over the place. Kind of numb at the moment, probably the best I can do. I'm trying to focus on you and our life there. I can't wait to return to normal, you know?"

"Would it help if I came out to be with you?"

"It helps me more to know you're there to help your dad. Reggie is great, but his skill set is narrower than yours."

Kat laughed. "That's one way to put it. I love the geek, but he's useless in public relations, or in public for that matter. God, I'm so relieved we can talk and feel close again."

"Me, too."

"Santi, this is all going to work out. You will have your life back and still get to visit your son. You're in the middle of this horrible thing, but you will get to the other side of it, I promise."

"Thanks, I needed to hear that. I think I'm unwinding enough that I could sleep now."

"I'll let you go so you can. Good night, babe."

"Good night."

"Hold on!" Santi yelled. He was bodyboarding at the Wedge at Newport Beach with Diego riding on his back. The waves became hollow and deep with an extreme backwash. He kept yelling at Diego to hold on so that he could get them to shore, but he hit a riptide. Diego was knocked off of him, and his board went flying. As they tumbled in the churning vortex, he managed to grab Diego's hand, but he couldn't get a good hold, and the force of the water tore Diego from his grasp.

"Hey." He woke to Agent McCoy standing in his doorway. "I heard you call out."

"I did?" He sat up in bed. "Just a nightmare. Sorry."

McCoy nodded. "Glad it wasn't anything else."

Santiago watched McCoy shut the door and realized there was not a chance in hell he was going to get back to sleep. Maggie's glow-in-the-dark wall clock said five forty-five. When he flung off the covers, the cold air pricked his sweaty chest. Surplus adrenaline from the nightmare made his muscles twitch. The beer-fueled state of calm he'd managed to attain last night was long gone. The dream—the feel of Diego's slippery skin on his back, his tiny hand sliding from Santi's futile grasp—felt so real. The loss of him tore through Santi like a meat cleaver. Where was Diego right that moment? Was he sleeping? Was he too terrified to sleep? Was he hungry or cold or physically hurt? Did he wonder why his daddy didn't save him?

He dressed, put on his jacket, and left the room. Except for the blast of the furnace kicking on, the house was quiet; darkness was gradually giving way to dawn. McCoy had returned to his bedroll on the couch. "You going somewhere?"

"My neighbor, Miguel Vigil—he'll be up. I'm going to see him."

The wind had died. The sun had not yet risen above the Manzano Mountains, so the light was muted. Yesterday's sleet had combined with a layer of frost that coated the grasses and the naked branches in a silvery sheath.

The sky was clear. Once the sun rose past its shield, it would ignite the frosty terrain into a shimmering wonderland. He felt a sudden urge to show this to his son, to share all the wonders of the natural world to a wide-eyed toddler still new to this planet. If only he could run back to the house, bundle up Diego, and bring him outside to witness the beauty the world was capable of, instead of the obscene ugliness he was now experiencing.

Walking past the empty place that once held his house accentuated his anger and helplessness. By Diego's age, he was already well acquainted with the ugliness in life, even though his mother had still been alive to protect him when she could.

He strode on, the subfreezing air scouring his lungs before being expelled in foggy puffs that would have been comical if Diego were there to play fire-breathing dragon with him.

After he crossed the service road and entered the Vigils' property, he could see light in the windows of Miguel's adobe workshop. Miguel called it that because he was not the kind of man to say he had an artist's studio. It was where he created his retablos and bultos, his wooden representations of saints. He carefully hand carved each one, delicately painted it with water-soluble pigments, and then varnished it with a combination of pure grain alcohol and piñon tree resin that he made himself in the traditional way. He had explained to a young Santiago that creating these sacred objects was how he practiced his faith, that when he carved or painted, he meditated on the santo, considering the suffering each had endured and how faith interceded. Miguel had told him they were not idols to worship; one did not pray *to* them, but rather prayed *with* them to God.

Santiago stood at the heavy door and knocked. His ungloved hand smarted in the cold and felt as if it could shatter against the hard wood. Miguel opened it. "*Mi'jo*, come in."

Miguel motioned to one of two chairs positioned in front of the wood stove, which contained a blazing fire and threw off so much heat Santi took off his jacket. Miguel handed him a cup of coffee and sat down next to him, holding his own mug between his rough farmer's hands.

They sat in silence, but for the popping of the burning piñon. Santi drank his coffee. Candlelight and the glow from the stove half illuminated the collection of santos that hung on the raw adobe walls and stood on makeshift shelves. Sometimes Miguel sold some at farmers' markets or gave a few to CeCe's friend Carmen to donate for the nuns' community projects. But most of them surrounded Santiago now, as if they were closing ranks in a protective formation. He knew some by name, recognizing San Ysidro, the patron saint of New Mexico farmers—Miguel's most personal santo—and Our Lady of Guadalupe, in her red gown and star-strewn blue cloak, surrounded by a nimbus of flames.

"Does it help?" Santi asked.

Miguel looked at him. "Does what help?"

"Believing."

Miguel's shoulders dropped as he let out a sigh. "Believing, for me, is a constant struggle. Believing does not come naturally to me. It is a choice I make every morning and every night. I want to believe, so I urge my stubborn mind to follow my soul. Does it help? *Mi'jo*, remember that summer four years ago when the drought nearly took my chile crop? I took to drinking; I turned my santos to the wall to punish them for their neglect. And yet the rains finally came in the nick of time, and our farm was spared. I have no idea if believing helps an outward situation, if prayers are ever answered. I can only say I am a better man for trying to believe. And at the risk of insulting these santos, finding out my mother was actually a Jew who had to hide her faith, furthered my certainty that it doesn't matter much what you believe in, the details, the rules man imposed along the way. No, I think it is the act of believing that matters. The courage and discipline to believe in something, whether it is God, or nature, or particle physics—it is about the journey toward faith."

"I'm so scared," Santiago whispered. "If I could believe in God, maybe I wouldn't be so scared. But I'm also full of rage. If there is a God, how could He let this happen to an innocent little boy who never hurt anyone? Is this some kind of lesson for me? Or punishment? That I fathered a child and didn't even know it and when I found out I was angry instead of grateful? That I saw Diego as an inconvenience? Because that's not how I feel—even before Diego was taken, I figured out that much."

Miguel squeezed Santi's shoulder. "I don't believe in a vindictive God. God is love. Don't confuse your own feelings of guilt or remorse with God's accusations. You came here to meet your child and provide for him as soon as you learned about him. I saw you begin to love him. There is no reason or purpose to his being taken. *Mi'jo*, sometimes we feel great joy in this life on earth, and sometimes we feel great pain and suffering—every life has both heaven and hell. Did you come to me to help you pray?"

Tears brimmed his eyes. "I came to you because you've always told me the truth."

"Then here is my truth: Mother Father God, I am certain you are looking out for our precious Diego and that you will bring him back to us safe and sound, to our loving arms where he belongs. I know you are healing Rosalinda, restoring her to health so that she will once again embrace her son. I know that you are filling Diego, Santiago, and all of us with the strength to endure this difficult time until he comes home. We are grateful for this truth."

Miguel's commanding voice resonated within the earthen walls. Santiago felt Miguel's words penetrate the deep layers of his fear and anger, and in that moment, in that sacred place, next to the man he loved and trusted most in the world, he believed.

Abby woke to find Agent McCoy at his post at the kitchen table.

"Any calls?" she asked, starting her coffeemaker.

"A few from well-wishers in the community. Some from reporters. They're all recorded if you want to hear them." Agent McCoy seemed even larger seated at her small table.

Ben came up the hall, his dark hair tousled from sleep. He kissed her and made his way to the coffeepot.

The phone rang, and the contraption hooked onto it blinked and flashed the caller ID as unknown. "Go ahead and pick up," Agent McCoy said. "It's on speaker."

Abby paused before reaching for the receiver.

"Do it like we've practiced," he instructed. "Just cooperate and get the information."

Abby answered it. "Hello?"

"Abigail Frasier?" The voice was mechanically distorted, robotic.

"Yes. Who is this?"

"You know who this is. You have cops listening, don't you?"

"What do you want?" Abby wanted to reach through the phone lines and strangle him.

"I have something *you* want."

"I need to know he's okay." Abby kept her gaze focused on McCoy, who nodded.

"He's sleeping. I'm keeping him dosed up. Kid, say something!" After a long pause, she could hear whimpering and then, "Mama!" Her hand went to her pierced heart, tears welling in her eyes.

"I want one million in nonsequential, unmarked one-hundred-dollar bills put into a black duffle bag. No fake money, no shorting me, no GPS trackers, no exploding dyes, no bullshit, or the kid is gone— get it?"

"By when?"

"I'll call back Wednesday with instructions. Follow those instructions to the letter, or I kill the kid. Tell your cop and FBI friends to back the fuck off. Either I get my money and get away, or you won't get the kid alive. You'll get him dead in a trash bag on the side of the road."

"We can do this sooner—I have the money now."

"What the fuck did I say? Show me you can follow directions."

"You'll call back Wednesday with instructions that I will follow to the letter. I'm telling my cop and FBI friends to back the fuck off. You'll get your full one million without any bullshit. You'll get away so that I get Diego back alive," Abby said forcefully.

She heard a click, and the line went dead.

Abby replaced the receiver, and Ben took her into his arms. The sound of Diego's terror had shaken her to her core.

"Burner phone, of course, no GPS. No way to get his location," McCoy said. "I don't know why he bothered with the voice distorter if he knows we've identified him. Probably already bought it and wanted to get some use out of it. Progress, though. I'll call this in to SAC Williams and the team."

A few hours later, Ramone and SAC Williams met with Abby, Ben, and Santiago to debrief and strategize. They sat down in Abby's living room with coffee and a tray of blueberry scones she had made. Santiago passed on having refreshments. His legs were already jiggling; more caffeine was the last thing he needed.

SAC Williams chewed his scone and made small talk with Ramone until Santiago wanted to slam the coffee table with a gavel to bring the meeting to order.

Finally, Williams washed down his scone with some coffee and said, "I thought we'd review what we've learned in the forty-two hours since Diego was taken. Based on DNA evidence, we believe Caden Todd Owens is holding Diego at an unknown location. He is also the primary suspect in the murder of Jesse Allen Schroeder and the attempted murder of Rosalinda Ortiz. How is she doing, by the way?"

"Critical but stable condition," Ramone responded. "Still sedated and on a ventilator. They might start easing back on the sedation tomorrow."

"Good. We'd certainly like to ask her some questions," Williams said. "At this point we know she and Diego lived with Jesse Schroeder up until her arrival here on October 6. We have evidence that Caden and Jesse were known associates, via witnesses and phone records, beginning in late September, when Caden was released from the state penitentiary. This activity increases between them in early October and throughout the month, culminating with Jesse's murder on October 31 at approximately four in the afternoon. Then Caden lies in wait in an unidentified vehicle—most likely stolen, since his own car is found later at his residence—in the cottonwood clearing on this property. The analysis of the tire tracks indicates the vehicle is most likely a full-size van or SUV. A little after 8:30 p.m., Rosalinda returns from the Halloween carnival with Diego. She settles him into bed. Caden breaks the glass on the back door and enters the house, where a chase and struggle ensues. Caden enters the back bedroom, where Diego is sleeping. Rosalinda tries to stop him and is shot twice in the abdomen. Caden takes Diego. You folks return home at 9:20 and make the initial 911 call."

Santiago nodded. "Yeah, we already know all of that."

"Contrary to Rosalinda's story, there is no evidence that Jesse Schroeder had gambling debts that placed her and Diego at risk, and there is evidence that Jesse Schroeder was not on the run from loan sharks, but rather was continuing to live at their formerly shared apartment. Also, Rosalinda received and made a total of ten phone calls to Jesse between the night of her arrival and October thirty-first, ranging from four minutes to the longest call, which was seventeen minutes and was made about two hours before Jesse's murder. There is no phone contact between Rosalinda and Caden Owens at any time. We don't know if she knew Caden through Jesse or if he kept that association separate and unknown to her."

"Rosalinda is the victim here," Santiago said. "She had nothing to do with this."

"She is most definitely a victim," Williams said. "But whether she had anything to do with it or not is still undetermined. Her story about the gambling could have been fed to her by Jesse to send her to you for safekeeping for his own reasons. She might have believed it and had no involvement or prior knowledge regarding the kidnapping scheme. At some point, we can surmise Caden Owens found out Diego had a rich grandmother and hatched his plot to take Diego for ransom, which is interesting, since Diego's paternity was not verified until a week after Rosalinda came here."

"She knew I was the only possible father to Diego before the paternity tests," Santiago said. "So she could have told Jesse at some point and he told Caden, who took it from there."

"We found Caden's fingerprints in Jesse Schroeder's apartment. We can't pinpoint if he left them the night of Jesse's murder or if he'd previously visited the place. We have yet to determine whether Jesse was part of the kidnapping scheme and things soured between him and Caden or Jesse found out about it and tried to stop Caden from going through with it."

Ramone stroked his silver moustache with an index finger. "Have you considered the possibility that this was a three-person conspiracy that included Rosalinda? The timing is awfully coincidental that she comes here with her danger story and is in regular, secret communication with the boyfriend she claims she has broken up with. Maybe Caden got greedy and didn't want to share the ransom with Jesse and Rosalinda. He used them to get what he needed for his kidnapping scheme and then tried to eliminate them."

"You think Rosalinda helped plan the kidnapping of her own child? That's insane," Abby said.

Ramone said, "You and Rosalinda were never friends—in fact, things were pretty tense between you the summer Diego was conceived. What if she came here as part of a con, get you on her side, have you fall in love with Diego, and then her friends take him for a few days? They make their big payday, and you never see any of them again."

"You just can't stop trying to make Rosalinda into some kind of monster, can you?" Santiago's gaze bored into Ramone. "She can't help what family she was born into. She hated them and their crimes. She struggled to make an honest living for herself and Diego. She would never do this."

Williams went ahead. "Jesse Schroeder, Caden Owens, and Rosalinda Ortiz are connected in some way. We can only speculate how at this point, until we know more. We don't have evidence that Rosalinda had prior knowledge, but we have to rule that out. Our agents went over Caden's residence and car; no DNA of Diego or Rosalinda found in either. We did find Jesse's DNA on a soda can, fingerprints, and a strand of hair in Caden's car, passenger side. Nothing useful has come from the tip line or AMBER Alert. We interviewed Caden's father, Richard Owens, in Arlington, Texas. He and Caden's mother,

Deborah, have been divorced since Caden was in high school, and Richard hasn't had contact with her since then. He and Caden are estranged, and they've had no contact in ten years. Deborah lives in Kansas with a second husband and is currently fighting a battle with breast cancer. She denies any contact with her son in over five years. Both agreed to contact us immediately if either hears from Caden. Now we have a demand for ransom, and we are anticipating Caden's call with instructions for the exchange on Wednesday. Our team is already formulating a variety of contingency plans to recover Diego and apprehend Mr. Owens."

"He said for you to back off and not try anything or he'll kill Diego," Abby said. "I have the money. We just want Diego back— that's our priority here, not apprehending Caden Owens."

"She's right," Santiago said. "We don't want you to do anything that puts Diego at risk. This guy is smart; he'll catch onto any tricks. Don't we have a say in this? Diego is my son. We want to do this exactly like Caden said."

"Our job is to rescue Diego and apprehend the suspect. If Caden gets away, what if he goes through your million and decides he didn't get enough? What if he decides to come back to get Diego again? Or snatch Maggie next time? Are you going to be able to watch them 24/7? Any of you could be at risk if Caden is at large," Williams said.

"Listen to the expert, *mi'ja*," Ramone said. "You have to trust the professionals."

"My money is why Diego was taken in the first place. I'll get rid of it if it puts my family at further risk, and don't think I won't if that's what it takes. But for now, it's my money that can bring Diego home, not your fake or marked money, not a GPS tracking device, or exploding dye canister, or whatever other tricks you think are so damn clever. You'll have to apprehend Caden later, by some other means, after we have Diego home," Abby said.

Santiago looked at his mother with profound respect. "Exactly."

"Isn't the primary mission here to get our boy back safe and sound?" Ben said. "I understand your wish to go all cops and robbers here, and grabbing up Caden to face his punishment would be aces. But don't we have to weigh that against any risk to Diego? His safety has to trump your trophy of Caden's head on a platter."

Williams smiled at Ben. "I understand what you're all saying. Diego's safety is our number one priority. Once we hear Caden's instructions, we'll scrutinize them for any holes and evaluate any viable opportunity for us to intervene before, during, or after the exchange. I appreciate and share your concerns. If there's nothing else, I need to get back up to Albuquerque. Ramone, I appreciate your help. Sounds like you're taking good care of McCoy, covering him for breaks and feeding him well. I appreciate it."

"*De nada.*" Ramone appeared grateful for the recognition.

Santiago stood up and walked away from the small talk. Abby followed him to Maggie's room. He gave her a hug, noticing how petite she seemed now that he was grown. His formidable tiger mother fit neatly in his arms.

Her hands searched behind his neck. "I miss your ponytail. I'd always give it a squeeze when we hugged," she said, pulling back from him.

"I saved it for you when I cut it off freshman year."

"You never gave it to me. I want it."

Santiago laughed. "I grew it here, in your house. It's only right that you have it."

She smiled and started to leave, but then turned back to look at him. "This house always was and is still *your* home, my son."

He nodded, suddenly too choked up to speak.

"You were ten years old, and you saved me," she said.

"We saved each other."

Chapter Thirteen

ROSE OBSERVED HER family's stress over the terrible kidnapping of little Diego and the near murder of Rosalinda. It was heart wrenching. Maybe it was because of her own failing heart, but she couldn't maintain the state of worry everyone else was immersed in; she sent up her prayers and let it go. Worrying would not change a thing. It wasn't lack of concern. She had other things to occupy her mind. The powerful pull to return to her past was undeniable, and all she had to do was close her eyes . . .

Rose is nine. A copy of *The Voyages of Doctor Dolittle* lays on the bench at the window where Rose likes to read on the fire escape; her dingy Raggedy Ann doll sits on a chair in the corner; its stringy red head flopped against its chest. Papa got her the doll on her fourth birthday, right before the Great Depression, when they had to move from the Lower East Side to Brighton Beach. She knows he scrimped and went without tobacco to buy the doll for her. That shows how much he loves her. She likes living here and not there.

What she remembers about the tenements is no one had any space. Relatives came and went and slept on the fire escapes. Mameh made money baking for the kosher baker, whose wife got the pox and died on the trip over to America, and the baker's son always ran back and forth from the store next door up to their apartment to pick up whatever Mameh baked. Rose had to drink stinky goat's milk from the stinky goat the baker owned. She rode on Papa's shoulders through the crowded streets to shul.

She has little hanging in her wardrobe but picks out a plaid jumper with plenty of room to grow. Mameh says soon Mrs. Galinsky's daughter, Murielle, will have a bag of clothes she has outgrown to give to Rose. Murielle's eleven and has already started to read Torah and prepare for her bat mitvah in a couple of years. Rose is still in the history phase of Hebrew school, but she can't wait until she starts with the Torah to make her Papa proud.

"Rose! Your father is leaving for work!" her mother yells from the kitchen. Rose loves summers, when she goes with her papa to the market where he sells produce. She earns pennies washing fruits and vegetables for Papa's customers and hopes one day to save two dollars to buy Mameh a pair of gloves and Papa a new pipe. She figures she'll have enough left over for a pack or two of gum.

She walks down the street with her papa, holding his hand and swinging it high and low. He remains stoic as they walk, not daring to look unscholarly. Even as Papa sells produce, there is no doubt he is a learned man. All the Jews treat him with respect because sometimes he stands in for the rabbi in shul. Rose sits on an orange crate, chin in hands, and beams with pride. She gives a respectful curtsy to all he introduces her to, and she sees in his eyes the love he has trouble showing physically. She is somebody special when she is with her papa.

Papa studies the Torah. He only sells produce to make money, but the Torah is his life. Back in the shtetl in the old country, Papa says, how learned you were about the Torah gave you status, but here in America, he says, "*Der mentsh trakht un Got lakht*. Man plans, and God laughs."

Papa's cousin, Hymie, takes the fruit truck, and she and Papa walk home after a long day of schmoozing. The sidewalks and beaches are full of people fleeing the city's heat. The beaches are infested with them. For the love of God, Papa doesn't remove his hat. She flounces her dress to create a breeze and feels the pennies and one nickel in her dress pocket jingle. She'll put them in her chalk piggy bank she won at Coney Island.

At home they find Mameh in the middle of fixing Shabbat dinner. The whole neighborhood is starting to smell like fish and chicken. Shabbat day, Papa says, is when Judaism is more *reyach* than *ruach*, more aroma than spirit. Rose notices the *Kos L'Kiddush*, Papa's wine cup, at his place at the table on top of Mameh's *Mapah Levanah*, or white linens. Rose is only nine, and yet she knows Jewish custom inside and out—and the way into her father's heart. When Papa and Mameh tell their stories of survival, Rose swells with pride because she came from a strong, unyielding group of people. The first thing Papa does when he gets home is put on his slippers and puffs on his pipe as he reads the daily *Forverts*, the Yiddish newspaper, which rides home with him under his arm. Rose runs to get his slippers and pipe. She lights Papa's pipe and smiles when the blue smoke takes flight out of his mouth. He smiles, too, his teeth yellowed like the old keys on the piano at the synagogue.

Eighteen minutes before sunset, Mameh will light the candles. Summertime sunsets are late, and it gives Rose's working sisters and her boarding uncles plenty of time to get home and relax like they're supposed to before Shabbat dinner.

After tending to Papa, Rose skips to the kitchen to help her mother, who is the one responsible for keeping their home a Jewish one. Rose knows all about the Talmud from Papa. He still has his shtetl mentality and is commanded by God to teach his daughter to be a good Jewish wife someday. And to keep clothes on her back. It is commanded that Rose be respectful, obedient, and a good Jew, and to marry and have children who keep the Torah and mitzvot, or commandments. Papa tells her this is true wealth. On Shabbat she shows her gratitude to the Jews released from slavery a long time ago. Rose doesn't need to be commanded to love and honor her parents. But it was a mitzvah anyway. How silly. She could not imagine anything that could force her to break that one. They are her everything.

Mameh greets her in the kitchen with a big hug and kiss on her *shayna gegrayzlt kop*, her pretty curly head, and hands Rose an apron. Mameh is a lot more affectionate than Papa. Not that Rose doubts her father's love for one second, but her mother always shows hers.

Rose's mouth waters with the thought of eating *kneydl* and chicken *polkes* right out of the sweet cinnamon *tsimmes*. Her favorite. Its scent wafts from the small oven, making promises that test her patience. She hasn't eaten much today, except fruit. But that is usual for the day of Shabbat meal. Everyone goes a little hungry during the day.

Mameh has her set the table and allows her to place the silver candlesticks and candles as the centerpiece. Rose feels special and can tell her papa is kvelling, peering over his newspaper at her, as she knows she is making his life wealthy, his home a sanctuary for God, and everything right in his world. Mameh says a man needs to be reminded of his Jewishness by wearing his *kippah* and *tallit* and by keeping the company of fellow Jews. But women, Mameh says, know from the inside they are Jews, and how lucky we are to be able to perform our mitzvahs from the comfort of home. And when Rose gets married, she will be able to keep a Jewish home, the biggest commandment a woman has in the eyes of God. Rose can't wait.

Her two uncles arrive first. They were rabbis in the old country but roll cigars in this country. They don't seem to care as long as they study the Torah. They down some vodka before the sun sets. At that time, Mameh will light the candles, and then no one can eat or drink anything until after Papa says *Kiddush*. Papa opens his old velveteen Hebrew bible, and the three men start their Yiddish chatter, which switches to Hebrew when they discuss the Talmud. Rose finds comfort in the predictability of her home and runs to light their pipes. The tobacco is moist and fresh and fills the room with a hearty aroma, their rings of smoke hanging inanimate around them in the light. One uncle is the *kitseler*, or tickler. The other slips her a nickel. It clinks against the small bounty in her pocket.

She runs to get the two loaves of challah ready for the table. She eats the ends that her mother surreptitiously leaves for her. They are thin and delicious and covered in poppy seed. Mameh fans herself with a dish towel and gazes out the window at the zigzagged fire escapes and laundry flailing on lines. Where does Mameh go in her wistful moments? Is she sad for having to leave her parents behind? Maybe she feels she has failed as a daughter. Rose runs over and hugs her mother tightly, hoping to make her forget any sadness. Not on Shabbat. Her mother is tender and yet hard as they come. Rose has never heard her mother complain, even in the Lower East Side, when there had been a lot to complain about. Other wives were called "real kvetchers," but not Mameh. America didn't change her. Some other women even stopped covering their heads, but her mameh kept hers covered. Papa makes the money, but Mameh is the brains of their finances. That's how it was in the old country. Even to Mameh, Papa's studies are more important than him having a great job.

Rose covers the challah with a white linen napkin and sets it on the table. By now her sisters have arrived. They both relax by the radio, listening to music before it has to be turned off for the night.

At sundown, when Mameh lights the candles, Rose quietly recites the prayer with her. Instead of covering her eyes with her hands, like everybody else, she closes them. Afterward, the adults start putting money in the *pushke*, or charity box, on the table. Rose reaches in her pocket for a penny, but with Papa watching, she chooses one of her nickels. Papa smiles. She'd like to tell him that besides being a good wife and mother, she would like to be a rabbi someday, but he would think that absurd. Women aren't meant to be rabbis.

After the prayer for the wine, Papa beckons her to his side, as he does every Friday night. This is her favorite part. The children's blessing. He puts his hand on her head, and it feels as if she is floating. The prayer is entirely in Hebrew. She has heard it all her life. It asks God to make her like Sarah, Rebecca, Rachel, and Leah, the mothers of the Jewish people. To shine down on her, favor her, and grant her peace. Papa lingers his hand on her head for a second longer as they gaze into each other's eyes. In them she sees the gleam of hope her people have had in their children for centuries. His hand drops tenderly from her head, his fingers caress down to her chin. He has never looked prouder, and she has never felt more loved.

After Abby took the ransom call on Sunday, a quasi routine fell into place. Abby stayed with Rosalinda at the hospital during the day when Maggie was at school. Santi covered the evening shift. CeCe's friends relieved them, usually Hazel. Abby secured the ransom money. Tomorrow, on Wednesday, they would hear the instructions for the exchange and soon after have Diego home. Santiago could almost imagine an end to this.

He closed his laptop. It was impossible to concentrate on the manuscript he was attempting to edit. The words became a meaningless parade of black lines, curves, and dots. He stood, placed the laptop on his chair next to Rosalinda's hospital bed, and stretched. Her color had returned to normal—in fact, her cheeks were downright rosy. The bruising on her face had begun to fade, her lip healed. Her kidneys had rebounded and were now producing brilliant yellow urine that the nurses celebrated every time they came into the room. He couldn't help but laugh. Cheering for pee. They were even talking about waking her from her sedation and removing the endotracheal tube and ventilator.

A young, scrubs-attired nurse came in smiling, but she frowned when she looked at Rosalinda and her monitor screen. She came to Rosalinda's side and placed a hand on her forehead. "She's burning up—and diaphoretic. Her heart rate is accelerating." She grabbed the thermometer and swiped it across Rosalinda's perspiring forehead. "One hundred and two point eight. I'll call the doctor."

Santi realized Rosalinda's rosy cheeks had been the flush of a spiking fever. *Shit!* He should have snapped. He had seen only what he wanted to see.

"You're going to have to step out," the nurse said as soon as she returned, trailed by the doctor Santi recognized as Rosalinda's chief surgeon, one of those older white men who seemed devoid of all color except subtle variations of gray.

"What's happening?" Santi asked, stepping back but not leaving.

The surgeon ignored him while he examined Rosalinda.

"One hundred and three point eight," the nurse said. The monitor alarm went off as Rosalinda's heart rate passed 120.

"Blood cultures times three, urine culture." He listened to her heart and lungs with his stethoscope. He pulled up Rosalinda's gown, donned gloves, and opened up her dressings, barking unintelligible orders to the nurse.

Rosalinda's flawless abdomen now had a freshly sutured incision starting just below her breastbone, circumventing her belly button, and extending beyond that. Santi could see the edges of her skin where the scalpel had cut through, now gathered back together with blue thread. On either side of the incision were two sooty circular bullet entry wounds, each surrounded by a field of gunpowder tattooing caused by Caden firing his weapon at such close range. The belly button ring she used to wear, with its twinkling gem, was absent.

He grabbed his laptop and jacket and fled the room just as several more people in scrubs and white coats brushed past him. He stumbled into the waiting area. One large family group took up half the chairs. A middle-aged man was saying something in Spanish. His family burst into laughter, up and down the line of chairs.

Santi wondered what the hell they had to laugh about in a place like this.

On Wednesday, Abby stayed home to wait for Caden Owen's phone call. Santiago had spent the night at the hospital while Rosalinda fought for her life. An infection had spread to her bloodstream and threatened every vital organ, including her heart. He called Abby in the early morning to report that her fever had broken and the doctors believed they had found the best combination of "big gun" antibiotics. The next twenty-four hours would tell if they were right and if Rosalinda was strong enough to survive the complication.

"Santi sounds exhausted," Abby said to Ramone, who was waiting with her for Caden's phone call. SAC Williams was also present with the excuse that he was giving McCoy the day off, but Abby suspected he wanted to be there for the phone call, also.

Ramone smiled. "*Mi'ja*, you have enough to worry about without adding a grown man who can fend for himself to your list. Santiago is fine."

Abby glared at him. "I don't care if he is grown, he's my son."

They sat in the living room, bright sunlight streaming through the windows. Williams was working on his laptop computer in the kitchen. Ben was at UNM prepping his students for exams. She was grateful Ramone was there, despite how irritating he could be.

"I saw you put Santiago's old room back together. The floors came out perfect, no?"

"I wanted it to be ready for when Diego comes home," Abby said. "It's going to be rough enough to try to explain to him why his mama isn't here. But later on, once she's ready to be discharged, I'm going to take care of her here. Ben and I already talked about it. It could be months before she's strong enough to live on her own and take care of Diego."

"What if she was involved in this? Will you still feel so generous?"

"Santi's right. You do have some kind of vendetta against Rosalinda—" The ringing phone silenced her. She ran to the kitchen, Ramone behind her.

SAC Williams nodded for her to answer it. "Hello?"

"Listen carefully," the mechanized voice said. "In the Sandia Mountains there is a trailhead called Tree Spring. You and you alone will bring the cash in a black duffle bag and place it in the trash bin next to the men's side of the restrooms. You will do this at first light Friday morning. Then you will go home. No surveillance, no FBI, no cops, no tricks. I get paid, and I get away. After that, if I am one hundred percent happy, I will call you to tell you where to find the kid. Better make sure I am in the mood to make that call, or he will die alone where he is—adios, Diego. Do you understand?"

"When will you call back to tell us where to find him?" Abby said.

"When I'm happy. Your job is to make me happy. Repeat my instructions."

"At first light Friday morning, I'll bring one million in cash in a black duffle bag to Tree Spring trailhead in the Sandia Mountains. I'll place it in the trash bin by the men's side of the restrooms. I'll go back home, and you will call to tell me where to find Diego."

"If I'm happy."

"You will be." The phone line went dead.

Williams already had a map of the Sandia Mountain National Forest recreation area up on his computer screen. He turned it so Ramone and Abby could see. Abby pointed to Tree Springs trailhead. "I've been there lots of times. Ben and I like to hike that trail."

"Close to eighty-five hundred feet elevation," Williams said.

"That storm over the weekend brought at least a foot of snow up there," Ramone said.

"It's open year around. We've snowshoed there. They plow the road to the trailhead, and it's a short distance from the highway. Ben's SUV will do fine," Abby said.

"You aren't doing this alone," Ramone said.

"Of course I am—you heard him. I told you guys, and Santiago agrees, we're doing this exactly as Caden says. He wants me alone at dawn on Friday with the bag of cash, which only weighs twenty-two pounds—I looked it up—so even a delicate girl like me can carry it."

"It could be a trap to take you or hurt you," Ramone said.

"He just wants his money, and he won't even be there."

"We don't know that for sure," Williams said. "What if you hand over the million and never hear from him again?"

"Then I've done everything I can. It's a risk I have to take. Fuck the money. Can I be any more clear?" Abby said.

Williams and Ramone exchanged that look men gave when a woman was being difficult.

"I'm going to bring these instructions to my team, and we'll do our research, run some scenarios," Williams said. "I think we should go up to Tree Spring now and assess the layout, pose as civilians in case he's watching the place."

"I could drive us in my personal truck," Ramone said. "It'll take about an hour and a half from here. It's eleven thirty now, and it's getting dark by four forty-five. We could dress like hikers, borrow Abby and Ben's snowshoes, take some pictures, like tourists."

"Let's do it. I'll run up and brief my team, change clothes, and head back down. I'll send another agent to be here while we're gone. I'll need to borrow some winter gear."

"I got you covered," Ramone said. "Abby, can we borrow your snowshoes?"

"I want to go with you. I'm the one delivering the money, so I should be able to check it out. I can wear Maggie's snowshoes."

"In case you've never Googled yourself, there are tons of pictures and articles about you online. If he is watching the place, he'd spot you, and that would compromise us." Williams attempted to temper his refusal with a smile. "Ramone and I will be able to pass as a couple of dudes enjoying a beautiful day snowshoeing in the mountains."

"I'll give in on this, but not about going alone to make the drop. No snipers hidden in the trees, no helicopters swooping in, none of your FBI secret mission crap. If you capture him before he gives us Diego's location, he'd never talk out of spite. He'd let Diego die. So I don't know why you're wasting your time even going up there."

"He's wanted for murder. If we are able to grab him up, we'll offer an enticing deal to get his cooperation. You need to trust us, Abby. We can bring Diego home safely and get a dangerous criminal locked up for good," Williams said.

"A deal? He knows the most he can get is life in prison for killing Jesse Schroeder. This isn't a capital punishment state. You have nothing to trade."

"The death penalty was reinstated for federal cases in 1988. He will be charged under federal, not state, law. If we have him in custody and he hasn't revealed where to find Diego, we can offer life in prison instead of the needle—that's an attractive deal," Williams said.

"You're gambling with my grandson's life." Abby felt dangerously close to tears, and the last thing she wanted was to act like an emotional female.

Ramone slung his arm around her shoulders. "Diego is the prize. We won't let anything happen to him. *Mi'ja*, you have my word. We just need to see Tree Spring trailhead. Caden chose this place for a reason. If we can figure out why, it gives us an advantage. It's routine police work. Now, will you loan us the snowshoes, or do we have to trudge through snow up to our asses?"

"You're sixty-two, old man. I don't need you dying of a heart attack on top of everything else. The snowshoes are hanging in the storage shed out back."

When Rosalinda's brain produced any images from her sea of darkness, they were terrifying nightmares. Even as her helpless psyche relived the moments prior to her gunshot wounds, her body lay pinned down, paralyzed into submission. Flashes of trying to run from Caden, Diego being ripped from her arms, her son's echoing cry, "Mama!", repeated in a sadistic loop.

Just as the attack had played out in real life, the assaultive images came out of nowhere, inciting panic and then ending the same way each time: with searing pain ripping through her core and instantaneous submersion into a dark void that provided no relief or comfort.

Awareness beyond this perpetual hell was impossible.

Rosalinda's team of doctors decided the infection was now under control, so it was time to bring her out of her medically induced coma and remove the breathing tube and ventilator. The longer a person was in a coma, the greater the chance of complications and difficulty waking up. The nurses had begun to follow the ventilator-weaning protocol and lighten the sedation over the last several hours. Santiago watched as Rosalinda's fingers began to twitch.

A plump Hispanic nurse stood next to her on one side of the bed, along with a respiratory therapist, a short man with a shiny bald head and huge black-framed glasses. The surgeon and his small flock of residents stood on the other side. Santi tried to position himself so that when Rosalinda woke, she would see one face she knew and trusted. He felt his breathing catch; his hands were clenched and sweating. He opened his fists and wiped his palms on his jeans.

As Rosalinda's eyes fluttered, the nurse held her hand and spoke. "Rosalinda, can you wake up for me? You're in the hospital. You have a tube in your throat to help you breathe, so you can't speak yet. You are safe. We're here to help you."

The doctor aimed his penlight into each of her eyes. "Pupils are equal and responsive."

"She's squeezing my hand," the nurse said. She took both of Rosalinda's hands. "Squeeze for me. Good. Grips are strong and equal."

Rosalinda's eyes opened. The doctor was listening to her lungs. Then he adjusted her ventilator settings. After a moment he listened to her lungs again and then disconnected the machine from the tube in her mouth. "She's breathing on her own. Let's get that tube out."

The respiratory therapist removed the strap securing the tube. "I'm going to pull out the tube—you'll cough, but that's normal." He put on gloves and laid a paper cloth under her chin. He quickly pulled out the tube. As Rosalinda coughed, her hands gripped her abdomen.

"You were shot twice and then had surgery, so you're going to be sore," the nurse said.

Santiago leaned in once the respiratory tech got out of the way. Rosalinda's eyes seemed to try to focus. "It's Santi. I'm here."

The doctor uttered some orders to the nurse about stat blood gases, neuro checks, and vital signs. "She can suck on some ice chips but nothing else by mouth. Keep the vent on standby, but I think she'll be fine. Call me ASAP with those results. If she stays stable, we'll move her to a regular room in the morning." He and his white-coated entourage left the room.

"Rosalinda, can you tell me where you are?" the nurse asked.

"Hospital."

"How old are you?"

"Twenty-seven."

"Do you know what month this is?"

"Halloween—where is Diego? I want my son!" Rosalinda cried out in her hoarse voice.

"Stay calm, Rosalinda. I don't want to have to give you any more sedation right now. I need you to wake up and remain calm. Slow down your breathing." The nurse watched as the red numbers on Rosalinda's monitor climbed. She motioned for Santi to come closer, and she backed off. "Santiago is here. He's been here every day with you."

Santi held Rosalinda's hand and looked into her frightened eyes. "Do you remember what happened?"

"Caden . . . took Diego."

"We're getting Diego back soon, I promise."

"What day is it?" Rosalinda's eyes fluttered again, but she seemed to fight against going back to sleep, blinking hard and refocusing.

"It's Wednesday night, November fifth, at eight thirty. You had surgery during the night after the Halloween carnival. The FBI is going to get Diego back. Abby's going to pay the ransom Friday morning, and then we'll have our son back. It's going to be okay, I promise."

Rosalinda's eyes filled with tears, and they overflowed, streaming down her face. Her cracked lips trembled. The nurse dabbed at her mouth with lemon petroleum jelly swabs and pulled up the blankets, tucking them around her. She raised the head of her bed slightly. "Want to try some ice chips?" Rosalinda nodded and the nurse left.

"Tell me everything, please."

"After Caden took Diego, we didn't hear from him for a few days, until he called Abby and demanded one million in cash. She heard Diego's voice, so we know he's alive. He called back this morning with the instructions to leave the cash in a black bag in the trash can by the men's restroom at Tree Spring trailhead in the Sandia Mountains on Friday morning at dawn. Then she's to leave, and he'll call back with Diego's location."

"Jesse was supposed to stop him. He promised me. Caden would have to kill Jesse to get past him." Rosalinda looked into Santiago's eyes, and he could feel her read the truth in them.

"Oh God," she whispered and began to cry. "Jesse."

"I'm sorry." Santiago tried to shake the intrusive images of Jesse's dead body shredded with stab wounds from his mind.

The nurse returned with a cup of ice and a plastic spoon. "I think you better go now."

"She remembers what happened," Santi said. "I was just trying—"

"Cabin!" Rosalinda interrupted. "Jesse said Caden had a cabin in the Sandias—maybe that's where he took Diego."

Chapter Fourteen

AFTER SANTIAGO'S LATE phone call filling her in about Rosalinda, Abby didn't sleep much. She was making coffee early on Thursday morning when Ramone and SAC Williams knocked on her kitchen door. Agent McCoy opened it for them. One glance told her Ramone hadn't slept either. Williams was younger and wore his fatigue better.

When Abby hit the button on her combination coffeemaker and grinder, the noise was like a jet taking off in the small kitchen.

"I used to hate that obnoxious noise, and I'll probably end up with work-related hearing loss," McCoy said. "But the damn thing makes great coffee."

Abby pulled out her largest mugs for the men. She was anxious to hear their news but knew not to ask before the coffee was ready. She heard Ben singing in the shower and smiled.

"Santiago still at the hospital?" Ramone asked.

"Yes. If Rosalinda had a good night, they're going to move her to a regular room this morning. What, no breakfast burritos?" she asked.

The chair legs scraped against the linoleum as they all sat themselves around the table. Ramone shrugged. "I thought you'd want to hear the news first."

"So talk," Abby said.

Williams took a gulp of coffee. "After hearing from Santiago last night, I called Caden's father, Richard Owens. He said he didn't think about the cabin because it belonged to his ex-wife's family. Since they'd been divorced so many years, he'd only been to the cabin a few times, when Caden was young. He described it as a one room cabin, about twenty by twenty-five feet. Woodburning cook stove, sink, and a small bathroom, pretty primitive, at least the last time he saw it. He told us his ex-wife's family name was Morgan, and her dad's name is Duane. Richard guessed the cabin, if they still owned it, would be in her dad's name. We looked them up through property tax records and bingo, Duane Morgan still owns the property, which, get this, is less than a mile as the crow flies from Tree Spring trailhead."

"So go there and get Diego." Abby set her mug down hard.

"We spent all night working out a plan. First we need to determine that's where Caden is holding Diego. We have to be careful not to tip him off. Later today we're sending in an undercover unit dressed as cross-country skiers to do some investigating, since it's high elevation and they've been getting lots of snow over the last week. Only one other cabin is on that road, and it's about a mile before you get to the Morgan place. It's a heavily wooded area, and the Morgan cabin sits at the end of the dead-end road. After we ascertain Caden has Diego there, we'll conduct a raid during the night, two or three in the morning, when it's most likely Caden is asleep. We have to catch him off guard—we don't want him using Diego as a human shield or a bargaining chip. We have to get in and get out before he knows what's happening."

"I'm supposed to deliver the ransom at dawn. Isn't that cutting it close?" Abby asked.

"Not at all," Williams said. "The timing is to our advantage. Caden thinks he's in control. He has the exchange set up and has his getaway plan in place. He has no idea we know about the cabin. He'll be sleeping with a smug smile on his face, quite certain he's covered all his bases, until we grab up Diego and arrest his ass."

"Diego should see someone he knows right away so he knows he's safe. I want to be there, and I know Santiago will, too," Abby said.

"We'll be staging the operation from the other cabin on the road. We need to keep our presence there to the minimum required personnel. We'll have some EMTs stationed nearby who will be taking Diego straight to UNM Hospital to be examined and treated, if need be. At the least, they'll give him IV fluids to help with dehydration. Even if he seems fine, the doctors might want to observe him for twenty-four hours. You and the rest of the family should wait for our call and then meet Diego at the hospital. Ramone will be with us—I'm afraid that will have to do. Remember, this is all conjecture at this point. You still may have to deliver the ransom."

Ben came in, dressed in professor clothes. "Good day, gents."

Abby poured him some coffee and gave him a quick kiss.

"Ramone, mate, where are you hiding the burritos?" Ben asked.

"Yeah, Ramone," McCoy echoed. "You can't just bring us breakfast burritos every day and then stop—you've conditioned us. We're drooling like Pavlov's dogs here."

Williams dug into his pocket and produced a wad of bills, which he threw on the table. "McCoy, you know the way to Bennie's. Make mine eggs, cheese, sausage, and green chile. You make the run, and then I need to head back up to Albuquerque. Don't forget my change."

"Yes, sir." McCoy started a list of everyone's orders while Abby updated Ben.

"I'm glad to hear Rosalinda is doing better," Ramone said to Abby after Ben left for work. "I think I'll pay her a little visit after they move her out of the TSICU this morning. I'd like to hear how she happened to know about Caden Owen's cabin."

"Let her get her son back before you start harassing her, Ramone," Abby said.

Ramone gave a quick rub to his silver moustache with his index finger. "I guess she isn't going anywhere, so for you, *mi'ja*, I'll wait. But I bet you a year's worth of free Bennie's breakfast burritos that I'm right about her."

"Prepare to cry into your chile, old man, because you will lose that bet. She told Santi that Jesse told her about the cabin. Jesse died trying to stop Caden, and Rosalinda almost died—what about that says she was on board with having her son kidnapped?"

"*El que engaña con apariencia de verdad es impostor*," Ramone answered. "He who deceives with a truthful appearance is an impostor."

The moon was little more than a curved white scratch in the black night sky, lost in a crowded sea of stars bobbing so close Santiago felt like he could reach up and pluck one. Away from the city lights, the night sky transformed into something alive. His breath puffed white vapor as he exhaled, standing on the back stoop of the staging cabin in the Sandia Mountains at one thirty in the morning.

One mile to the west his son was being held captive by pure evil. It was all he could do not to charge through the woods, storm the cabin, and rescue his son. If it became necessary to kill Caden with his bare hands, so much the better. But that would violate the agreement he had to swear to uphold before Williams would even allow him to come this far in their rescue operation. He was ordered to stay put. No matter what.

He went back inside the cabin, a rustic but well-constructed and maintained log structure with one large, open room. The team was going over their plan, compulsively checking their weapons and equipment, and waiting for the go-ahead command. They fiddled with their top-of- the-line military-grade night-vision goggles, night-vision weapon scopes, and thermographic cameras. They were dressed in black, spoke in monosyllables, and looked like clones created in a secret government lab.

SAC Williams appeared focused as he spoke by radio to the pair of agents who were literally up a tree to gain line-of-sight surveillance of Caden's cabin. Santi watched Williams for signs of doubt or worry but couldn't find any. He looked like a competent professional executing his job.

Ramone caught Santi's eye. "How are you doing?"

"Pumped. I hope they can do this soon." Santi also hoped Ramone couldn't tell how nervous he was, how terrified something could go wrong. His son's life hung in the balance.

Food was laid out on the long wooden table, but it didn't interest him. Who knew FBI raids were catered? But it wasn't party food; it was sensible fare, like protein bars, cheese sticks, bottled water, and a large carafe of coffee.

At 2:00 a.m., Williams spoke. "Okay, circle up. Here's the status. A van reported stolen is parked close behind the structure. The cabin is dark except for the light from the fire in the wood stove. One adult confirmed via night-vision equipment, after a period of upright movement, is now supine along the north wall of the structure. Child presence strongly suspected but not confirmed due to small size and limitation of equipment, with ambient heat from wood stove contaminating the field. Possible position along south wall of structure, no movement detected since surveillance began, meaning the child is most likely sleeping and/or drugged, as previously indicated. Agent Swanson, is your team ready?"

"Yes, sir."

"Then it's a go at your command," Williams said. "Remember,

recovering the child alive and well and apprehending the suspect, alive or dead, is the mission. Be safe, and let's do this."

"Mic check, one two three," Swanson said to his team. Thumbs went up, and the other five repeated the exercise.

"They can talk and hear each other through headsets in their helmets, and Williams can also communicate with them using his radio, like he's doing with his agents who are in the tree," Ramone explained to Santi. "So we should hear the play by play as it happens."

Santi nodded. A huge lump was forming in his throat as he imagined the terror Diego had already experienced these last six days and the additional terror about to unfold without his ability to understand he was being rescued. He thought of Abby and Ben awake, anxiously waiting for word. He thought of Rosalinda alone in her room at the hospital, the body that had carried and nurtured Diego for nine months now torn by bullets and scalpels and held together with thread. He thought of Miguel and CeCe praying for them and of Rose just trying to keep breathing around her enlarged and failing heart. He thought of his little sister Maggie, safe in her second home with Rachel, Charlie, and Hattie. Whatever happened to any one of them happened to all of them. *La familia*. It gave him strength. He was not alone, not for the last twelve years. Before that, he had known what alone was. He knew the terror of being at the mercy of a dangerous man. Just like his son was now. His hands formed fists as he registered the fact that his happy little boy had been robbed of his innocence, his peace replaced with fear, his trust in the world shattered.

The team moved out. Ramone and Santiago stepped outside to see them off. In a single line they shuffled their skis to build momentum and then disappeared into the trees.

Ramone clapped him on his back as if they were spectators at a ball game. If they were women they would hug. Ramone cleared his throat. "I have some donuts stashed in my truck."

"You? Mister I-Lost-Forty-Pounds-by-Not-Eating-Carbs?"

"I know, right? I remembered how it is to wait in these situations, and it took me back to the old days on stakeouts, eating all those donuts, and I figured, why the hell not, on a night like this, eat a goddamn donut while you can't do anything else . . . but wait."

"I'll get us some coffee and meet you at your truck." Santi clapped him on the back.

"Williams said if we want to listen in on the raid we better come back in fifteen minutes. So I set my phone for ten minutes," Santi said as he handed Ramone his coffee. Ramone's personal truck was hidden in the trees near the staging cabin. It was cold in the cab, but they couldn't risk running the engine for heat. Santi set his coffee on the dashboard so he could take off his gloves to eat his donut. A bite of its spongy sweet goodness washed down with some surprisingly good hot coffee felt like just the thing he needed to get through the next ten minutes.

Ramone's eyes were closed in reverential bliss as he chewed his forbidden fruit. "Don't tell your mother. I'd never hear the end of it."

"Okay, but you'll owe me."

"I'll owe you? Forget it."

"I should take a video. I would own you. We both know you'd do about anything to keep Abby off your ass."

"Fair enough." Ramone sighed and peered into the empty donut bag. "Worth it, though," he said, licking powdered sugar off his thumb.

Santi finished his coffee. "We better get in there." He felt his nerves tighten.

Ramone wadded up the bakery bag. "It's only been seven minutes, but okay."

The pickup truck door squealed when Santi opened it. Some nearby coyotes replied with a series of short yips culminating with a long howl. The men's boots slid through the snow as they rushed back to the cabin.

Inside, Williams was talking with his assistant. He paused and nodded to them as they approached. "The team just passed our surveillance position in the tree. No change at the Morgan cabin. They should arrive at the edge of the trees momentarily and check in with us before they proceed."

Santiago felt panic rise in his chest. It must have shown on his face, because Ramone said, "It's going to be fine. Seems like just yesterday you were the kid who needed saving. Now, you're the dad. Tough to tell which is harder, no?"

"It's always harder to be the kid."

Williams held up his hand and spoke into his radio. "Roger that. It's a go."

Unintelligible shouting, loud banging, and then an explosion of gunfire that reverberated through the trees with no need of radio transmission. Santi bolted before anyone could react. He sprinted to Ramone's truck, where he knew the keys dangled from the ignition. He fired it up and threw it into gear, driving too fast over the snow-covered rocks and logs through the trees until he connected with the road, speeding toward the Morgan cabin, swerving through snow.

Completely void of thought, he executed his actions in mindless determination. He pulled into the unplowed driveway at the end of the road. As the truck struggled over the foot or two of drifted snow, he could see lights were now on in the cabin. He rolled down the window and heard no more gunfire. Except for the rumble of the truck and whine of its tires, it seemed quiet. When he was maybe thirty feet from the cabin, he parked and flew from the truck, slogging through the snow. An agent posted outside drew his weapon on him, "Stop where you are!"

"I'm Diego's father—Santiago Silva! You met me!" He held up his hands.

The agent approached with weapon still raised. "What the fuck do you think you're doing? I could have shot you!"

"I'm here for my son." Santi's voice was strong, though his legs threatened to collapse.

The agent lowered his weapon and spoke into his mic. "I have Santiago Silva, the father, outside. I'm sending him in." The clone agent actually smiled at him and shook his head.

"Thanks, because you were going to have to shoot me to stop me from going in there."

"I know. I have a kid. Go ahead, Dad."

Santiago lurched as fast as he could to the open door to see Caden Owens sprawled on the floor to his right, bullet ridden, still holding his handgun. Probably the gun that shot Rosalinda. Caden's pasty white face with staring eyes looked fake, like a crude, low-budget movie effect. Agents were photographing him and beginning to process the scene.

A sudden burst of loud wailing came from the back of the room, and Santiago ran to his son. An agent was trying to wrap him in a shiny silver thermal blanket as Diego struggled and screamed. "Diego, Daddy's here. We're going to get you out of here—"

Diego stopped screaming. His sunken eyes connected with Santi's face. "Daddy?"

"Yes!" Santiago reached for him and the agent moved out of the way. The blanket fell as he scooped up the small, shivering form, still in his wet, soiled pajamas. Santi unzipped his borrowed parka and pulled Diego inside its warmth. Diego clung tightly to him, with his arms around his neck and his bony legs hugging his waist, so small in the oversized jacket that Santi was able to zip it up around them both. Diego's head protruded from the jacket to rest against Santi's neck. Santi kissed the top of his head through matted hair as Diego snuggled against him. Santiago's arms cradled him over the jacket as if he were wrapping his arms around a big pregnant belly. He had been denied attending Diego's birth, had not heard his son's first cry, but he was there now. "I'm so happy you're safe, son. I'm so happy I have you back."

"Mama?" Diego said, his voice wavering.

"Mama is going to be fine. She is safe in the hospital. You'll see her soon."

An agent stood in front of them. "Congratulations. It was a good outcome. He went for his weapon, so we didn't have a choice. The bad guy can't hurt anyone anymore."

"Thank you—I don't know how to thank you," Santiago said through the tears that wouldn't stop. These clone agents were now his best friends for life. He wanted to give them Abby's million dollars and take them out for beers.

"No need, sir, this is what we're trained to do. The ambulance is here. The EMTs want to examine your son and get him to the hospital."

"I'm going with him," Santi said.

"Who's going to try to stop Rambo Dad?"

Rosalinda looked at the clock: 2:30 a.m. Santiago had promised he would call as soon as Diego was rescued. Between her extreme anxiety and the constant searing pain in her abdomen, sleep was impossible. Anyway, she'd had enough sleep over the last week to last her a lifetime. And besides, sleep brought nightmares.

She was in her own room, out of intensive care. The police still had her cell phone, so she had given Santi the number of the room's landline. Now she held the phone in her hand, willing it to ring.

Her physical pain was nothing compared to her mental and emotional anguish. Jesse was dead, and it was her fault. Her son was kidnapped and has gone through God knows what, and it was her fault. All of this traced back to the night she had stupidly told Jesse about Abby. And then, Jesse had stupidly blabbed to Caden. And then she had stupidly thought if she pretended to cooperate with Caden's demands and threats, she would think of a way to stop him. After witnessing her entire family of criminals and the lengths they would go to get other people's money, how could she have so completely underestimated Caden's capacity for evil?

After Ramone was done with her, he would have everyone believing she planned her own son's kidnapping, and they would all turn against her. Santiago would probably take Diego away from her, and who could blame him? She cried when she realized her son might be better off without her. She might even go to prison, like the rest of her worthless family. Maybe that was what she deserved.

She prayed to God: As long as He spared Diego, He could do whatever He wanted with her. Crying set her abdomen on fire. She had refused her pain medication until after her call from Santiago, so she could have a clear head. Every part of her seemed connected to her abdomen; she couldn't move a muscle without feeling it in her wound.

The night nurse came into her room and saw her crying. "Rosalinda, I don't want to delay your pain medicine any longer. Effective pain management depends on staying ahead of the pain. It's not about being tough. It just isn't good for you to be in pain because you won't breathe or cough as deeply as you need to, and that sets you up for pneumonia."

"I'm not crying from the pain. I want my baby back. I can't take this anymore!"

The phone began to ring its loud, landline ring. She grabbed it. "Santiago?"

"Diego is safe. I'm here with him in the ambulance headed for UNM Hospital so they can check him out, but he seems pretty good, considering. The connection is bad—we're still in the mountains—but I wanted to tell you that you'll be seeing him soon."

Her bitter tears of exhaustion, pain, and fear transformed into the sweet tears of relief and joy. Before she could speak, after another burst of static, the line went dead. Rosalinda hung up the phone, wiped her tears, and looked up at the nurse. "I'll take that pain medicine now."

When the ambulance arrived at University Hospital's Pediatric Emergency Room, the personnel allowed Santiago to stay with Diego. After assessing he was stable, with no significant injuries aside from a rash on his bottom from languishing in wet and soiled clothing, the first order of business was to bathe him. "I want Daddy to do it," Diego told the female tech. They were in a treatment room with a sink large enough to fit Diego. The tech handed Santi the soap and washcloth. "Wash his cleanest areas first. When the water gets too filthy, let it out and put in fresh. Here's shampoo, extra washcloths, and towels here. I'll check back in a few minutes."

Santiago lathered up the washcloth with some serious institutional soap and began to wash Diego's face. The feel of the warm water, the soapy foam running down his forearms, took Santiago back to when he used to help bathe Maggie when she was a baby and toddler. Diego stared at him with a solemn expression as Santi carefully worked the cloth around his face, trying not to get soap into his eyes. "Why did you let that man take me?"

Santi stopped. "We didn't let him take you; Mama tried her hardest to stop him. We've been trying to find you every minute of every day. We've all been so scared and so sad until we finally found you."

"I was scared and sad."

"I know, and I'm so sorry the man took you. You're safe, and we're going to keep you safe. That bad man is dead now, so he's never coming back. I promise."

"He tied me with this foot to the bed so I couldn't get to the potty." Diego lifted his right foot a few inches out of the quickly darkening bathwater. "So I peed and pooped my pants." The shame in his voice brought fresh tears to Santiago's eyes.

"You couldn't help it. Anybody else would have done the same thing, even grown-ups."

"My butt got sore," Diego said. "And it hurted."

"I know. That was mean of him. The doctor is going to give us medicine to put on it so it can get better fast," Santi said. "I need to shampoo your hair."

"I put a washcloth over my eyes, and Mama uses a cup to pour the water on me, like this." He tipped his head back to show Santiago how to do it.

Santi grabbed a paper cup from the dispenser and handed Diego a clean, dry washcloth to fold against his eyes. He supported Diego's back with one hand and lathered up Diego's scalp with his other, his fingers sliding through Diego's silken hair, which seemed longer than he remembered. He poured water with the cup to rinse Diego's head and had to admit it was a handy tip.

Just as he was finishing, the nurse, the ER resident, and the attending physician returned. Santi gathered up Diego's seal-slick body into the towels to dry him. The resident motioned for Santi to bring him to the exam table.

The resident spoke. "Blood work and urinalysis show some mild dehydration. We did a toxicology screen, but that isn't back yet. The EMTs said they found liquid Dramamine and cold medicine at the scene. The guy was using them to sedate Diego, but any effects seem to have worn off. His neuro checks are good. What did you eat and drink at the cabin, Diego?"

"I drank water from a water bottle. I ate peanut butter and crackers. I don't like peanut butter anymore."

"I bet not. What sounds good to you? A hamburger? Fries? Pizza?"

"Yes."

The doctors laughed. "Well, we're going to get you some food, and we want you to drink a lot of the special juice Nurse Sherrie is going to bring you. We'd rather not have to start an IV, Dad, so if you can get two or three bottles of this flavored electrolyte water into him, we can probably avoid it."

"I want my mama," Diego said to them, his face crumpling as he thought about it.

"Now that you're all cleaned up, I just want to check your rash and see you drink one bottle of your juice. Nurse Sherrie will put some cream on your rash and get you into some clean pajamas. Then your daddy can take you up to see Mommy for a little visit." The doctor looked at Santiago. "He can visit with his mom for about a half hour if she's up to it, and then bring him back. We'll have food for him and more liquids. We don't think he needs to be admitted to the hospital; we'll just monitor him here. We want to see he's eating and drinking well before we let you take him home later today." He turned back to Diego. "Guess what? When you get back here, Nurse Sherrie has some cartoons you can watch on that screen right there while you eat your food and drink more juice."

"Spider-Man?"

Nurse Sherrie handed Santiago the clean underwear and pajamas.

"I do have some Spider-Man cartoons." She gave Diego his bottle of flavored electrolyte water with a straw stuck into it. "Make this disappear, and you can go visit your mom."

Santiago carried his son through the hallway to the bank of elevators. Diego was preoccupied with his ID wristband, turning it around on his slender wrist. As they waited for the elevator, he asked, "Is my mama dead?"

Santi tipped up Diego's chin to look into his eyes. "No. No, we're going to see her in a minute. I talked to her on the phone in the ambulance. Why did you ask if she's dead?"

"The bad man told me she was dead. I saw him shoot her with his gun." Diego's eyes filled with tears.

"Your mama did get shot, but she's strong. After she heals, she'll be all better."

"He said he was going to shoot me, too, if I didn't do what he said."

Santiago felt his stomach fall. "What did he tell you to do?"

"Shut up and be quiet and go to sleep and don't bother him."

"Did he ever hurt you, like, hit you or touch you where he shouldn't?" Santiago asked.

"No. But I didn't like him."

The elevator arrived, and they boarded it alone, since it was four fifty in the morning. "Diego, no kid should ever have to go through what you did. When you remember the bad stuff that happened—you might feel mad or scared or sad—I want you to talk to someone, me or Mama or Grandma Abby, anyone. Talking about it helps to get it out of you. You'll think about it less and less. You're safe now, and you don't have to worry."

Diego laid his head on Santiago's shoulder and yawned. The elevator stopped on the fourth floor. "Here we are." Diego's head popped back up.

After checking in at the nurses' station, Santiago walked down the darkened hallway to room 417. The door was ajar; he pushed it open until Diego could see Rosalinda, the head of the bed partially raised, a small lamp illuminating her while the rest of the room was cast in darkness. Her hair was in one braid now, and it lay across her shoulder. She opened her eyes and broke into a wide grin. "*Mi'jo!*" She reached for him.

Diego practically dove from Santi's arms. "You can sit next to her on the bed, but be careful you don't climb on her belly—she has a big owie there," Santi said. Diego nestled cautiously against her, his head on her shoulder.

Rosalinda put her arms around him, kissing him all over his head and face until he was giggling. "I've missed you so much."

Diego's face grew serious. "Is this your big owie?" He pointed to her stomach. "Where the bad man shot you?"

"Yes."

Diego leaned forward, his lips brushing the hospital gown over her dressings. "I kiss it and make it better."

"Thank you, *mi amor*. It's just what I needed." Rosalinda looked up at Santiago as Diego cuddled next her, and mouthed the words *thank you*.

Diego began to weep quietly, holding onto his mother, nuzzling his face into her neck. Rosalinda's tears streamed down her face as she held him in her arms.

Santiago sat down in the chair off to the side, feeling like he was intruding on something intimate. The power of their bond was so palpable, he could almost see it as an aura surrounding them in the shadowy light. Soft, wordless murmurings in their private language, silent tears mingling; it was the most beautiful thing he'd ever witnessed.

He'd be damned before he would let Ramone, or anyone else, separate them again.

Santiago woke. He had crashed out in the recliner next to Diego's bed in the Pediatric Emergency Room after their predawn visit with Rosalinda. The last thing he remembered was Diego eating his meal while watching Spider-Man cartoons. He looked down to see his son curled against him like a sleeping cat, half under the hospital blanket. The wall clock said ten fifteen. Relief poured over him as the events of the night replayed in his mind. He wanted to gather up Diego, hug him, hold him tight, and never let him go, but instead he let him sleep, watching the slight rise and fall of his small back.

Nurse Sherrie appeared. "I found him like this right after you guys went down for your nap. I didn't think you'd mind, so I didn't put him back in his own bed." She ran the temporal thermometer across Diego's forehead. "Still normal. He's doing great. They'll probably be kicking him out of here in a few hours."

"I thought you were the night nurse. Shouldn't you be out of here?"

"We're a little short staffed, and I need the overtime. Besides, I didn't want Diego to have to get used to another new face after all he's been through. There's a circus of news reporters out front; I guess the story broke about his rescue."

"I don't even care. Nothing could ruin how happy we are."

Diego squirmed and suddenly sat up, blinking and rubbing his eyes.

"Good morning!" Nurse Sherrie said. "What do you like for breakfast, Diego?"

"Pancakes and bacon," he said, a huge smile spreading across his face. "I tricked you, Daddy. I snucked into your bed."

Santiago began to tickle him lightly, inciting raucous giggles. "You did trick me—you little trickster coyote."

Diego began to howl and roll around next to Santiago. "Hey, Diego, can you stay here with Nurse Sherrie for a few minutes while I hit the bathroom and call Grandma Abby?"

"I'm not Diego, I'm trickster coyote!"

Nurse Sherrie scooped him up from Santiago's lap. "We'll be fine, won't we? We'll put on your Spider-Man cartoons and have breakfast."

"I'll be back soon," Santiago said and watched for signs of separation anxiety in Diego. But he was engrossed with the remote control Sherrie had given him to turn on his cartoons.

Santiago found a quiet spot in the adjacent Pavilion food court, where he ate his breakfast burrito and phoned Abby. "Mom?" he said through his mouthful. He gulped some coffee.

"Santi! How are you guys doing?"

"Great. He'll be coming home this afternoon. Isn't that unbelievable?"

"I can't wait to see him. Ramone is heading over here, and he's hell-bent on talking to Rosalinda at the hospital. I asked him if she should have a lawyer, and he said he just wanted to talk. I told him I was coming with him, and I think you should be there, too. If he starts badgering her, we can stop it."

"There's no way I'm letting him bully her into anything. Let's just get it over with, and then we can take Diego home. Caden's dead, case closed."

"Right. See you after a bit," Abby said.

"Oh, Mom, reporters are all over the place."

"SAC Williams is holding a joint news conference with APD and Ramone's department at one this afternoon in Albuquerque, so that should clear out some of them. That's probably why he's chomping at the bit to talk to Rosalinda."

"Diego needs things to get back to normal. No more bad guys, no more cops."

"Ramone is family, Santi."

"Then he better act like it."

Santiago downed his burrito and checked on Diego, who was working on his breakfast tray while engrossed in Spider-Man. Nurse Sherrie said she would stay with Diego.

When he got to Rosalinda's room, her bed was empty. Just as he was about to panic, he heard the toilet flush in the bathroom. The door swung open. Rosalinda hung onto her IV stand and rolled it forward, taking small, slow steps. She was hunched over, perspiration dotting her face from the effort.

He came to her side, and she held onto him as he helped her back to bed. He could see the pain in her face. "How's Diego?" she asked.

"Perfect. I can take him home later. But don't worry, we'll be back up to visit you."

"They said I might get to go home Monday if I can eat and drink better and get this IV out. Thank God they took the urine catheter out, but it's a bitch to get to the bathroom, and it's only right there. I'm supposed to walk more, like all the way to the nurse's station and back." She leaned back on her pillows, still breathing hard, and wiped the sweat from her forehead. She looked up at him. "This is Friday? A week ago from right now, none of this had happened yet."

Santi pulled over a chair and sat next to her. "Ramone and Abby are on their way to see you. Ramone wants to talk to you, but if you want a lawyer—"

"No. Let's just get it over with."

"Abby and I are going to stop him if he tries anything."

"Thanks, but I can take care of myself."

"Says the woman with two bullet wounds and a missing spleen."

She smiled at him and reached for his hand. "Just means I'm tough."

His thumb lightly traced her long, tapered fingers. "You and Diego."

She shook off his hand when the knock came. "Come in."

Abby entered first, her light auburn hair brushing the shoulders of her teal wool jacket. She smiled and came over to kiss Rosalinda's forehead. "It's good to see you out of intensive care. You look so much better."

"My son is safe. I'm so grateful to you, Ramone, and the FBI agents."

Ramone nodded. He pulled over the last chair and offered it to Abby, but she made a point of sitting on the bed next to Rosalinda's legs. So Ramone sat down on it.

"I'm going to tell you everything I know," Rosalinda said. "Abby, remember when you were on the news about your literacy project?"

"Yeah, that was early October."

"Jesse and I were watching, and before I could think about what I was saying, I go, 'That's Diego's Grandma.' He started saying I should tell you, that here you were giving money to other people's kids when your own grandson could use some. That kind of thing. I was pissed at myself for blurting it out like that. I told him I didn't want Diego's father or his family to know about him.

"I thought that was the end of it, but then a few days later he brings Caden Owens to our apartment, saying he'd run into him at the bar. I didn't know him, but I knew he was a hard-core criminal that Jesse used to run with before Caden went to prison, before Jesse went straight. Caden said he had this plan where they would take Diego and pretend he was kidnapped to get money. I told him no way. That's when he threatened me and Diego, and he said I had to do what he said or he would do it another way. Plan B, he called it, and he said I wouldn't like it, basically threatening he would hurt or kill us. Jesse said he owed Caden and I had to go through with it. I knew he was dangerous, so I was scared. They told me to come to you with the danger thing, the gambling debt story. But I only came to stall them, to give me a chance to figure out how to stop it."

Abby's eyes widened. "You knew about their kidnapping plot when you came to us?"

"I was going to stop it—I would never let them take my son! I was breaking up with Jesse, and I was going to move back to Esperanza and start a new life—that's the truth, I swear it. That's what I told Jesse. He was going to call it off with Caden and then leave for Nashville. When we went to the carnival, I thought it was all over and we were free."

Abby stood up from the bed. "If you'd told us, we could have protected you and Diego. Look what happened, all because you didn't tell. You could have been killed! Diego could have been killed!"

"You don't think I know that?" Rosalinda began to cry. "You don't get it."

"We were all so good to you, trusting you, when you were lying to our faces! Putting Diego and all of us in danger—it's so selfish! How could you? You're right—I don't get it!"

"I do," Santiago said. "You expected Rosalinda to trust us? Are you nuts? She knew you never approved of her. Growing up, even when she was as little as Diego, she couldn't even trust her own mother to give her food or keep her safe—she had no one. She only survived by fending for herself. And you wonder why she couldn't trust us? Trust that we wouldn't take her son away from her if she told us what was really going on? Trust that you wouldn't turn on her like you are right now? How could she risk that? I get it, because I lived it, too. How long did it take me to trust you? Months? Years? Countless hours of the best therapy your money could buy?"

"I'm sorry!" Rosalinda said, tears still flowing down her cheeks. "I wish I could have told you. I tried my best to stop it. Hate me if you want, just don't take my son!" She buried her face in her hands.

Santiago put his hands on her shoulders. "Rosalinda, look at me. No one is taking Diego from you. I won't let that happen, I swear to you."

Abby stood there shaking her head, looking as if she'd been sucker-punched. Santi knew in his mother's world, kindness and trust should beget kindness and trust, and anything else was incomprehensible.

Ramone cleared his throat. "It wouldn't be difficult to allege you were in league with these men, that you came to the Silvas' with the intent to worm your way into their sympathies, use your son as a pawn to score a million dollars. We could pursue a whole list of potential charges: child endangerment, conspiracy, obstruction of justice, to name a few. I have to report this to Williams, but I'll tell him it's my position that justice would not be served by pursuing charges against you. Under severe duress, you used terrible judgment, made stupid decisions. I think you know that. I think you need to take to heart the very serious consequences of your bad judgment and use your second chance to atone in some way. I'll let you know what

Williams decides." He got up and replaced the chair against the wall. "I need to get over to the press conference. Abby, call me later if you need a ride home."

"She can ride home with Diego and me," Santiago said.

Abby faced Rosalinda, her fair complexion flushed red. "I hope you don't think any of this affects the agreements we made—you and Diego will stay with us while you are recuperating. After you are strong enough to lift him and take care of him by yourself—and that could take months—we'll see about finding you a place nearby. Will that still work for you?"

"I know you're only doing this for Diego, but thank you."

"I'd like to see Diego, now," Abby said to Santiago. "I'll wait for you in the hall."

"How could you defend me?" Rosalinda demanded once the door was closed.

"You didn't want me to?"

"I thought you'd hate me, like Abby does. I hate myself."

"I wish you could have trusted me. During one of our late-night talks, when it was just you and me, I wish you could've let me in, let me help. I could sense something was going on, that you were hiding something. Trust is the absolute hardest thing for me, so how could I condemn you? We're just damn lucky Caden didn't kill you both. I don't know what I would have done . . ."

"I wanted to tell you. But I couldn't imagine that you wouldn't want to get your son far away from someone like me. Abby's right, it was selfish. I couldn't risk losing my son, and I almost lost everything. And poor Jesse."

"Jesse brought this on himself."

Rosalinda took a ragged breath. "He wasn't a bad person."

Santiago leaned down to kiss the top of her head. Her hair smelled like the same industrial soap he had used on Diego. "I'm sorry for your loss."

"Go be with Diego," she said and turned her face away from him.

Chapter Fifteen

BY THE TIME Abby and Santiago got Diego home, it was almost four in the afternoon. Diego looked apprehensive as they unlocked the kitchen door. Abby watched Santiago carry him through the house, reintroducing him to the place, showing him there were no more bad guys lurking in the closets or behind the drapes.

What a good father he was, so cognizant of what Diego might be feeling. And yet it also unnerved her, seeing their growing attachment for each other. Santiago needed to start weaning away in preparation for his return to San Francisco, for both their sakes.

When the phone rang, Abby jumped. McCoy and the other agents were wrapping things up in Albuquerque and then would return to their homes out of state. Aside from a few of Ramone's men posted at their road near the highway to turn reporters away, they were on their own. She picked up the wall phone's receiver, noting the black box had been removed. "Hello?"

"Abby, you guys got home—Diego's with you?" Rachel said.

"We're all here."

"We're so anxious to see him. Maggie and Hattie are harassing me to let them come over, but I told them to give you some time to get him settled in. If you're up for it, how about you guys come over here for a low-key dinner? I have lentil soup in the Crock-Pot, and I'll get the girls to make cornbread."

"That sounds perfect. Ben will be home soon, and we'll be over. You're a lifesaver. I didn't know what we were going to eat, and none of us slept last night, and I really need to talk to you," Abby said, dropping her voice on the last part so Santiago wouldn't hear her.

"Everything is not hunky-dory?" Rachel asked, using one of Rose's expressions.

"You could say that."

After Abby hung up, she found Santi and Diego sitting on the bed in his old room. Diego was pointing to the floor. Abby stood in the doorway.

"That's where Mama was," he said. "His gun shot *bang bang*—so loud. And I saw blood on her. He took me, and I didn't want to go. I tried to fight him, but I'm too little."

"I know. When Abby and Ben and I got here, we called the ambulance to get Mama to the hospital, and the police came to look for you, lots and lots of police."

"And they shot the bad man so he's dead."

"Yes. Dead and gone and never coming back," Santi said.

Diego let out a big sigh. "Why didn't Mama come home with us?"

"She's still getting better at the hospital, and she'll come home very soon. You and Mama will share this room again, and you'll both be safe."

"But . . . will you stay in this bed with me?" Diego's eyes were wide and unblinking.

"Sure, buddy. Until Mama comes back, I'll sleep in here with you. How's that?"

"Good," Diego said. "Let's read books now."

"We're going over to Rachel and Charlie's for dinner," Abby said. "Your Aunt Maggie is very happy you're home and wants to see you. I think I'll go on over, and you guys can come when Ben gets home."

"Sure," Santi said as Diego dumped books into his lap.

As she walked over, Abby soaked in the comfort of the sun. All traces of their recent storm had melted away, leaving the ground soft and yielding under her steps—such a contrast from the normally dry, hardened earth. The Manzano Mountains' white cloak was shrinking fast up its broad shoulders.

Abby hadn't spoken directly to CeCe in the past couple of days, but she knew Rachel would have passed along the updates. She wondered how Rose was doing. Now that Diego was home, she'd make time to visit her.

Fury thrummed inside of her. She was not quick to anger, but once she was, look out, Ben would say. Rachel would understand, and the thought made her jog the rest of the way to her door. She opened it and was immediately accosted by Maggie and Hattie. "Where's Diego?"

"He's reading books with Santi. It's scary for him to be back where it happened, so Santi's helping him with that." She saw they had hung up their Welcome Home Diego banner. "They'll be over after a while."

Maggie put her arms around Abby for a hug. "I'm so happy! Aren't you?"

"Yes, honey, it's wonderful. I'm just really tired. I'll go get some coffee and hang out with Rachel. You guys might as well relax, do your homework or something."

"Mom! Homework? It's Friday!" Maggie said.

"Oh, right. What was I thinking? Why would you ever want to get your homework out of the way when you could panic Sunday night at bedtime?" She smiled as she walked past them to the kitchen, where she found Rachel tossing a salad.

"How's Diego?" Rachel asked, pouring Abby a cup of coffee.

"Okay physically, pretty traumatized emotionally, which I can totally relate to about now." She held the steaming cup to her nose, inhaling the scent. New Mexico piñon, her favorite.

Rachel's dark eyebrows rose. "What's the deal?"

"Rosalinda knew about Caden's plans to kidnap Diego. Her boyfriend was part of it, at least initially."

"No way."

"She says Caden forced her to come to us, threatened to do it with or without her cooperation. She says she was trying to stall until she could figure out how to stop him, that she never would have cooperated with a kidnapping, even a fake one."

"But you don't believe her?" Rachel scattered a handful of grape tomatoes onto her salad of baby greens.

Abby leaned on the island. "The point is she didn't tell us. They both could have died—it pisses me off!"

"What does Santi say?"

"He defends her. He says she couldn't trust us for fear we'd take Diego away from her. Is this some kind of Hispanic perspective that I don't understand? Am I being the insensitive rich white woman, thinking there's no excuse for not asking us for help?"

"Maybe a little," Rachel said. "I can see how it would have been really intimidating for Rosalinda to take you aside and say, 'By the way, my boyfriend and his criminal associate want to use Diego to bilk you out of a shitload of money, and they forced me to come here to set it all up.' When she came to you, she did say it was because they were in danger, so that's true. I think you feel betrayed, but you didn't really trust her either. You and Ramone—hell, all of us—have thought there was something she was hiding."

"Well, she was."

"I guess I'd tell you to try to put yourself in her shoes. Not as you, Abby, with the whole white privilege thing, but as a brown girl raised by criminals telling her to never trust 'the Man.'"

"I'm 'the Man'?"

"Yes. You and your millions of dollars and being joined at the hip with the sheriff makes you 'the Man' in her eyes. A nice and generous one, but still not to be trusted."

"You're right; my feelings are hurt that she couldn't reach out to me for help, after everything I was doing for her."

"She lives for Diego—it would kill her to lose him. She probably thought you and your high-priced lawyers would have taken her to court for putting him in danger and accused her of being an unfit mother. Santiago gets custody, and the court cuts her out of his life. You have the power. Someone like her doesn't."

"I don't look at the world like that."

"I know, but how could Rosalinda be sure when so much was riding on it? She saw you and Santiago bond with her son. She might have felt replaceable. She did try to stop the kidnapping. Isn't that why her boyfriend got killed and she was almost killed? The fake kidnapping turned real."

"Well, that just shows how in over her head she was."

"What does Ramone say? Is he going to go after her?"

"He's going to tell the FBI about it, but he's against pursuing charges. Which I agree with. She's been punished enough, just not by me, I guess," Abby said with a guilty shrug.

"Well, she put you and the rest of us through hell. But she paid a huge price, and she's truly sorry, right? And now she knows we all know about it, and we'll be judging her—it's humiliating to screw up that bad—I should know, right? She blew whatever trust you did have in her, and it's going to take time for her to rebuild it. But she's the mother of your grandson, so like it or not, it's a package deal."

"I know I have to get over it. I need to get Santiago back to his real life as soon as possible, and that leaves Rosalinda and me. We have to find a way to make it work."

Diego dozed off during the second book, a cautionary tale about giving a cat a cupcake. Santi carefully got up from the bed and pulled his phone from his pocket. He stood in the open doorway so that he could keep an eye on Diego as he phoned Kat.

"Santi? I've been going crazy waiting to hear from you. It's all over the news that Diego was rescued and they killed the kidnapper." Her voice was so clear it was as if she was standing right in front of him. He could almost feel her warm breath in his ear.

"We have him home. I'm watching him nap. I was there right after they rescued him and rode with him in the ambulance to the hospital. He's okay—they just needed to be sure."

"Oh, thank God! That's wonderful. You must be so relieved."

"After the week we've had, I'm just starting to feel the relieved part. Anyway, Rosalinda is still in the hospital, but she's supposed to be discharged early next week. I need to be here with Diego until she gets home and then help my mom get Rosalinda settled in. She's going to need a lot of help at first. I'll fly out by next weekend. How does that sound?"

"Like a week too long, but I understand. Just plan on some long hours after you get back. Between work and your starved-for-affection girlfriend, you're going to have your hands full, babe." Her voice was like melting butter.

"Oh? I like the sound of that." The unfamiliar sensation of a smile spread across his face at the thought of holding her in his arms under her vintage satin quilt and the way she had of making the world disappear.

"I miss you like crazy. But I need to go—I have someone on hold, if they're still there."

"Tell Gordon and Reggie I'll be back soon and thank them for all their extra work. I'll make it up to everyone, I promise."

"Especially me?"

"Most especially you."

"I'm really happy, Santi, that everything worked out. Talk to you soon?"

"I'll call to say good night," he said. "Bye." He was still grinning when he looked over to see the little bundle of Diego sleeping on his bed, like a perfect gift, like a miracle.

Rose slipped away to her room while CeCe and Miguel toasted Diego's rescue. They had been invited to Rachel's for dinner, but when Rose decided she was not up to it, CeCe grilled Reuben sandwiches for the three of them. She settled into her chair and turned on the television, but not to watch it. When CeCe checked on her, she didn't want to explain why she sat in a dark room by herself, so the blare of an old movie along with her crocheting on her lap provided her cover. Rose regarded her forays into the past as nobody's business but her own . . .

When Rose and Nick arrive at Nick's parents' house, it is sprinkling. All that secret preparation at her Aunt Ruth's, and now she is wet. She can feel her hair cringing back into tight curls as she stands on the doorstep. She has never been to the Bronx, and now she stands in the Belmont area of the West Bronx, Little Italy. She wants to tell Nick she is sweating like a *nafke* in shul, but catches herself. He puts an arm around her and opens the door.

They are greeted by Nick's smiling parents, full of hugs and sloppy kisses on the cheeks. Rose tries to smooth her hair, as she is sure it screams her ethnicity, but notices another dark, curly-haired woman bustling about the house. This could work.

"Mama, Papa, this is Rose." Nick ushers Rose inside as if she is a frightened deer.

"Pleased to meet you," Rose says, putting out her hand to shake. But Nick's mom yanks her into a bosomy hug. She is even shorter than Rose, her salt-and-pepper hair twisted in a bun. She smells of oregano and garlic and simmering tomatoes. Nick's father plants a kiss on her cheek. His moustache tickles, and he has a shock of white hair like Albert Einstein.

"Welcome to our home. Let's get you out of that wet jacket. Make yourself comfortable," Nick's mother says. "And call me Lucia." Her pudgy arms help Rose shed her jacket.

"Any friend of Nicola's is a friend of ours," says his papa. "I'm

Frank, by the way." He takes their wet jackets. He doesn't have the serious intensity of her papa. And her papa would never offer to hang up someone's coat.

They have a modest home, yet from what Rose understands, when Nick's family first immigrated they lived in the Lower East Side, too. Nick grew up in the Bronx. How does a Jewish girl from Brighton Beach get hooked up with an Italian Catholic guy from the Bronx? It has to be *beshert*, destiny. Only destined love can move mountains. She hopes it can move her papa.

Nick holds her hand practically the entire time as relatives look on with knowing smiles. His sister Madonna is married to Vito, and they have three unruly children who can do no wrong in their grand-mother Lucia's eyes. Madonna is very pretty, and she sits bloated and pregnant with baby number four. Unfortunately, Nick's other sister, Febe, looks as if she could not possibly have come from the same nest as Nick and Madonna. Like Rose's Aunt Ruth, Febe has a very large nose and a dark mop of hair that looks as if it doesn't know if it wants to be straight or curly. Her glasses are thick; she is the oldest, unmar-ried, and still living at home. The youngest son, Salvatore, is "out with the boys."

Before they sit down at the large dining table, Frank brings out an old lady, bent over a cane. Her white hair is held up in combs, and when she is seated, Rose sees her eyes are as blue as Nick's. Nick brings Rose over, his arm around her waist, to introduce them. Nonna takes Rose's hand. "You sure know how to pick 'em," she says, wink-ing at Nick. Rose is taken aback and laughs along with Nick. He kisses her in front of everybody. He loves her in front of everybody.

"Not everyone could make it this time, but you come back next time and you meet everyone else, eh? A real celebration," Lucia says. "But now we eat."

So far, they are not so different from a Jewish family. The women are much louder, which Rose likes. And they eat a lot more. She's lost track of how many courses she's had and how many are left to go. She doesn't know a *secondo* from a *contorno*, but Nick explains Italians believe being at the table with family and friends keeps you young, so dinners are long, drawn-out affairs. His dad leans back and unbut-tons his pants and waits for the next course. The grandchildren are launching pieces of green beans at each other with their forks. She had always wanted to do that as a child, but her papa would have spanked her before she could get in a good flick. She finds herself smiling at their antics. She never had that kind of freedom.

"What do your parents do, Rose?" asks Lucia, twirling her spaghetti on a spoon.

She is prepared for this question. "My father was a teacher, but he's been ill for a while now. My mother cares for him."

"Oh, my," Lucia says. "Febe, we send them home some dolce, eh? Remind me." Rose squirms in her seat. She has rehearsed only so many lies. And what the heck is dolce? "You let us know if there is anything we can do to help your mama and papa? Right, Papa?"

Nick squeezes her hand. "That's very kind of you, but we get by, really," Rose says.

Frank moves on to his cheese and fruit and never answers Lucia. It seems "Right, Papa?" is rhetorical. Madonna's husband helps her up from the table. How sweet. "Jesus, Mary, and Joseph, if this baby doesn't get off my bladder . . ."

Lucia claps her plump hands together and rocks them in prayer. "Blessed Jesus, thank you for another bambino." Lucia wears a simple thin gold band, like Mameh, and does everything in the household, like Mameh. They cook and bake different foods, but essentially they are the same. Nick's papa, too. Surprisingly, she feels right at home, despite the Jesus remarks. She tells herself Jesus was a Jew. And they called him "Rabbi," just like Papa. Nick's family has the same comforting energy Nick has. Something that's hard to leave. Something she could get used to.

Wine flows like water around the table. Rose notices Nonna is on her third glass, and Lucia moves the decanter away from her reach. Rose feels light-headed and happy. Nick is by her side, and she is his showpiece. "Look, Mama, she looks like Rita Hayworth," Nick's papa says. The wine helps Rose forget there is another side to this fairy tale. She allows them to fawn over her and assume she is the one for Nick. Damn it, she *is* the one for Nick.

Next thing she knows she's in the kitchen with Lucia and learns *dolce* means "dessert" as they set out various cakes and pastries. Strong coffee percolates on the stove. But a kitchen is a kitchen, and Rose dives in, sprinkling powdered sugar over pastry like she does with Mameh's kichel. Something like a gooey strudel sits in a baking dish waiting to be cut and served. It is weighed down with honey and nuts.

"My boy, Nicola, he's a good man. A blessing for any woman to have as a husband," Lucia says. "Why, she could stay here while he travels and have bambinos. Save up money for a new house. Always plenty to eat and a roof overhead. He's not so hard on the eyes, no?"

Rose smiles. "No, not at all." She feels herself blush. Especially all this talk about bambinos. Lucia's arms waggle as she whips heavy cream with a whisk. It is as if Rose is in a parallel existence. Nothing is so different. Could this be her home?

After the desserts are prepared, Lucia shows Rose around the house. Just as she suspected, there are Jesuses dangling over every bed. "You religious?" Lucia asks.

"No" is all she says, hoping Lucia thinks she is some kind of diluted Christian.

"No matter. Catholic, Protestant—we are all the same to God, no?"

When Rose returns to the dining room, Nick is still at the dinner table, sipping sambuca. He throws her a kiss across the room. She likes this casual life with Nick. It feels right. No one has even asked her about her background. Or scolded Nick for not bringing home a good Italian girl. It is obvious his family is bending over backward to make sure she feels welcome. Something she knows would never happen in hers. All of her childish idealism toward her father crumbles as she realizes there are other good people in the world besides good Jews. And that some people believe America to be a melting pot, where we let go of the old and embrace the new.

Rose rejoins Nick, who is now smoking a cigar with Frank and drinking his sambuca. Nick pulls her on his lap and offers her a small glass, like a shot glass on a stem, of sambuca, which tastes like licorice.

"Sambuca is an after-dinner drink, or what we call a *digestivo.*" Just in this short evening, she has learned several Italian words. The muddling, yummy liquor makes her forget that Papa and Mameh would *plotz* if they saw her now. But she doesn't care. She feels more herself here than in the constraints of her father's household. Here where *amore* is celebrated and cherished.

Instead of grabbing the Torah after dinner and secluding himself, like her papa does, Frank picks up a mandolin and begins to play and sing a ditty in Italian. His eyes are glassy from drink, but his voice is like an opera singer's. Febe, who has barely spoken all evening, joins him with such an angelic voice it shocks Rose, who begins to giggle in delight. Then Madonna joins in, her voice coming out more through her nose and carrying more of a Bronx accent. Everything she says sounds like a kvetch. The kids and Vito are conked out on the davenport. Nick holds her tight on his lap as he sings the Italian song, too. Her head is whirling with happiness and sambuca. Nonna claps along, and Lucia comes dancing out of the kitchen. No wonder Nick turned out to be musical. She feels as if she was born to be in Nick's arms and this family.

"Bravo!" Frank says after they finish. Madonna and Febe kiss their papa; Lucia embraces him from behind his chair. Nonna sits with a gapped-toothed smile. Love flows like the wine. Nick picks up a cannoli and gives her a bite, but her teeth come down on something hard. She spits the ricotta cheese into her palm and sees a ring covered in cream. A diamond ring.

"*Mi vuoi sposare?* Rose? Will you marry me?" Nick asks. The next thing she hears are screams of joy from everyone at the table, and Lucia is suddenly hanging around her neck. Rose trembles holding the ring. Hardly anyone gets an engagement ring in her community. Not that it's forbidden, but it's considered a waste of good money. Nick slides it on her left ring finger, ricotta, whipped cream, and all, promising everlasting happiness.

"Yes," she says.

She dare not wear her ring on the subway for fear a thief might cut off her finger, so she holds it in her pocketbook and stares at it. This night has felt as if it were right out of the Hollywood movies she and Ida hug themselves and swoon over in dark theaters. Rose knows this is right, more than ever after meeting his family. If she doesn't marry Nick, she will regret it for the rest of her life.

Before her stop she tries to summon the right words to tell her parents, while she still has the taste of garlic on her breath, the stickiness of Nick's sambuca good-night kiss on her lips, and the feel of him as she sat on his lap. She is an Italian at heart, so excited about love. They sing about it, laugh about it, and scream about it. The Jews, not so much. Jews believe in marrying for love, but it's a different kind of love, something one is supposed to grow into over time.

She snaps her pocketbook shut, grabs the metal pole, and swings herself off of the subway car onto the platform. There is a confident spring in her step. Engaged to Nick! Will marry Nick! She repeats this warrior chant all the way to her apartment, where her parents wait, unaware they have the worst daughter ever.

She finds her parents sitting at the dining table, holding a letter. They look pleased when Rose walks in. "We have good news," says Papa. "My cousin's wife has a nephew coming to New York. We want you two to meet. It's time you start to pick a husband."

"What if I want to pick my own husband? Marry for love?"

"You do not have to marry him if you don't like him, but eventually one will be a good match for you," Papa says. "Love deepens as time passes. Then comes children, your biggest mitzvah." He took Mameh's hand.

"I grew up in America, Papa. Kids today have different ideas about things."

"Some things, yes, but not about this. Not about what is written in our laws."

"But what if, Papa, I was to choose the man I date and fall in love with? What if I were to love a non-Jew? What if he makes me happy? Wouldn't love count for something?" Mameh looks down and examines the letter's envelope, turning it over and over.

"Love a non-Jew? What talk is this? I will tell you what you want to know. Rose, you are my daughter, and I love you. I taught you the best I knew how. But if you could turn your back on me and the history of suffering our people have endured, it would be as if you stuck a knife up into my ribs and my heart. I would writhe with pain inside, but I would do what I must. You would be dead to me. I would never want to set eyes upon you again. Your pictures would be burned. Mameh and I would sit shiva for you, and after, your name would never be spoken again in this house. The community would know, and I would feel disgraced. My disappointment in you would send me to my grave an unhappy man. But, yes, you do have the right to choose."

"I'm sorry you feel that way, Papa." Rose tries to keep her lip from trembling.

Papa stands up and slams his fist on the table. Mameh jumps a mile. "This is nonsense! I won't hear you speak of this again. We have arranged for you to meet prospective husbands, and you will go out with them. Jewish men. That's final."

Rose storms to her room. She takes her suitcase from her wardrobe and flings it on the bed. Tomorrow she will call Nick and have him meet her. Papa has a choice, too. He can choose to keep her in his life or shun her forever.

With her suitcase packed, she climbs onto her fire escape to write her good-bye letter to her parents. In it she will tell them about Nick and how wonderful he is and what an accepting family he has, unlike them. And how this is her life and her happiness that are at stake. Then when she meets up with Nick, she will tell him everything.

The moon is a smirk in the dark sky as she writes. Her tears flow out of frustration, anger, and sadness and hit the page as proof. This is the last time she will ever sit on her fire escape and pour out her deepest thoughts. How hard it will be to look at Mameh for the last time in her life. Rose rocks herself and cries, humming the Yiddish lullaby her mameh sang to her as a child. The pain cleaves her heart. Mameh will be devastated. Aunt Ruth said there are no happy endings.

How long before she feels happy again? She will get over losing her Jewish family with the love given by her Italian family. Can she dance at her wedding without wishing her parents were there? How she wishes she could have it all, like other brides. Will she cry out for her mameh when she births her first child? But Lucia will be there for her, eager to hold the new bambino. And the proud papa look on Nick's face will be enough. Won't it?

She reassures her parents in the letter that regardless, she will love them forever, and she hopes that in time their feelings will change. She folds the letter and climbs back in the window to her room. She can hear the surf tumbling and waving farewell as she shuts the window.

The apartment is dark as she walks around it for the last time. Rose is startled to see her mother sitting at the table. "Mameh, what's wrong?"

"Your father isn't feeling well."

"Indigestion again?"

"No, Rose. When he came over on the boat, he got an infection. It left his heart weak."

"How come I didn't know about this?"

"We didn't want to worry you. Children should be carefree. But you aren't a child anymore, are you?"

"Has he seen a doctor?"

"When Papa gets overexcited, he has one of his spells, and his heart has trouble working. He gets chest pains. He just needs to calm down and rest." Mameh's face looks so tired from worry. Her head is not covered, her hair mostly gray. She has had a hard life so Rose wouldn't have to, and it shows.

Rose sits next to her mother and holds her in a tight embrace, hiding the tears stinging her eyes. Mameh clings to Rose as Rose rocks her and softly sings a traditional Yiddish lullaby that Mameh used to sing to comfort Rose: "The goat will trot to the market, while mother her watch doth keep, bringing back raisins and almonds. Sleep, Mamehleh, sleep."

The next morning, Rose slips out of the apartment. She jumps onto a subway headed for 59th Street–Columbus Circle, where she told Nick to meet her. That is where he confessed his love under the full moon and presented her with her moonstone pendant, which she feels against her heart under her dress. Her nerves rattle along with the subway whirring on the tracks.

He waits at their bench by the light post. She falters behind a vendor selling red-hot frankfurters before she approaches him. He has a fistful of flowers and looks around eagerly for her. She reaches into her pocketbook and slips on her engagement ring. She is sick to her stomach as she sneaks up on him. He jumps to his feet. "Where's your suitcase?" he asks.

In that moment she takes in everything about him, the distinct blue of his eyes, where he parts his hair, the curve of his jaw. His smile flattens as she stares. "I can't" is all she says before her tears spill. She knows she should have thrown herself in front of the subway train when she had the chance. It would have felt better than this.

"What, sweetheart? You can't what?" He holds her up as her knees weaken.

"I can't marry you. I'm sorry. I thought I could, but I can't." The words burn her throat.

"Are you saying you don't love me?" He looks as if she has blasted him in the chest with a shotgun.

"No, I love you more than you could ever know. I'll love you forever, Nick."

"Then why, Rose? We can go to City Hall right now. Don't let my family scare you off."

"It's not your family, it's mine. They're Orthodox Jews, Nick. If I marry you, I will lose them forever."

"So you choose to lose me forever? They've already had you for a lifetime. It's my turn! I love you. Let me meet them, I'll convince them. I can't lose you."

"I will be dead to them. I will never be able to see or talk to them again." She takes off her ring, opens his hand so she can touch it one last time, and places the ring in his palm.

"Rose, no." He tries to give it back. "I'm begging you."

She walks backward, and he follows. "It's no use. It's not going to work," she says, sobbing so hard he is a blur. "You'll find someone else. I'll always love you." She sees him stagger, covering his face with his hands, before she runs through a crowd of people to disappear.

She decides to walk to Greenwich Village in case Nick runs down to the 59th Street subway to catch her. She holds her arms around herself as if she had fallen on a hand grenade and is keeping her guts from spilling out. How could doing what's necessary feel so wrong? She forces one foot in front of the other down the seemingly endless blocks toward the Village. This is how she will spend the rest of her life, head down, trudging one foot in front of the other, resigning herself to a life of duty. And loss. She will go home and date the men her parents have picked out, going through the motions of *shadchan* but never finding one to love.

By the time she catches the subway to Brighton Beach at Fourth Street in the Village, she is numb. Nick has no idea where she lives or how to find her. He doesn't even know her real name. Dehydrated from her walk, she has no more tears to shed, only a deep pain in her chest where her heart used to be.

The usual people say their hellos as she walks home. She cannot force a smile but nods in acknowledgment. Funny how her life can change so drastically, yet everything around her remains the same.

Her tired legs climb the several flights of stairs to her parent's apartment, where she will stay until she marries a nice Jewish man. She will never tell her parents about Nick or the sacrifice she has made, and everything will go back to normal. To everyone but her. She will silently and privately mourn for the rest of her life. She produces her moonstone pendant, warm from her breast, kisses it, and puts it in her pocketbook, where her engagement ring once hid. This reminder of Nick's moon, and his promise of eternal love, is all she has left.

As she enters the apartment, her mother comes running to meet her. "Oy, Papa and I have been so worried! You didn't leave us a note," Mameh says.

Rose thinks of the good-bye letter that is torn to pieces in the trash can in her bedroom and embraces her mother, hoping she'll have the magic cure, like when Rose would skin her knee or be sick in bed. Mameh smells like the schmaltz she has rendering on the stove. "Don't worry, Mamehleh. I'm home now . . ."

Rose snapped up in bed awake. Her eyes stung and were practically swollen shut. What had she done? Her heart raced as if she was running to catch a subway train. *Nick, Nick! I've changed my mind!*

Her broken heart squeezed in her chest. The lamp tipped and crashed as she tried to turn it on. It was still dark. If she hurried, she could fix this. Running to the bathroom felt as if she was wading through mud—what was wrong with her? She had to get ready quickly. She brushed her wavy, dark hair as determination reflected back in her young eyes. Her parents had blinded her to the truth, but no longer. She deserved to be happy, with or without their consent. Anything to be Nick's wife. Certainty swept over her. Swoony, panic-stricken, and a bit off balance, Rose bounced off furniture like a pinball gathering speed to get to her closet. She wouldn't take much. She'd be living out of a suitcase, traveling with Nick. Her breath quickened as she searched for her floral dress, the one Nick loved. Urgency pummeled her chest. Their kids would be musical and outspoken. Their life full of laughter and love. Maybe she would sing in Nick's band. She knew every song by heart. The thought of wearing tight sweaters and high-waisted pants to show her figure tickled her. Nothing as drab as what hung in front of her in her closet. She would take art classes in the Village and sip sambuca with Frank every Sunday. Maybe even go to Mass with Nonna. Or start her own religion based on love. Nick would want her to be anything she wanted, because he loved her. Her mind flooded with all the names of big band leaders and musicians she and Nick would rub elbows with as they hung out in smoky clubs around the country, envied by the other wives because Nick always wanted her near. She needed to tell him right away that any other life would not be worth living. She was not confused anymore. *Don't worry, Nick. I'm coming.*

She collapsed into her chair to catch her breath. In her lap she saw an old woman's hands. The hands made their way to her face, where she felt deep wrinkles wet with tears. A rooster crowed in the background, sounding her new awakening. Frightened, Rose looked at her hands again to see another man's wedding ring hanging on her thin finger.

Rose pulled clothes out of her closet, flinging them behind her on the bed. She wanted that life with Nick she once threw away. She wanted it more than anything. Next came the boxes from her closet floor, as her hands became bulldozers. And where was her damn suitcase? She stopped and held her head, which felt as light as a drifting balloon. The room spun her, pieces of dreams fraying. From the deep corner of her closet, she excavated a lacquered jewelry box. When she opened it, a tiny princess popped up and twirled to "Someday My Prince Will Come."

She unwrapped a pale-blue Bakelite box hidden in tissue paper under the once-revolving princess, now stuck and silent as the music box eked out one last distorted note. When she opened the box, her moonstone pendant lay in a bed of cotton like a perfectly preserved artifact. She had not seen it since the day she laid it to rest along with her love for Nick. The silver had tarnished, like the black sky outside her window, but the moonstone was as luminous as the day Nick gave it to her.

It was as if she held the sacrifice she had made in the palm of her hand, the delicate chain knotted and hanging like a noose. That sacrifice, all those tortured years with Mort, had tarnished her like the pendant in her hand. She had become bitter and hateful, everything she despised in others when she and the moon had been new.

Papa had dedicated himself to being so correct that it forced him to be wrong about so much. He died two years after she married Mort, and she was pregnant with her second child. Mameh went to live with Aunt Ruth. Mameh changed under Ruth's tutelage, but Rose was stuck with her choice. She became like Papa, for somewhere deep inside she was driven to have her sacrifice mean something. Rose demanded in her children what Papa had demanded in her. Even when it caused CeCe to hate her, the way she had ended up hating Papa.

What was the meaning of all this? Why relive an agony and longing she would never wish on anyone? Why couldn't she die and slip away on a cloud of ignorance? A pain shot through her heart, and all the grief buried within burst out as breath-defying sobs for that hopeful girl she once had been. Sitting on the floor, she rocked back and forth and finally heard her anguish.

"Ma! What are you doing? What's the matter?" CeCe stood over her, Miguel at her side.

Rose heaved a shuddering sigh as the sobs subsided. But the pain remained, searing and red as hot coals. "My heart is broken."

CeCe knelt in front of her. Rose looked into her daughter's face, contorted with worry, her eyes wide and searching. Her once-dark hair now streaked with gray tumbled around her shoulders; her baby was suddenly a sixty-four-year-old *bubbe*. Where did all those years go? Rose reached a shaking hand to rest on CeCe's cheek. "I failed you."

CeCe looked up to Miguel. "Help me get her back to bed. She needs her oxygen."

Rose shook her head but allowed them to help her up and walk her around the wreckage to her bed. Miguel righted the lamp with its dented shade and switched it on while CeCe untangled the oxygen tubing and positioned the cannula into Rose's nostrils. The cool breeze began to sweep through her head, clearing her mind.

CeCe sat next her, holding her hand. "Better now?"

"Cecelia, Miguel, with the breath I have left, I need to confess. That's what you Catholics do, right, Miguel? You confess in the hope you'll be forgiven?"

Miguel was picking up clothing and boxes from the floor and putting them back in the closet. He stopped and sat down in the chair near the bed. "Why do you feel you need God's forgiveness?"

"It's not God's forgiveness I'm after. It's yours. I see the love you have for each other, and I thank God you married despite how I acted. I wish I could have been brave like you. I lost the love of my life because I didn't have the chutzpah to stand up to my papa. Then I turned around and tried to do the same thing to you—I'm so ashamed. Miguel, you are everything a mother wants for her daughter. I'm sorry I treated you so badly."

"Rose, I forgive you. I forgave you years ago. You reacted the way you'd been taught. My father was the same way." Miguel's kind face caused her eyes to fill with fresh tears.

"What do you mean, you lost the love of your life?" CeCe asked.

Rose pressed her hand against the pain in her heart. "I've been remembering things—more than remembering, reliving things from my past. Before I married your father, I was in love with an Italian Catholic. He asked me to marry him, and I said yes. Long story short, my parents would have shunned me forever if I had gone through with it, so I broke his heart something awful. And mine. I've missed him every second of my life, and I miss him now. My point is, more than anybody, I should have understood when you brought home Miguel. Instead I was a selfish hypocrite. I pray you can forgive me deep down, not just saying the words, so I can finally have some peace."

One look at CeCe's face told Rose her daughter was not ready. CeCe looked as confused and hurt as she had more than forty years ago. "Ma, I don't know what to say. I don't know what to think."

Rose nodded her understanding. "We'll talk in the morning. I spent decades hurting you, so take your time. It was my apology that couldn't wait, not your forgiveness."

The sun was rising while CeCe sat drinking her cup of coffee. She called Rachel, whom she knew would be feeding and milking her goats.

"Hey, Ma. What's up, besides you?" CeCe could hear desperate, hungry goat screams in the background. She wanted to scream along with them.

"When you're able to come over, I need my wise and supportive daughter."

After Rose told the details of her story, CeCe could only stare at her mother, trembling with rage. Rachel had a hand on CeCe's arm, trying to calm her. The pound cake sat untouched between them on the kitchen table.

"That's such a sad story, Bubbe," Rachel said. "Isn't it, Ma?"

"You're sad for her? What about me? And you! Look what she put us all through. You're right, you're a hypocrite." CeCe leaned back in her chair and crossed her arms. "I'll never get back those years, Ma. And neither will you. You missed the birth of my daughter and her whole life after that. You made her feel like an unwanted half-breed."

"At least you went ahead and married Papa despite her and lived the life you wanted. At eighteen, back in that rigid time, she caved in to her parents. She paid a huge price."

"And then she passed that price on to me. My whole adult life without my mother—do you know how much that killed me?" CeCe turned toward Rose. "Do you?"

"That's what I'm trying to tell you. I do now. Your anger is justified. I deserve it."

"Did you ever love Papa?" CeCe asked.

"We had our moments. He was a difficult man, your papa, but that's old news."

"So why did you marry him if you weren't in love with him?"

"After I gave up Nick, I gave in to the whole deal. Jewish men courted me, and over and over, I turned them down. My parents were fed up with me not making a choice. Then, Mort came along from Treblinka, skinny and haunted and in desperate need for someone to take care of him. I felt sorry for him. It gave me a kind of purpose. Trying to save Mort was my crazy way of trying to make up for what I'd done to Nick."

"Whatever happened to him?" asked Rachel.

"I never knew. I guess he's dead by now; he was older than me. CeCe, I wanted you to hear the whole story. Now you can decide if you're still going to hate me."

"I don't hate you, Ma. I hate what happened. I hate that a lot. You shamed and punished me for following my heart. Something you couldn't do."

"I'd go back and change things if I could. I'll be out of your hair soon enough."

"Bubbe, don't say that," Rachel said. "I don't hold anything against you. I'm no one to talk when it comes to making mistakes. And I've been forgiven." Her eyes met CeCe's.

"CeCe, I didn't want to die with things like they've been between us—that would leave you holding the bag. Even if I don't live to see it, forgive for yourself, not for me," Rose said.

Witnessing her parents' marriage was what had given CeCe the determination to marry for love. What a hard, lonely life her mother had endured. She began to feel something like sorrow for that young girl in Rose, who couldn't defy her parents. That girl, she could feel sympathy for. The mother who turned against her? Forgiving her might take some time.

Chapter Sixteen

ROSALINDA FELT SHAKY and weak after her first shower at home at Abby's house. She hung onto the pedestal sink waiting for her dizziness to pass. Who knew toweling off could feel like running a marathon? She gathered up her dripping hair and wound it into a towel, wincing from the pain in her abdomen triggered by the movement. She looked down, half expecting to see her guts spilling out onto the floor. Instead she saw the long, lumpy incision running the length of her middle. She used to wear midriff-baring tops and low-slung jeans to show off the flawless, flat plain of her stomach and her pierced belly button with its sparkling gemstone. Santi had been mesmerized. Those days were over.

"Fuck it," she said. Cursing helped with pain, according to Hazel and some scientific study she'd read. Hazel was her self-appointed home-care nurse. She had designed an eating plan that Rosalinda had to admit was helping with her constant nausea and lack of appetite. Hazel said since the surgeons had had to remove part of her stomach, it would take time to be able to eat a normal-sized meal, so frequent small snacks throughout the day helped her to digest. Hazel also gave her an exercise plan that involved walking for fifteen minutes two to three times a day to build up her strength, increasing to twenty minutes after one week. Rosalinda was grateful for anything that would enable her to move out from Abby's house as soon as possible.

She reached for her clothes, which hung on the towel bar, and slowly dressed, careful not to drop anything, since bending over was the worst. Abby acted polite, but Rosalinda could feel her anger.

Santiago's presence helped buffer things, but he would be leaving soon, so with Hazel's help and her own determination, Rosalinda was working toward the goal to be out on her own in no more than one month, after her next doctor's appointment.

Hazel had told her to get dressed every day and put on makeup to get back to normal, instead of shuffling around in her robe like a patient. So she put on a little mascara, eyeliner, neutral eye shadow, and a subtle lipstick. She had to admit the reflection in the mirror was more recognizable.

Still breathing hard, she opened the door and walked back to her and Diego's room, running her hand along the wall for support. She could hear Diego and Abby in the kitchen. Santiago came up the hall behind her. "Need any help?"

"I'm okay," she answered. He followed her into the room.

"I made the bed while you were in the shower," Santi said.

"Thanks. Hazel told me to make the bed so I wouldn't be tempted to crawl back into it."

Diego came running into the room, grabbing her legs from behind and nearly knocking her off-balance. She put her hands on Santi to steady herself.

"Hey, buddy, slow down around Mama, remember?" Santi said.

Diego looked up at her. "Sorry, Mama. I forgot."

Abby appeared in the doorway. "I thought I would go to the grocery store and take Diego with me. I have the list Hazel made for your snacks. Do you need anything else?"

"No. Thanks, though."

"I want Daddy to go to the store, too," Diego said as Abby helped him on with his jacket.

"Daddy needs to stay here and help Mama," Abby said. "You can help me with the shopping and ride in the cart."

"Bye, *mi amor*. Be good for Abby." Santiago lifted him so Rosalinda could give him a kiss without having to bend over.

After they left, Rosalinda pulled the towel from her head, and her long, damp hair tumbled free. Santiago guided her to the desk chair and helped her to sit down. She handed him her brush, and he began to gently work it through her hair, starting from the bottom, near her waist. After he had the tangles out, he picked up her hairdryer, which sat on the desk. She nodded, and he switched it on, directing it to the sections of hair she lifted with her fingers for him to dry. He used the brush with his right hand as he handled the blow dryer with his left. She closed her eyes, feeling the brush glide through her hair, the air swirling around her like a hot summer breeze. "If this editor thing doesn't work out, you could always do hair," she said when he turned it off.

"I used to do Maggie's hair for school when she was younger. She would only let me do it. She has her father's hair, so thick and curly, just getting it brushed was a challenge, but I even learned how to do complicated French braids from Rachel."

"Hazel says I should cut it off like hers while I'm recuperating."

He looked at her in mock horror and then laughed. "Just kidding. You'd look great. Short, long, bald, whatever."

She looked up at him. "Your hair has already grown a lot since you've been here. I always liked it long. Why did you cut it?"

"I cut it the first week of college. I thought I looked ethnic enough without adding long hair in a ponytail."

"I bet you cut it so you could do better with the white girls."

"Possibly."

"Did you have a lot of girlfriends in college?" she asked.

"I dated around. Sometimes I found myself sort of accidentally in a relationship, but the girls eventually broke up with me. They said I was holding back, that I put up walls. I just didn't want anything deep. It's corny, but I saved my passion for my classes. I loved learning, I loved college. I want to go back and get my MFA someday."

"Diego loves learning. He's really smart, too, just like his daddy."

"You always said you were going to go back to school."

"Until I got pregnant."

Santiago sat on the edge of the bed opposite her chair. "When did you find out you were pregnant, exactly?"

"I knew in August."

"But I was still here—I hadn't left for college yet."

"I know."

He blinked and shook his head. "Then why didn't you come to me? I thought you found out after I was gone and that's why you didn't try to track me down."

"I couldn't do that to you. You would have sacrificed everything."

"You were only twenty-three and all alone. Did you think about not having it?"

"When I found out I was pregnant, I wanted the baby more than anything I'd ever wanted in my whole life. I wouldn't be alone anymore."

"What was it like, being pregnant with him?"

"I loved it. After the morning sickness passed, I never felt better. I read all about it and took care of myself and went for all my prenatal appointments. I'd moved to Albuquerque by then and qualified for Medicaid and WIC, the nutritional program; I had good care. I worked as a hostess at a restaurant and lived in a tiny efficiency apartment. I didn't hang out with anyone. I slept, worked, read baby books, and tried to eat right. I just wanted a healthy baby."

"Tell me about his birth."

"I had him at the Lovelace Women's Hospital. A nurse midwife delivered him, Tilly—she was awesome. I didn't have any drugs or epidurals or anything. It was snowing, even though it was March, that real pretty kind with big fat flakes. I was watching it from my sixth-floor window. Eee, I was in so much pain, but I remember being in awe of how beautiful it looked with the city lights and the snow coming down. The nurses kept saying how good I was doing, and when I pushed him out they put him up on my chest and he didn't cry, he was just looking around, taking it all in. I was the one crying. I'd never been so happy."

Santi leaned forward and reached for her hand. "I'm sorry I wasn't there for you. And for me—I didn't get to experience any of that. Do you have pictures?"

"Oh no! Where's all my stuff from the apartment? Did the police take everything? Did it get thrown away? Diego's baby book was there—" How could she be so brain-dead as to have forgotten that? Panic gripped her.

"It's okay—Ramone said the apartment is still sealed by APD. When they unseal it, I can drive you up there, and I'll box up whatever you want to keep."

"You'll probably be gone by then."

"I don't leave until Saturday. It's only Tuesday. I'll call Ramone and make sure we can arrange to do it before I go. If you know how to reach Jesse's brother, we could send him anything of Jesse's he might want."

"Maybe his guitar; I think his brother gave it to him. His car's a beater, and he didn't really have anything else of value. Neither did I, just some clothes and kitchen stuff, mostly junk. But Diego's baby book is priceless. I can't believe I haven't even thought about it."

"Well, you've been kind of distracted, what with the kidnapping, getting shot, nearly dying, and then there's the whole coma thing."

"When you put it like that." Rosalinda smiled into his kind face and then felt her smile fade. Three more days until Santiago returned to his life and she and Diego would begin to count the days until his next visit.

After lunch, Abby read to Diego to settle him in for his nap. Santiago washed the dishes while Rosalinda sat in front of her small plate, the tiny serving of cottage cheese and peaches only half-eaten. "That's all I can do."

He nodded and took her plate, the dishcloth slung over his shoulder. She hadn't even eaten as much as Diego. It worried him. Hazel said Rosalinda would have delayed healing if she didn't consume enough nutrients and calories.

"Just cover it and put it in the fridge. I'll try again after my walk."

From the corner of his eye, he saw Rosalinda grimace as she stood. Though they had discharged her with a week's supply of pain pills, she told Santi she wouldn't take any, as the narcotic in them made her feel too out of it.

"Let's go out the front for a change," she said.

They had been taking walks through the Bosque behind the house. He showed Rosalinda the spot where Caden had hidden the stolen van the night he shot her and took Diego. She had stood there, staring at the ruts the tires had made and the crime tape that still fluttered between the trees, and said nothing.

Santi followed her to the seldom-used front door. It opened onto the flagstone patio, which was encircled by a low wall and gate. Rosalinda sat on the banco, the adobe bench connected to the wall. "Let's sit here for a minute before we walk," she said. The sun, high overhead, radiated warmth against the flagstones and glinted against her hair, reminding him of the blue-black sheen of a raven. He sat next to her.

Along the interior periphery of the low wall were about a dozen terracotta pots holding the skeletal remains of last summer's flowers. "Abby always plants red geraniums," he said. "I helped her—it was our spring ritual. We'd pick out the biggest and prettiest ones and transplant them into these pots. They're for Bobby. The first year, when he was missing, she planted them as an affirmation, that they would be the first thing he saw when he got home. I knew he was already dead. But even after she knew it, too, she kept on planting them, year after year. Even though she loves Ben now, she'll always love Bobby, and every spring she plants red geraniums."

"You're lucky you had Abby to teach you about love."

"Yeah . . . you're right. I never thought about it like that. The Bacas sure as hell didn't teach me anything good about it."

"Why red? Geraniums come in other colors, like white and pink, don't they?"

"Red was their color. When they got married, Bobby was in the navy, a communications expert on nuclear submarines. His sub tours lasted months at a time. When he finally got home, he always carried an armful of red roses for her."

"Abby hates me now. I deserve it, but I miss feeling her like me."

"Abby is the most forgiving person in the universe, or how would I even be sitting here right now? My dad and I took Bobby away from her."

"You were a little boy. Your dad took Bobby away from her."

"The point is, she'll get over it. It's just a little awkward right now. Abby's love is like a force of nature. She loves intensely . . . she'll do anything for you. But that means if you let her down, it hurts her. Believe me, I've been there. She feels betrayed, but then she eventually forgives. All you can do is try to rebuild the trust day by day and wait. She'll come around."

Rosalinda gripped the low wall to stand up. "Let's walk about seven minutes down the road toward town and then turn around and come back."

Santi reached for her arm, but she pulled away. "Hazel says if I lean on you, it's cheating. I have to do it myself," she said.

"Am I allowed to pick you up if you tip over?"

"Probably not."

He let her set the pace, and they fell into what he would call "a mosey." Her face was mostly stoic, though he did catch a few grimaces when she wobbled on the loose gravel. They walked past the empty place where his house used to be, and he thought of his mother, Juanita Baca. When he was applying to colleges, he sent off for the required copies of his birth certificate. He learned his mother, a Mexican national, was only seventeen when she gave birth to him, making him wonder if his thirty-year-old father had won the teenage girl cockfighting. His memory of her was elusive, since she was already gone by the time he was five. His father had told him she didn't love him and had left. In truth, his father had beaten her to death and buried her under the earthen floor of the rooster house when she was only twenty-two, about the age he was now. It would be five years before Bobby was murdered and buried next to her—she would never have been found otherwise. But now, gazing across the field, he remembered her playing tag with him, darting just out of his grasp, her rare laughter, his desperation to catch her.

His fleeting memory dissolved when Rosalinda spoke. "Earlier you said you didn't have a serious girlfriend in college. What about Kat?"

"Kat and her brother have been my best friends since freshman year. I never thought of her as someone to date—I didn't think she was my type and our friendship meant too much to me to risk it. I confided in her about almost anything. She made me laugh and lighten up when I needed to. I didn't find out until after graduation that she had been crushing on me since we first met. I was clueless until Kat started giving me some pretty unmistakable signals. We have a lot in common and already love each other as friends. We'd just started to date when Abby called about Diego, so it's new. And I've been away all this time, but I have a good feeling about it."

"Do you think she'll be good with Diego?"

"Sure," he said. "Yeah, she'll be great with him." The truth was, he hadn't even thought to imagine Kat and Diego in the same room together. As they walked on, he tried to picture it. Kat seemed more like a kooky aunt than a substitute mother. The one who would start pillow fights at bedtime and ruin dinner with candy. Maybe that was okay. Diego had a mother.

"Has it been seven minutes?"

He looked at his watch. "In five, four, three, two, one."

She pivoted around to walk back, her hair flying with the sudden movement. "Ow!" she said and grabbed her belly. "Shit! I forgot I couldn't do that."

"You okay?"

"Except for the goddamn pain, I'm great. Hazel says just to cuss at it and keep going."

Their view held the mountains now. White clouds nestling along the crest, sepia-toned autumn colors of the bosque in the foreground, all under a strong blue sky. Santi stopped to soak it in. He'd seen some beautiful places in his travels in Europe with Kat and Reggie one summer, and he had explored all the varied splendor that was California, but nothing beat what was in his own backyard. "I'll miss this when I go."

Rosalinda hooked her arm through his, and he could feel her leaning on him as they walked on. "You're cheating," he said.

"Yes. I'm a cheater." She sounded weary, her voice breathy. "Don't tell Hazel."

The delicate weight of her leaning on him, the grind of their shoes against the gravel, made him think of their shared journey. The start had been rocky and terrifying, but they had survived to make it this far. They were Diego's parents, his mama and daddy. Between the sharp head wind that had kicked up and his sudden, dumbfounding joy, his eyes began to water, blurring the road ahead.

Maggie had decided since Santiago was leaving soon, she would spend the evening at her "real home." After dinner, she spread out her homework on the kitchen table.

"You can use your desk in your room," Santi said, sitting across from her. "You might be able to concentrate better. Diego's tearing through the house on his after-dinner wild streak."

"I don't want to be shut away. I came over here to be with my family," Maggie said.

Abby was doing the dishes. "And we're very glad you're here."

"If you'd built that big house you were going to build, we could all fit. I hate this stupid little house." Maggie folded her arms over her chest. Her curly hair was tousled from her walk over in the wind. Even Santiago, who had seen Bobby in the flesh only once, the night he was murdered, could recognize his face in Maggie's expressions. At twelve now, his little sister was transforming from the little girl he'd helped raised into something foreign: a teenage girl. How fast the last twelve years had gone. And in the same amount of time moving forward, Diego would be nearing sixteen.

Abby wasn't taking the bait about the remodel, so Maggie persisted. "If we had a house like Rachel and Charlie and Hattie, we could fit the whole family and all my friends."

"At the time, it didn't seem to make sense to build a big house when Santi was going to go to college out of state. And in a few quick years, you might decide to move away, too. Ben and I don't need to rattle around in a big house when it's just the two of us," Abby said without turning around from the sink.

"Have you ever heard of a thing called visits? What if Santi and I want to visit and bring people? And maybe I wouldn't ever move out if we had a decent house."

Abby shot Santi a look of faux alarm at the thought of Maggie never moving out, and he had to suppress his laugh.

"Rosalinda and Diego could live with us," Maggie went on. "They're our family now, too. Everyone is all '*la familia*' all the time, except here. It's this house's fault. It splits us up."

"I'm out of here in two days, and you can have your crib back," Santi said.

Maggie rolled her eyes. "That's another thing. You shouldn't even be going back. You should stay here. You have a kid who needs his dad. I didn't get to have a dad until Ben came, and it sucks—you should know that. It isn't fair to Rosalinda, either."

"What isn't fair to me?" Rosalinda asked as she walked behind Diego into the room. Diego scrambled into Santiago's lap, exhibit A in Maggie's case.

"That Santi is bailing on you and Diego and going back to California," Maggie said. "See, Diego loves his daddy." When Diego heard that, he began to silly kiss Santiago's hand, giggling so hard he couldn't maintain his pucker.

Rosalinda sat down at the table. "Maggie, Santiago is not bailing on me. His life is in San Francisco. He's going to be helping me financially, and he's going to come back for lots of visits. Diego and I will be fine. And we'll be nearby, so his Auntie Maggie and everyone else can see him all the time. It'll work out, you'll see."

Abby came up behind Maggie and put her arms around her. "I love how you care so much about your family."

Maggie grabbed her books and shrugged off Abby's embrace. "If you would just listen to me for once and do what I say, we'd all be better off. But no, I'm just the kid." She strode off in the direction of her room, apparently having had an adequate dose of *la familia*.

After giving Diego his evening bath, Santiago decided to say his good-byes to the Vigils and Rose in case he got too busy to on his last day. The closer Saturday came, the more eager he was to get back to

Kat and his job. Knowing he'd be back next month for Christmas made leaving easier.

He found Miguel outside chopping wood. He'd stripped off his jacket, switched on the porch light, and hung one of his lanterns on a post, since the moon was hidden by thick clouds. Santi marveled at how this sixty-six-year-old *viejito* could swing his heavy antique ax and land it with a crack that sounded like a line drive hit.

He stopped when he saw Santi. "Hey, *mi'jo*, good to see you."

"What are you doing out here in the dark swinging that ax?"

"Oh, you know. A man has to do what a man has to do. Besides, I get all antsy in the off-season." The off-season Miguel spoke of was not baseball but chile farming.

"I'm going back to San Francisco day after tomorrow."

"I was about to enjoy my one cerveza for the night. Would you like to join me?"

"A beer sounds good, but I want to see Rose before she turns in."

"Oh, she doesn't go to bed until after the ten o'clock news. We have time."

Santi followed him to his workshop, where he kept a little fridge. He lit the wood stove and grabbed them each a bottle. They settled in, having a drink, watching the light and shadows play on the walls and dance across the faces and forms of Miguel's carved saints.

"I was thinking about you, Santiago, and how so much has happened to you in your young life. And even with tragedy and anguish, you always prevail."

"Well, everyone's okay, and that's what counts."

"Except for the perpetrator, no? He got what he deserved. You've been in my prayers."

"I appreciate it. How has Rose been doing?" Santi took off his jacket as the wood stove turned the small space into a sweat lodge. The cold beer hit the spot.

"She's holding her own. She gets around on that scooter. Uses her oxygen most of the time now. She's been reflecting on her life, which has been interesting, I guess you could say."

Santiago thought back to when Rose and Mort had first descended on them four years ago, the summer he was with Rosalinda. Rose had a fervent love for him, her "adopted" grandson, ever since Santiago had half carried Mort from certain death in the bosque fire and then, with Rosalinda's help, had cleared Mort's name from the accusation of having started the blaze with his matches and cigar. He loved Rose, too, despite her ignorant comments about Hispanics when she had first arrived. She told him what Mort suffered during World War II as a prisoner in the Treblinka death camp, spurring Santi to read extensively about the Holocaust and to incorporate what he learned into one of his more successful short stories, the one Gordon Hopkins had published.

"I wanted to be sure to see her before I left," Santi said. "I'll be back at Christmas, but you never know."

"No guarantees for any of us," Miguel said, draining his beer. "But for an old woman with a failing heart, time is not her friend. So I will relinquish you to her."

Santiago found Rose in her room watching an old black-and-white movie on television. She sat in her recliner, legs raised, pink fluffy slippers on her feet. Her cloud of red hair hovered over emerging white roots. An oxygen cannula was inserted into her nose, its tubing curving along each pale cheek and then trailing to the oxygen tank parked next to her.

"Rose," he said. "It's Santi."

"It's my heart that's bad, not my eyes. Who else would you be? Mario Lopez?" Rose's mischievous twinkle in her eyes had not dimmed in the slightest. "Here, take a load off." She turned off the movie.

He sat in the armchair next to her. "I leave early Saturday morning. I need to get back to work and everything."

"Everything includes a girl, I hear. How does this work? You live and work in San Francisco with your girlfriend, and what, you fly back here some weekends to be a father?"

"For now, while Diego is still too little to travel, I'll be flying back and forth a lot."

"Sounds like you are trying to have the best of both worlds." Her gaze was challenging.

"It's new, this being a father thing. But I love him like I've never loved anyone."

"I want to show you something." She dug around in her pockets and produced a piece of jewelry, blackened ornate silver with tiny diamond chips surrounding a vivid white round stone. She put it into his hand. "Moonstone."

"It's beautiful. Where did it come from?"

"The love of my life gave it to me." Rose's smile came from somewhere deep inside of her, and for an instant he caught a glimpse of the girl she once was.

"Mort?" he asked.

"Nick was his name. He was a Catholic Italian. I was eighteen, raised in an Orthodox Jewish household. If I'd married Nick, I would have been dead to them. So I did the 'correct' thing and sacrificed Nick, broke both of our hearts. Later I married Mort, a perfect Jewish match, but it never felt right. It was the 'correct' thing to do, but it wasn't right . . . for my soul, you know? Every day, every night, my heart was with someone else. That's probably why it finally turned on me."

"I'm sorry."

"The pendant you're holding, I want you to keep it."

"Rose, I couldn't—it's from the love of your life, and why me? You should give it to CeCe or Rachel or Hattie."

"Don't worry about them, they're getting the good stuff. No, this is from Nick, and that's outside my life with Mort, so it has nothing to do with them. When Nick gave this to me, he was going away for a few weeks, playing in his band. He told me that every night we were separated, we should look at the moon and send each other love. Right there on the street, beneath the streetlamp, he played me a song on his sax that was popular during the war, called 'I'll Be Seeing You.'" Her voice was surprisingly strong and clear as she sang the lyrics about yearning for a missing loved one while looking at the moon. He recognized the song as a jazz standard from his music appreciation class.

"Here's what you do, Santi. You take Diego outside to look at the moon and tell him that while you guys are apart, he should look at the moon, the same moon you'll be looking at, and you'll think about each other, send each other love, that kind of thing. It helps, trust me," Rose said.

Santiago rubbed his thumb against the white gem as if it were a worry stone. "Thanks, Rose, but I feel bad taking this—don't you want to hold onto it? It's your connection to Nick."

"My connection to Nick is stronger than ever. I don't need it anymore. But you do."

CeCe appeared in the doorway. "Knock knock."

"Who's there?" Rose replied.

"Your daughter!" CeCe joined them.

"If you're trying to tell a knock-knock joke, it isn't very funny," Rose said. "Unless being my daughter is some kind of a joke."

"You said it, Ma, not me. Time for your medicine." CeCe's long, dark hair was generously seasoned with gray now, but her face remained nearly wrinkle free.

Santi slipped the pendant into his pocket. He leaned over to give Rose a kiss on her cheek and a hug. "Be good. I'll see you at Christmas."

"I'm making no promises on either count," Rose said, holding his hand. She looked up at him. "God, you've turned into a handsome man. Let's hope you'll be as smart as you are pretty."

"No promises." Santi laughed. He hugged CeCe good-bye and left them to their sparring.

After saying good-bye to Miguel, Santi walked home. The cloud cover had thinned and ripped in places, exposing a bright half moon. His hand found the pendant in his pocket. He thought about Rose, forced to make the hardest choice in her life when she was only eighteen, the same age he had been when he unwittingly cocreated Diego.

The moon seemed different somehow; he couldn't take his eyes off of it. Maybe because Rose had spent her lonely life searching its face for the love she had lost, or maybe because he was anticipating living more than a thousand miles away from his son, with only the moon to share between them.

He brought out the pendant. The glowing moonstone seemed to be lit from within, but like the moon, it could reflect only borrowed light. Rose said she didn't need it anymore, but he did. He tucked it back into his pocket.

Santiago never slept well before an early flight. He spent the night intermittently napping and checking the time on his phone. His alarm was set for 4 a.m., which would give him just enough time for a quick shower before Charlie picked him up at 4:30 for the half-hour drive to the Albuquerque International Sunport. At 3:50, he gave up trying to sleep and started getting ready.

The day before, he and Rosalinda had explained to Diego that his daddy had to go back to his job in another state and that he wouldn't be seeing him for about five weeks, until he came back for Christmas. They used a map and a calendar to show distance and time.

Diego had drawn a line with his red crayon between Albuquerque and San Francisco. When they talked about Santi coming back for Christmas, Diego had said, "Like Santa!" Then he, Rosalinda, and Diego had put on their jackets and walked outside to look at the moon together. Santi had explained that wherever you go on earth, there was only one moon to see. He said that they could both look at the moon and send love to the other person every night. Even if the moon was hidden by clouds or not up yet, it was still there, just as when Santi was away, he was still there, sending Diego his love. He even sang a little of Rose's song. Diego had laid his head on Santi's shoulder and tried to hum along. When Santi looked at Rosalinda, he thought he saw tears in her eyes. Or maybe it was just a trick of the light.

But as he showered and dressed, he decided he would look forward to what he was returning to and not focus on what he was leaving behind. He began to list everything in San Francisco he could think of: his apartment overlooking Columbus Avenue; his own bed, coffeehouses on every corner; his favorite Chinese restaurant; the way the bay looked when the sun shone, dazzling the water with spangled light; and the way the fog materialized and crept in on Carl Sandburg's little cat feet. Kat's softness, her laugh, her sharp, creative, wholly unique mind. Catching up on his editing—able to immerse himself into those astonishing manuscripts without distraction. Tending only to his own needs, without having to consider a dozen other people or provide the constant attention a three-year-old requires. He could return to being the single young man he was before the interruption, go back to launching his career and enjoying his girlfriend in one of the most extraordinary cities on earth.

He had actually worked up a sense of giddy relief by the time he headed to the back door to watch for Charlie's truck.

As he tried to avoid the squeaky floorboards on his way up the hall, Rosalinda opened her door and stood in the semidarkness. Her hair was loose and wild from sleep. Through the open doorway, in the glow of the night-light, he could see Diego sleeping, sprawled on his back in the new flannel pajamas Abby had brought home for him.

"I wanted to thank you, Santi. For everything you've done for me and Diego and will still be doing. I thank God for you." Her voice trembled. She looked down, avoiding his eyes.

He set down his bags and took her into his arms. They held each other a long time without speaking, until he could he hear the rumble of Charlie's truck. He kissed the top of her head and released her. She ducked back into her room as he picked up his bags and walked out the door, not looking back.

Chapter Seventeen

WHEN ABBY WOKE she was startled to see the sun was up. She hadn't heard Santi getting ready—surprisingly, given what a light sleeper she was. Ben slept beside her. No surprise there. The house could explode around them, and he would not be disturbed.

After splashing cold water on her face and brushing her teeth and hair, she found Hazel in her kitchen eating breakfast with Rosalinda and Diego. Hazel had made them one of her mystery hot cereal concoctions, a combination of flax, oats, chia, amaranth, quinoa, toasted piñon nuts, and God knew what else, sweetened with agave syrup. "Good morning," Abby said.

"Grandma, Daddy is gone," Diego said.

"Yes, he's in San Francisco. When is he coming back?" Abby helped herself to a large mug of coffee and a small bowl of cereal.

"Christmas!" Diego said.

Rosalinda kept her eyes on her cereal, her face half-hidden by her hair.

"How are you doing?" Abby asked her.

"Okay, thanks." Her tone was flat, and she made no eye contact.

Hazel picked up Diego's empty bowl. "Rosalinda and I are going to take advantage of this perfect weather and take a nice long walk, aren't we?"

Rosalinda actually smiled at Hazel. "Yes, ma'am."

Abby wondered how long it would take them to get over their rift. They were stuck on stilted small talk. "I thought I would hear Santi getting ready and I'd get up to say good-bye, but I slept right through it. Has he called to say he got in?"

"His plane was supposed to get in at ten thirty California time, so with the time difference, he's not there yet," Rosalinda said.

Diego had climbed off his chair and was playing with the toy jet plane his father had given him, flying it down the hallway, making a roaring sound to accompany the flight.

Abby gripped her coffee mug with both hands while Hazel grabbed whatever wasn't nailed down to throw in her dishwater.

"I can watch Diego if you guys want to start your walk," Abby said, getting more coffee, her sluggish brain starting to spark to life. "I need to wash the sheets so Maggie can sleep back in her room tonight."

"It'll be nice to have her back," Rosalinda said.

"I wonder if we'll have to peel Hattie off of her or if they're finally ready for a break from each other. We've never reached a Maggie-Hattie point of exhaustion."

"She told me it's been twenty-nine days that she's been in exile," Hazel said. "She also mentioned she's studying Mary, Queen of Scots, in school and could identify."

Abby laughed. Maggie quips were the best.

Hazel hung up the dishtowel. "Well, chica, ready to roll?"

Rosalinda slowly stood, one hand bracing her middle. "Sure, *viejita*, if you think you can keep up with me."

"Honey, if I moved as slow as you, my seventy-seven-year-old joints would lock up on me," Hazel said, throwing a wink to Abby as Rosalinda laughed. They grabbed their jackets and left.

Abby realized that was the first time she had ever heard Rosalinda laugh, except maybe when playing with Diego. Never had she heard her laugh with another adult. It was a good laugh, hearty and real. And it was Hazel who had drawn it from her.

Rosalinda had to push herself to keep up with Hazel. Hazel didn't baby her the way Santi did. She could feel sharp tugs deep inside and wondered how that could be good.

Though the trees were bare and the leaves beneath her feet had already half decomposed after the rain and snow, the sun was so warm she had to unbutton her jacket and then remove it and tie it around her waist. It felt good to cinch it around her middle, splinting her muscles.

Hazel fell back a step and linked her arm through Rosalinda's. "I haven't told you about Santiago when you were away in la-la land."

Rosalinda jabbed her lightly with her elbow. "So tell."

"He was frantic. He stayed for hours and hours at the hospital to get his ten minutes with you. He held your hand and cried and talked to you in whispers."

Once Rosalinda had awakened and remembered to tell him about the cabin, the focus had been on rescuing Diego. "I think you're telling stories."

"And the way he looked at you. Even after you woke up, you had to have seen it."

"What you saw was pity, which is more than I deserve."

Hazel snorted. "And I've seen the way you look at him."

"Get your eyes checked, old lady."

"I won't tell a soul. But if you ever want to talk . . . Hey, you're starting to hunch, stand up straight."

Rosalinda lifted her head and squared her shoulders. The pull in her abdomen as her spine straightened made her gasp.

"See? Those muscles want to tighten up and curl into a ball if you let them. It's a constant battle. I have to do an hour of yoga and an hour of weight training followed by a half-hour swim every day just to keep my posture and flexibility. Old people who stop moving lose their posture, their strength. Next thing you know they get osteoporosis, break a hip, and that's all she wrote."

"You're intense with all that working out. You got your eye on a younger woman?"

"Remember the nurse, Joan? She said she was getting ready to retire?"

"She was pretty, with that silver braid and blue eyes. Nice, too. I didn't get the gay vibe, though. You might be barking up the wrong tree."

"I'm not the one barking. She slipped me her business card with her private cell phone number written on the back."

"Did you call her?"

"Thinking about it."

"Do it! What good is having a hot bod and looking way younger if you don't follow up when someone notices? Are you some kind of tease? Put your money where your mouth is."

"Wow, for someone unwilling to talk about your own love life, you sure have a lot to say about mine," Hazel said.

"I don't have a love life. But you could, unless you're chicken. *Brk brk.*" She flapped her free arm.

"I liked you better in a coma. I could wash your hair and brush it and talk to you, and you never talked back."

Rosalinda laughed. The Manzano Mountains had lost any long-distance evidence of snow, though much was still there, hidden behind the tree cover and concealed inside canyons. But down here in the valley, the temperature had to be in the sixties, no clouds in sight. This weather would not hold for long; even in New Mexico, winter was inevitable. Santi had told her about all the rain and fog in San Francisco. As the sun warmed her face and tingled her scalp along the part in her hair, she knew she could never live in a place like that. She needed sunshine about as much as she needed oxygen. And chile. Red or green, she could never live without chile. She remembered when Santi would come to her at night, after working a long day in the chile fields, how she could smell it on him, as if it was exuding through his pores and clinging to his hair. She could taste it on his skin. How could he be happy so far away from home? Away from the people and things he loved? Her sigh was audible.

Hazel patted her arm consolingly, as if she could read her thoughts. Rosalinda wanted to crawl into Hazel's lap, the grandmother, the *abuelita*, she never had. It surprised her that she felt such a thirst for female nurturance, when she'd never known it. She felt the skinny, lonely little girl inside of her reaching for it, like a plant in the shadows leaning toward the light.

Santiago felt his consciousness returning. He opened his eyes in the dim light. Kat slept, her leg over his, her head on his chest. Her pale skin seemed to glow in the semidarkness, while his darker skin seemed to absorb the light. As he wondered how long they had slept, he heard his phone vibrating in the pocket of his pants, which were somewhere in the pile of clothes on the floor next to the bed. They hadn't wasted any time.

He eased out from under Kat, who rolled onto her side and continued to sleep, and found his phone. It was Abby. "Hello?" he said as he walked to his adjoining bathroom so as not to disturb Kat.

"I didn't see any reports of planes going down, so I guess you got there in one piece."

"Sorry I didn't call. I actually crashed out. I didn't sleep last night. How is everyone?"

"Good. Maggie is back in her room, reorganizing everything, rearranging the furniture with Ben's help. Diego took a nap. He played with that plane you gave him all morning and then insisted on napping with it. I told him he'd poke his eye out with that thing and tried to get him to cuddle one of his stuffed animals, but he wasn't having it. I meant to wake up and say good-bye before you left. I'm like a kid—I didn't see you leave, so you must still be here."

"How's Rosalinda?"

"Hazel was here when I woke up, feeding them breakfast. Then they went on a walk while I watched Diego. After they got back, they hung out in her room like a couple of teenage girls, laughing and carrying on."

"You sound jealous. Why don't you just forgive Rosalinda and get it over with?"

"I'm not there yet, Santi."

"Well, I really appreciate what you're doing, taking care of them like you are."

"Anything for you and Diego," Abby said. "I'll let you go. I'm glad you finally got back to your real life, after everything. You know how proud I am of you, right?"

"Thanks. Love you. Say hi to everyone."

He walked back into his bedroom and picked up his clothes to get dressed. Something fell from his pocket and hit the wood floor. It was Rose's pendant.

After he dressed, he walked to the window, parted the heavy drapes, and looked at the pendant in the light. The round white stone contained subtle striations within it that he hadn't noticed before. The sun lowered over the bay. Beneath the cloud layer, it angled bright light horizontally, igniting windows on buildings.

"Santi?" Kat sat up in his bed. "What time is it?"

He slipped the pendant back into his pocket and pulled out his phone. "Four forty. I'm starved. Want to go to Franchino's? I'm craving their gnocchi with gorgonzola sauce."

"Sure. But I better have the chicken piccata, it has about a thousand fewer calories. I ate too much while you were gone. The lonely kind of eating, where you stand up at the sink and pretend the calories don't count that way."

"You look perfect to me. Let's just go enjoy our food and celebrate that I'm back."

"Fine for you; you don't have to worry about it." She pulled up the sheet and modestly wrapped it around herself before retrieving her clothes. "I'll go get ready."

Santiago attacked his work with intensity and focus. Within a few twelve-hour days, he had completed his editorial notes on all five manuscripts and sent them electronically to his authors. He had lengthy clarification phone calls with each one. Two manuscripts had needed only light editing, and the authors both agreed to turn their revisions around in two to three weeks. Two other manuscripts required more intensive work, and he requested those be returned in four to six weeks. The last one involved structural changes, additional character development, and an altered ending. That author assured him she understood and agreed with his vision and would have her rewrite completed in two to three months. Meanwhile, Santiago had an ever-increasing stack of new submissions to begin to plow through, many of them requested by Kat or Gordon at the writer's conference they had attended in his place.

Gordon commended him for hitting the ground running and expressed relief that the preproduction and release calendar would be within the timeline he had projected. All five books would be produced as trade paperbacks. Kat had completed her cover designs for each novel, and after a few minimal adjustments, all five authors had been happy with the previews she had sent. She then worked on the back cover designs and contents. After each manuscript was returned to Santiago and he gave his final approval, Kat would tackle the copyediting. Reggie would then transform each manuscript into page proofs, the final opportunity for each author to review and comment. Kat would review these and begin her marketing strategies for each book, coordinating with the authors and eventually sending advance reading copies to reviewers. Reggie would submit the final page proofs to the printers for their first print run. In the meantime Gordon would work with distributors, libraries, and booksellers—independent bookstores and chains, both brick-and-mortar and electronic—to make plans to get the books to consumers in every available format.

The five of them, along with Gordon's longtime assistant, Bev, celebrated Santi's return at Gordon's favorite restaurant, Restaurant Gary Danko, a short walk from Columbus Avenue to North Point Street in Fisherman's Wharf. Specializing in New American cuisine, the restaurant was said to be harder to get into than heaven, but of course Gordon Hopkins had managed.

After caviar and the appetizer course, Santi noticed it was near Diego's bedtime, so he excused himself and stepped outside to make his call. He'd been away one week, and because of his work, it had flown by. He figured it must feel longer to Diego.

"Diego!" he said, after Rosalinda gave his son the phone. "I'm looking at the moon and sending you love."

"I see it. It's getting bigger and brighter. Do you see that, Daddy?"

"The moon will be full next week for Thanksgiving, like we'll be from eating turkey."

"But I want to see you." Diego's voice grew softer.

"I'm sorry, buddy. But I'll be there for Christmas, remember? Did you have your bath?"

"Grandma gaved it to me because Mama can't."

"Mama is getting stronger every day. Pretty soon she'll be able to do everything she used to do, like pick you up, bend over the tub, and chase you when you run around the house naked."

"Maggie chased me, but she can't catch me because I'm too fast."

"Yeah, you're about as fast as the jet that brought me here." Santiago watched as thin, dark clouds streaked across the moon's face. The breeze was turning damp and cold.

Diego puffed breath into his ear. "Then I will come see you right now, really fast."

"I'm sorry, buddy, but that isn't possible. It's too far."

"I want you," Diego said, his voice dissolving into snuffling tears.

Santiago ducked back into the alcove by the glass door to try to escape the increasing wind. He saw Kat approaching. "I love you, Diego. And I will see you at Christmas. I miss you, too. I'm sorry you're sad—"

"Santi? Diego is crying. I need to settle him into bed," Rosalinda said.

"I didn't mean to upset him. I'm sorry."

"He's just overtired. He had a great day. Charlie let him help with the horses, and he even got to sit on one while Charlie led him around.

I made him wear his bike helmet. He's fine now, sitting on Abby's lap having some milk and a cookie. How are you doing?"

Kat stood on the other side of the glass door, her eyebrows raised.

"Working a lot. We're at dinner now, so I need to go. Tell everyone that I miss them."

He ended the call after their good-byes and opened the restaurant door, allowing a gust of wind to hit Kat in the face. "Sorry," he said, feeling like all he was doing was apologizing.

"This dinner is expensive, and each course is timed." She turned away to lead him back to their table.

"You know I have to call Diego before he goes to bed," Santi said.

She turned around to face him. "You could have called earlier. I get that you need to call him every night, but work with me here. Sometimes you need to think ahead if we have plans." Before he could respond, they reached their party, and she turned on her smile.

How could he explain he wanted to wait until the moon had risen? How could he explain to Diego that his daddy loved him even though he wasn't there? Abby had assured him that Diego would get used to this, that he would adjust.

Hearing his son cry for him left him shaken. He took a gulp of wine, which was now a red, to go with his main course: the juniper-crusted venison with braised red cabbage, cranberry compote, chestnut spaetzle, and tangerines. The servers simultaneously lifted the lids from their entrées to a chorus of appreciation. His plate was beautiful, the scent was tantalizing. But what he craved more than anything was some milk and a cookie with Diego on his lap.

While Diego napped, Rosalinda fell asleep reading on the living room sofa. Abby pulled the throw over her and set her book on the ottoman. Rosalinda didn't stir. She seemed younger and more innocent asleep, and Abby could even work up some tenderness toward her—until the memory of Rosalinda's deception wiped it away.

Abby paced around the house, listening to the wind rattle loose windowpanes and whip the canvas tarp covering the roof-mounted swamp cooler. After Mort had died and Rose had her heart attack, she and Rachel and CeCe had agreed to keep their Esperanza Café closed until spring. CeCe didn't have to say it, but Abby and Rachel knew she meant the café wouldn't reopen until after Rose passed.

At first Abby had enjoyed the time off. She organized her recipe binders. She supervised the thorough cleaning and painting of the empty café. She pitched in to help Rachel with her goat cheese business. Since October 6, when Rosalinda and Diego had arrived on her doorstep, she had diverted her time and energy to them and Santiago, especially during their week from hell.

Now, though, she felt her restlessness returning. She looked forward to reopening the café. She scribbled new spring menu ideas in her notebook. The café hours were 11:30 a.m. to 3 p.m., so it was an easy schedule.

Abby stood in front of her closet and remembered the abandoned house plans that were stashed behind the crowd of clothes and shoes. She reached into the back, stirring up dust, and felt around for the cardboard cylinder that contained the blueprints. She pulled the tube out and spread the curling papers on her bed. Carefully, she examined each page: north, south, east, and west elevation drawings, the electrical and utility plan, the foundation plan, the roof design plan, and finally, the floor plan. She and Ben had spent hours with the architect designing it all but hadn't taken the next step of choosing their builder. Ben was all set to proceed; she was the one who had gotten cold feet. The four bedrooms, two offices, library/music room, home theater, chef's kitchen, laundry room, three-car garage, and attached greenhouse had suddenly seemed grandiose, traitorous to her values. Even though it would be built with money she had earned and would fit inside only one wing of the house she grew up in, in her mind it was contaminated with the memory of her parents' obscene wealth and twisted racist mentality. Though she had amassed considerable wealth, she was most comfortable giving it away and living in her old, small house with its connection to the past. Maybe clinging to this idea of living so humbly was an indication she was still rebelling against her parents, trying to prove some point. To whom? Her husband and daughter were the ones inconvenienced. Her austerity had not been noble; it had been self-indulgent.

Now when she looked at the floor plan, she saw Maggie entertaining her friends. She saw the office space Ben and she sorely needed. She saw the end of the morning lineup outside the one bathroom. She saw the greenhouse alive with herbs and vegetables. She saw not having to do her laundry in the small kitchen. She saw a dining space large enough to host her friends and growing family. Her fingers slid over the thin, smooth paper, going room to room, imagining how much life such a house could hold.

Just as she found their notes about the builders, she heard an unintelligible cry from the living room. She ran to find Rosalinda, still apparently asleep, crying and calling out, "Jesse!"

"Rosalinda, wake up. You're having a bad dream," Abby said, gently squeezing her shoulder. "Rosalinda, wake up."

Rosalinda woke and looked around frantically, still crying. Abby sat near her on the ottoman.

"Oh, my God," Rosalinda said. "It was so real." Waking did not stop her flood of tears and anguished sobbing.

Before he left, Abby remembered, Santiago had taken Rosalinda to their old apartment to box up her things. He said she had been stoic as she stepped around the large, dark blood stains on the carpet, the evidence of Jesse fighting for his life and losing.

Rosalinda sat up, her shoulders still heaving as she seemed to try to compose herself, her arms wrapped around her abdomen. "When Jesse was going to stop Caden, I told him to be careful—I knew how dangerous he was—"

"Who brought Caden into your lives?" Abby asked.

"Jesse."

"Then that's who's responsible for what happened after that. Did you love Jesse?"

"I didn't love him, but he was good to Diego and me."

"Until he found out he could cash in on Diego."

Rosalinda wiped the tears that were still coursing down her face. "He'd been supporting Diego, working shit jobs, trying to go straight. At first, he just wanted me to tell you about Diego. He said he thought it was unfair that his father's family didn't even know about him, and child support would help us. Then, Jesse ran into Caden at a bar, got drunk, and told him about Diego. It was Caden's plan to go for big money with the kidnapping con."

Abby walked across the room to grab some tissues and handed them to Rosalinda.

Rosalinda dabbed at her eyes and blew her nose. "I wanted to tell, but I had no proof. It would have been my word against theirs, and they hadn't done anything yet—it was only talk. I was afraid of Caden. Can you imagine his reaction if some cop showed up at his door, with him just out of prison and on probation, saying I accused him of planning to kidnap my son? He'd already threatened me and Diego. When I came to you and said we were in danger, it was the truth. Each day I didn't tell made it harder to tell you; the more time passed, the deeper I was in—it was like quicksand, like I was sinking and getting more and more trapped. Finally, I begged Jesse to stop it once and for all, and he admitted he wanted out, too. He thought he could reason with Caden, since they used to run together. Jesse thought they were friends, because he has— *had*—a big heart. He never would have believed Caden would do that to him." Rosalinda looked up at her when she didn't fire back another question.

Abby let out the breath she had been holding and looked into Rosalinda's tear-filled eyes. "I don't know for sure how I would have reacted if you'd told me, how far I would have gone to make sure Diego was safe. If you had told me your boyfriend and his criminal associate had sent you to us in order to set up a fake kidnapping to extort money from me, I would have found it hard to believe you weren't part of it. I don't know that I would have been able to trust anything you said after that."

"I don't give a shit about money. Look at me, I have two pairs of jeans and maybe five tops, the same clothes I've had since Diego was born. My bra is held together with a safety pin. Anything I had, anything Jesse had, went to giving Diego nice clothes to wear, toys to play with, books to read, decent food to eat. Jesse got greedy under Caden's influence. The thought of getting all that money from someone who was famous for giving it away, no one getting hurt— he got sucked into it, but I never was. I was forced to come here under threat, or you still wouldn't know about Diego. I'm sorry it went so wrong." She held Abby's gaze without flinching.

"I believe you. You've sacrificed for Santiago in the past, and even now, you aren't trying to hang onto him or interfere with his new life. I have a lot to thank you for."

"I just hope that someday we can be friends again. It would mean a lot to me."

"Friends screw up sometimes, you know? Then they cry, hash it out, and get over it—at least that's how women do it. Men might throw a punch and then go have a beer or settle it on the basketball court. Look at Rachel and me, we started out as, well, definitely not friends, and now we'd do anything for each other."

"Santi says you are the most forgiving person in the world."

"I believe in forgiveness. But I can take the long way around to get there, sometimes," Abby said. "Now, I was about to make some tea. Want to join me?"

Chapter Eighteen

AFTER RELIVING HER last moments with Nick, Rose found her excursions into the past jumped forward into her life with Mort. When she rested in bed and felt herself start to feel drowsy, it was with trepidation she surrendered . . .

Sometimes a mother's intuition is a curse. A horrible gnawing in Rose's gut keeps her busy in the house, wiping, dusting, cooking, and baking. Mort sits in his easy chair watching Walter Cronkite's grim face report about the war in Vietnam.

She isn't surprised when the doorbell rings in the house they bought in a Brooklyn suburb a few years back. She peeks out the window to see a small truck parked in front, the motor still running, as if ready to make a fast getaway. The doorbell rings again, but Rose is still in no hurry. She holds her breath and opens the door. "Western Union, ma'am," says the young man, not quite looking her in the eye. She is sure it is not one of those new Candygrams that is all the rage. She takes it, signs for it, but the courier doesn't stay around for a tip.

"Mort." She runs her thumb under the gummed edge. She turns off the TV, sits down next to him. Her hands shake. She knows. She's known since it happened. "You read it."

Mort takes the telegram. His face pulls down as if the gravity in the room is turned up. "Our Samuel, they regret to inform us, is missing in action, presumed dead." He folds the letter and takes off his reading glasses.

The words begin to kill her. She lets out a mournful wail and doubles over. She grabs the telegram from Mort and crumples it in her hand. "No," she screams. Mort is not comforting her. He remains stoic in his chair. Rose sobs, holding herself, bent over. Her tears spill onto the carpet. Her Samuel. Her baby! He didn't have to go. He got good grades in college, but being a first-generation American on his papa's side, Sam felt he needed to prove something. So what did he prove? How much a mother's heart can be broken?

Friends and relatives bring food, but Rose cannot eat. Mort has retreated into that dark place where he goes with his Holocaust memories. She hates him for that. Her daughters are gathered around her, crying, begging for comfort. The world has stopped. Rose's heart has stopped. Life has stopped.

She knows Sam is dead, although the telegram said "presumed dead," and wants to start shiva right away. Mort doesn't. Jewish law is hazy about this, but Mort will not grieve his son until they learn exactly what happened to Sam. She knows they will never be told the details, and why would they matter? She hates Mort for holding out, delaying the inevitable good-bye to their son. After two weeks of suffering, with Mort hiding in his room, Rose takes it upon herself to make shiva arrangements with the rabbi, friends, and family. She cannot keep Sam waiting. She can't wait any longer. Limbo is too lonely a place to be.

Mameh and Aunt Ruth are getting food out of the refrigerator for shiva. People will bring more food that will make Rose sick to look at. And instead of being comforted by the boiled eggs representing the cycle of life, the dead-fart smell gags her. Her feet are lead weights, and she is useless to help in any way. "CeCe, light the shiva candle for me," she says. She goes through the Jewish motions, like she has all her life, but no way in hell does that wick and flame represent Sam's body and soul to her. The girls put up folding chairs for visitors as the practice of sitting shiva begins. Mirrors are covered. Mort is still in hiding, the son of a bitch.

For years she and the kids have tiptoed around Mort, afraid to disturb him. But no more. Rose flings open the door of Mort's study, where he sits with the heavy curtains drawn shut, closing out any speck of light. "Leave me!" he says.

"Leave you? Who the hell do you think you are? The king of Persia?" She pulls open a curtain panel. "And you're not fucking Bela Lugosi. Our son is dead. Our son. Yours and mine." Mort stands, and she is in his face. "I hate you! You and your sick, dark soul!" She pounds on his chest as if to start up a heart that is missing, presumed dead.

He holds her at a distance, hard, by the shoulders. "I'm sorry," he says. His eyes are dark and empty, his expression flat.

"You're sorry? Is that it?" She may laugh or cry—it could go either way. Her breathing changes, and she explodes into hysterical laughter. "You're such a coward, Mort. I pity you," she spits the words. "And I'm the one who's sorry, because I wish it were you instead of him."

Rose opened her eyes, and there was Sam, plain as day. He stood at the foot of her bed, a shy smile after all this time, a wave like he was passing on his bike. He wore a nice suit and tie. "You look so handsome," said Rose. She wanted to hold him, feel the weight of his arms around her, smell the aftershave he always wore. His fair face, so young, with its smattering of light freckles, his blue eyes like Rachel's, his hair almost strawberry blond.

"It's been a long time. I wanted to impress you," Sam said. He did a funny J. C. Penney catalog pose, and she laughed.

"It's so good to see you, son." Rose was afraid to blink. "I got old, and you didn't."

"I love you, Mom. Don't worry, we'll see each other again soon." Sam slowly dissipated into a small bright orb and then vanished.

"Such a terrible time when we lost Sam. The rest of us kids, we weren't allowed to talk about it. I remember feeling so alone, and yet we were all going through the same nightmare," CeCe said to Rose over their morning coffee. Rose had been up earlier than CeCe and had spread old photographs all over the kitchen table, retrieved from her dilapidated hatbox. "We saw what you went through with Papa. He provided no comfort to you or to any of us."

"I haven't looked at these for years. Look, here's one of Sam holding you. He was almost eight by the time you were born." Rose smiled now, remembering Sam's appearance in his suit and J. C. Penney pose. The pain of losing him had subsided, replaced by a longing to see him again. She didn't want to diminish Sam's visit by speaking of it, so she didn't tell CeCe.

CeCe held the photograph a moment and then picked up another one. "I worshiped my big brother. Look," she said, reaching into her plaid work shirt and pulling out Sam's dog tags. "When you and Papa were so mean to Miguel and me, I stole these after our wedding at the courthouse. I wear them most days, to keep him close."

"I wondered where they went. I think I even accused your father of hiding them from me or throwing them out. I'm glad you took them. I would never tell your sisters this, but I think you were Sam's favorite. He'd like that you have them."

"Ma, what do you believe in—I mean, for an afterlife? Do you think you'll see loved ones, maybe be with Sam again?"

"I'd like to think so, but I'm not making any plans. You know, 'Der mentsh trakht un Got lakht'—'Man plans and God laughs.' That one was a favorite of my papa," Rose said. "I do think that for me to die in peace, I have to forgive your father," she added. "It's not going to be easy."

"I had to find my peace with him, too. It took a while."

"I don't have that much time," Rose said. She saw the color leave CeCe's face. "Sorry, but it's true. I'm getting my affairs in order." She laughed, but the slow, suffocating congestion in her chest caused her to cough and gasp. She caught a blob of phlegm in her flowered hankie. It felt like a warm hatchling in her palm. "I think I need to graduate to an industrial-sized man's handkerchief." CeCe took it from her and handed her some water, which was hard to drink when she already felt as if she was drowning.

"You signed that living will, saying you don't want any more medical treatment. But Ma, what if you have only a mild heart attack, or maybe just a touch of pneumonia . . . what if they can make you better? We could have more time."

Rose's heart twisted in her chest. In a good way. In a way that told her how much her daughter really loved her and that Rose was sorry to have to leave her. "CeCe, I'm ninety-one years old. I love you, but it's the end. *Finito*." God, it felt good to speak Italian again.

Her daughter sighed, pain etching her face and causing her to look her age. "I know I have to respect your wishes."

Rose almost blurted, "Well, that would be a first." But they were moving beyond the barbs, so she caught herself. Instead she squeezed her daughter's hand. "We have now, *bubeleh*."

Rose hooked her trifooted cane onto her scooter, wrapped her lunch in a tea towel, and headed down her ramp and into the bright November day. It was the closest to running away as she could get. But why was she still running?

The peacock, Pretty Boy, flew from the top of the barn to get a better gander at her. He cocked his head and stared. "What are you looking at?" Rose said. Whenever she came out to the barnyard, she thought of Mort and how he had found solace there in his last years. They made quite a couple in Esperanza. Probably the best years of their lives. She guessed she had loved him by then.

Rose nibbled at her cheese and crackers. The horses had come to the fence to watch her. She threw cracker crumbs for the doves that rained down from the trees. A crow flew by with a pecan in its beak. The chickens scratched rhythmically through dry leaves around her, making contented clucking sounds. She closed her eyes against the beacon of the warming sun. It was all so beautiful. She felt swaddled by radiance . . .

Crash! Mort stomps on the wineglass, and everyone yells, "Mazel tov!" Rose and Mort sit in chairs that are held high in the air by celebrators who parade them around the room. She laughs with Mort as they reach for each other. He is not the man he used to be when they first met. She has nursed him back to humanity after a torturous past. He is forever grateful to her. He smiles now with a full set of teeth. He gives her purpose. Who is the grateful one?

Rose flies through time as if she is caught on the wind. Mort walks into her parents' apartment, where he and she are living until they can save enough money to get a place of their own. He holds something behind his back. She is fat and heavy with child, and her back aches. "What are you hiding?" she asks. "Did you trade rationing coins? Is it a pair of nylons?"

"Better," he says in his thick Yiddish accent. He produces a fat envelope, but it doesn't look like nylons. "Mr. Seinfeld is retiring and moving to Florida. I bought his shop. It comes with the apartment. You'll be in the same building as your Aunt Ruth." Mort has worked for Mr. Seinfeld as a top-notch tailor since he arrived in New York. This is their dream. Rose jumps into his arms and gets as close as the baby will allow. "It is all because of you, my dear Rose." The baby kicks and squirms. She takes his hands and places them on her belly. His eyes widen as the tiny feet dance.

When she goes into labor, Mort doesn't leave her side, even though he is strongly urged to stay in the waiting room. He brings in a copy of Psalm 121. That is why Papa loves Mort. He knows his Jewish education. After Mort's torture by the Nazis, he is more determined than ever to keep his Jewish way of life. Mort holds her hand when the pain grips her.

When he sees the baby is a boy, he cries. She cries, too, and reaches to hold her baby. She grasps Mort's hand. He is beaming, and she is deliriously happy. Together they name him Samuel, to open his soul to the universe.

She is lifted up and away to twelve years later, and Mort's tailor business is doing well. She is in a rented car, sitting in the passenger seat. All five kids are in the backseats of the station wagon, singing some annoying song. Mort is driving them to the Catskills, where they can now afford to vacation. Mort is not a sociable man, but he feels most comfortable surrounded by other Jews speaking Yiddish. Henny Youngman will be there. He makes Mort smile. "Take my wife, please!"

Mort and Sam take golf lessons. The girls follow a handsome tummler around the resort, the recreation guy who conjures up activities for the kids. Rose sits drinking a Tom Collins with the other wives while keeping one eye on the kids. They compliment Rose on her hair, which she has finally been dyeing red. At night, Sam babysits his younger siblings in the hotel room while she and Mort go to the comedy clubs or out to dance the mambo. Mort hates dancing, but he does it for her. He is more lenient than Papa in his ways, especially as he gives the children in money what he cannot give openly with his heart. On vacation, he tries hard to make Rose happy. And she is.

"Bubbe, are you all right?" Rose woke to Hattie standing in front of her. "I'm just checking. Looked like you were about to slip off your scooter," Hattie continued. "Pretty Boy might land on your head while you're sleeping." Hattie made kissing sounds at the iridescent blue bird, like Mort used to. She looked like Red Riding Hood in her red hoodie, holding her basket of pinecones.

Rose had no idea how long she had been out. "What are you going to do with those?" she asked.

"Maggie and Diego and I are going to make Thanksgiving decorations. Little kids always need something to do." As her great-granddaughter stood there, Rose realized Hattie was a part of her and Mort.

As were Rachel and CeCe. And the other kids and their children. Together she and Mort had created a continuing stream of life. She and Mort. Her husband.

Hattie and Maggie had gotten out of school early on Wednesday before the long Thanksgiving holiday. They entertained Diego at the kitchen table as he learned the magic of drawing a turkey by tracing the outline of his fingers on paper. He colored it before Maggie cut it out with blunt-nose scissors.

Hattie showed him her pinecone turkey. "Can I have it?" He reached for it.

"You can make your own, how about that?" said Hattie.

"And finish your milk, please," Maggie said, taking her role of aunt seriously.

CeCe watched and thought about when Abby had adopted Santi—how adding him to their extended family had enriched everyone. He had changed them all. And now Diego was doing the same thing. Too bad Santi had to miss out on Thanksgiving at home this year, especially when they had even more to be thankful for. CeCe promised to send him some pumpkin pecan cookies but told him they wouldn't taste as good as he remembered because he wouldn't be eating them at home. A nudge of Jewish guilt.

Miguel came in the door carrying one of the chile *ristras* that had been hanging on the back porch since October. He could not have turkey without red chile. He went to the children and tapped each of them with a kiss on the head, duck, duck, goose style. Rose came from the other direction, pushing her walker. Her portable oxygen tank hung on her shoulder like a small gym bag. "Boy, this oxygen makes me high," she said with a big smile. "What can I do to help?"

By now Miguel was at the sink, running the water to rinse and remove the stems of the chile pods. "I'd have you peel potatoes, but there's no room at the sink," CeCe said. "Here, let me make room for you at the counter."

"Don't be silly. Miguel and I can squeeze in here together." Rose pushed her walker aside, stepped up to the sink, and bumped Miguel aside with her small butt. "Miguel, have I ever told you about my best friend, Ida Goldblatt, and the things we used to get away with? You girls cover your ears," she told Hattie and Maggie.

Rose babbled happily at the sink with Miguel, who still had on his cowboy hat, his head bent to listen or thrown back in laughter. CeCe imagined Rose slowly fading from Miguel's side until she had vanished completely, leaving only silence and an empty place behind.

Santiago had worked eleven long days—each one punctuated only by the number of hours of sleep he could count on one hand—since his return. As he crossed items off his protracted to-do list, a sense of competence returned. No longer was he the unavailable slacker whose messy personal life interrupted and threatened their shared venture. He was restored as the wunderkind in whom Gordon had entrusted his faith.

When Gordon arranged the annual Hopkins Thanksgiving ski trip to Aspen, Kat convinced Santiago they should stay behind, take advantage of Reggie's absence, and celebrate their own private holiday at home. Santi loved to ski and had been to the Hopkinses' ski chalet in Aspen several times over the years, but sleep sounded good, too, as did not disappointing Kat.

He'd assumed they would attend some obnoxious Thanksgiving buffet, so he was surprised on Wednesday evening when he heard cussing and banging outside their door. He put down the manuscript he had been reviewing. He found Kat struggling up the three flights of stairs with her roller cart piled with groceries. He hadn't even noticed she had gone out.

He watched as Kat retrieved a pomegranate that had made a run for it, chasing it down half a flight of stairs. She held it up in victory. "Ta-da!"

"What is this?" he asked.

"It's our Thanksgiving dinner." She wheeled the cart past him into the apartment.

"But you don't cook."

"You do. And I'll be your capable assistant. I have recipes from online magazines," she said. "It'll be fun." She batted her huge eyes at him; her face was flushed but smiling from her struggle up the stairs. With her short black bangs and her hair in two high pigtails, she looked like a kid. Cute, but young. Her hopeful expression persuaded him to go with the plan.

"Okay, well, let's see what you have here," he said, lifting the bags onto the kitchen island.

Kat read from her list as he unpacked. "We'll have turkey, of course. See, it's a cute little twelve pounder. With fresh herb dressing, sweet potatoes, mashed white potatoes with gravy, roasted brussels sprouts with bacon and pine nuts, cranberry-orange-pomegranate sauce, and the pumpkin pie is from Stella Pastry & Café." She hugged him from behind. "With Reggie gone, we can do whatever we want, wherever we want, for four whole days and nights."

He hugged her back. "We shall cook up a feast to rival all feasts in the land, m'lady."

"You've been reading that sixteenth-century historical mystery submission, haven't you? What do you think about it—no, don't answer that. You are hereby banned from further work until Monday next. Only supping, slumbering, and great frivolity will be allowed, as decreed by Queen Katrina the First."

"Am I the king?"

"The king is elderly and infirm. You are my dashing consort, Prince Santiago from Spain. Once the king shuffles off his mortal coil and receives his heavenly reward, we will unite our kingdoms." She began to kiss him deeply, blotting out his thought that her scenario seemed to reflect an underlying agenda.

Over the years Santiago had assisted Abby, CeCe, and Rachel in preparing sumptuous Thanksgiving dinners for more than a dozen hungry mouths, so this Thanksgiving for two was a snap. He instructed Kat how to properly use a chef's knife, something Abby taught him when he was ten. With double ovens, a six-burner professional stove top, and plenty of prep space, this kitchen made it all the easier. In Abby's kitchen, they had made do with a cutting board atop the washing machine and a four-burner 1950s-era gas stove and oven. Still, she managed to turn out some of the best food he'd ever tasted.

He and Kat woke on Thursday morning to a cold drizzle and dark skies, conducive to staying in and cooking. Kat turned on the old movie station with the sound muted and played Django Reinhardt jazz albums on her turntable.

"I wish I'd thought about bringing back some of Magdalena's sage," Santiago said.

"Whose what?"

"Magdalena Silva, Bobby's mother—my sister, Maggie, is named after her. You know Abby lives in Bobby's parents' house, right? Magdalena had these sage plants, shrubs actually, that are still going strong. It produces the best sage, and it's a tradition to use it when we make Thanksgiving dinner."

Kat put her hand on top of his as they stood side by side in front of the island. He met her eyes. "Santi, the whole point of this—cooking Thanksgiving dinner together—is to start making our own traditions. New traditions."

He wanted to tell her that traditions are passed down, that he treasured the traditions Abby carefully introduced him to when he moved into her house following his father's death. His father had committed suicide when he was surrounded by cops and unwilling to surrender. Even as she grieved Bobby in the final difficult weeks of her pregnancy with Maggie, she turned her attentions to his needs, reading to him at bedtime, cooking their meals together, planting red geraniums in the spring, and snipping the velvet leaves from Magdalena's sage bush in the fall. After Maggie was born they brought her into their traditions. Abby encouraged him, as the big brother, to help care for her, read to her, feed her mashed peas, rock her. He saw now it wasn't about teaching him to be helpful—it was about forging their bonds as a family. It was about love.

What was he teaching his son? What traditions was he passing on to him?

"Why do you look so sad?" Kat asked. "Is Magdalena's sage so much better than what I brought home?"

"No, no. I was just thinking about some of the family traditions I grew up with, after Abby took me in. I'm glad Diego will experience a lot of the same things I did." When he saw the look on her face he added, "I like this, cooking with you, starting our own traditions. I guess I'm just a little homesick. This is the first year I haven't been home for Thanksgiving."

"Or maybe it's the first year you're home for Thanksgiving with me."

Kat set the table with her great-grandmother's china. She lit long tapered candles in the silver candelabra. She decided they would dress for dinner. She emerged from her room in a vintage cocktail dress, black satin with rhinestones, with a low-cut neckline that accentuated her voluptuous figure. Her hair was loose, her lips were red. The little girl look was vanquished.

He'd chosen black trousers and a white shirt. He found a vintage tie looped onto his doorknob, light green with an Art Deco leaping antelope design in rust and black, so he put it on.

She was making martinis in the shaker. Nineteen-twenties Parisian jazz played in the background, a female singer with a nasal, high-pitched voice crooning. "Josephine Baker," Kat said, handing him his drink. The turkey rested under foil. The gravy yielded slow, luxurious bubbles as it thickened on low heat. Santi gave it a stir to make sure it wasn't trying to stick.

"Do you want to carve the bird while I transfer everything else to serving dishes?"

"We could just fill our plates here," he said. "Saves on dishes."

"We are not bohemians."

The turkey appeared moist; the knife slid through the meat like butter. The convection oven had produced a crisp caramelized skin. He placed a selection of white and dark meat onto the platter she provided. He saw that it was four o'clock, five in Esperanza. His family would have eaten by now. If the weather was good, Charlie and Miguel would be tossing horseshoes, perhaps commenting on the fact that Santi was not there for them to beat. He knew they were at CeCe and Miguel's this year, so that Rose could comfortably join them. Would Rosalinda be hanging out with the women, or would she be watching Miguel teach Diego how to toss a horseshoe?

He finished his martini and ate the olive—his first nibble of the day. Kat opened a bottle of Pinot Noir for the meal. "Daddy brought this back from France last year, from the Nuits-Saint-Georges region." She had been teaching him about wine and handed him a glass for his approval.

He closed his eyes and sniffed, swirled, swished, and tasted. "Raspberry, vanilla, cloves, with a light oak finish."

"Very good. It's anchored with some wet leaves and mushroom notes, sometimes called autumnal undergrowth, the earthiness that adds so much complexity to a good Pinot Noir."

After the gravy was ladled into its boat, the turkey platter garnished, and the serving dishes transferred to the table, he pulled out her chair. Since the Hopkinses were atheists, instead of a prayer, Kat raised her glass for a toast. "Happy Thanksgiving to us."

"Happy Thanksgiving to us." He clinked her glass.

After they ate, they lingered at the table and finished the bottle of wine. "God! Everything was so incredible!" Kat said.

"Those Brussels sprouts were addictive. Well, everything was. Thanks for arranging it—it was a fun day. And thanks for saying you'd do all the cleaning up."

"I never—Santi! At least we have a dishwasher for everything but the china."

"Or we could leave it for Reggie," Santi said. For all of Reggie's otherwise slovenly ways, he was a renowned kitchen-cleaning dish-washing ninja.

"I don't think even I could stand the mess for three more days. We'll just do it fast and then slowly help each other get out of these clothes," she said. "Why don't you go make your call to Diego and I'll get started? But I don't want to get any grease on this dress." She stood up, unzipped and slithered out of the dress. She stood in her black lace bustier, garters attached to black sheer stockings, still in her black stilettos, and tied on an apron. "Hurry back."

He called Rosalinda's cell, and she answered on the first ring. "Hi, happy Thanksgiving."

"Yeah, you, too. How did it go?" Santi asked.

"Abby and I went over to CeCe's to get started cooking by eight thirty this morning. Ben and Maggie stayed with Diego until later. After they came over, even Diego helped. I felt really good—it might have been the first day that I didn't even think about pain, and I was able to eat a little bit of everything. Abby's been so much nicer since we talked. Oh, Diego and Hattie did the wishbone pull, since they're the two youngest, and he got the big end, so his wish will come true. He was so excited."

"Did he get to play horseshoes?"

"Yes, it was a beautiful day. Charlie and Miguel let him stand like three feet away from the stake when they were teaching him to pitch." She laughed. "He managed to throw a ringer."

Her laugh warmed him. "Hey, before you put him on, could you take the phone around so I can say, 'Happy Thanksgiving' to everyone?"

"Santi, this is the first time I've ever really celebrated Thanksgiving. Your family is so good to me and Diego. I have so much to be thankful for."

"They're your family now, too, you know."

After Santi visited with everyone—except Rose, who was napping—Diego got on the phone. "Daddy, the moon is a ball. Miguel says it's Frost Moon because the frost comes at night when it gets cold, like frosting."

Santi stood at his window. "The moon is hiding behind clouds here, but I can see the bright spot, so I know where it is."

"Is it playing hide-and-seek? I play it with Maggie and Hattie."

"Yes, it's hiding, but I found it. Did you eat lots of turkey?"

"I ate a leg with Charlie. We chewed it like dogs."

"I'm glad you're having a good Thanksgiving."

"I made a ringer! The horseshoe is heavy, so I have big muscles."

"Mama told me. I'm very proud of you. I love you, son."

"I love you, Daddy." He heard kissing noises, so he made some, only to hear Rosalinda laugh. "It's me. Diego ran off to find the girls. He said he wants to play hide-and-seek."

"I'm counting the days until I can be there with him—with everyone. I miss you guys."

"We miss you, too. Hey, I didn't even ask, how was your Thanksgiving?"

"Good. We cooked, too. Now I have to help clean up, so I better go. Kiss Diego for me. Tell him his daddy loves him."

"We—I mean—*he* loves you, too."

"Good-bye, Rosalinda." He ended the call, standing in the dark, looking out on the city lights, savoring the fresh sound of everyone's voices.

His bedroom door opened, sending a shaft of light into the darkness. Kat stood silhouetted in the doorway.

"Why are you in the dark?"

He switched on his bedside lamp. "I was trying to see the moon, but it's behind clouds."

"I thought maybe you fell asleep in here, it's been so long."

"I talked to everyone, since it's Thanksgiving. I hope you left something for me to do."

She walked over to him and put her arms around him and spoke into his ear. "Food is put away. I loaded the dishwasher and hand-washed and dried the china. You can go check to see if I missed anything, if you really need something to do."

"I can think of something I really need to do right here." He kissed her.

"And then, pie," she said, pulling him down on the bed.

December

LONG NIGHT MOON

Chapter Nineteen

SANTIAGO COUNTED THE days until his Christmas trip home. Through his college years, winter break had lasted an entire month, and he'd always spent it at home. He assumed he'd have about two weeks off, but Gordon decided they would close only during the week of Christmas and be back to work the following Monday, so as to have a few days to conduct business before the end of the year. In that case, Santi would fly home Saturday the twentieth and fly back on Sunday the twenty-eighth, to carve out as much time with his family as possible.

As he was perusing his flight options online, Kat hung at his elbow. "Before you do that, let's talk." She handed him his mug of coffee, reheated, which he must have abandoned somewhere in the apartment. She sat next to him at the kitchen island.

"It's the sixth already. If I'm flying on the twentieth, that's only two weeks from today—peak travel time—so I'm already pushing it." He took a sip of his coffee. "I needed this, thanks."

"Santi, I think I should go with you."

He looked at her, shocked into silence.

"It's time I meet your family."

"You've met them—and my sister."

"In college. And not in our present context. I haven't met your extended family or seen where you grew up. I haven't met your son." Her tone was level but firm.

"Look, that's really nice you want to do that, but we only have a week—it'll be rushed. My house is too small for everyone as it is,"

Santi said, wondering why he felt such a visceral reaction against her suggestion. His stomach clenched, his heart pounded.

"I could stay with your neighbor friends. I didn't think we'd be sharing a bed, anyway. I could crash on the couch—it doesn't matter. The point is we'd spend Christmas together."

As he looked into her pleading eyes, he thought about how young she was. She had graduated from her exclusive private girls' school two years early and had started at UCLA at sixteen, when he was eighteen; he had turned nineteen in their freshman year. Reggie was his age, but his younger sister had caught up to him, and they were in the same class. While she was advanced academically, her emotional maturation had stayed age appropriate, one of the reasons he'd never looked at her as more than a kid sister. "As much as I'd really love to have you there, I don't think this is the right time. This trip is for me to spend time with Diego, my first visit home since he and I met for the first time and since the trauma that happened right after that. It's just too confusing to introduce a new person right away. He needs to see that even though I live far away and he doesn't get to see me for weeks at a time, when I am there, he has my total focus. He's only three and a half. I'll take you home to meet everyone after Diego trusts we have a schedule he can rely on and that he's my top priority. What he needs has to come before what we'd like."

"You act like I'd be in the way—that I'm some selfish girl who would compete with a child for your time and attention. That's total bullshit, Santi. I can hang back, give you guys some space. I'd take walks, read, hang with your friends." Tears began spilling from her eyes.

"You're taking this too personally. I can't give Diego anything new to deal with right now. I'm still building trust with him, and it's going to take longer because I'm away so much."

"Is this about Rosalinda?"

"What? No. This is about Diego. Why isn't he reason enough?"

"Because I see you talking to her, your expression. You never look at me that way. And you talk about stuff that isn't about Diego—like what she's been doing, how far did she walk, how much did she eat, laughing with her and going on and on. Don't even deny it."

He shook his head, shocked. "We had a lot to work out while I was there, but we're on good terms now. It's better for Diego and for us, since we have to find a way to coparent. We went through hell together. She almost died, and I care about her a lot. Please don't do this."

"Me? You treat me as if I'm just some friend with benefits, not even significant enough to spend Christmas with—"

"Why do you care about Christmas? You don't even believe in it."

"I don't have to believe in Santa Claus or the Big Daddy in the sky to want to be with the man I love on the most important holiday of the year. I knew you were going to be against it."

"Is this some kind of loyalty test? I already chose to be here in San Francisco with you."

"Only because your precious job is here, and if you want that, you're stuck with me."

"Look, I'm going home for one measly week to be with my son for Christmas, and no, it isn't a good time to bring you along. That's all this is. It's not about me dissing you or not caring about your feelings. We just had a great Thanksgiving together. Why can't you trust me?"

Kat blew her nose and seemed to be trying to pull it together. "I've been your friend for over four years. I've watched how you treat girls. You hold back and then act all innocent when they get hurt. I thought I had an edge because you cared about not hurting me, you cared about not fucking up your friendship with my brother or damaging the high regard my father holds for you. I thought you'd finally grown up and were ready for something real."

"You're extrapolating all this shit because I'm not willing to take you home for a week when I visit my son. I'm not doing this to you. If you're choosing to be hurt and read all this crap into it, I can't stop you. But if we can't get past this, it won't be because of me."

"Ever since I met you, you were all about getting away from where you came from, launching a new life far away from there. Now you are hooked back in because you have a kid there, and a baby mama—your first great love—hell, your only love, as far as I've seen. How am I supposed to compete with that?"

"You can believe what I am saying—it's about trust, Kat. I get that when we started this, I wasn't a dad. You didn't sign on for that. But now I am a dad, and I'm going to do it right, because my dad fucked it up and I'm not going to be like him. I know how that feels, and I'm not doing it to Diego. Where my kid is concerned, there is no competition."

Kat let out a sigh that sounded like defeat. "My whole life I competed with Reggie, older by twenty months. I was really little when I realized I had two strikes against me: I was female and I was younger. I saw what was important to our dad, to our family. When I was three and Reggie started kindergarten, I taught myself to read and write. I was already better than him, and my dad noticed and started tutoring me—mom had left us by then. When I joined Reggie in elementary school, I kicked his ass and skipped a grade. In middle school and high school, we went to separate schools, but I was still kicking his ass. I skipped another grade. He got accepted to UCLA, and I got accepted to all five Ivy League schools I applied for, but I went to UCLA to be with him because he asked me to. See, he wanted his little sister to be with him after years of going to different schools. He missed me. To him, it had never been a competition." She smiled and shrugged her shoulders. "I don't know why I'm this way. I've been driven to win for as long as I can remember. A shrink told me it was because our mother left us and I'm still trying to win her back. I spent four years trying to win you, and now that I have you, I'm fucking it up."

Santiago reached for her, and she stepped into his open arms. He held her for a minute or so before speaking. "You don't have anything to worry about. I'm here. I'm sorry my life got so complicated. I was away for a month last time; this will only be a week. And then I'm back on the twenty-eighth. We'll have New Year's. You can plan whatever you want for our celebration. All I care about is we'll be together."

Her arms tightened around his waist.

Reggie emerged from his room after a late Friday night of video gaming, open robe over boxer shorts, black-framed glasses askew, curly russet hair and beard considerably past due for maintenance. He shuffled over and put his arms around the two of them, laying his head on Santi's shoulder, not one to pass up the chance for a group hug.

Abby drove down the interstate south to Esperanza after she and Rosalinda had been Christmas shopping in Albuquerque. Abby glanced in her direction. "How are you holding up?"

"Better than I thought I would. At least the crowds weren't too bad." Rosalinda didn't tell her it was hard to be back in Albuquerque, that she had developed a kind of phobia about returning to where she had lived, first alone and then with Jesse. Her heart palpitated and her palms sweated as she looked at the wide-angle view of the Sandia Mountains, their looming presence defining Albuquerque. When she gazed at their snowy crest, she knew that somewhere up there, on the east slope, stood the cabin where her baby boy had suffered and could have died. She had to remind herself that it was Caden who perished there. But now, as they headed home, putting miles between them and the fast-paced, stressed-out hordes of city dwellers, she began to relax.

"You're sure Santi will like the new shirts and slacks we got him?" Abby asked.

Rosalinda shrugged. Santiago looked handsome in his professional attire, but it seemed unnatural. She preferred his Esperanza work clothes: old jeans, boots, pearl-covered snaps on his body-hugging shirt. She used to love to rip those snaps open. "He can use them for his job."

"Let's cross him off as done. For Ben I ordered those books he wanted and a new field backpack; his old one is falling apart and smells like river muck. Maggie's list is long, but I've found a few things. Except for stocking stuffers, are we done shopping for Diego?"

"You got him all those clothes, books, and toys. I'd say he's done. You know he has a birthday in March already." Rosalinda let out a big sigh as Abby exited the freeway to Highway 47, which would return them to Esperanza. Now her view was of the Manzano Mountains beyond the Isleta Pueblo. The landscape, dormant farm fields in the valley and the surrounding rugged high-desert terrain, appeared dry beneath the bright sun. Yesterday, snow had teased them with sparse flakes that disappeared even as she and Diego wished for them to multiply. She longed for the beauty of snow, a silent, thick layer to cover the relentless sea of brown. Even that kind of snow never lasted long, shrinking away to a day of mud before drying up altogether and making one question if it had been real or merely a winter's dream.

Last night, after Santi talked to Diego, he had stayed on the phone with her for another half hour. Abby gave Diego his bath while she stayed in their room, listening to him talk about his day, how the fog was so thick you needed an umbrella and raincoat or you were soaked by the time you reached your destination, and even then, your eyelashes and hair became slick with it, your face enveloped in a fine sheen. He described the sagging clouds that seemed suspended between the taller buildings like a blanket fort. She listened, her eyes shut, drinking in his voice. Wondering why he sounded lonely; wondering why his loneliness felt in tune with hers.

Back when they were together, after making love, she was the one who always fought sleep while he became talkative, his words droning into something like music or like a priest delivering Mass during one of the rare times someone took her to church when she was young. She couldn't imagine who that would have been—certainly not her mother or any other relative. Maybe one of the neighbors, who sometimes fed and bathed her when no one else was getting around to it, had taken her in some righteous attempt to save her soul. What she had really needed was someone to save her from her family.

Rosalinda wished she knew the words to tell Abby how grateful she was that she didn't have to worry about providing for Diego anymore. She thanked Abby repeatedly. But repeating her gratitude sometimes felt like it diluted instead of strengthened her sincerity. She had always had ample love for her son, but trying to meet his physical needs had been a relentless strain, a struggle whose victories included finding day-old bread for a quarter, scoring garage sale clothes that fit him and weren't too stained or faded, and then meeting Jesse, who made good on his promise to help provide for them both. Jesse, who would still be alive if Rosalinda had never uttered Abby's name.

"We'll go straight to Rachel's to store our gifts, since there's no room at our house—she usually gives me the guest room closet. Later on, we women will have a wrapping party there with Carmen, Bonnie, and your girl Hazel, CeCe's cabal. They always show up, bearing trays of homemade Christmas cookies and CDs of holiday music," Abby said. "Bonnie always smuggles in some margarita fixings. No kids or men allowed. Miguel will host them for their own wrapping party at the same time. Some bizarre packages come out of that soirée, let me tell you. You should have seen the time Charlie wrapped a new saddle for Rachel."

When Rosalinda pictured the men's wrapping party, she saw Santiago with them. "Maybe Santi will be home in time to join them."

"Our wrapping parties are usually pretty close to Christmas Eve to allow for last-minute shopping, and he'll be home on the twentieth, so he'll be there." Abby pulled the car onto the lane leading to Rachel's house. "When Santiago first moved in with me, right before Maggie was born, it took him a few years to be able to enjoy Christmas—or any holiday, for that matter. I had to be patient, wait for him to make some new memories and let go of some of the old ones that gave him dark circles under his eyes. It was so gradual, like watching him thaw. But he did, and it was a beautiful thing to witness."

"You did more than witness it. It never would have happened without you."

Abby looked at her and then back to the road as she drove slowly through the gate. "That's what you think?"

"That's what I know."

Abby parked next to Charlie's truck. "Well, that's sweet of you to say."

"Abby, it's not something sweet to say! It's the truth. You're so giving and loving, and you don't even realize how much people need that, people who don't even know how much they need it until you give it to them. And it's so powerful it's scary, but even though you're scared, you grab onto it like some kind of life preserver, and words . . . words just aren't enough to express how much it means—" she stopped when she realized she was crying. "Shit," she said, wiping her face, turning away from Abby's startled expression.

She felt Abby's hand on her shoulder. "Words are enough."

Later, when Rosalinda suggested to Abby that she felt ready to start looking for a place to rent, Abby put her off with some excuses and then said, "Besides, I think it's too soon. The doctor hasn't cleared your lifting restriction yet, and you know you'll end up having to pick him up if it's just the two of you."

"But it might take a month or so of looking before we find the right place. I don't want to have to move again for a long time. I think Diego needs stability." She almost added that she needed stability, too, a place she could fix up for the two of them. Somewhere safe, private, with a yard for Diego to play in and for her to dig a vegetable garden and plant flowers. Somewhere not too far away. Something she could afford once she was working, along with Santi's child support. It was bad enough Abby would have to pay her rent until she could work, but it was either that or be underfoot until she could save up for her own place.

"I figured we'd start looking after the holidays, after Santiago goes home and things settle down," Abby said. "What do you think—will that work for you?"

"I guess it makes sense to wait."

And then Abby shocked her by saying, "I'll be so sad to see you guys move out. And I mean both of you. I'll miss all the time we have together now, shuffling around in our pajamas before breakfast. It's so different from a visit. It's never the same."

"After we move, I hope it can be like how you and CeCe and Rachel are, how you just go between each other's houses like they are different rooms in one giant house, like family."

Abby smiled. "You *are* family."

"Do you want me to wait so you can help pick out his bicycle?" Rosalinda said over the phone to Santiago. Hazel was hanging on her every word as they walked in the bosque along the arroyo.

"That would be great. It's going to be his Santa present, right?"

"That's what we said. He'll need training wheels for a while and a helmet."

"And elbow and knee pads. Let's just wrap him in bubble wrap for the next decade or so." Santi laughed. "I can't wait to see him. One more week."

"I wish you could stay longer," she said as Hazel raised her eyebrows.

"Me, too, but I think once we get into the rhythm of monthly visits, it'll get easier. Well, Kat's waiting on me. Take care. Hug and kiss our boy for me. I'll call him tonight."

"Bye," she said and put her phone back into her pocket.

Water rushed through the arroyo after the recent rain and the few inches of melted snow, but Esperanza would still be ending the year in a moderate drought. In this part of the bosque, the cottonwood trees were thick and gnarled. Even without their foliage, the sunlight dappled through the dense canopy, creating scattered splashes of light.

"When Santiago comes home, tell him how you feel," Hazel said.

"Horseshit," Rosalinda said, stepping around the recent evidence that Charlie, Rachel, and the girls had been riding on the trail.

"Funny. If you don't tell him, maybe I will."

"You better not, old lady. You don't know how I feel."

Hazel laughed. "Chica, it's all over your face every time you talk to him. You are going to have to wear a bag over your head if you don't want people to know."

Damn that Hazel. Rosalinda handled her feelings for Santi by distancing herself from them. She was good at it. But how could she remain detached with Hazel constantly stirring things up? She stopped in her tracks. "Reality check: Santiago has made his life in San Francisco, with his girlfriend, Kat."

"I hear Kat's a real pussy."

Rosalinda ignored her. "Santi and I have a great relationship now. I'm not going to make things all awkward between us."

Hazel put out her hand. "I'm going to bet you, right here and right now, on this the thirteenth day of December, Santiago feels the same way about you as you do about him."

"You've been reading too many bad romance novels." Rosalinda walked past Hazel's outstretched hand.

"I don't read romance novels. Heterosexual sex is a bore. Joan gave me some lovely lesbian erotica to read."

"You and Joan are getting serious fast."

"Carpe diem, chica. Snooze, you lose."

They walked back in silence. Rosalinda's thoughts moved on to imagining her new, independent life and feeling grateful that Abby was facilitating her transition into it. She would live modestly, as she always had, working hard and saving whatever money wasn't spent on Diego's needs each month. She would go back to school to set an example for her son. She would not squander the opportunities before her, and she would not become distracted by wanting a man who did not want her.

As December's chill set in, Rose felt increasingly confined to the house. Getting around became more difficult. She felt as if she had lived her whole life over in the past months, and it exhausted her. Yet it also shifted everything she had experienced into a different perspective and caused her dying heart to feel new again.

She was now addicted to the old western channel. She threw her fists against the bad guys and chewed on her thumbnail, wondering if the good guy would get rescued in time. She imagined slinging her leg over a horse, and eating beans out of a tin plate, and shooting like Annie Oakley. Watching *Cheyenne* and *Maverick* brought back memories of when the kids were young and so was she. She sang along to the familiar theme songs, remembering how the kids would cover their eyes when Cheyenne would take off his shirt, showing his forty-eight-inch chest and tiny waist, Rose's favorite part.

She skipped her afternoon nap to watch *High Noon*. She couldn't help herself. Gary Cooper resembled Nick so much. She couldn't take her eyes off the screen.

Her bedroom door opened a crack. Rachel peeked in. "Bubbe?"

"Racheleh! Come see what Nick looked like," Rose said proudly. She welcomed the chance to share him.

Rachel sat down next to Rose on the bed. "He's really handsome," she said as she played nervously with a folded piece of copy paper. "This is weird timing."

"*Vas?*"

"I thought I'd give you an early Chanukah present, but then I thought maybe you wouldn't want it, that it might upset you, but Ma told me to let you decide . . ."

"Oy! *Shpayen es aoys*, already. Spit it out."

"I Googled Nick," Rachel said.

"Women ogled and googled Nick all the time. Who wouldn't, looking like that?" Rose pointed at Gary Cooper.

"I searched him on the Internet," Rachel said, handing her the piece of paper. "If you want to know."

Rose took the paper. She opened it up and saw his picture. He was older, but she'd know him anywhere. His eyes gave him away, and he had kept his full head of hair. Her heart swooped up into her throat. The words became too blurry to make out. "Read it to me, please."

Rachel took the paper. "Nicola Giuseppe Mancinelli, former celebrated Big Band Era and studio saxophonist, died Tuesday, May 9, of complications from pneumonia at Mount Sinai Hospital," Rachel stopped. "This is from 2005, Bubbe."

"I didn't know his middle name was Giuseppe," said Rose. "Go on."

"Known professionally as 'Nick Mann,' he married in 1942, but divorced in 1943. He is survived by his brother, Salvatore, and a son, Angelo."

"He had a son? Oh, I bet Lucia and Frank were thrilled. Angelo, that's a good name, Nick." She briefly considered all the faces she'd met who now were gone. Including Nick's.

Rachel continued. "He never remarried. Friends and relatives described him as married to his music. He was cremated, and the memorial was held at the Church of St. John in the Bronx."

"That's where Nonna went to Mass and where all the children were baptized," Rose said. They still felt like family. It felt good to remember them rather than try to deny they ever existed. Nick married in 1942, the year after she broke his heart, and then divorced after only one year? One year did not a marriage make. He never remarried. Had she left him too broken for anyone else? Or had she really been his one and only? She knew full well he had been hers.

"Bubbe, are you okay?" asked Rachel, taking Rose's hand.

Gary Cooper's big, innocent blues in high definition were like two huge moons she longed to get lost in. "Watch the rest of this with me, Racheleh. The end is the best part."

"Hurry! It'll be sundown soon. We have to be there to light the menorah," Rachel called out to Charlie and Hattie, who lagged behind on the quick jaunt to her parents' house. As they walked past the chicken coop, the chickens were cozying in for the night. Hattie, who benefited from Chanukah more than anyone, now skipped ahead, eager to collect her gelt, the gold-foiled chocolate coins that were doled out one night at a time over the eight nights of the holiday. She would also receive money as a present, which she had already mentally spent.

"You look beautiful, Ma," Rachel said as she stepped inside the door, admiring CeCe's deep-blue Navajo velvet shirt with silver buttons worn over her broom skirt.

Rachel and Charlie went to Rose and kissed her. "Happy Chanukah, Bubbe."

"My handsome cowboy grandson," Rose said. "Rachel, you did good."

"Aw, shucks, ma'am," Charlie said, with a wink to Rachel.

CeCe prepared to light the candles. The menorah sat in the front window to publicize the Chanukah miracle. Ma had picked a blue shamash candle with which to light the first white one. Rachel, Rose, and CeCe positioned their lace scarves on their heads. Miguel wore Mort's yarmulke, in honor of the first Chanukah without him. Ever since Miguel had discovered he was descended from Sephardic Jews on his mother's side, he had been an active participant in the lighting of the Chanukah candles. When Rachel was little, it was something she felt forced to do alone with CeCe. If it didn't include her papa, she wanted nothing to do with it. Now, the ritual united them.

Even Charlie covered his head during the prayer. Rose and Hattie sang the prayer with Ma. They had to sing fast, as there was only one candle to light on this first night of the holiday, and they ended up sounding like Alvin and the Chipmunks, inciting giggles from Hattie that became contagious. It was a time to celebrate, to be joyous and even silly.

"I miss that old geezer, Mort," Rose said. "As much as he lived in la-la land, he could sure tell the story of Chanukah. Usually more than once in an evening."

"He loved the Rugrats' story of Chanukah. Remember how he went around saying, 'A Maccababy's got to do what a Maccababy's got to do?'" Hattie said with a grin, but her eyes glistened with tears.

Zeyde Mort never knew the profound awakening he had stirred within Rachel. He called her Zophia, after the woman he had loved who had been murdered in front of him by Nazi soldiers. In his flashbacks, he saw Rachel as Zophia, and he felt calmed with her words and her touch on his fevered brow. Both Rose and Mort had lost their first loves, their soul mates, before resigning themselves to making a life together. Rachel looked around her. None of them would be standing together in front of the menorah if they hadn't.

Hattie dumped out a bag of chocolate coins in the middle of the table. "Ladies and gentlemen, rev your dreidels, place your bets. Hey—Zeyde Mort would make us sing the song, so we should sing it. 'I have a little dreidel, I made it out of clay,'" she sang in her pure ten-year-old voice as the rest of them joined in. Charlie and Papa sort of moved their mouths. "C'mon, Mom! Play dreidel with us."

"Oh, no," CeCe said. "She's coming with me to make latkes."

Rachel followed CeCe to the kitchen. "You're not going to grate the potatoes by hand, are you?"

"Hell, no. Not when there's my handy-dandy food processor. I did enough hand grating as a kid. If Mort were here he'd be grating by hand."

"Here, let me do it, Ma. I don't want you to mess up your shirt," said Rachel, taking her mother's place at the counter. She put the grater attachment on the food processor and shredded the peeled potatoes CeCe had ready in a bowl of cold water. She turned the burner under the oil on medium high. "Soon Hattie will be too old to be the center of attention on Chanukkah and will be in the kitchen with us cooking," Rachel said with a sigh. "We'll have to rope Diego in next year. Chanukah needs little kids."

"I can't believe this is my last Chanukah with my mother," CeCe said with a break in her voice. "She always made a big deal about Chanukah when we were kids. The synagogue would have a carnival, and she'd give us wrapped presents for eight days straight. Can you imagine, with five kids? She was always trying to make up for Mort. I never appreciated it enough."

Rachel patted the shredded potatoes with a cotton tea towel and put them in a mixing bowl with egg, grated onion, salt, and pepper.

"If they're too wet, add some matzo meal to it," CeCe said.

"I know, Ma." Rachel smiled, shaking some matzo meal from the box. She used to find her mother's unsolicited advice irritating. Now she found it endearing. It was Ma.

"It's so hard. Looking at her and knowing . . . her looking at me and knowing. She has this peaceful smile . . ." CeCe trailed off, dabbing her eyes with the tea towel.

Rachel set down her spatula to put her arms around CeCe. They both began to laugh as they heard Hattie saying, "Ante up!" from the dining room, referring to the pile of chocolate coins in the middle of the table. She sounded like one of Rose's gambling western gunslingers. "Give me your IOUs or your horse!"

"I hope Ramone doesn't show up and bust our illegal gambling ring in there," CeCe said.

The potato pancakes popped and sputtered as Rachel put them in the hot oil, which was to remind the Jews of the miracle oil that lasted eight days instead of one.

"Tomorrow I'm making fried jelly donuts for Miguel, which I learned is a Sephardic Jewish tradition," CeCe said.

"Oh, the irony of being shunned for decades only to find out he had actually been the genuine article all along," Rachel said. She turned over the crisp and golden-brown latkes. Charlie called them hash browns, which he would eat with ketchup if no one was watching. Rose lovingly referred to him as the true goy of the family. But following tradition, Rachel put some sour cream and applesauce in two separate bowls to have with the latkes. "We're set," she said. "Grab some forks, Ma."

Hattie had a ring of chocolate around her mouth, reminding Rachel of Bluto from the old Popeye cartoons. Rose had little gold nuggets of crumpled foil in front of her and was wearing a sheepish smile, with telltale chocolate between her teeth. The menorah candle had burned halfway but flickered with life. It was Charlie's last spin of the dreidel. He rolled it between his palms like dice. "Remember the Alamo!" he said, giving the top a quick turn.

"*Shin!*" Hattie yelled as the dreidel finally fell. "You lose! Your candy or your life!" She definitely had been watching TV with Rose lately.

"Okay, clear the table." Rachel held the plate of latkes and balanced the bowls of applesauce and sour cream on her forearm. After she set them down, she snuck the bottle of ketchup from her apron pocket to Charlie under the table.

"I saw that," said Rose, pointing an arthritic finger. Charlie and Rachel stopped in their tracks. "But who am I to judge? My papa insisted on sour cream, Mameh, applesauce. Let's live a little. Racheleh, pass the ketchup."

Chapter Twenty

SANTIAGO HUNG DIEGO'S bulging Christmas stocking next to Maggie's after he and Rosalinda filled them with an orange in each toe, then layers of nuts, candies, and toys for Diego and cosmetics and perfumed soaps for Maggie. Diego's Santa gift, the two-wheeler with training wheels, was parked next to the tree, a seven-footer loaded with lights and ornaments, topped with a hand-drawn angel cloaked in a metallic blue gown Maggie had created when she was four. The angel had a winking eye and a crooked grin that gave her a devilish expression. It still cracked him up to look at it.

"I'm too wired to sleep. How about some spiked eggnog and we sit in front of the tree for a little bit?" he said. Everyone else had turned in while he and Rosalinda were finishing the last Christmas preparations.

"Sounds good." She headed to the kitchen.

"I can't wait to see his face in the morning."

She looked over her shoulder. "I think you're as excited as he is."

"I've never been this excited about Christmas, not even when I was the kid."

Rosalinda pulled the jug of eggnog from the refrigerator. "I know what you mean. He makes everything new. Even going to the laundromat, he finds a way for me to enjoy it, only because he is there. He makes anything and everything more *meaningful*, no?"

"That's it. That's what he does. I didn't know how to say it."

"And you call yourself a writer." Rosalinda smiled a teasing smile reminiscent of when they had been together, when she'd liked to bust his chops, back when the age difference was apparent.

He laughed as he poured a shot of rum into each of their eggnog glasses. "You've had longer to experience this, to find the words."

Rosalinda clinked his glass. "To Christmas, together with our son."

They brought their beverages to the living room, switched off all the lights but those glowing on the tree, and sat together on the sofa. Santiago looked at Rosalinda. The tiny white and blue lights from the tree bathed her face and reflected in her eyes. He didn't imagine she'd had much in the way of Christmas trees in her life or anything that went with them. The thought of her deprivation made him want to hug her, comfort her, because he knew how it felt and because Abby had done that for him. His first Christmas with her had been overwhelming. Maggie was about six weeks old. Hattie wasn't born yet. Rose and Mort were still in Brooklyn, not speaking to CeCe. So it was Miguel and CeCe, Rachel and Charlie, Abby, baby Maggie, and him. After all the presents, and food, and constant merriment with everyone, he had grown quiet and then slipped away to cry in his room, because he had never imagined Christmas could be like that. He had cried for all he now had and for all he never had before then. He knew Christmas wasn't about the presents or the food or the merriment. It was about love. Realizing that made him cry all the more. Abby found him and didn't say a word. She put her arms around him and held him until he was cried out, limp and exhausted. From the other room, they heard tiny Maggie erupt into angry newborn yelping, and they both began to laugh.

Rosalinda sunk into the sofa. "It feels so good to relax." She took another sip of eggnog.

"You and Abby have been whirling dervishes, getting everything ready."

"While you get to fly in and enjoy the fruits of our labor."

"Hey, who put the bike together? 'Some assembly required,' my ass."

"Ben?" she said with that smile again.

"He may have loaned me his tools and given me a pointer here and there."

"They're so sweet together, Abby and Ben. I swear they never argue or have a nasty vibe or anything. He's wonderful with Maggie and Diego, too."

"Ben is a godsend." He finished his eggnog, feeling the light buzz from the rum. "It's funny how you and I got together about the same time they did. It was kind of rough for him at first, a biologist who studied the endangered silvery minnow. The farming two-thirds of our family thought he was there to steal their water, their livelihood."

"So I wasn't the only black sheep that summer." Rosalinda's head nestled against his shoulder. She yawned. "And yet, here I am."

"See how they are? A bunch of rule-breaking renegades who love beyond all reason." Without thinking, Santi's hand found hers, their fingers intertwined.

She yawned again. "I better go to bed—it's almost two. Your son will be getting us up in a few hours." She slipped her hand from his and stood.

"It's already Christmas morning," Santi said. "Merry Christmas."

She hugged him. "Merry Christmas, Santi." Her face tilted toward his, his arms still around her. Their lips met in a quick kiss, just a peck, really, he would assure himself later. Her index finger came to his lips, lightly pressing. "Good night." She turned and walked away while he used every ounce of his self-control to not reach for her.

Instead, he decided to check on the luminarias. He looked out the front window to see the sacks filled with sand, each holding a lit votive candle; they were placed about a foot apart, circling the flagstone patio and lining the walkway. So simple and so elegant, their yellow glow breaking the darkness. He, Diego, Maggie, and Ben had arranged them in their formation while Rosalinda had sat on the banco, dipping into the plastic bin and filling each sack with a scoop of the sand they reused every year. The paper sacks were recycled as well, used each year until they wore out. He and Ben lit each candle with their propane lighters at dusk. It had been cold, well below freezing, but at least there was no wind to blow the sacks into self-immolation. After the luminarias were lit and they were all chilled to the bone, they trooped inside for traditional posole and tamales. Rosalinda and Abby had made the posole. The tamales—red chile pork and green chile chicken—came from the cabal after their annual tamale-making party. Hazel also made her vegan *calabicitas* tamales, filled with squash, onion, corn, and green chile.

He decided to sleep on the sofa instead of going to CeCe and Miguel's and risk waking someone at that hour. He grabbed the throw and stuffed a pillow under his head. He left the tree lights on and stared at them instead of closing his eyes. Intense longing for Rosalinda persisted. He felt like he had when he first met her, completely knocked off his feet. He grappled for an explanation. Was this some emotional flashback to that time? Had the past somehow boomeranged into the present? Had there been a rip in the fabric of the space-time continuum?

All he knew was, more than anything, he wanted to hold her and never let her go.

His weakness for nostalgia and capacity for intense emotion combined to fuel this phantom desire. More than one writing professor had advised him to rein it in, while his classmates were prodded to plumb their feelings with greater abandon. It made sense that his passionate history with Rosalinda would collide with the loaded present situation of sharing a child at Christmas, triggering this blast from his past.

He realized he had forgotten to call Kat. On Christmas Eve. Shit. Kat had accused him of wanting Rosalinda; perhaps she planted the notion in his suggestible mind. He checked his phone and found it dead. He could plug it in and call her, but his charger was in his bag in Miguel and CeCe's guest room. He could go to the kitchen and call Kat from the landline. But his body melted into the sofa, and his fatigue overcame the urge. As his thoughts were freed of wakeful control, the enduring image of Rosalinda's smile eased him into sleep.

"That's everything," Maggie announced, checking behind the tree one more time. Diego darted through the waves of wrapping paper thrown into the center of the room. Bows were stuck randomly to his pajamas, and a green one clung to the top of his head.

"I have one more," Abby said. She set down her coffee cup and headed to her bedroom. Reaching into her closet, she retrieved the tube, now wrapped in Christmas paper, with a bow on top. She grinned in anticipation.

Abby returned to the living room, where Santi, Rosalinda, Maggie, and Ben all looked at her. She held the wrapped tube like a baby. "This present is for everyone, but I'd like Maggie to open it." She handed it to her as if passing a baton.

"What is that?" Diego asked Maggie.

"It's a Diego bonker." Maggie playfully tapped Diego on the

bottom with it. "Here, you can help me take off the wrapping." Diego grabbed the side where it was taped and pulled, the wrapping giving way with a satisfying rip. Maggie stuck the red bow onto Diego's head next to the green one. She pulled the round plastic cap from one end and peered inside. "It's a bunch of rolled-up paper."

"Pull it out," Abby said. Ben squeezed her shoulder to signal he knew what it was.

Maggie pulled out the papers that were bound along one edge, unrolling them to their full size. She held them like an oversized menu she was perusing. "House plans?"

"It's your new house. We break ground next month and should be finished by summer. I've already lined up the builder," Abby said.

Maggie began to shriek and jump up and down, sending wrapping paper flying. Diego laughed and jumped with her. Maggie dove at Abby and Ben, who sat next to each other on the sofa, smothering Abby with kisses. "Thank you! Thank you!"

"What about this house?" Santiago asked. "Are you going to bull-doze it?"

"No!" Abby said. "We'll live in it while the new house is being built two acres over. I want to offer this house to Rosalinda to live in with Diego, if she wants it. We can update the kitchen or fix it up however you like."

Rosalinda appeared stunned.

"Rosalinda, remember how you said you wanted to live nearby, so we could go back and forth like we do with Rachel and CeCe? Is this too close?" Abby asked.

"It's perfect . . . are you sure?"

"I've been telling you we needed a bigger house," Maggie said.

"Yes, Maggie, you're the one who started me thinking about this. You were right. The timing seems perfect now. I never wanted to destroy this house that Magdalena and Ricardo built to raise your father in. It's a good house, all adobe. They don't make them like this anymore. I think they would approve of it becoming Rosalinda and Diego's home." She didn't add that her spirit companions had already given their blessings.

Rosalinda stood and waded through the wrapping to Abby. Abby got up to hug her and whispered into her ear, "Now you can concentrate on what you want to do with your future, instead of worrying about where to live."

Abby felt Rosalinda's breathing become ragged as she began to cry. Abby held her, patting her back.

"Why is Mama crying?" Diego asked.

Santiago picked him up and held him close to Abby and Rosalinda.

"Because I'm so happy," Rosalinda said, letting go of Abby to face Diego. "The last time I was this happy was when you were born, *mi'jo*. I cried then, too."

Maggie threw the torn wrapping paper over them like confetti. Diego squirmed out of Santi's arms to help.

Ben stood next to Abby, his arm around her shoulder. "Well played, love."

She leaned into him, watching Santi, Maggie, Rosalinda, and Diego begin to ball up the paper for an indoor snowball fight. The gifts were stacked in their boxes next to the tree, momentarily forgotten. "You buy all those gifts, and they play with the wrapping," she said.

Ben grinned. "I want to update the electrical plans to incorporate more solar and wind-generated energy—the industry has made a lot of advancements since we made these plans. And there's some improved water conservation features available—"

"I already told the architect you'd be calling him," Abby interrupted.

"You know me too well," he said.

A loud dinging interrupted the melee. Abby held up the egg timer she had in her robe pocket. "Breakfast is ready."

She and Rosalinda had put together a spinach and cheese frittata the day before to bake while they opened the presents. Dinner would be posole and tamales left over from the night before, so they could enjoy the day together without having to cook.

Rosalinda joined Abby in the kitchen. "Looks good," said Abby, removing the frittata from the oven. "I know you've been worried about finding a job. And maybe you want to do something with children again in day care or preschool, but hopefully some of the pressure you've felt about that is gone now. I was wondering if you'd consider working with us in the café when we reopen. You have a talent for cooking and baking, and you seem to enjoy it. I mentioned it to CeCe and Rachel, and they said they'd love to have you. Rachel can always use a hand with her goat cheese business, too, and she runs that from the back kitchen of the café. Of course, Diego would be welcome, too. We raised Maggie and Hattie underfoot until they started preschool, and they still hang out there after school. Just more options, that's all. Don't feel like you have to, just something else to consider. Or maybe you'd rather be a full-time student. Ben could help you apply at UNM—"

Rosalinda grabbed plates and utensils to carry into the dining room and then dumped them back down. "Why? Why are you appointing yourself my fairy godmother? The other day I called the hospital to set up an installment payment plan to pay off my gigantic medical bills that the insurance didn't cover, and you'd already paid it in full. Santiago told me the million bucks you didn't have to give to Caden is now in trust for Diego. I didn't even know how to thank you for all of that, and now you are giving me a house? And you want me to work with you—I didn't ask for any of this."

Abby walked over to her and smoothed her hair and looked into her fiery eyes. "No, you didn't ask. You would never ask. You are tough and independent like I was at your age. I like to solve problems. I like to take care of my family. But Rosalinda, everything is up to you. You decide what is best for you and Diego. I'm only offering. You can tell me to back the hell off anytime you want—Santiago and Maggie do it all the time. You've had to overcome so much in your life. You've been alone, and you've had to struggle. I just thought you deserved a break."

"You didn't used to think that."

"No, well, I changed my mind. You know, when Bobby and I first came here, the first time I saw this house it was a wreck. Bobby's father, Ricardo, had been alone since Bobby left for the navy, and he became a hoarder. CeCe and Miguel took me in, four months pregnant, while Charlie and Miguel cleaned it out. Then they headed up all the repairs it needed, a new roof, reconditioning the floors, painting. Fixing up this house, preparing it for Bobby, gave me a purpose when I needed it most. And when I had to face he was never coming back, this house became my bedrock, my foundation, to build a new life with my children. It's been there for me these twelve years, and now it's here for you, if you want it."

"I love this house. I just don't know how to thank you."

"You could let us live here with you while our new house is being built," Abby said.

"I'll think about it," Rosalinda responded. Abby smacked her with a kitchen towel.

During the next few days, Santiago spent nearly every waking moment with Diego. He set his alarm to wake up early at CeCe and Miguel's so that he could have breakfast with him. He played Candy Land, read books, and made Play-Doh ice cream cones. After Maggie was awake, they met up with Hattie to ride bikes on the hardened dirt paths, Diego zooming after them on his new two-wheeler with training wheels. Santiago found his old bike in the storage shed and rode behind Diego, who thought he was beating Daddy in a race.

He bathed him and tucked him in at bedtime with Rosalinda. On his last night, after bedtime reading, he reminded Diego that he would be leaving early in the morning, but that he would be back in a few weeks.

Diego's face crumpled. "I don't want you to go."

"I don't want to, but I have to get back to my job. I'll call you every night, and we can talk and look at the moon together."

"I want you to be here, not the stupid moon." Diego began to cry. Rosalinda tried to comfort him, but he pushed her away. "I want my daddy."

"I'll be here as much as I can, buddy, I promise." But even as he said them, the words tasted foul in his mouth. The truth was he would be there as much as it was convenient for him to be away from San Francisco. He would be there when his career allowed, when Gordon gave his approval, when Kat could tolerate it. He told himself the words he used were easier for a three-year-old to understand. The words he used spared his child from hearing his daddy had made a choice to live far away from him. When he chose San Francisco, he hadn't known about his son, but he couldn't let himself off the hook for that. It didn't change the impact on Diego.

"He'll be okay," Rosalinda said as Diego buried his head to bawl.

"No, I will not!" Diego's words were muffled by the pillow.

"Diego, kiss Daddy good-bye. You'll feel worse later if you don't," Rosalinda said.

Diego sat up, his face red and wet with tears and snot. Santiago tipped his chin up to look into his big, dark eyes. "I love you, Diego. I will miss you. I will be back soon."

"I love you," he said, only *love* sounded like *luff*.

Santi kissed him and hugged him, which Diego allowed but did not reciprocate. He was like a floppy sock monkey in his arms.

Diego crawled into his mother's lap. She nodded to the door, indicating he should leave, so he did.

He said his good-byes to Maggie and Ben and found Abby in the kitchen.

"I could hear Diego crying," Abby said, dunking her tea bag in her cup.

"I feel like shit."

"It's just the transition. He'll have so many distractions, so much attention from everyone, he'll be fine."

"What does that say about our relationship?"

"It says that even though he doesn't like it when you go away, he has a deep, trusting bond with you. He knows you're always coming back. You'll show him every month. So he's allowed to be happy in between seeing you. And so are you. Go home, enjoy your job, your city, your girl. You're allowed."

He hugged her. "Mom, I'm always blown away by your generosity."

"Come on, Santi, giving the house to Rosalinda is the most selfish thing I've ever done. I started to think about not getting to bathe Diego, or talk with Rosalinda when we're waiting for our coffee in the morning, or watch Maggie mother her little nephew when she doesn't know I'm noticing. Ben and I want them as close as we can get them. So does Maggie—not to mention everyone else who has adopted them, just like they did me and, well, eventually, Ben."

"It helps me, more than anything, to know you love them and want to take care of them for me. It's hard to leave them like this." His throat constricted around the words.

She kissed his cheek. "It's the transition, remember? Look forward."

Rosalinda appeared in the doorway. "Good, you're still here. I wanted to walk you over . . . I need to get some fresh air."

Maggie walked past him on her way to the fridge. "I thought you left already."

Santi laughed and shook his head. "Thanks, I needed that. Bye for real."

"Bye, now, go!" She began to play shove Santi toward the door, giggling. "Leave already!" Santi pulled her into a hug that she tolerated only briefly before fleeing the room.

"Do you have everything?" Abby asked. Ben came in to stand next to her.

"Yeah. Thanks again."

"Diego is asleep. I'll be back in a few minutes," Rosalinda said.

He put on his coat and followed her out the door. The night was cold and dry. The air, still. The moon was a few days past full. "Long Night Moon."

"That's its name for December?"

"For the winter solstice, the shortest day of the year, the longest night. I'm sorry about Diego. It kills me to see him cry." His breath puffed out his words, visible in the bitter cold.

"He's not the only one who misses you . . . we all do." She put her gloved hand on his arm.

He looked at her and felt her trying to tell him something. Something he wasn't sure he should hear. She didn't need words; her eyes drew him in until his face was inches from hers, their frosty breaths comingling. He kissed her, a real kiss this time, and she kissed him back. He watched them from above himself, yet his eyes were closed. He couldn't hold her close enough with the layers of thick wool pressed between them, gloves covering hands and fingers. Only their mouths met. She pulled back and looked at him in horror. He could feel the same expression freeze his face.

"Why did you do that?" she said, her voice loud in the darkness.

"*You* did it! I can't do this!"

"I know you don't want me—I don't know what's happening." She paced in front of him.

"I'm with Kat. I'm not that guy. I'm not the guy who would do that."

"I know you aren't. I don't even know what this is," she said, gesturing to the charged air between them.

"It can't happen, that's what it is. I'm sorry, Rosalinda."

"You better go. I better go." Instead, they flew into each other's arms for another desperate, utterly wrong kiss.

When they broke apart, they stood looking at each other, too dumbfounded to speak. Eventually Rosalinda said, "Good-bye. Have a good trip." She turned and began to walk away.

"Good-bye," he called after her. He watched her go until not even the Long Night Moon could find her in the darkness.

He walked around the Vigils' property, trying to pull himself together before going inside. He toggled between giddy joy and shameful humiliation. What was wrong with him?

After accomplishing nothing except making the animals nervous, he let himself in the back door. He found a note saying CeCe and Miguel had retired to their room but would get up early to see him off, since Miguel was taking him to the airport at 6 a.m.

On his way to the guest room along the polished brick-floored corridor, he saw Rose was still up in her chair. He nodded at her through the open doorway of her bedroom, and she waved him in. "It's only nine thirty. They roll up the sidewalks early in these parts. Me, I sleep so much my days are nights, and my nights are days, who knows from which. So sit down, talk to me. You leave in the morning." Her oxygen assisted her breathing with pulses of air each time she took a breath.

He sat while she fumbled with the remote, accidentally switching channels before finding the off button. "Yes, back to San Francisco."

"You look terrible."

"I feel worse than I look."

"I'm guessing it has to do with trying to live two lives at once."

"I'm trying to be there for my boss, my girlfriend, my son, Rosalinda, and I end up disappointing all of them. It's killing me to leave Diego. Rosalinda and I just kissed. We couldn't stop, and I think about her all the time. My girlfriend, Kat, picked up on it before I did."

"You either keep things the way they are, with this traipsing back and forth. Or you decide your life is here with your son and Rosalinda."

"My life is in San Francisco."

She gave him a hard look. "Tell me your most perfect day in your San Francisco life."

"Kat is either in my bed or I'm in hers. We get up and have coffee. If it's a workday, we walk through the neighborhood to the offices. I'm busy, lots of meetings, phone calls, emails, staying on top of a million details, trying to review new submissions in between things. After work we usually eat at a restaurant—so many great ones it's hard to choose. I love walking, the sea air, the beautiful buildings, the tourists, the history, the art—San Francisco is a great city."

"But unlike Tony Bennett, your heart isn't there. Not anymore. Don't get me wrong, you have a great setup—I know what it is to love a city. I loved New York; God, I miss the old days there. Now, tell me about your perfect day here in Esperanza."

"I have breakfast with Diego. He's silly and happy every single morning; it cheers you up just to see him. Rosalinda is there. She looks at him the same way I do. And Abby and Maggie and Ben. We laugh and talk. Then we play. Ride bikes, build a blanket fort, ride horses, visit the goats. He naps in the afternoon. I don't know how much longer that will last after he turns four. He's already changing and growing so fast. While he's napping, Rosalinda and I go for a walk."

"You should see your face. So bright I need sunglasses, or I could get a cataract."

"I love Diego. I love him more than I thought was possible."

"Close your eyes. You're sleeping and you're just about to wake up. When you open your eyes, whose head is on the pillow next to yours? Quick, who do you see?"

He saw Rosalinda. He tried to make it Kat, but she morphed back to Rosalinda. "Rosalinda. But I can't. It's impossible."

"Santi, my boy, you are at a crossroads. You've reached a fork in the path. You go one way, you get that life. You go the other way, you get *that* life. The hell of it is, when you choose one, you lose the other. Forever. I can't tell you what to choose. I only know not choosing isn't going to work."

"At least if I live in San Francisco I can still visit here." Santiago felt panic grip his chest. He might need to take a hit from Rose's oxygen tank.

"You've already told me this visiting thing is hurting everyone, and how can you live like that, one foot there, the other foot here?"

"I don't know what else I can do."

"Crossroads, *oy vay*! Your first thought is to try to get out of it. You can put it off, stand there like a schlemiel, but to move forward, you have to choose which road to take. And I tell you, the one thing I've learned is, you only get the one life. You can base it on your job, the city, the promises you made before you knew about Diego, and stay in San Francisco. Your kid will still love you. He'll survive. Here's the tricky part: to do right by everyone else, you have to be selfish right now. What do you want the most? *Who* do you want the most? If you don't choose based on that, you cheat yourself, and you cheat everyone else. You can't be real in a life you choose to please other people. They'll smell it. It goes bad, like day-old fish."

"But I'd be hurting Kat and letting down her dad, sacrificing a great career. I'd lose my good friend, Reggie. I'd lose San Francisco." He felt the pain of it.

"That's your sacrifice. Great love requires great sacrifice. What would you get?"

He thought about it in a way he hadn't allowed himself before that moment. "I'd be there for my son, all those little moments: loose teeth, school programs, skinned knees . . . I wouldn't have to miss out on everything that already goes so fast. I could look into graduate school, work on my MFA, either at UNM or a low-residency program somewhere. I could write my own stories instead of revising other people's work. I could be with my family, Maggie, everyone else." He stopped and looked at her. "I'd be free to love Rosalinda. We could be together. We could raise our son and be a family. But I don't even know if she wants that."

"I don't hear that you love Kat. You care about her; you don't want to hurt her because you are a good man. But a good man does not inflict himself on a woman he doesn't really love. That's the worst kind of hurt, and it sounds like she's already feeling it. Who do you love?"

"Rosalinda," he said, with such certainty it startled him. "But what if she doesn't love me? What if we're just hormonal or something."

"What if I told you that Rosalinda loves you, and she's been trying not to? She's been trying to stay out of your way, not mess things up for you, because when you really love someone, you want for them what *they* want."

"How do you know?" Rosalinda had just said: *I know you don't want me.*

Rose looked at him, her eyes as focused and intelligent as ever. "Because I watch, I observe. I'm smart that way. And maybe Hazel said something."

He sat back in the chair and began to chuckle. Tension erupted out of him as laughter. He should have known the cabal, spreading their *mitote*, their gossip, would have the inside scoop. Rose laughed with him but then coughed into her handkerchief. She sputtered and hacked and spit. "I reveal the secret of life to you, and this is the thanks I get?"

He reached into his pocket and pulled out the pendant Rose had given him. "I've kept this with me. I look at it all the time, trying to figure stuff out, trying to find peace."

"What are you going to do?"

"Fly back to San Francisco, think some more. So much is riding on this, I have to be sure. Can you please not say anything? No hints to Hazel, no *mitote* for the cabal."

"Tick a lock," she said, twisting the imaginary key to her mouth.

He stood and then bent down to give her a kiss and a hug. "Love you, Bubbe Rose. I can't thank you enough. I want you to do one more thing for me. Be here when I get back so we can celebrate."

Her mottled hand gripped him tightly. "Don't take too long, then."

Chapter Twenty-One

AS SANTIAGO WALKED up the three flights of stairs, his wheeled bag thumped against each step like a drumbeat counting down the seconds until he faced Kat.

When he reached the apartment door, it swung open. "God, that was the longest nine days ever." She pulled him through the doorway. Though it was noon, she wore a black negligee.

"I love my present, Santi, see?" She pointed to the vintage ruby earrings dangling from her ears. He had bought them for her before he left.

"They look nice," he said, starting to wheel his bag to his room.

She followed. "I bet you're exhausted. Reggie is still in Maui with dad. He doesn't get back until late tonight. What do you say we go back to bed for the afternoon?" She opened the ribbon ties on the skimpy matching robe, revealing the negligee's transparent bodice.

"You're beautiful, Kat. I wish you could believe that."

"As long as you think so," she said.

"I do," he said, throwing his bag on top of his bed. "But we need to talk."

She put her arms around his neck and tried to kiss him. He turned his head so that her lips brushed the stubble on his cheek. "What?"

"Let's go sit in the living room."

"You're scaring me." She fumbled with the ribbons on her robe, tying them back together.

"When I accepted the position at Polydactyl, moved here, and started a relationship with you, I had no idea what was going to happen in my life. I'm sorry, really sorry, but I can't do this anymore. I never wanted to hurt you or let down your father and Reggie, but I can't live here when my son is in New Mexico."

"Move them here. Set them up in an apartment. Then we could see Diego whenever you want." She put up her hands. "There! Problem solved."

"Their home is in Esperanza. My family has taken them in. It's the best place for Diego to be, and it's where Rosalinda wants to live."

"You have it all here. A great career—you get to bring new books into the world. You have San Francisco, and you have me. It's the life you've always wanted. It's a great life."

"It *is* a great life. It's just not mine."

"It still could be, you can have everything here and still see Diego on visits—I promise I won't give you shit about it anymore. Go as often as you want and stay as long as you need."

"I can't do that to Diego. Not anymore," he said. "And I can't do it to me."

"If you sacrifice everything for your kid, you'll end up resenting him—don't deny who you are."

"I figured out who I am: I'm a father who loves his son. I'm a writer, not an editor. And it turns out you were right. I do have feelings for Rosalinda. I'm in love with her. I guess I never stopped loving her. I'm sorry to hurt you, but it's the truth, and I can't change it. I'm sorry, Kat."

Kat began to cry. "I should have known I couldn't compete with her. I knew she wanted you back—I told you. I saw this coming and still I loved you. God, I'm so stupid."

"Rosalinda doesn't know anything about this—I don't even know for sure if she wants me. But I want her. And I want my son, day in, day out, every moment I can get, because it goes by so fast, and I'm not going to miss anything more. I rented a van; it's parked on the street. I'm going to start packing my clothes, my books. That's about all I want, so it shouldn't take long. You can keep the furniture, rent the room as furnished. I'll talk to Reggie soon, and I have a letter I wrote for your dad, apologizing, explaining why I have to do this, and wrapping up some work business. If you could give it to him for me, I'd appreciate it." He reached into his inner coat pocket and handed her an envelope.

She took it, sobbing, holding it as if it were her death sentence. "So that's it. You're just going to leave me?"

He stood before her, wanting to comfort her, wanting to help. But he was the cause of her pain. "You're only twenty, Kat. You're so young and amazing—someday the right guy is going to be incredibly lucky—"

"*You* were the right guy. I wanted you." Kat shook her head, her sobs subsiding, replaced with ragged breathing. "If Rosalinda hadn't gotten pregnant or never told you, and you never saw her again, do you think you could have ever grown to love me?" Her eyes peered into him, trying to read the truth.

"Yes—of course." He decided she needed to hear certainty more than the truth. The truth was he had no idea. He knew he had wanted to love her. But that wasn't the same.

"I believed we were meant to be together, all those years. I believed it more than I've ever believed in anything. How could I be so wrong? We were *this* close." She held her finger and thumb a hair's breadth apart. She began to cry again, "It's so unfair."

Santi reached for her, and she sobbed into his shoulder. After a moment she stepped back and looked him in the eye. "I think it would be better for me if I can try to hate you now. At least for a while . . . I don't know, maybe forever." She turned and walked away, in the direction of her room. "Leave your key," she said before shutting the door behind her.

After an hour of packing and loading the van, Santiago realized he was too sleep deprived and emotionally spent to set out on the eighteen-hour drive to Esperanza. Instead, he decided to spend one last night in San Francisco. He drove up Columbus to Beach Street, then turned onto Hyde and Jefferson and checked into the Argonaut, a nautical-themed historic hotel with views of the bay. He walked through Fisherman's Wharf, stopping to eat cioppino out of a sourdough bread bowl. He watched the sun go down. The night was cold but clear. He looked up at the Long Night Moon that he and Rosalinda had kissed under not even twenty-four hours before and smiled. When it was time, he called Diego and did not let on that he would be home soon. Rosalinda didn't say much except that when Diego wouldn't believe his daddy had left, she had taken him to Miguel and CeCe's to see the empty room. But after that, he played with Maggie and Hattie and seemed back to his happy self.

Santiago walked up the Embarcadero to Pier 39 to say good-bye to the noisy, smelly sea lion colony. He dodged street performers, throngs of tourists, and locals going in and out of restaurants and bars to head back to the Argonaut. After a hot shower, he climbed into the comfortable bed. Before sleep claimed him, he thought about the circuitous path his life had taken, from his birth parents to Abby, from Esperanza to Los Angeles to San Francisco, from charting one future to discovering his destiny.

The next morning, after grabbing a quick breakfast at the hotel, he left by seven thirty. He traveled over the Bay Bridge to Oakland, the San Francisco skyline in his rearview mirror. He hit Bakersfield by noon, had a quick pit stop, and continued on to Interstate 40, which would take him all the way to Albuquerque. But by Williams, Arizona, he hit snow. He'd been on the road for twelve hours, it was dark, and snow was coming down faster than his wipers could clear it. The weight of the van helped, but when conditions got worse he was forced to pull off in Flagstaff and check into a motel.

When he woke at 6 a.m. it was still dark outside. He looked out to see a silent world of snow, luminous under the parking lot lights. It buried cars a good foot deep, and it was still coming down. He turned on the television to learn I-40 was closed at Williams all the way to the New Mexico state line and beyond. His mood plummeted. Here he thought he would have Diego and Rosalinda in his arms after only five or six more hours of driving; instead, he was stranded in Flagstaff for at least another day. Tomorrow would be New Year's Eve. If the interstate reopened by then, he still had a chance to make it home in time to celebrate with his family.

When he spoke to Rosalinda that night, she told him about all the snow they had gotten, more than ten inches by Ben's yardstick. They had built snow creatures and snow people, and the girls had helped Diego build his first snow fort. Diego took the phone and talked about how fierce his snow dragon was, "with big teeth and big claws, but it can't breathe fire, or it will melt."

Santi kicked himself for spending the extra night in San Francisco; if he had left right away he could have beaten the storm, could have helped his son build his first snow fort. He consoled himself by realizing he would never miss anything ever again.

By the time Rosalinda got Diego home from Rachel and Charlie's

New Year's Eve party and ready for bed, he was so tired he fell asleep as soon as she began reading the first storybook. At the party the fact that he had refused to nap that afternoon was evident. By seven thirty, he was yawning and irritable. Hattie and Maggie gave up trying to engage him in play.

Rosalinda was relieved for the excuse to leave early. Not that the party wasn't fun, especially with Hazel and her girlfriend, Joan, in attendance, and Charlie playing old Motown and 1960s rock music for dancing, and watching CeCe and Miguel able to cut loose while Carmen sat with Rose back at their house. Rosalinda wanted some time to be alone and not need to expend the energy to act cheerful. She missed Santiago, and though she was grateful that the house she now walked aimlessly through would be hers, the thought of not sharing it with the man she loved—of only seeing him when he visited Diego, of keeping her love for him hidden—grieved her.

The kisses they had shared the night before he left, the passion she'd felt and thought she felt from Santiago, now seemed like artifacts from their past. Add in the intoxicating moonlight and his impending departure, and it all combined to create the moment for their irresistible kiss. She was sure he was back in his San Francisco life, in the arms of Kat, wondering why he had ever behaved like that.

Her mistake was to open herself to love, something she had sworn to avoid. But since her heart had awakened to feel her vast love for her son, it was harder to shut it down when required. Immersed in this place where love flourished everywhere around her—Abby and Ben, Rachel and Charlie, Miguel and CeCe, and now Hazel and Joan— heightened her sense of not having what everyone else cherished most.

She put her hand over the ache in her chest and willed it to subside. Santi had only been gone a few days. With time, and before he returned, she would knock off this nonsense.

She looked in on Diego and watched him sleep. He looked so much like his father that her eyes brimmed with tears. Lights flashed across the bedroom window. Maybe Ben and Abby had come home early.

When she parted the curtains to look out of the kitchen door window, it was not Ben's car but an unfamiliar van. Fear gripped her. She knew it couldn't be Caden, but her terror was not rational. Maybe he had an accomplice who had come to avenge Caden's death or to try to succeed where Caden had failed. The new alarm system was engaged, the security cameras were rolling. She switched off the inside lights, found the baseball bat that Ben kept in the broom closet, and held it ready at the door.

Peering through the gap in the curtains, she saw a figure emerge from the van. The bright lights of the security system leached all color from the scene. The figure stretched and turned his face to the door, blinking in the glare. Santiago.

She put down the bat, punched the code into the alarm panel, and opened the door, not stopping to put on her coat. She nearly slipped on the ice as she ran to him, then stopped short. "What are you doing here?"

"I had to come home."

"You just left."

"I couldn't get back here fast enough—and then I hit the snow-storm in Arizona—"

"What about your job? What about Kat?"

"I traded them for you and Diego."

"Are you sure? Because—"

He kissed her. She pulled back from him to finish her sentence: "Abby will not like this one bit, and you know who she'll blame."

"I'll just sit her down and tell her how much I love you and Diego and that I can't stand to be away from either of you one more minute."

She let this sink in. "You quit your job and dumped your girl and drove through a snowstorm because you love me? You're awfully sure of yourself."

"I'm committed. That's what my cross-country coach used to say. He said I wasn't the one with the most natural talent, but I was the most committed."

"I can't believe you want me." She blinked tears that seemed to freeze on her face.

"I've always wanted you, Rosalinda Ortiz."

She felt her inner fortress crumble. "I loved you even when I knew I had to give you up that summer. It was the hardest thing I've ever had to do in my whole shitty life. And after I found out I was pregnant, I wanted to call you so many times when I felt weak and alone. But once they put Diego in my arms, I was strong. I knew I had to be for him."

"Were you really never going to tell me about him? It kills me to think—"

"I had to wait until you were through college. Diego was getting old enough that he needed his father, so I knew it was time to tell you, but I was afraid, so I kept stalling, until Jesse found out." Her teeth chattered as she shivered in the cold.

"Let's get you inside," he said.

She pulled open the door and turned on the kitchen light. The bat leaned against the wall. "I didn't know who you were, with that van."

He shut the back door behind him. "I scared you. I'm sorry. I was trying to surprise you." He hugged her and then pulled out a chair. He grabbed Abby's shawl from a coat hook and wrapped it around her. "I'll make us some hot tea."

She watched him pull out two cups and light the fire under the kettle, still unable to fully grasp that he was there, he loved her, and they would be together.

He leaned against the counter. "What if you hadn't blurted to Jesse that Abby was Diego's grandmother? What if he hadn't told Caden? What if they hadn't forced you to come here?"

"You'd still have your life in San Francisco. I would have told you about Diego eventually. I guess we'll never know how that would have played out."

The kettle began to rumble. Santi caught it before it could whistle and poured the boiling water into their cups over the tea bags. He set them on the table and sat down near her. "The whole ordeal we went through, it's like it stripped everything down to the bare truth of what's important—at least it did for me."

They blew on their tea and took tentative sips. "I saw the doctor yesterday for my two-month check. Can you believe it's been two months? It's already starting to feel unreal. Except for this." She raised her sweater to reveal her scar. It had calmed down some, had settled into her skin and become a part of her. "He said the scar would fade over time until it's a silver line."

He knelt before her and traced the scar lightly with his fingertip. "In Japan, there's this art form that's been around for over five hundred years, called *Kintsugi*. When a piece of pottery or porcelain is broken, they mend it with a lacquer mixed with real powdered gold or silver or platinum. The idea is to make the broken place beautiful and not try to disguise it or pretend it never happened, but to honor the mended place, because it is part of its history, its fate."

She reached for him and cradled his head against her, stroking his hair. What she felt overwhelmed her ability to form words. In her twenty-seven years, she had never experienced this from anyone, not from her mother, her family, or any of the men she had been with. And yet here he was, her Santiago, kneeling in front of her, wanting her and all her imperfections.

Santiago stood and reached into his pocket, pulling out Rose's pendant. He had polished the silver setting and chain in the motel room with some toothpaste, a trick Abby had taught him. The prominent part of the design now gleamed in the light, the diamond chips sparkling, while the deeper layer of silver remained blackened, in shadow, contrasting against the white radiance of the moonstone.

"It's beautiful. Help me put it on."

She lifted her hair while he hung the silver chain around her neck and fastened the clasp. The pendant reached her heart.

He told her the story Rose had shared with him when she had given it to him in November. "I've kept it in my pocket, pulling it out to study it and rubbing the stone like a magic lamp but not knowing what to wish for. And then, three days ago, right after you and I kissed, I went to Rose all torn up, and we talked. She told me I was at a crossroads, and I only get one life, and I had to choose. When she put it like that, it was a no-brainer."

"In the morning we'll go over and thank her."

"Yeah, I can't wait to see her face when she sees us together," he said.

"You made me lose a bet with Hazel. She'll never let me hear the end of it."

Just before midnight they checked on Diego and then bundled up and went outside. The Long Night Moon loomed overhead, casting its silver light onto the shimmering snow, transforming the snow creatures into a ghostly gathering. They stayed close to Diego's window and watched Santi's phone screen for the countdown. As midnight arrived, they kissed to the sounds of fireworks, distant guns discharging, dogs barking, and, from Rachel's house, the unmistakable racket of his extended family out on the porch, hollering and banging on pots and pans with cooking utensils to drum out the old year, with its disappointments and grief, and to welcome in the new year, with all the brave hope they could muster.

Santiago could see the coming year unfurl its three hundred and sixty-five days before his mind's eye. He saw a new house being built, a summer wedding in CeCe's flower gardens, and losing Bubbe Rose. But most of the days he saw were filled with routine things: walking the chile fields with Miguel, working the horses with Charlie, hanging out at the café with Abby and Rachel while CeCe slipped him a cookie, helping his little sister navigate the tricky terrain of adolescence, and tromping the Rio Grande riverbanks with Ben, searching for silvery minnows. And at the center of everything, the singular privilege of fathering Diego and of sharing it all with Rosalinda, the love of his life.

And as the first year completed its circle, the second year, and then all the rest, a lifetime of years, tumbled forward, and all he could do was catch quick glimpses of fragmented moments as they washed over him in waves, seemingly endless until they ceased, and he knew whatever their ultimate sum, they would never number enough.

Midnight's din faded away, and it became merely another cold winter's night, ordinary and exquisitely irreplaceable. "We should head back inside the house," he said.

"*My* house, you mean? You know, if you play your cards right, there's a chance I might let you live in it with me."

"I could be your renter in the spare room." He opened the door for her.

"That seems like wasted space. The practical thing would be for you to sleep with me. The spare room could be your study." She took off her coat, hat, and gloves. The moonstone seemed to wink at him when she turned in the light.

"A study? I've always wanted my own study. Well, that's reason enough to sleep with you."

"Oh, I'll give you reason enough."

He reached for her. "You already have."

Rose made it a point to kiss everyone good night before they left for Rachel's New Year's Eve party. As she had promised herself, she made it through the holidays, right up to the New Year. But she felt tired. A warm bath and a good night's sleep was all she asked at the moment. Her lungs, like saturated sponges, hung heavy in her chest. She had to ride her scooter to her room; her walker was an old horse put to pasture. Carmen followed with a tray of chamomile tea.

She could undress herself but needed Carmen's help getting in and out of the tub. Her arms felt like flailing noodles. She could feel her bones and muscles dissolving like an Alka-Seltzer plopped into water. She sat on the edge of the tub while Carmen turned on the faucet. She poured the last of her lilac bubble bath into the roaring water. Lilacs were rare when she was growing up in Brighton Beach. Their heady scent wafting in the breeze on a New Mexico spring day was one of her favorite things. These last years with CeCe and the family had been the best in her life. Family here didn't disown, or break up, or give up. They stuck together, circled the wagons, and survived.

"I hope it's not too hot," Carmen said, testing the water so the bath wouldn't simmer Rose into a Jewish stew. She turned on the cold water, and Rose frowned to see some of her fragrant bubbles give in and die. When the temperature suited Carmen, she helped Rose into the tub. Even with Carmen's gold crucifix dangling in her face, Rose adored Carmen. *See, Papa, what you missed out on?* Her life lesson? That hearts speak to one another beyond biases. The heart knows what a thick head doesn't.

Carmen said, "Rose, you need to eat more. Look how thin you are." True. Rose's skin hung like Spanish moss. And her body was completely hairless, like one of those yappy little dogs. But her *kishkes* found food painful to digest, so she ate as little as possible. She was disappearing. With little body fat, she felt like a lead weight, her bony *tuchas* pressed against the cast-iron bathtub. She held some bubbles in her palms and tried to blow them off, but she didn't have the oomph. They hissed and glistened in her hand like exotic life-forms. Some of them kissed her face as they popped.

Carmen washed her and then helped her out of the tub. She gently dried her with a fluffy towel as if Rose were her young child. She rubbed lotion on her so she wouldn't split apart like old parchment. Her body had become a shackle. She could hardly identify with the girl who had Lindy Hopped and twirled on Roseland's dance floor. Except in her heart. Carmen let the nightgown envelope Rose like gossamer wings and settled her into bed.

"Bonnie told me to tell you she'll be over to color your hair and clip your toenails in the next couple of days," Carmen said, sipping chamomile tea in the chair next to her.

"Oy, tell her not to bother," Rose said. She couldn't imagine trying to breathe while Bonnie applied hair color. *Alter kocker* women who colored their hair were trying to hold onto something from their past. Letting go required far less energy. As far as her toenails went, they say the *momsers* would still be growing after she was dead in the ground.

"I understand," said sweet Carmen, who had never worn a stitch of makeup in her life, but her exquisite spirit transformed her face to that of an angel. When Carmen smiled, Rose saw a golden aura burst out of her like the *esplendor* from Carmen's beloved Lady of Guadalupe.

"So beautiful," Rose said, captivated as Carmen attached the tubes in her nose. Suddenly she saw the big ballroom lights of Roseland as the oxygen swirled to her brain. "Thank you," she told Carmen and touched her face good-bye. Carmen kissed her forehead and left.

She turned her attention to the television. The news was on low, the only light in the room. Toddlers with guns killing parents, cops shooting young black men, *shmegegge* politicians, stampeding religious know-it-alls, who's *shtupping* who: Rose had had enough news. Nothing was new. She switched to her western channel. Cowboys killing Indians, Indians killing cowboys . . . Rose turned it off. *What idiots we all are. It wasn't just you, Papa.*

Rose had asked Carmen to open her curtains so she could see the night sky. She gazed on the lopsided moon and the stars as bright as flickering flames. It was hard to see stars growing up in the city. A child without stars. As she stared, her vision blurred. The stars and the moon were expanding, obliterating the darkness, their lights twirling and combining. Such brightness. Suddenly she could breathe it in, as if drawing in bracing springtime air after a long hibernation. The light filled her, imbuing her with more joy and more life than a mere body could hold. Somewhere in the distance, a subway train rattled down a track. A familiar melody from a lone saxophone carried her as if she were a wisp of smoke, lifting her into the dazzling sea of light and sound.

She had no idea where she was headed, but it was one hell of a start.

Acknowledgments

WE ARE FILLED with gratitude for our lifelong friendship and our creative collaboration, which has so enriched our lives and sparked into existence the characters and the world of Esperanza, New Mexico. It is a world we have come to love, populated with characters by now so real to us, we will miss them as long-lost friends. We imagine them continuing their lives, wrapped in one another's arms, ready to face whatever life throws their way. After all we've put them through, we wish them peace.

Our longtime cherished friend and trusted first reader, Corinne Armijo, provided invaluable feedback and encouragement, as always. We also are thankful for the generosity, inspiration, and writerly expertise of our friends and colleagues at Women Writing the West (we're looking at you, Dawn Wink and Susan Tweit), Southwest Writers Workshop, New Mexico Book Co-op (especially Barbe Awalt and Paul Rhetts), and Wordharvest (Jean Schaumberg and Anne Hillerman). You have all taught us more than we can say.

We are incredibly fortunate to have the work of Corrales artist extraordinaire Barbara Clark grace our book covers. Visit her website at bacpastels.com and prepare to be amazed. We thank our favorite local independent bookstore, Bookworks, for their ongoing support of our books.

For nursing and medical competency, we received helpful guidance from Sheena Ferguson, MSN, RN, CNS, at the University of New Mexico Hospital. For help with our kidnapping plot, we consulted extensively with Supervisory Special Agent Jonathan Zeitlin,

Investigative Publicity and Public Affairs, Federal Bureau of Investigation. Both went out of their way to assist us with essential technical support. For all things Jewish and for Brooklyn history, we learned valuable information from the Brooklyn Jewish Historical Initiative (brooklynbased.com), the Brooklyn Public Library (brklynlibrary.org), and AskMoses.com. Any mistakes are ours alone.

We count our lucky stars for our beloved agent, Liz Trupin-Pulli (JET Literary Associates, Inc.), for her tenacity, fierce loyalty, and her ability to convince us anything is possible. Copyeditor and *comadre*, the amazing Diana Rico, saves us from ourselves time and time again.

Our love for UNM Press knows no bounds. Thanks to Director John Byram for his strong support and sly humor. Thanks to our editor, Elise McHugh, whose insightful editorial guidance helped *Long Night Moon* find its potential. The production team, headed by Maya Allen-Gallegos, and now James Ayers, is a joy to work with. And thanks to Katherine White, marketing and sales manager, for getting our books into the hands of readers. Everyone at UNM Press expresses their passion and commitment to the written word by tirelessly bringing beautiful books into the world.

Long Night Moon tackles themes surrounding religious and ethnic biases, the consequences and rewards of crossing familial dictates, and the universal dilemma of confronting inescapable crossroads. As we conclude our Esperanza Trilogy, a story of hope and *la familia*, we celebrate the gift of our families: the Pearls and the Overturfs, who raised us (and put up with our young shenanigans); our supportive husbands, Mark McCarty and Breck Boggio; and Sue's daughter, Holly Glazebrook-Gonzales, her son-in-law, Tim Gonzales, and her granddaughter, the spectacular Josie Gonzales.